# MY BLUE PENINSULA

## MAUREEN FREELY

Published by Linen Press, London 2023

8 Maltings Lodge

Corney Reach Way

London W4 2TT

www.linen-press.com

A CIP catalogue record for this book is available from the British Library.

ISBN: 978-1-7391777-1-3

# About the Author

Maureen Freely was born in the US but grew up in Turkey. After graduating from Radcliffe College, Harvard University, she moved to England, where she teaches at the University of Warwick. She has, in addition to authoring eight novels, translated many classics of twentieth century Turkish literature as well as five books by the Nobel Laureate Orhan Pamuk. Formerly Chair and President of English PEN, she continues to campaign for freedom of expression worldwide.

# Praise for Maureen Freely's novels

## *My Blue Peninsula*

'In Freely's multi-layered and richly beautiful novel, Dora's search for the truth about her own family is also a journey into the nightmare of history. Freely understands that truth is always provisional, identity always a series of camouflages, and the past is never over. What matters is the struggle to find meaning in chaos, and to endure. My Blue Peninsula is profoundly intelligent, moving and brave.'

– Nicci Gerrard

## *Sailing Through Byzantium*

Sunday Times Books of the Year 2013
'The 1962 Cuban missile crisis provides a threatening hinterland to this novel focused on Istanbul's raffishly bohemian American expat colony. Comic mishaps and painful predicaments are silhouetted against the old imperial capital's melancholy, mouldering grandeur.'

– Peter Kemp

'Freely's roman à clef is compulsively readable, thought-provoking and entertaining.'

– The Independent

'Sailing Through Byzantium glints with ironic wit...Haunting vignettes heighten the melancholy that coexists with sardonic flair and narrative bustle in this engaging novel.'

– Sunday Times

'In Sailing through Byzantium, Maureen Freely's Istanbul is an absorbing Never-Never Land, a place of wild parties and refuge for social pariahs. This book is full of surprises...the cover with its moody close-up of a solemn child gives no clue about its level of intrigue, or its clear eyed prose.'

– TLS

'Finely calibrated, compassionate and compellingly observed, Sailing Through Byzantium is a triumph.

– Jason Goodwin, Cornucopia

'History pours through this wonderful novel, but refracted through a young girl's enchantment and dread. This is the story of a country, a city, a family, a scared child, in which memory throws the past into a kaleidoscopic pattern, vivid and always changing. In other words: quite fabulous!'

– Nicci Gerrard

'Rich, seductive, exciting.'

– Maggie Gee

'What Freely does succinctly and memorably is conjure up the picture of Turkey in the 1960s – how odd, how romantic and how mysterious it must have seemed to a young child from distant America. And what a gift to the reader.'

– Bookoxygen

*Enlightenment*

'A dark Conradian drama, set in a beautifully illuminated Istanbul, where the past is always with us.'

– Orhan Pamuk

'A complex, often riveting novel...quietly stunning.'

– Publishers Weekly (starred review)

# Books by Maureen Freely

of Sait Faik Abasıyanık
*A Useless Man* (with Alexander Dawe)
of Hasan Ali Toptaş
*Shadowless* (with John Angliss), *Reckless* (with John Angliss)
of Sema Kaygusuz
*The Well of Trapped Words: Selected Stories*
of Tuba Çandar
*Hrant Dink: The Life and Death of a Turkish-Armenian Intellectual*
of Suat Derviş
*In the Shadow of the Yali*
of Sevgi Soysal
*Dawn*
of Tezer Özlü
*Cold Nights of Childhood*

It might be easier
To fail – with Land in Sight –
Than gain – My Blue Peninsula –
To perish – of Delight –

– Emily Dickinson

# Table of Contents

# THE FIRST NOTEBOOK

# This morning

I was standing at my window this morning, sipping my tea, when all at once the sun broke through to chase away the winter. The Bosphorus turned silver, and the long black tanker that had been churning past – slicing the rough waters and scattering ferries – seemed to be gliding across a rumpled satin sheet. Then the clouds closed up again. But not securely. As I made my way down Istiklâl, pushing through the crowds, there were other shafts of unexpected light, rescuing storefronts and wet paving stones from oblivion, and in due course alerting me to a ragged row of bright white banners on the approach to Taksim Square.

The demonstration was small but noisy. Beyond, I could see the usual wall of police. Or at least, I could see their helmets. So I slipped into a side street. It took me past Aghia Triada. There was not much green left in its courtyard, but in muffling the chants, it offered a sort of peace. Glancing up, I caught the last shaft of light I would see all day, playing on its lovely silver cross.

It was while I was negotiating the broken pavements of Sıraselviler that the dread descended. I kept it at bay by banishing all thought. But then, having arrived at the building that still houses our office, I saw a young woman waiting for the lift. And in spite of myself, I screamed.

In fact, all I'd seen was her red headscarf. When she turned, I immediately saw my mistake. I must have raised a hand to my mouth, because now, with genuine alarm playing on her open face, she asked if I was all right. I stupidly pretended to have twisted my ankle, so she insisted on seeing me into my office. Even then, she would not leave me. Her mother also suffered from weak ankles, she explained. Before I knew it, she was placing my foot on a chair, and darting into our little office kitchen, and making me tea, and telling me that it was only her second day at her new job with one of the dentists upstairs. I can no longer remember which.

Politely, but without much curiosity, she asked what sort of work we did here. Carefully, I explained: we'd been forced to shut down. Before that, we'd run a sort of digital history platform. But even when she glanced up at the logo featured in so many news reports during the hate campaign, even when she found me in the poster beneath it – 'Dora,' she said, 'What a pretty name for a foreigner!' I detected not a glint of recognition. It was with some relief that I noted this as a sign of the times, after all, the raids and bombs and purges of recent years, our own small bloodbath had faded from public memory.

She left me at last, with a promise to return. 'I could bring in your lunch,' she said. 'I could save you the trouble.' And how my heart ached to meet her daughterly gaze. I wondered, as I so often did with covered girls, what colour her hair was. But even more, I wondered how I could have confused her with that other one, and why it was that I saw covered girls as suspect.

I stood up, banishing that thought too. But the shell had cracked. I could no longer pretend, even to myself, that I was fine, just fine, absolutely fine, or any of the other variations of fine with which I had managed, so far, to fend off the kindly and concerned.

There was, nevertheless, a job to be done. I had just one more day to clear this office and to archive as best I could our own little pocket of history before it, too, disappeared.

I had already done the bookshelves. I was leaving the walls for last. So it was time for the desk drawers that we'd all treated in the same random way. After assembling the assorted contents on their tops, I lingered unnecessarily over the yellow velcro watchbands, the heart shaped sunglasses, the bent business cards, the receipts from a previous life. I picked up a rough and wrinkled piece of paper, torn from the sort used as table coverings in simple restaurants. I turned it over to find the words:

WE WERE HERE

And the date. And the place. And our signatures, merged into one.

I cannot say what exactly I had in mind as I bolted down the stairs, buttoning my coat as I went. I knew only that I had to get to the sea, the sea, wherever I could find it. It had begun to rain, but in my haste I hardly noticed. Having reached the bottom of the hill, I boarded a ferry, with no other aim than to cross the Bosphorus. I must have taken a dozen ferries. I must have walked five miles along each shore. I have memories only of the obstacles: the heavy machinery around the road works, the sudden, ear splitting calls to prayer, the cars parked on the pavements, the busses that wanted to run me over, the fishermen who almost blinded me as they cast their lines, the winds that whipped around the promontories, the ancient potholes, and the iron bars that rose up from the pavement to trip me up.

Then, late in the afternoon, I had my meeting with the sea. I was standing on the wet steps at Kuzguncuk, watching the approaching ferry, one of the old ones, cutting through opaline currents that seemed, just then, to be made of liquefied marble.

I could not help but gasp at the beauty of this illusion, short lived though it was. My fellow travellers gave no indication of having seen a thing. They just stood there on the landing, lost to the opposite shore. It was, I think, their placid expectation that gathered up what was left of my fury. You fools! I thought. You fools!

At once, the reprimand turned inwards. For who more foolish than we?

All the way home, as I battled with the crowds and hills and wet cobblestones, I chastised myself. If only. If anything. If nothing else. It was not until later, when I was standing at my window, watching the Bosphorus which was just a black expanse by now, traversed by ever-shifting lights, that I was able to still my mind.

And then, for the first time since his death, I felt his presence. His arm, cradling my shoulders. His silence, speaking.

I listened, as best I could. I listened, as he summoned all the others. Together they crowded in. First consoling, then chastising. And finally, guiding me to this little table that is only just wide enough for the dark, stark notebook to which I am consigning these words.

I would have preferred something prettier, with marbled covers perhaps. But my ghosts won't have it. They have run out of patience. And I have run out of time. This story they've bequeathed me – it is not mine to keep.

It belongs to you, dear girls. For better or worse, it is your legacy.

So first, let me clear up a few misunderstandings that perhaps arose from that unfortunate altercation we had, just after your father's funeral. Do you remember? We'd decamped to the back of that rather lovely café near Tünel. We had your stepmother with us, and she'd ordered us stiff drinks. And it was, I think, while we were waiting for those drinks to arrive that one of you, I can no longer remember which one of you, found the truth on your phone.

By which I mean the tableau that your father's assassins had left in their wake. Why I'd thought I could spare you this horror, I cannot say. In this day and age, it's not enough to hide the odd newspaper. Of course it was going to go viral. It had, after all, been arranged for just that purpose, for who was going to look away from a scimitar arranged so artfully beneath those three severed heads?

'Tell me this was photoshopped.' Clem, I think that was you. Maude, you spoke at the same time. 'Tell me it isn't true.' Alas, I could not. Neither could I tell you how it had come to this. As you may recall, I was unable to say a thing.

Your stepmother couldn't speak either. Until those stiff drinks arrived and she offered up that strange toast. To our health, she said, to our courage, she said, and then, screwing up her face, she added, but most of all to our refusal.

Whereupon one of you asked, in a harsh and strangled whisper, 'Refusal of what?' Upon which Anais crumpled. You'll remember, I'm sure, how she took hold of my shoulder, how her own shoulders shook as she hid her face and wept. How, once she had collected herself, she said, 'But I can no longer refuse. From now, I lack the strength. Perhaps the time has come,' she said, 'to accept that we are cursed.'

No sooner had she left – the moment she vanished from

view, in fact – you girls both turned to me. On me. At least, that was how it felt.

You wanted to know what Anais had meant by a curse.

You were not impressed by my answer.

I was lying to myself, you said. All this airy talk about history and justice. It meant nothing. It was just a clever way of shunting the blame. I was afraid, you said. Afraid of admitting that I had let this happen, with this mad crusade of mine. All, you said, in the name of some hundred-year-old secret that no one except me would ever have cared about, if I hadn't made such a ruckus.

Of course, I protested. But seven years have passed now since that day. As I sit here at my desk, thinking back and back and back, I'm ever more inclined to accept your verdict. I could have chosen differently. We could all have chosen differently. Instead, we pulled each other in.

By which I mean to say: if our family is cursed, it is not only because of what the older generations passed down to us. It's what we made of it, and failed to make of it. It's what I'm still struggling to understand as I retrace my steps, consumed once again by a desire I cannot name, and unable, even now, to imagine the roads not taken.

# What I knew from the beginning

*Delphine*
|
*Dora*

From a very young age, I knew there were things my mother wasn't telling me. Things she refused to explain. Like who my father was. Or why she didn't like me calling her Mother. Why she insisted that I address her, most especially in company, as Delphine. Why I had two birth certificates, the first placing me in Istanbul on the 18th of November 1949, and the other placing me in New York City on the same date.

I would have been seven when I spotted that anomaly. This on a typical Saturday morning, when Delphine was sleeping late, and I was doing what all girls that age love doing when their mothers' eyes are closed – going through her chest of drawers.

I found the two certificates rolled up inside a sock. I took them to the dining room to examine them with my magnifying glass – a gift from one of my mother's so-called gentleman callers.

I knew all about dates by then. We'd been doing them in school. Although I could not read most of the words on the Istanbul certificate, the name of the city was clear. As was my name. And most of my birth date: the day of the month, and the year. It was definitely official. I could tell that from the stamps. But when I took my incriminating evidence to my mother, she just peered at it with a single, half-closed eye, before heaving herself over and planting a pillow over her head.

Later, when I asked her if both birth certificates were mine, she said of course they were. When I asked her how I could be born in two different places at the same moment, she said, 'Don't be so literal-minded, Dora. That's just paperwork.'

Paperwork was something my mother was an expert on. From as early as I could remember, she'd been working as a secretary for the UN. But the salary was not enough for us to live on, and that, she said, was why she also had to work for a man called William Wakefield, who had her on some sort of allowance that was never enough either.

She called him our saviour in those days, and later she would call him our man for all seasons, but I could tell she was afraid of him. They'd first met in at the US Consulate in Istanbul where she had worked in the last years of World War II, and where he had briefly been stationed. In those days, he liked to tell me, Delphine had been the belle of every ball. 'And isn't she still,' he would say, but in a distant way that set him apart in my mind from the gentleman callers.

He would drop by every month or so, always without warning. Flying in from one continent, he'd say. About to shoot off for another. When I was old enough to ask him why, he told me he was a diplomat.

He'd bring me presents. By the time I was seven, the toys had given way to books, I recall. Books I almost always liked. When I asked him why he was such a good guesser, he said it was because he had a daughter of his own. We'd talk about whatever I happened to be reading while my mother was getting dressed, and then, if she was still not ready, which was almost always the case, he'd take me down to the nice Polish lady who picked me up from school and babysat for me a fair number of nights as well, and while we waited, he would talk to this lady about her homeland, of which he knew a great deal.

When at last, long last, my mother was ready, William would shake my hand and say it had been good knowing me, and usher my mother out the door. They never lasted long, these dinner dates. But a few days later, Delphine would have to leave town for a few days. If I asked her why, she'd make as if to zip her lips. Even now, it's a gesture that provokes an instant fury.

We were still living in Manhattan the autumn I turned eight, but had just moved from the Upper East Side to something a lot lower. I had just started at my third private school, having had to leave the second (and the first) for non-payment of fees. My mother had picked me up early on this particular afternoon in late November, in her words to take me out for a treat, and in my own estimation to make it up to me, after parking me with a new classmate's family over Thanksgiving while she went off on one of her assignments.

In the Russian Tea Room she leaned across the table – beautifully, even I knew that. Lovingly – I knew that too. Eyes shining, she prodded me for details: the exact location of the house in the Berkshires where I had felt so pitied, and so lonely, throughout that very long weekend, the names and possible professions of my classmate's relatives, the number of servants, the size of the turkey I had not so much as touched.

'I hope you realise that I left you with the crème de la crème,' she said. 'They've founded so many colleges and museums, I've lost count.' Met with sullen silence, my mother sought refuge in the menu, the mirror in her powder case, and, finally, with gushing gratitude, the waiter.

'A champagne cocktail for me,' she told him. 'And a Shirley Temple for the millstone.'

It was after he left that I asked my question. 'Why don't we have a family?'

'Oh, but we do, my little chickadee. You know we do.'

'Why don't we ever see them?'

'You have that back to front, my dear. The problem is that they won't see us.'

'Why not?'

'Because. They cannot bear it.'

'Why not?'

'Because. With our very presence, we speak louder than words.'

'Why, though?'

'Because they judge me,' she said. 'For having a daughter, with no husband in sight.'

She'd said this before, but it made no sense to me.

'Why does that matter, even?' I asked.

'Oh, it does. It does. If you're a pillar of society, nothing matters more.'

That made no sense to me either. So I reminded her: a pillar was not a person.

'If only, my little chickadee. If only.' Looking over my shoulder, she let her tears well over. Then, with a sigh, she dabbed her eyes, dried her fingertips on her napkin, and took out a cigarette. When she turned her head to let out

23

the first plume of smoke, I saw that her whole entire cheek was glistening with tears.

'How much do you know about the empire?' she asked.

'Which one?'

'The Ottoman Empire, you silly little turnip.'

I kicked my feet against the table. 'Don't call me a turnip. And stop going off the subject. I asked you why we don't have a family. And you start talking about empires. I'm not interested in empires. Empires are boring.'

'Well, this one isn't. This is the empire that made our family rich.'

'So what?'

'What do you mean, so what?'

'I'm not interested,' I said.

'Well, isn't that a shame now. To think that you spent a whole weekend with those museum people, never suspecting that in our world, they're just new money. Never knowing that your family, our family – by which I mean, my father's family – directed the business of one of the greatest empires the world has ever known, not just for a puny generation or two, but for four long centuries! And all that, without ever, not for a single instant, giving up on being French! What would you say, my little chickadee, if I told you that our original French ancestor set sail for the Ottoman Empire in 1536? And oh, if only you could see his portrait. A lady killer if ever there was one! Oh, the tears that were shed by the fine ladies of Marseille as his ship slipped over the horizon. He would be back, of course! Bearing silk from Smyrna. The fine ladies were still there waiting. They couldn't have enough of this strapping young lad who'd braved untold dangers to make his fortune. But he had eyes only for the fairest…'

'Mother! Stop exaggerating!'

'Believe you me, I am telling you the gospel truth. Where do you think we got our good looks? Noses like ours don't come from just anywhere. But anyway. I'm not conjuring up the facts out of nowhere. Families as great as ours keep records, I'll have you know. And we never stopped speaking French. We started in silk, as I just said, and then we married into figs and wool. By the time I was born, we'd moved into shipping. Shipping and hypocrisy. My grandfather took care of the first part, and my aunts took care of the second.' Sighing, she let out another billow of smoke. 'I've told you they brought me up, these two. After my parents fell off that ledge.'

'When did they do that?'

'What a question! When they died, of course!'

'But you said they died in a plane crash.'

'Yes, of course. But it was that kind of crash. It fell off a ledge. You know. At the end of a runway. Why anyone would think to build a runway at the edge of a cliff though. I guess they thought it would make take-off easier.'

'But it didn't,' I said.

'No it didn't. Down they plunged, right down to the sea floor, leaving me at the mercy of the ugly sisters. And oh, were they ever cruel.'

'Is that why you ran away?'

'Is that what you think – that I ran away? Not at all, my little chickadee. I never ran away. I was pushed.'

'Just because you had me?'

'Let me put it like this, my little chickadee. If we'd stayed, they would never have let me keep you.'

# Mysteries and magazines

For all its thrilling drama, this story didn't make sense to me either. But because I was already reading the mysteries and magazines my mother left scattered across our apartment, I soon came to understand that almost everyone else in the world believed children born outside wedlock to be doomed and damned. Even in New York City. Just as well, I thought, that even here, we hid the truth. We told anyone who asked, and even those who didn't, that my father, like my mother's father, had died in a plane crash – yet another plane crash – just days before my birth.

Where was he, though, if he was, in fact, still alive? Why did my mother fob me off every time I asked? Trained in detection by Dorothy Sayers and Ellery Queen, I could not help but notice that her evasions didn't add up. It wasn't him, she sometimes said: it was his family we had to worry about. It wasn't how he felt, it was who he was. It didn't matter how he felt, because my mother had never once entertained the idea of sharing me. What mattered most, my mother said, was never, ever to breathe his name.

'Why not?' I asked.

'I promised.'

'So what?'

'It was a sacred promise. Do you happen to know what happens, when you break a sacred promise? No? I didn't think so. So let me tell you. They roll right over you. They stamp you out.'

They. It was the icy, ominous way she said it. And what this implied: my mother had made a sacred promise not just to one man, but to an entire league of them. Why?

I pondered this question most deeply whenever she parked me with my latest babysitter and disappeared to parts unknown, for reasons never specified, beyond what she blithely called 'the obvious'. Namely: that it wasn't for nothing that she worked at the UN. And it wasn't just her six languages. In any event, having six languages was not at all remarkable in Istanbul, as she so liked to remind me. Everyone had six languages at least. The things that set her apart, she said – the thing that made her a real treasure – was that she could spot a Communist a mile off. No matter what they said they were or even how they dressed.

'And I don't need to explain to you how important that is.'

As indeed she did not. Every child attending American schools in the 1950s was steeped in horror stories about Soviet spies and Communist infiltrators, plotting together to steal our nuclear secrets, building bombs so powerful as to bring about the end of the world.

Like every other child in America in the 1950s, I took those horror stories to bed with me each night. And if I woke up before dark to a dark and deadly hush, my first thought would be – they're here. The Communists. Giving my mother the third degree.

She would never crack. Of that I was certain. But what if these evil traitors managed nevertheless to divine my mother's true identity? What would become of her? What would become of me?

I would have been nine when I woke up before dawn to the sound of a glass smashing, against a wall or a floor. But when I peered out into the hallway to find out which, I saw my mother standing at the entrance to our living room, holding a high-heeled shoe in each hand but still wearing her fur coat. Beyond her, in our favourite armchair, was our saviour, later to become our man for all seasons. William Wakefield. He was sitting where my babysitter had been, and redder in the face than I had ever seen him.

'What the hell do you think you're up to?'

'At PJ Clarke's?' my mother said. 'What do you think?

'Happy hour ended a very long time ago, my young friend.'

'What can I say? One martini leads to another. Especially on Friday nights.'

'So tell me,' William snarled. 'Who was buying? Was it Michal, or was it Sven?'

'You know them?'

'How could I not?'

'Sven from the Social and Economic Council?'

'That's a front,' William said, 'as you well know.'

'That's a given.'

'So let's move on to Michal. Do you happen to know what he's calling himself these days?'

'He didn't say,' my mother said. 'In any event, we weren't talking about work.'

'What were you talking about?'

'Oh, you know. Gold.'

'Oh really? What kind of gold?'

'You know full well what kind of gold,' my mother said.

'Aha. How interesting. So you spent the evening prattling on about gold to our fine pair of known operatives. And at no point did you wonder if they were playing on your weak spot, to reel you in? What did they promise you?'

'Oh, for God's sake, William. Nothing.'

'Nothing but all those martinis.'

'You've got it.'

'Plus a few leads on your favourite conspiracy theory.'

'That gold exists, William!'

'Yes, but where?'

'That's what I intend to find out one day.'

'And that,' bellowed William, ' is how they intend to play you.'

'No one plays me.'

'That is very good to know, Delphine. Music to my ears, in fact.' Standing up, he sighed heavily, before taking himself over to the sideboard, there to pour two tumblers of bourbon. Handing one to my mother, he said, 'I take it they had questions to ask about a certain friend of ours in a certain Soviet consulate. You know. From the old days.'

'I don't know who you're talking about,' my mother said.

'Oh, yes, you fucking do.' He pointed at our sofa. 'Sit down.'

She sat down.

He did the same. First to savour his drink, then to lean forward and ask, 'So tell me. Whose side are you on?'

'Our side. Your side! Of course!'

'Then what are you doing spending Friday night with a pair of Soviet spooks, lapping up tall tales about Armenian gold?'

'It j happens to be an interest of mine, William! As you well know.'

'I can't believe I'm having to spell all this out for you. But, Baby, if you don't want to end up electrocuted or at the bottom of a lake, I'd advise you to put a lid on that particular fetish. For the time being, at least.'

'Can you at least tell me why?'

'It marks you out. Raises questions. Attracts the wrong sort of attention. Need I say more?'

'I still don't get it,' my mother said. 'I speak to known Soviet operatives all the time.'

'Not to talk about Armenian gold, you don't.'

'I wasn't the one to mention it! They were! And so what if they did?'

William sighed and shook his head. 'Maybe I should buy you an atlas. Maybe then you'd remember that there happens to be a Soviet republic called Armenia.'

'That's not where the gold is,' my mother said.

'Exactly. So tell me. Did they happen to have any ideas as to its current whereabouts?'

Pressing her lips together, widening her eyes, my mother reached over for the handbag she had thrown on the sofa next to her and dumped out its contents.

'Now we're getting somewhere,' said William in a happier voice. He sat back, lit up a cigarette, and waited for my mother to rummage among the lipsticks, the mints, and the pencils, the matchboxes and the keys.

'Here,' she said finally, handing him a rumpled napkin. 'This is all I got.'

With his free hand he straightened it out on his knee, crumpling up his nose as he read the notes she had jotted down on it. 'Interesting,' he said. He sounded almost impressed. 'Yes, I think we can use this.'

'As leverage, you mean.'

'Yes, if nothing else, as leverage.'

'Turn the tables on them, in other words.'

'Hmmm,' said William. 'Now there's a nasty thought.'

'It hadn't occurred to me until this very moment,' my mother said, a bit too eagerly.

'But it's worth considering, certainly. My friend, this could be the moment.'

'You think so?' she gasped.

William sat back, to think, inside a cloud of smoke. 'Let me mull it over. Talk it through with A N Other.'

'Not that A N Other?'

'The very one. The next time he and I meet, I mean. Which could be a while. So I wouldn't pack my bags quite yet.'

'No, of course not. I couldn't go now, anyway. Not while a certain friend of ours is still based there.'

'I take your point,' said William, 'But a little bird told me he's not long for Istanbul. They want to move him to the Embassy in Ankara.'

'Poor boy. That's not his style at all.'

'But as you and I both know, it's not his choice, either.'

William Wakefield never did buy my mother an atlas. So I used the one at school. And there it was: the Armenian Soviet Socialist Republic. I looked it up in the encyclopaedia too and it was here, amidst the bare facts about this republic, that I first read of Armenian massacres in what later became Turkey, in the middle of the First World War. There was no mention of gold, so I widened my search, eventually discovering that there was no private ownership in any part of the Soviet Union, that everything, including precious metals, was owned by the state.

Aha, I thought. So that was why my mother had said that the Armenian gold she was so interested in was no longer in Armenia. It must, I decided, have been moved to the coffers of the Kremlin, in Moscow.

So far, so good. But who was this old friend in Istanbul they kept mentioning? And whose side was he on? Reviewing the conversation I had overheard, I was inclined to think he (a) worked for the Soviets while also (b) working for us.

Acquainted as I now was with Eric Ambler and Ian Fleming, I could not help but worry for this man's safety. And also for our own, if – as I now suspected – William planned to send my mother and me back to Istanbul. Was this wise? Bearing in mind all the things my mother had told me over the years, about the sacred promise she had made, and what they would do to her, and to me, if she broke her vow?

Was this unnamed Soviet friend one of them? Or had he too made a sacred promise? Why did my mother call him a friend at all, if she didn't want to risk returning to Istanbul while he was still there?

I was sitting in my school library, reading up on the population, religions, and major industries of Turkey, gazing at a picture of Mustafa Kemal Atatürk, who was the father of the modern republic, even though he himself had never had any children, when suddenly a rogue thought flew in at me, out of nowhere:

The unnamed Soviet friend whose name my mother dared not breathe must be my father.

Who was he? Who was he really? Did he know of my existence, or had this, too, been hidden from him, and if it had been, why? How had he and my mother met? Had they ever been in love? Who and what had torn them asunder? Was I destined never to meet him, or would a return to Istanbul offer us the chance, at least, of a brief, even accidental, encounter?

What did it say about me, if half of me was Soviet? Even if I knew nothing about it, even if I could never be sure, how could I ever trust myself, knowing one of my hands lived in eternal ignorance of what the other hand might be doing?

What was worse – to know or not to know? Some nights I considered begging my mother never to take me back to the city where the truth might lurk. But then, upon waking the next morning, I would remind myself what so many of my mother's paperbacks had taught me: no good can come of running away from the truth. Best to face the facts. And first, to prepare.

*From Russia with Love* is probably the only book my mother ever bought in hardback. She might even have bought it on the day it first came out. She just couldn't wait, she said, to find out what James Bond made of Istanbul.

That had been a year ago, when I was eight. I'd read it then, too, in the manner the author might have intended though perhaps not for a girl my age, and in the space of one long night. Returning to it with my new suspicions on the eve of turning ten, I viewed it more as a guidebook to the thrilling terrors now awaiting me: a city straddling Europe and Asia, cut through by an unsheltered Bosphorus, a fabled skyline of minarets and imperial palaces, beneath which lay a labyrinth of secret passages – an underworld of rats and hell cats. And under every rock, a Russian spy.

Another two years would pass before I heard another word about Istanbul. By now I had almost if not quite put it out of my mind. At least, I'd stopped believing that the world described by thrillers and mystery stories was entirely accurate. But then, one sodden, steaming August morning, the doorbell rang, and there, before me, was a dowager – no other word will do – draped in silks and jewels, her white hair swept up into a bun topped by a tiny hat with a tinier veil, and clutching an embroidered portmanteau. After looking me up and down without affection, she announced,

'You must be Dora.' Her English was heavily accented, but fluent. Without waiting for an invitation, she stepped inside. 'Where's your mother? She's not still in bed at this late hour?'

She was. Or rather, she had been until that moment. Entering her bedroom, I found her hunting frantically for a dress. 'That's not who I think it is, is it?'

'I have no idea,' I said.

'I wish I didn't either,' my mother said. She fished two stockings out of the laundry basket. 'Her name is Karine. Madame Karine, I should say. Go out there and buy me some time, while I put on my face.'

Out I went to ask Madame Karine if she'd like some coffee. She waved the offer away. 'Just clear that table for me,' she said, gesturing in the direction of our dining alcove. I did as she asked, whereupon she plonked her portmanteau on a chair and told me to go back and tell my mother to hurry up. 'I don't have all day, and I am not a man for whom she must put on a face.'

By the time I returned, still without my mother, Madame Karine was busy removing documents from an accordion file and spreading them across the table, like a fan. Some looked like bank statements. Others looked like contracts or deeds.

'What are these?' I asked.

'These,' said Madame Karine, 'are the papers your mother will need when she and you return to Istanbul. If, that is, she is to claim her rightful legacy from those ugly aunts of hers.'

'We're returning to Istanbul?'

'Oho! Did this disgrace to modern motherhood neglect to tell you? You're leaving any month now, I understand.'

'How do you know all this?' I asked.

'Don't you have a sharp tongue now! Quite impressive for a girl of eleven.'

'Twelve,' I said.

'Twelve, then. But never fear. I happen to like a sharp tongue on a girl of whatever age.'

'Who are you?'

'Aha! Oho! So this too has been kept from you! Never mind. Or should I say, better late than ever.' She offered me a limp, bejewelled hand. 'I am – how shall I put it? – your mother's great aunt. As for you – you are my great grand niece, or my grand great niece, though I would prefer to avoid saying either. It is too too depressing. I'm barely in my seventies, after all! What matters is that we are related. And after the same thing. Or perhaps not,' she said. She glanced at her golden watch. With an impatient sigh, she began gathering up the documents and returning them to their accordion file.

'Perhaps your mother would prefer not to claim what is her due – or shall I say, what little part of her rightful inheritance she can claim under that catastrophe of stolen fabrications we call Turkish law. Though even this small part is far from insignificant. Nevertheless. I can deduct from her absence at this moment that perhaps she does not wish to distract herself with mere millions, or a modest portfolio of fine properties, bent as she is on following that gaggle of wild geese to their pot of gold.' With that, she put the accordion file back into her embroidered portmanteau and sailed off to the door. 'You can tell your mother I'm in New York until Tuesday if she can find her face before then.'

'Aren't you even going to leave an address?' I asked.

'She knows where to find me. You can be sure of that.

But tell her not to bother, unless her answer to my other proposal is yes.'

In answer to my question – what proposal was that then? – she merely laughed.

My mother's answer, when I asked her the same thing: 'Oh for God's sake. Who cares?'

I did. But that was the last I heard of it. As for Madame Karine, all my mother would say was that we were indeed related, 'but only sort of, in a manner of speaking'.

'What does that mean?' I asked.

'It means that because she married into a petroleum fortune she thinks she can spout lies like one of her husband's oil rigs. You are not to believe a word she says!'

Except about Istanbul. And the inheritance. Some eight months later, in April 1961 to be precise, we were on our way back.


## The City

Throughout our ocean crossing, and even after we had changed ships at Genoa, my mother shared her apprehensions about returning to the city she still called The City. Every night, over supper, she would tell me that if it weren't for this inheritance, she would have been tempted to ask the ship to turn around.

'I'm doing all this for you,' she would say. 'You and your future. That's it. If I thought I had any choice in the matter, if I could claim this legacy in absentia, I would never go back to Istanbul, not even with a barge pole.'

But when our ship rounded Palace Point on that bright spring morning, my mother could barely contain herself.

After pointing out the grand monuments of the Old City, and the bridge at the mouth of the Golden Horn, she pulled me to the railing to point to the hill rising up from its northern shore. This was the European quarter, she told me. Our birthplace, no less. There on the left was the great Galata Tower. There, almost next door, was the Swedish consulate. And there, further down the Grande Rue de Pera, between St Antoine and the Soviet consulate, was the grand apartment that had witnessed my entry into the world. Or at least, one of them.

I was not the sort of twelve-year-old who cared much about luxury or splendour, but the dusty, dirty avenue that was no longer known as the Grande Rue de Pera was nevertheless a disappointment. Arriving at the building that had ushered me into the world, we'd found the free spirit I would come to know as my Great Aunt Hümeyra. She was waiting in its shabby entrance, draped in more shawls than the warm day warranted, and when she opened her arms in effusive abandon, they slipped off her shoulders, en masse, to be swept up by an unkempt man who turned out to be our porter. As he carried our bags inside, she strode out to the middle of the narrow avenue to perform for the traffic. By now she had re-draped herself in her bright and clashing shawls. And though I could not yet follow her Turkish, I gathered from her gestures and her occasional forays for our benefit into French and English that she wanted this motley assortment of drivers and pedestrians to know how much she appreciated their patience, and how much she longed for them to share her joy in welcoming us home.

Home, I remember thinking. Since when was this home? The wrought iron door slammed behind us like a prison gate. The marble steps were uneven and the stairwell stank of damp. The air in the third floor apartment that this great aunt had bequeathed to us was stale and still. There was nothing in the front room but an overstuffed sofa and a table that was missing a leg.

'Never fear!' said Hümeyra. 'There is more on the way!' Leaning forward, she added, in a stage whisper, 'My thieves are busy combing the city for us, even as we speak. And look!' She gestured at a pile of red satin in the corner. 'I have managed to liberate for you the most precious drapes!'

I was already at the window where I would spend so much of the next eighteen months, watching, wondering, dreaming, and standing guard.

But that morning, the scene before me was almost too much to take in. Accustomed to the narrow rectangles of sun and sky above our Manhattan apartments, I was unsettled, but also mesmerised, by this tableau that would not stand still. There, beneath our hill, was the unsheltered Bosphorus, crisscrossed with ferries, fishing boats, and ships. There, beyond it, was the greying Asian shore. Here, just beneath our building, just slightly to its left, was a courtyard, fronting a dark stone edifice, before which stood a taciturn armed guard. Above him fluttered a red flag with a white hammer and sickle.

The Soviet Consulate.

No one had seen fit to warn me that we would be this close.

Why was that? I wondered, while behind me, my mother and this great aunt I was to call Hümeyra continued with their inventory like two chirping birds. My mother was charmed by the four-poster bed. Hümeyra apologised for the sparseness of kitchen utensils, as she made yet another list for her thieves. They were almost dancing, these two, as they went from room to room, fiddling with the hot water heater, moving the full length mirror, winding up the clock. As we left our new apartment for Hümeyra's own next door, they were arm in arm.

Waiting for us in Hümeyra's great room, perched on the edge of the ancient chaise longue, was a broad-faced man with ginger hair that stood up like a brush. With a slow and anxious smile, he rose to meet us. My mother stopped short, as he bowed. My mother turned to Hümeyra. In French, she asked her what on earth she thought she was doing.

'I thought you would want to see him,' she replied.

Upon which I was told to return to our new apartment. When I protested, my mother pressed the key into my hand and said, 'Now.'

She said this in a tone I had never before heard her use before. I was too shocked to disobey.

It did not take me long, though, to find the side window that looked across a shaft and into the alcove I would come to know as Hümeyra's morning room. There I stood, watching the two women stabbing the air, while the man whose short ginger hair stood up like a brush wandered back and forth between them, shoulders hunched, face fallen, hands on ears.

At one point, he stopped near the window. For a long time, he kept his eyes fixed on the ground. But when he looked up and saw me standing there, his face lit up, as very slowly, he bowed.

# A new suspicion

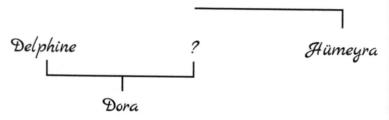

*Delphine*               ?                    *Hümeyra*

*Dora*

Could Sergei be the one? The man my mother wished never to acknowledge as my father? My suspicions deepened over supper that same day, in Rejans, a nearby restaurant run by White Russians, when Delphine informed me that I was never, ever to speak to this man, who was not just a Communist, but a provocateur, and not just a Soviet, but a Soviet spy. 'If I'd known he was going to be here, if I'd had the faintest inkling, I would never have brought us back.'

I asked where she knew him from.

'Here,' she said. 'Isn't that obvious?'

'Not really,' I replied. 'Not if you weren't expecting him not to be here.'

'Of course I wasn't expecting him to be here. For God's sake, they should have moved him on by now. Or not moved him back.'

'So which is it?' I asked.

'I don't know.'

'You could ask him, you know.'

'In fact, Miss Priss, I could not.'

'Why not?'

'He could be trying to draw me into something.'

'Like what?'

'Didn't you hear me? This man's a Communist. Which is

40

why I don't want you speaking to Sergei, ever. Not unless you want to spend the rest of your life locked up.'

'If you say so,' I said. But only to fob her off. It wasn't that I didn't believe her. This was the Cold War, after all. If this man whose name I now knew to be Sergei was a Russian, then it followed – did it not? – that he was a Communist. Or at least, pretending to be one. Either way, he could still be my father. Either way, there were things my mother wasn't telling me. Things I both longed to know and feared. It was, perhaps, this curious dread, this itching curiosity, that drew me to the side window each Friday evening, to watch the ebb and flow of Hümeyra's soirees.

It was a rare Friday when I did not see my mother in conversation with the man who was not to be spoken to. They were easy with each other, contemptuously easy, like brother and sister, almost, in the way they would exchange looks, or shrugs, or laughs. I often saw my mother cut this Sergei off mid-sentence or shake her fist at him. Once she put her hands around his neck, as if to strangle him. As he pushed away her hands, he kissed her on both cheeks.

A few other regulars I came to know from this distance: A very large blond woman with an accordion. A man they called the Society Photographer who had been in some sort of car accident, they said. It had left him too severely brain damaged to hold down a job, but he came religiously to every soiree, to take more pictures than anyone could count. Some of these he would give to Hümeyra. Most she would cut up for her paintings. A few she would keep, to frame one day, she said, but she never did.

There was also a man named Baby Mallinson who'd been a celebrated jazz pianist in New York and a card-carrying

Communist before being blacklisted during the McCarthy witch hunts. If he was not three sheets to the wind when he arrived at a soiree, he provided us with the most enchanting music. If it was a three-sheet night, though, he would pick a fight with Sergei. And then he would crawl into a corner, to cry and cry and cry.

According to Vartuhi, the maid, these two lived together. Sharing the same bed. She would say this and raise her eyebrows to indicate she did not approve, but also sighing to indicate that she forgave them. A relation of Vartuhi's cleaned for Sergei and Baby Mallinson, but no matter how hard she worked, Vartuhi reported, the household remained in disarray. Had our return thrown these two off balance? Did Sergei and my mother still love each other, I wondered, somewhere deep inside? Had they been driven apart by the Cold War? Would they be together still, joining hands with their beloved daughter, had patriotic duty not called? I would conjure up scenes to illustrate my hypothesis, but then I would remember: this Sergei was on our side somehow. If our secret bond were discovered, it would blow his cover. I did not want to blow his cover. And neither did I wish to blow my own. If my mother gained the faintest idea of my suspicions, there'd be hell to pay, and so I said nothing. I waited, and I kept my eyes peeled, and not just on Hümeyra's soirees. There was also the courtyard of the Soviet Consulate. I knew, from Sergei's comings and goings, that he had to be on their payroll.

I guessed, from the way my mother held him in her arms once, in the late hours of a soiree, that his heart wasn't in the spying life. That he longed to defect. That he was probably asking my mother to arrange it. When they sat down to

42

converse intently, backs bent, and heads bowed, I guessed that they were puzzling together over the best case they could make for him. They wouldn't bring him over – would they? – unless he had something very valuable to offer.

What could that be? I asked myself. Until at last I saw the obvious. Of course. What else? Our Sergei would buy his release from the Soviet yoke by solving for the West that most dangerous mystery: the enigma of Armenian gold.

Such a good idea! Why, then, were Sergei and my mother still shaking their heads and sighing? Oh yes, I thought. Again, I was staring at the obvious. It was not enough to solve the enigma. Sergei's information would be of no use unless he led them to the gold itself.

Would he ever dare to attempt a feat this dangerous? If he did, what were his chances of surviving? Or ours? No, this was a bridge too far, I told myself. Silently, I tried to convey my qualms across the gulf between us. Willing them to accept that the odds were against them: never would they succeed in freeing this gold from the coffers of the Kremlin. Until at last, they seemed to hear me. Nodding sadly, raising their heads at last, but still holding hands. I could not lip read. I could not be sure. But it seemed to me that this was the moment when they dropped that plan and returned to the woes of the here and now.

When it was my mother's turn to cry in Sergei's arms, I knew, without a shadow of a doubt, that she was crying about the humiliations she and I had been suffering at the hands of her cruel family, and that family's vast network of spiteful friends.

# My mother's cruel family

During the many weddings that comprised our doomed attempt to re-enter polite society that first summer, there were always exceptions: the brides who insisted on our sitting at the top table, under their mothers' dark glares; the nephews who made sure my mother was the first to dance; the kindly uncles who kept her glass full; and the younger men who rushed across the dance floor with arms outstretched, because once upon a time, they'd worshipped my mother but also because their wives and aunts and mothers had not yet chastised them for daring to acknowledge a woman who should never have been invited in the first place – a woman who'd had the audacity (as my mother let slip in an uguarded moment) to bring along the daughter who should never have been born.

Sundays were the hardest. We would walk into St Antoine to a forest of frowns. We would sidle into a crowded pew only to watch its other occupants slip away.. The priests were kind to us, but they pretended not to see.

'That was my aunt, by the way,' Delphine would say afterwards, as we sat with our cakes and coffees beneath the Art Nouveau nymphs at Markiz. And then, as if I needed reminding, she would add, 'I'm referring to that woman the size of a tractor who looked right through us. She's the one who tried to terrorise me into getting rid of you. And she calls herself a Catholic! Promise me you'll never do that,' she would add, as she glowered through her smoke.

'Never do what, exactly?'

'Never let anyone terrorise you into doing something you know is categorically and absolutely wrong.'

'Mother! Do you honestly think anyone could?'

A smile, at last. A hand, extended. 'We're a good team, aren't we? In spite of everything, at least we're that.'

We were getting nowhere, though. We must have wasted half of that summer with lawyers in smoke-filled rooms with leather chairs so hot they seemed to be sweating. Hour after hour, the men who could not help us reclaim our rightful legacy bowed their heads in studied resignation, as my mother leaned forward, chest first, and pleaded. The boy would come in with the tea tray. My mother would accept another glass and the boy would take away the glass she'd allowed to go cold. As she stirred three cubes of sugar into the new glass, she would make a good show of fighting off tears, before launching her next argument. Watching her get nowhere was tedious so to pass the time I wrote down the words she repeated the most, and afterwards, back in the apartment, I looked them up in the dictionaries and grammars I'd amassed for myself. Once I'd learned the words, I'd record them in a lovely marbled notebook.

*Allah aşkına.* That was the first phrase I recorded, and the words my mother used most during those long sessions with unhelpful lawyers. It meant 'for the love of God'.

Then there was the day my mother walked me up four flights of stairs to a smoke-filled office whose floors were stacked high with newspapers in a script I'd never seen before and where my mother, having stunned the men behind the desks to silence, delivered a desperate or angry or impassioned plea in a language I was unable to identify.

'I suppose you're going to ask me what just happened up

there,' she said afterwards, over cakes at Pelit. Before I could speak, she added, 'Unfortunately I can't tell you.'

'Why not?'

'For your own safety.'

'Why did you take me with you, then?'

'Hah! What do you think?'

'I don't know what to think,' I said.

'Okay then. I'll tell you that, at least. I needed you there as protection.'

'Why?'

'Never you mind.'

'What language were you speaking?'

'It's better not to say.'

'Was it Russian?' I asked.

'Hah! That's funny. But no. Just for your information, it wasn't Russian.'

'Then what was it?

'Something else.'

'If you don't tell me, I'll ask someone else,' I threatened.

'How exactly do you plan to do that?'

'With this,' I said.

I took out the newspaper I had skimmed off one of the piles while no one was looking.

The moment my mother saw it, she grabbed hold of my wrist. 'How dare you! 'Do you want to get us killed?'

Back in the apartment, she offered an explanation of sorts. She told me we had just visited the offices of an Armenian newspaper and she had been speaking Armenian.

'How do you know Armenian?' I asked.

'I just do.'

'That's not an answer. It's an evasion.'

'Too bad.'

'Can you tell me at least what were you saying to them, up in that office?'

'I was telling them not to print something.'

'What something?' I asked.

'A vicious lie.'

'About us?'

'About me.'

'Why did you need me there with you, then?'

'I wanted them to know who you were, and who would come after them, if they messed with me.'

'I don't understand,' I said.

'I know you don't. And honey, believe me, it's better off that way. We're not staying here forever, you know. We're here for a reason, and once we get what we want and deserve, we'll be off.'

'With the gold?' I asked.

Grabbing both my shoulders, my mother cried, 'Who's been talking to you about gold?'

'No one!' I said. 'I just thought...'

'For God's sake, Dora. Tell me. Who's been putting ideas in your head?'

'No one,' I said. 'Oh for God's sake. Christ. Dora, you'll be the death of me. Of us both. All right then. Just this once, I'll explain. And when I'm done, you're going to have to wipe the slate clean. Pretend I've never said a thing. Do you understand?'

'I understand.'

'Okay then. It's like this. They were going to name me. In an article about gold.'

'Armenian gold?'

'Shush. And anyway. Gold knows no nationality. And also. As those shit-for-brains editors now know. Their story was

47

totally false. But that's not the important thing. The important thing is for you to remember this: for as long as we are here, you are not to use or even think the word Armenian.'

'Why?' I asked. 'Because of the massacres?'

'God almighty! Who's been talking to you about them?'

'No one,' I said haughtily. 'I read about them in the Encyclopaedia Britannica.'

'When? Where?'

'At school, of course. Back in New York.'

'Heaven help me. Well, let me tell you. You won't find it in any encyclopaedia here.'

'Why not?'

'Because. Officially, it never happened.'

'But it did happen!'

'Shush!' This time, she grabbed my collar.

'Let go! You're choking me!'

'Better me than the mob outside,' she snarled. 'They'd tear you limb from limb if they heard what you just said!'

'Why?'

'Because what they've all been told, all their lives, in every school and newspaper, is that it never happened. That whoever says differently, is a traitor. Is attacking the national honour. Is asking to be lynched. This is not a free country, in case you hadn't noticed. You can go to jail just by thinking something. Most of all, for thinking this. It's every bit as bad as thinking like a Communist. In fact, it's one and the same thing. So Dora, I mean it. You are going to wipe your mind clean. Forget we ever had this conversation. Keep careful watch on what you say.'

'For the love of God,' I said.

'My thought exactly.'

During my early peregrinations around our neighbourhood, I had to ask for the love of God on a number of untoward occasions. I was tall for my age – which had been a plus in New York where I'd thought nothing of going out to eat by myself, day or night, and spent many happy afternoons wandering around the Met or Central Park unescorted, without anyone stopping me to ask where my mother was. But in Istanbul, a twelve-year-old who could pass for fourteen was the centre of grasping and hectoring attention wherever she happened to go. If I was so foolish as to wander around the back streets near our apartment of an evening – or even before it got dark – I would be met by lewd stares outside every bar and store front, while behind me others whispered words I knew to be obscenities, even if I didn't know what they meant. Even when I was shopping for food, early in the morning with all the maids and housewives of our neighbourhood, there would be urchins lingering around the butcher shops and the delicatessens, the fruit and vegetable and fish stands, waiting for me to step within range, so that they could poke their fingers between my legs.

Until, one day, the man with whom I was never to speak saw it happening. Draping a protective arm around me, Sergei shamed the urchin with a righteous dressing down, and soon there were a dozen or so other good citizens gathered around us, shaking their heads in consternation.

He took me back to the apartment, waiting outside while I checked to make sure my mother was there to greet me. When I returned with the news that my mother was not yet back from wherever she'd been the previous night, he thought for a moment, and said, 'Let's take this one risk.'

With that, Sergei took me across to Hümeyra. Which was

not unusual or risky in itself because I was in and out of that apartment all the time, but this was the first time I'd been there in the company of Sergei.

We found Hümeyra in her studio, which overlooked the avenue, and which barely had room these days for the easel that sat at its centre, what with all the paintings and photographs stacked against the walls, and the great piles of old magazines and newspapers, and the glasses filled with old coloured water, and the half used tubes of paint strewn across every available surface. When Sergei told her what had happened back at the market, it was Hümeyra's turn to embrace me with effusive sorrow. Pulling back to look me in the eyes, she told me, in French, that she was going to make sure such an outrage never happened again.

Quickly Hümeyra threw on an assortment of shawls and led us down the stairs and out into the avenue. For the next three hours, we went from shop to shop, greengrocer to delicatessen, red light hotel to red light bar. In each, she was greeted with warmth and delight. In each, we were offered tea or coffee or sweets, and sometimes we accepted. Though I could not yet fully follow a Turkish conversation, I could tell that she was impressing upon them that I was a relative, and not just a relative, but a very precious one.

From then on, I had the protection of the entire neighbourhood. Wherever I went, people stopped me, and invited me in for a coffee, or a tea, or a sweet, and because I always took my phrase books with me, I would use these visits to practice my Turkish. And before long, I could converse about anything that might come up in polite summertime conversation. Which is another way of saying that my vocabulary was rich in some ways, and poor in others: I knew everything there was to say about humidity or heat, but it was not until much later that I learned the words for snow and rain. I had no religious vocabulary whatsoever, but I was getting quite good at following conversations about money, politics, and the law, thanks to having spent so much time that summer at my mother's side, listening to all those important and pontificating men in law offices and in bars, identifying words and committing them to memory, so that I could figure out later how they might be connected. And when I think back on those imaginings, I can only marvel at the ease with which I was able to assemble a dastardly and watertight plot from no more than a word or two. Combining the world for shipment or bribe with the word for night or treason, I would conjure up the worst and then lie awake at night, preparing for it.

I think back on those silent and solitary exercises in self-preservation and wonder if I have ever known a life without extreme anxiety.

## A change of plans

Lacking an inheritance, and fast running through our reserves, my mother had no choice but to take on more work. This meant going against the sacred promise she'd made me before leaving New York, that it would be just the two of us from here on in, facing the world together.

Taking on more work meant most nights at Kulis, a bar favoured by journalists and diplomats, just down the avenue from our apartment. The bartenders were kind to me but I hated having to go there: it was smoky and stuffy and too dark for me to read.

So I started staying at home in the evenings. Making the most of my mother's absence. Reading and then rereading *And Quiet Flows the Don*, the Soviet novel in English translation that Sergei had given to Hümeyra to give me, without a word of explanation. Though perhaps (I conjectured) he thought none was needed. Perhaps he knew how important it was for a half-Soviet girl to understand that, beneath the threats and the propaganda, the country still possessed a living, breathing soul she could love and devote her life to rescuing.

Soon afterwards came another present – a transistor radio. This ostensibly from Hümeyra who was sad I had to spend so much time alone, who knew that the studio where she worked day and night was not enough for a girl my age, even though I was always welcome. If I preferred to sit somewhere else, more comfortably, then a radio might make for good company. She was right. It did. Before long I had extended my research into the secrets of the Soviet soul by listening to the nightly broadcasts in English on Radio Moscow.

Soon this broadcast alone was not enough. Intrigued by the sound of Russian, I asked Hümeyra to ask Sergei if he could find me a Russian grammar. The grammar arrived with a dictionary which allowed me to deploy the same method I'd devised with the hapless lawyers and the pontificating men. I jotted down words that turned up with any frequency in the Russian broadcasts I was now also listening in on.

It did not take me long to notice how often these words seemed to echo my favourite passages in *And Quiet Flows the Don*.

Meanwhile, my mother was cultivating new friends. From

time to time she brought one back from the bar with her. I didn't like that, and I told her so.

And she would say: 'Why do you have to be such a killjoy?' Or: 'Can't I have a little time off now and again?' Or: 'What? I'm supposed to be a nun now?' Or: 'Can't a gal have a friend back to the house more?' Or, most cutting of all: 'Why can't you find some friends of your own?'

Even in New York, I'd never mastered that art. I was liked well enough in school, but I'd soon learned that it was not a good idea to bring classmates home. And anyway, I preferred my own company.

By the end of my eighteen-month stay in Istanbul, I had one friend I could call my own. Though she was more like a disciple, a girl four years younger than me who was grateful for the smallest kindness and believed every word I said. But her parents were strict. Our time together was limited. The rest of the time, I was left to make do with the makeshift group my mother referred to as 'the cousins'. We were hardly friends, though, not in those days. We barely acknowledged each other. For the most part, we were fellow sufferers, skirting the edges of all those weddings.


## The cousins

*Sinan   Suna   Haluk   Anais*

It was at one of those weddings that I came to discover what it means to be related not just to the hostile congregation of a church or two, but to absolutely everyone. And how much it can hurt to look in any direction as you can see, and know that each and every person at each and every table knows more about you than you know yourself.

Let me set the scene for you: we are at some sort of club, possibly the Anatolia Club on Büyükada, in fact, almost certainly. The Sea of Marmara is choppy, as it often is towards the end of a summer afternoon. The sunbathers are gathering up their things and in their wake come the waiters with their hoses and brooms. They work around me, because I'm deep into a book that I am loath to leave mid-chapter. Until I hear my mother's voice.

'Honey, come here! Give those boys a break!'

I look over my shoulder and spot her at a table that has already been prepared for the wedding we shall be attending that evening. She has exchanged her scanty bikini for her red knock'em-dead dress which means she has already been back to the house where we are staying as slightly unwelcome guests. On the tree-lined terrace behind her, the afternoon bridge players have not yet given up the fight, but they are adjusting their ties and their preposterous linen suits in preparation for their return to their villas, to change into whatever their wives have chosen for them to wear this evening.

Sitting with my mother is a portly man with sad and liquid eyes who jumps to his feet at the sight of me, to bow and kiss my hand. Silently, he pulls out a chair for me. Silently, he watches me settle.

Then he turns to my mother. "Would you be so kind as to introduce us?'

'Yes, of course,' she says, and I can tell from the edge in her deferential tone that she is somewhat reluctant to do so. 'Dora, this is your Uncle Melih.'

And he says, 'At long last, we meet.'

There follows a long silence, which my mother ends. 'You

need to go back to the house and get ready.' she says brightly.

'I don't think so,' I say. 'I'm fine wearing this.' This being the sundress I have been wearing all day.

'Oh honey, don't be awkward. Why can't you let yourself be pretty? That taffeta looks so good on you. And the violet brings out your eyes. I had the maid iron it for your specially...'

'Well, you shouldn't have.'

'Why ever not?'

'Because she's not our maid.'

'She comes with the house, my dear. She was more than happy to...'

'It's still wrong,' I say.

'Who says?' she says. 'The Communists?'

Here Melih leans forward to put a gentle but still firm hand on my mother's shoulder. 'Let her be, my dear. Let us make the most of our opportunity.' Draping his arms across his ample belly, he proceeds to quiz me on my studies, interests, and future plans.

My mother interrupts from time to time, to speak of achievements I've forgotten to mention. He is very pleased to hear that I have picked up Turkish, seemingly without effort.

'She's a chip off the old block, in other words,' my mother says.

And Uncle Melih, beaming, says, 'How could she not be?'

But now we are joined by another man about his age. This one is lean and angular. No smiles. He pulls up a chair. No one speaks as he settles himself into it. He inspects us each in turn.

'Are you not going to introduce us?' he finally asks.

'There is no need,' says Uncle Melih.

'Well, just in case,' says my mother. 'Dora, this is your Uncle Semih.'

Semih laughs unpleasantly. In Turkish, he says, 'So, we have come to this.'

In Turkish, Melih says: 'Our girl, who is highly intelligent, can understand your every word.'

'Impossible. She has only just arrived.'

'I urge you to undertake your own investigation. Citizen, speak to the girl in Turkish.'

This the man proceeds to do, and although I can understand his every question, and answer each question in full sentences, my performance seems to upset Uncle Semih just as much as it delights Uncle Melih, who keeps goading the man on, urging him to find 'a question that this lovely creature cannot answer perfectly.' Until my mother reminds me, first in French and then in English, that I still need to change for the evening. And off I fly to the house where we are not entirely welcome, but instead of changing into the violet taffeta that the maid should never have ironed, I take my book out to the hammock in the garden, where I soon fall asleep.

By the time I get back to the club the sun has set and the moon has risen. The judge is taking off her robes, having made the couple man and wife, and waiters are running amongst the tables with wine and rakı and buckets of ice. As always, I have been consigned to the teenager table, and tonight the sufferer to my left is Sinan. Of all the cousins, I know him best because his mother, Sibel, likes to bring him along with her whenever her lugubrious diplomat husband is out of town, thereby freeing her to raise hell at our great aunt's soirees.

I say I know Sinan best, though in fact we have hardly

conversed. Instead, we've suffered side by side on Hümeyra's ancient chaise longue for many long hours, Sinan reading his book and I reading mine, until someone trips over his outstretched foot or spills some wine on my sleeve or mistakes my shoe for an ashtray or turns up the tango music so loud we can barely hear ourselves think. At which point, Sinan says, 'I can't bear this any more. Can you?' Whereupon we take our leave, retire to the relative quiet of our apartment next door, and again open the books we both use as shields.

Also sharing the humiliation of the teenager table this evening is Haluk. On other occasions, when it has been just the three of us similarly marooned, Sinan and Haluk have amused themselves by dropping into a water glass a small morsel of each type of food we are served, then to discuss at length the degree to which each morsel does or does not resemble an obscene body part. All this under the mistaken assumption that I cannot understand them.

This evening they are playing the same game, but more subtly, on account of the two girls who have been consigned to us. The one with the wild hair and the piercing blue eyes and the officious manner is Suna. The other is a fragile creature much younger than the rest of us – six years old, seven at the most – who speaks Turkish haltingly on account of having been brought up in Paris. Her name is Anais.

Sitting next to her is an American boy who looks like all the boys I used to know in New York, blond hair growing long before it gets chopped off the day before he heads back to school. Good bones, which seem too large for him. Ill at east in his shirt and tie, but friendly in that disarming way that is already breaking my heart. Does he genuinely think that everyone around this table likes and accepts him? His name is Tallis and he is here with his father who is here for a meeting.

'What kind of meeting?' I ask.

'A board meeting,' he says.

He and Sinan have known each other off and on for almost their entire lives, he says, on account of their fathers being friends. 'And our grandfathers, come to think of it. We go way back!'

He relates all this in an affable, by-the-by sort of voice, and either he doesn't notice the new darkness in his friend Sinan's eyes, or – in spite of all those years they have allegedly spent together, if only off and on – he does not yet know Sinan as well as I do.

'So how are you two related?' he asks the two other girls.

'We are cousins,' Suna replies.

'What kind of cousins?'

'Our fathers are brothers. And we share a grandfather. With these others,' she says, with an imperious wave of the arm, 'we share only a great-grandfather, the infamous Adnan Pasha…'

Here Haluk stops her to berate her in Turkish.

'As you wish,' she replies, also in Turkish, before returning to Tallis with a pleasantly officious smile. 'You will have heard of our famous and distinguished great grandfather, I am sure.' And she is right. Tallis' grandmother has told him a great deal about this Adnan Pasha. 'She knew him, of course. Way back when.'

The conversation is left to hang there, because now the orchestra strikes up. It looks and sounds like all the orchestras I've suffered at all the other weddings. Ponderous and very slow. Lugubrious, even.

The happy couple has been dancing for a few bars when

the infamous playboy I know as Uncle Teddy, dressed in his signature baby blue, leads my mother onto the floor. Having stolen the show, he takes my mother back to her chair, returning with Sibel, Sinan's mother, who is wearing a dress even more décolleté than Delphine's.

Haluk guffaws. Suna hits his shoulder. 'Shame on you!' she says. Sinan glowers at the water glass into which he has deposited small morsels of everything we have been served. Picking up a spoon, he begins to stir.

Anais turns to Suna and asks her in French what is going on.

'*Rien*,' Suna replies.

Tallis, who seems oblivious to the contretemps, asks, 'Why doesn't Anais speak Turkish?'

'Aha!' says Suna. 'Oho! Now that is a story!' She then proceeds to tell it. 'Once upon a time, there were two brothers called Melih and Semih. One became a toady for the Americans, and the other, a humble doctor, gave his life to the betterment of the nation...'

Here Sinan interrupts her. 'Enough with your nonsense,' he hisses in Turkish. 'Stop, before I throw this glass at you.'

'My apologies. Let me choose my words more carefully,' she replies in Turkish. And then, returning to English, she says, 'It might be said that both brothers were serving the motherland, each in their own way. But Melih, the elder son, he was a diplomat, after all, was more concerned with peace in the world, while Semih, the doctor, devoted his life to peace at home. This Semih went on to father two sons. Both of these sons of the good and patriotic Semih, born in the early years of the Republic, wished to follow in his footsteps, into medicine. The younger son, my father, made the wise decision to pursue his studies at Istanbul University. The elder, the father of our little Anais, ent to Paris, never to return.'

'But he must be here now,' says Tallis. 'At this wedding, I mean. Otherwise, why would Anais…'

'Of course they come back for visits,' Suna says. 'But these visits are very short. In Turkey, we call this the *Haluk problem*.'

A remonstration here from the Haluk at our table.

Suna blinks before scanning the table with a teacherly smile. 'But of course we are not speaking of the Haluk at our table.'

She then spins a long tale about a great but nameless poet, 'one of the greatest our republic has ever produced' who addressed his very greatest poems to his son, who just happened to bear the noble name of Haluk, imagining the great feats this son would achieve one day, all in service to the nation, once he had come back from his studies in America. 'Alas, the wretched boy then fails to live up to his noble name. Like the father of little Anais, he never returns.'

'How did you learn such good English?' Tallis asks.

'I study at an American school, the same school the poet's son s went to, before he abandoned us.'

Here Sinan interrupts again, in Turkish: 'Stop telling lies.'

'What difference does it make?' she says in Turkish, before turning back to Tallis to explain that her school is in fact the sister school of the one the poet's son attended.

'Tallis knows all that,' says Sinan, this time in English. 'His father is a trustee.'

'Of course,' says Suna, eyelashes fluttering. 'I knew this, from the outset. Nevertheless, you deserve a more nuanced answer, dear Tallis. My English is as it is because, I am, despite my age, an accomplished and widely-read intellectual.'

'Enough!' cries Sinan, throwing a piece of bread at her.

'You know,' said Tallis. 'It's a little rude of us, to be leaving Anais out of the conversation. Does anyone here know French?'

'I do,' I say. I change places with Tallis, so that I can sit next to Anais. I begin by explaining to her who I am, a second cousin, if not a cousin once removed. I always get these things mixed up, I say. But the long and the short of it is that I had only just come back to Istanbul with my mother, and that we live on İstiklâl, next door to an artist named Hümeyra who is also my great aunt.

Whereupon Sinan snorts, before saying, 'She is not your great aunt.'

'Are you okay?' Tallis asks. When I decline to reply, he tries again: 'I really don't think Sinan should have said that. It's none of his business, for one thing. He's a great guy, really. But sometimes...' Here Tallis lets his voice trail off. We had, at his suggestion, left the club to stretch our legs.

I not in the mood for talking, I inform him.

'Okay, then. Fair enough.'

We go to get some ice cream, for which he insists on paying. And then we go to sit on a bench overlooking the harbour. A late ferry is coming in, churning up the water, all lights ablaze.

'Do you mind if I talk,' he asks, 'even if you don't want to?'

'Suit yourself,' I say.

And so he does. He tells me where he's staying: at Robert College, downalong the Bosphorus. His father is a trustee, like Sinan said. The board is based in New York. His family has been associated with this school for three generations, beginning with his great grandfather who taught at Robert

College all his working life. This great grandfather also happens to be Tallis' major role model, on account of his having helped to found the Robert College School of Engineering. Engineering is the career Tallis is considering for himself. 'I like to make things. I like to see things happen.'

'What do you think you'd like to do as a career?' he asks, before saying, 'I'm sorry. I forgot you can't talk.'

'It's not that can't,' I say. 'I'm just not in the mood.'

'Well, it's nice just sitting here.'

'A lot nicer than over there,' I say, nodding in the direction of the club. Whereupon we both fall silent, until he points at the line of lights in the far distance.

'Is that Asia over there? Or Europe?'

'Asia.'

'I guess we'd better start thinking of getting back,' he says. Standing up, plunging his hands in his pockets in a way I have not seen a single boy or man do since coming to Istanbul,' he says, 'Listen. Would you like to go on a date some time?'

'I don't go on dates,' I say.

'Why not?'

'I'm too sophisticated.'

'Really? Wow. I'm not sure I know what you mean by that.'

'What I mean,' I say, as we amble back towards the club, 'is that I have my mind on higher things.'

'Like what?'

'Like Communism.'

'Communism?'

'I'm not a Communist,' I exclaim. 'If that's what you're asking! I just want to know why people come to believe in it.'

'You know?' Tallis says. 'I wonder about that myself sometimes. Listen, maybe I can come over one day, and we can talk about it.'

'Not if you bring Sinan,' I say.

Whereupon Tallis stops. Putting an awkward hand on my shoulder, he blinks as if for courage, before looking me in the eye. 'He really did upset you, didn't he?'

Later on, I will thank Sinan-who-was-not-really-a-cousin for refusing to play along. In fact, I will come to trust him and depend on him for just this reason. But that night, on returning to the wedding and the teenager table, I could not bear the insolence in his eyes, or the smirk on his face. So I left, without saying goodbye to anyone. I went back to the house where we were not entirely welcome. And there, instead of sleeping, I wrestled with the dark.

Until the sun came up, and I went out into the garden, to sit on the swinging chair, and wait.

When my mother came through the gate some time later, her high heels dangling in her hands, her hair dripping water, and her knock-'em-dead dress further deadened by damp spots, she was so intent on protecting her bare feet that she didn't notice me until she reached the porch.

'Oh,' she said. 'What are you doing out here?' Met with silence, she came down to join me.

'Not so close!' I hissed. 'You're sopping wet.'

She sat in the other swing chair whose movement seemed at first to surprise her. When she had steadied herself, she gave me a bleary-eyed smile. 'What's wrong, my little chickadee?'

'Stop calling me that. I won't stand for it!'

'But chickadee – '

'Did you not hear what I just said?'

With an anxious glance in the direction of the unwelcoming house, my feckless mother put her finger to her lips. 'Darling. I'm sorry. But I'm going to have to ask you to keep your voice down.'

'Why should I?'

In a stage whisper, she reminded me that everyone else in the household was asleep. 'But listen. Tell me. Something's happened. What's wrong?'

'Everything,' I said.

'How do you mean?'

'I need you to tell me who I really am.'

'What on earth do you mean by that, my little ...'

'Don't!'

'Dora! Please! Keep your voice down, would you? 'No I would not!' I shouted. 'Not until you tell me who I am.'

'Shush!' my mother cried.

And so I shouted louder. 'Who am I?' I cried. And louder still, as if the unwelcoming house itself had the answer: 'Who am I? Why won't anyone tell me?'

Whereupon my sopping wet mother jumped up and fairly flew across the grass to pin me down with one hand and to clamp the other over my mouth.


## Silence

Thus began the first of our silences.

I had not spoken to my mother, or to anyone else, for going on a fortnight when she announced, in writing, that she had to leave town for a week, or maybe two, and that I was to move across to Hümeyra's apartment for the duration, so that Hümeyra could keep an eye on me, 'now that it has become clear to us all how childish you really are.'

Once she was gone, though, I refused to decamp to the bedroom they had prepared for me in the other apartment. But I had no quarrel with Vartuhi, Hümeyra's maid, who insisted on bringing over the beautiful food she made in my honour, first for breakfast, and then for lunch, and teatime, and supper. And last thing at night, a glass of linden tea.

It was to avoid making extra work for her that I consented to eating with Hümeyra on the second day. And because Hümeyra had no quarrel with my silence and went out of her way to respect it, on the third day I began to speak again, if only to say please and thank you.

For a few days, we kept our exchanges to that minimum. I found the quiet soothing. So soothing that I began to linger after meals – me on the chaise longue reading, Hümeyra wheeling solemnly between the low tables on which she had begun to assemble parts of a collage. She rode a tricycle that one of her thieves had recently liberated for her, for this express purpose.

From time to time, she'd peddle across to the chaise longue, to squeeze my hand or my shoulder, or pat my head.

Never a question when I headed back to my apartment of an evening – though these were hot August nights, airless even with all the windows open. When she appeared at her side window before turning in, to wave across to me at my side window, she never once asked why I was sitting at my mother's vanity table, taking notes while Radio Moscow blared.

We would have been well into our second week of this routine when I came in for supper one evening to find

Hümeyra standing at the window, watching the passing ships. And there, on the chaise longue, was the man I now believed to be my father. He stood up and bowed, before taking my hand to kiss it.

Vartuhi brought supper to the card table beside the baby grand. We sat down to eat. At first Sergei tried to strike up a conversation, but then Hümeyra reached across the table and said, 'Sergei. The girl needs silence.' It was something about the way Hümeyra squeezed his hand, and the way he squeezed it back, something about the thoughtless grace with which they passed each other food, and filled each other's glasses, letting words hang happily unspoken in the air between them; it got me thinking. But it wasn't until late that night, hours after Radio Moscow had gone off the air, that it struck me.

Hümeyra was not my great aunt but my grandmother. For Sergei was her son.

With that I drifted off into agitated but ecstatic slumber. I'd cracked the mystery. I'd cracked it! But with morning came the terrors of logic. If Sergei was my father, and Hümeyra was his mother, why then was Hümeyra so close to my mother? More to the point, why had Hümeyra wanted me to meet Sergei, but not until my mother was out of town? Late the following afternoon, the worst-case scenario presented itself. Not only was Sergei Hümeyra's son. But Delphine – my mother – was her daughter. By another man, perhaps? But still related. Much too closely related. What all this meant, I now decided, was that I must be the product of incest.

Incest!

Suddenly, everything made sense – why people looked at me the way they did. Why they thought of me as the child who had never been born.

When Vartuhi came in with my afternoon tea, she found me in bed. When Hümeyra came in some hours later, to check in on me, I was still there. So she sat on the side of my bed, combing my hair with her fingers, comforting me now in Turkish, now in French or English. Until I asked:

'Are you my grandmother?'

With a smile, she bent over to kiss my forehead.

'Yes, my one and only. Yes. I am.'

'And is Sergei my father?'

'Sergei? Your father? Is that what you think, my poor sweet girl? *Mais c'est fou, ça. Qui t'a dit ces conneries?*'

'No one,' I replied. 'I worked it out myself.'

'*Mais ce n'est pas vrai, ma chère. Pas du tout!*'

'Then what really happened? And why won't anyone tell me?'

My newly confessed grandmother stood up. Wrapped the shawl she surely didn't need in this heat around her shoulders. For a long time she stared out of my side window into her own. And then, speaking very softly, she said, 'We shall tell you. The whole story. It's for the best.'

# THE SECOND NOTEBOOK

# Hermine

I awoke the next morning to find an old postcard propped up against the lamp on my bedside table: a tinted photograph of the Grande Rue de Pera as it no longer was. On the flip side was an invitation to a *vernissage chez Hermine*. When Vartuhi came in with my breakfast, I asked if she could tell me who this Hermine was, and where she lived. Her face fell so fast she almost dropped her tray. She scurried away without offering any answer, returning minutes later with a note in my newly confessed grandmother's hand:

> *Ma chère,*
> *Hermine c'est moi.*

I waved the note at Vartuhi. Could she tell me how I was to understand this?

She could not. Again she rushed from the room. I followed her out with my tray of untouched food, but she stopped me on the landing. Somewhat roughly, took the tray from my hands.

'Please,' I cried. 'Tell me what is going on.'

'I shall ask.'

A few minutes later she returned with yet another note from my grandmother, begging me, in French, for patience. She was composing her thoughts. They would be ready at eight sharp if I could grace her with my presence at that same hour.

But when I walked back onto the landing at the appointed time, it was Sergei waiting at the door. 'May I welcome you to the *vernissage*,' he said, with a bow and a great sweep of arms that directed me to the back wall, every inch of which was covered with paintings whose wild shapes and exuberant colours were at war with their sombre frames. Baby Mallinson was seated at the baby grand, rustling sheet music. 'Follow me, please,' said Sergei, directing me to a card table drowning in outsize linen and laden with food and drink. With old school ceremony he sat me down, pouring me a lemonade, before dropping an ice cube into a rakı glass that was already half empty.

'No top up for me?' Baby asked.

'Later,' said Sergei. 'First you must serve the muse.'

With a sigh, Baby began playing. First, it was something akin to *Pictures at an Exhibition*. Then he moved on to what I would later know to be the composition that made his name, though for me, on that evening, it was simply a piece I'd often heard at my mother's favourite supper club back in Manhattan.

For a time we listened in silence, eyes fixed on the plates between us. White cheese and melon, smoked fish, and aubergine puree. Broad beans in sauce. Four little sheep brains on a bed of lettuce.

Until Sergei waved for Baby to stop playing. 'Do not fear,' he said. 'The Divine Hümeyra is never on time, as you know. But she will arrive. And while we wait...there are a few things I am desperate to say and enquire. The first...'

He reached out for my hand and kissed it.

Without a word, I drew my hand away.

He let out a sigh.

'You are right, of course you are,' he said. 'It is not fair, in fact, it is cruel, to leave you lost in ignorance. Whatever others might say, it is my sacred view that every child deserves

71

to know her father. So tonight, we shall make our best attempt. But first…'

'Just tell me,' I said.

He raised a gentle hand. 'I understand your impatience. In my own life, I have similarly suffered. This is why I am here: to ensure that you need never sleep again without the truth. But first,' he said again, 'there is the larger canvas we must paint for you. Your grandmother has been hard at work on it. She will join us soon.'

'Stop being so melodramatic,' said Baby.

'My dear boy, you must shut up.'

'Then top me up, why don't you,' Baby said, waving his glass.

With a sigh, Sergei obliged.

'Thank you kindly,' said Baby.

'Did I detect sarcasm?' Sergei asked.

'Just a tad,' said Baby. 'Just a dribble.'

'If you keep acting up, dear boy, I shall send you home.'

'You just try.'

'You promised.'

'That I did.'

'Then behave!' Sergei cried.

Whereupon Baby turned to me, to say, 'You see how this man treats me? I don't know why I put up with him. We're lovers, you know.'

'Baby!' Sergei cried.

'She needs to know this!'

I informed them both that I knew already.

'Then why on earth,' Baby cried, 'did you get it into your head that this flaming queen could be your father?'

'People can change,' I said.

'Baby,' said Sergei. 'This is your final warning.'

'Okay, okay. But here's the deal. You have to keep to your promise, too. Stop beating around the bush and tell her.' Turning back to me again, he said, 'Listen, hon. I'm here to make sure he tells it to you straight.'

'And *I* am here,' Sergei bellowed, 'to speak in my own fashion!' As he turned back to me, he cleared his throat, joined his hands, attempted a smile.

'I would like to begin, dear child, by saying how much joy it brought me, to hear that you had mistaken me for your father. I regret to say that I did not have that privilege...'

A snort from the baby grand.

'...but I was there at your birth, you know! From the very moment of your arrival, and despite the vast distance that there was soon to be between us, I have always kept a place for you in my heart of hearts.'

'So who is he, then?'

'How do you mean?'

'Who's my real father?'

Sergei gazed down at his hands. 'We shall come to this. I promise. In the meantime, what I can say is...all I can say is...your mother should never have taken you to that wedding.'

That surprised me. In spite of myself I looked up.

'Of course I know she intended no harm to you,' Sergei continued. 'To the contrary, she wished her beloved daughter to be recognised by one and all! But she should have guessed that those cousins could not be counted on to remain discreet. Which one was it who upset you, my dear little one?'

'He didn't upset me,' I said. 'He told me the truth.'

'Sinan, you mean.'

'Yes, Sinan.

'That boy,' said Sergei, shaking his head. 'That boy. What exactly did he say by the way?'

'That Hümeyra was not my great aunt.'

'Aha. I see. Did he say anything else?'

'No.'

'Hmmmm,' said Sergei. I could not help noticing the relief in his voice. He was already on his feet. 'Let me see what is keeping our divine hostess,' he said as he headed for the hallway. He returned some minutes later with my grandmother at his side. Together they approached me, as solemn as mourners before an open casket. Hümeyra had a large sketchbook pressed again her chest.

It stayed there until Sergei had given up on getting either of us to eat. Once the food had been cleared away, she set it on the table and opened it up.

Inside were watercolours, all of the same view. Our view, by day and by night. In sunshine and rain and snow. The paper was brittle and yellowing at the edges. Each time my grandmother turned a page, there was another whiff of mould.

These paintings, Sergei informed me, were the work of my great-grandmother, whose name was Anahid.

'The apartment you now share with your mother was once her studio,' Sergei informed me. 'As for the apartment in which we are sitting at this very moment – it was the home Anahid shared with her husband – a banker! – and their dear daughter. And here, I fear, we come to the crux of the matter: the name of this daughter was not Hümeyra, but Hermine.'

'Hermine. Hermine!' That was my grandmother, not so much whispering the name so much as breathing it.

'But I don't understand,' I said. 'Why did she have to change her name?

'Hermine is an Armenian name.'

'So we're Armenian, are we? I thought we were Levantine.'

'Yes,' said Sergei sadly. 'There is also that.'

'How can I be Levantine and Armenian at the same time?'

'Because your lovely mother's father – your grandfather – was Levantine.'

'He was?'

'Yes, he...'

'*Attendez!*' This was my grandmother, who was already racing across the room. Vanishing for a few moments, she returned holding a pile of framed photographs topped by old sketchbook.

Dropping the photographs onto the table, she rifled through the sketchbook until she found what she was looking for: a charcoal portrait of a handsome if wild-haired young man looking madly upwards, encircled in what looked to be great shafts of light.

'Charles,' she said. Not to me, but to the portrait. '*Ah, mon cher. mon Charles,*' she cried, '*Qu'as-tu fait pour me mériter?*'

'What do you mean by that?' I asked. 'What happened to him?'

Sergei and my grandmother exchanged looks. Sergei's asking, *Shall I?* My grandmother saying, *No.*

'This too is an important story for you to know,' said Sergei finally. 'Though not for today. It would be a distraction from the story we are here to tell you.'

'The story about my father, I hope you mean.'

He raised a gentle hand. 'Yes, we shall come to that. But first, we must pass back to the days of loss and terror.'

Here he stopped to wrap his arms around my grandmother, who had begun to rock back and forth, moaning. Only when he had calmed her did he return to his story, and it was perhaps because he wished to spare her as much anguish as possible that he drew so heavily on metaphor and image.

First the silver spoon that should have remained forevermore in Hermine's mouth – for her family had numbered amongst the wealthiest Armenians of Constantinople. Tigran, her grandfather, the jewel of all jewellers…

From the pile of photographs, Sergei retrieved a portrait of a man with a narrow face punctuated by dark, sharp eyes and a drooping moustache. Although he was wearing a fez, his suit looked European. There was another picture of Tigran standing in front of our building. It had been taken in 1901, the year, Sergei informed me, of its completion. A third photograph from the same year showed a young couple sitting stiff-backed and unsmiling on our own chaise longue, before it was ancient.

This, Sergei told me, was my great grandmother Anahid, and her husband, who at the time of their marriage had, as already hinted, been the Ottoman Bank's fastest rising star.

But then, in 1910, there had arrived the first cruel bolt of lightning: Anahid – Hermine's mother – was struck low by consumption. She was dispatched to a Swiss sanatorium, leaving Hermine motherless from the tender age of four.

'Instead she was consigned to the clutches of a wicked French governess…'

My grandmother grabbed Sergei by the arm. 'Please!' she begged. 'No more of this witch today. My constitution cannot bear it.'

'As you wish, my dear. Of course, you are right. There is enough pain to endure, even if we do not stray from the path. We come now, dear Dora, to the moral of our story:

never let anyone persuade you that lightning cannot strike twice in the same place.'

For the second assault on the family fortunes had not been a single bolt of lightning. It had, instead, been the first strike in a firestorm that would claim the lives of a million or more Armenians in these lands before it was over.

Of course, no one could have known what lay ahead on the 24th of April, 1915, when Constantinople's 235 most prominent Armenians were summarily removed from their homes in the middle of the night, to be sent to parts unknown. All were well-connected, with many strings to pull. All had assumed they would be home within days. But only a handful would return. Most, like Hermine's father and grandfather and uncles, would perish in the hinterlands of Anatolia.

'As for Hermine – the poor girl would have starved, had it not been for a certain Aleph.'

'What's an Aleph?' I asked.

'Ah. Let me show you.'

He picked up the last of the framed photographs. It showed four men, all in European dress, sitting at a table overhung by palms. Only one was wearing a fez.

'Here they are, in happier days,' said Sergei. 'One of them Ottoman. The second Levantine. The third Armenian. The fourth and youngest, young enough to be their mascot, is American. But in those happier days, he has much to offer his friends from his desk at the American Embassy. As does our Ottoman Aleph, Adnan Pasha, from his desk at the Ottoman War Office. Add to this pair Achille the Levantine Aleph who commands a great fleet of ships, and Artin the Armenian Aleph, who is in their happier days the Ottoman Bank's fastest rising star. Until the Great War undoes them, there is nothing these four cannot do!

'For as long as the happier days last, they are virtually inseparable. Hardly a day they do not meet at the Bourse! Hardly a night they do not share at the tables of the Cercle d'Orient! But then comes the firestorm. Their Armenian Aleph has vanished, seemingly from the surface of the earth. Of course, the others go in search of him. Week after week. Far and wide. Until our Pasha pays a visit to his friend Artin's home, to discover that, wherever he has gone, Artin has left behind his daughter. Thus it comes to pass that – in a single and magnificent flash – our Pasha he takes the poor waif under his wing.

'And that, dear Dora, is why you are not only Armenian and Levantine, but Ottoman also.'

'Well maybe, in a manner of speaking,' I said. 'But not by blood.'

Again, Sergei turned towards my grandmother, but she was already vanishing into the hallway. This time she came back clutching a large frame.

It held a family portrait, dated 1919. A single glance was all it took for me to see it had been taken in the room where we were sitting. The same copper vase full of peacock feathers. The same chaise longue, its gilded edges gleaming and its wooden frame untarnished. Sitting at the high end was an angular man in a fez. Next to him was Hermine, who looked to be twelve or thirteen. Beside her sat two boys of the same age: one affably smiling, and one with eyes downcast. At the low end of the chaise longue was a woman in European overdress – a ruffled high-necked affair so elaborate that I did not immediately notice that someone had cut out her face.

'What happened to *her*?' I asked.

A hand on my arm. My grandmother, with a finger on

her lips. She lowered it to point out the others each in turn.

'My Pasha,' she said first. Pointing at her own likeness, she added, 'The Pasha's little imp.' Her finger passed next to the boys. 'You met them both, I think. At the wedding. They are older now, but still the same. This sad boy. He is Semih. Still so very gloomy. He never liked the Pasha's little imp. Not then, and not now. But Melih...' Her finger wavered over the smiling boy. 'My Melih has always loved me. And so many times he, too, has saved me! It is thanks to my Melih that we are here at all, in this house of my birth. He has risked everything for us. And for you, too, my dear Dora. You owe him your life.'

At this, my grandmother looked up at Sergei. 'Shall we wait for him?' she asked in French. 'Has he called? Is he perhaps delayed?'

A knock on the door. 'Melih! Is that you?'


## Melih


In came one of the elderly gentlemen to whom my mother had introduced me at the wedding. The friendlier of the two. No smiles now though. He looked anxious and contrite. Behind him was the boy who'd started it all.

Taking Sinan firmly by the arm, the man to whom I had been introduced as Uncle Melih led him across the room, before commanding him, in Turkish, to do what decency demanded.

His eyes firmly on the ground, Sinan said he was sorry.

'Again!' the man cried. 'And this time properly!' He had switched to English for this but then he switched back into Turkish to inform Sinan that if his mother couldn't be bothered to teach him his manners, he would be learning them now, from his grandfather.

So Sinan looked straight into my eyes, with the slightest flash of insolence, to apologise for the second time.

Whereupon the man pushed him away. 'Go now,' he barked into Turkish. 'Do not let my eyes see you.'

'May I read?' Sinan asked.

'You may do as you wish,' said the man. 'So long as I can no more hear you than see you.'

After Sinan had slunk off to the alcove we called the morning room, the man added his own apology: 'My grandson has much to learn about polite society. But tonight, at last, we can make up for lost time.' He took my hand to gaze deeply into my eyes. His own eyes unctuous. Then he turned to my grandmother. 'How far have we come?'

'This far,' said my grandmother. She passed him the portrait of herself with the Pasha and his two sons, one of whom must be this Melih – and the European lady whose face had been cut out. Melih burst out laughing when he noticed its absence. *'Mais c'est génial, ça!'* Then he turned to me to say, 'You must feel so very proud, to be descended from a great artist.'

'Ah!!!!' said my grandmother. 'You flatter me to no end! Who am I, dear Melih, beside your own mother!'

She turned to me, 'She was the greatest poetess of her age, you know.'

Her words left Melih looking perplexed. 'Have we come that far?'

At which Sergei jumped in. 'Not yet! Not yet! But soon! Perhaps,' he said, speaking so rapidly now that he was stumbling over his words, 'perhaps I should quickly move our story forward.'

'Only if you top me up,' said Baby from the baby grand.

This Sergei did, before returning to the table to race me through a string of tragedies and triumphs, mishaps and scandals stretching across three decades.

First the early 1920s. The dawn of the new republic and Hermine's artistic career. The kindly Pasha who had taken her under his wing, to raise her alongside his own two sons, Melih and Semih. Who was so kind as to furnish Hermine with the best art tutor in the city. Who had in turn been so impressed by her budding genius that he secured her a place at the new Academy.

But then the kindly Pasha was called away to serve the patriotic cause. The witch, who was once Hermine's governess and had now become the second Mrs Pasha, cast her out of house and home. Hermine was forced to decamp to the Princes' Islands, to stay with the family of poor mad Charles, who had long been Hermine's dearest friend but who had by now become an embarrassment to his father, Monsieur Achille, the shipping magnate, for a multitude of reasons, not least because he now believed himself a horse.

His mother, a Madame Odette, who had at first been simply indulging him in this delusion, had slowly come to believe it herself. The art tutor – a Maître Refique – had been the only person of consequence to keep an eye on this demented household, which was made stranger still by the community of Russian vegetarians occupying its large and overgrown garden. The Maître had done his utmost to remove her from this compromising situation, until events overtook him.

For before the summer's end, poor mad Charles had galloped his mother into the sea. On arriving to claim the bodies, her older children had discovered that Hermine had been impregnated, perhaps unwillingly, by their demented brother. So the two ugly sisters had claimed Hermine too, keeping her incarcerated until the moment of the birth and then showing her the door.

And so it was that Hermine had been deprived of her beloved daughter, who would be named and raised by her Levantine aunts. They'd told her that her mother died at birth. She would be eighteen before she met her mother.

'As for the kind soul who contrived to reunite them...'

Sergei paused, to look everyone present, even Baby, in the eye.

Until my grandmother broke the silence with a terrible sob. 'It was Melih! Dear Melih! *Ah, mon cher, sans toi nous ne serions rien!*'

Melih lowered his eyes to smile sheepishly at his hands.

My grandmother reached across the table for my hands. 'If only you knew, dear girl, how many times – *how many times* – this man has saved me from myself! And even more, from the gallows!'

'The gallows?' I asked.

Prompting Baby at the baby grand to laugh.

Causing Sergei to fix him with a venomous glare.

Whereupon my grandmother took my hand.

'The sad truth, *ma chère*, is that I am not only a very naughty creature. I am also a murderess. Not a triple murderess, as some claim. I was not the instrument of Charles' demise, nor of his mother's. But I did shoot my Maître.'

'But my dear, he deserved it!' Sergei cried. 'For was it not a crime of passion? And did you not do your utmost to nurse him back to health?'

'I'm sorry,' I said. 'You've lost me.'

Sighing and apologetic, Sergei suggested that this too might be a story for another day. 'For the moment, suffice it to say that this Maître was not all bad. He saved her from the streets, after all. Gave her two sons. Nurtured her art, in his fashion. But the fact remains he was a trigamist.'

'A trigamist?' I said. 'A *trigamist?*'

I stood up and went to the window. Breathed in the hot and humid air.

'Shall bring you some water, dear child? Yes, of course I shall,' Sergei said. 'All this must be a shock. You must need some air. Do take your time. And Baby, if you can play us a soothing tune, I shall top you up.'

This time Baby chose a spiritual, about the trouble he'd seen. Too much, too much. Clutching my water glass, I went into the alcove we called the morning room and sat myself down next to Sinan.

I asked him what he was reading.

'*Fathers and Sons,*' he replied.

'I love that book,' I said.

And he said, 'I have yet to decide.'

'Why don't *you* tell me who my father is,' I said.

He looked up from his book, to study me carefully.

'I *think,*' he said, 'you know already.'

And how right he was, I thought, as I returned to the great room to sink into the chaise longue, to bury myself in its cushions and shawls. *Of course* I knew. My father was this unctuous old man who'd saved my grandmother from the gallows. Relaunched her art career. Reunited her with her long-lost daughter, and then...It turned my stomach to think what had happened next. How could he? How could *she?*

As Baby continued his musical accompaniment – it was Porgy and Bess now, but how dare he – and why were the others looking at me so sadly and beseechingly – had they really expected me to hear the truth and rejoice? My mind was whirling. A lifetime of jigsaw pieces, spinning and colliding and falling into place.

Sergei came over to sit beside me. 'Oh, my little onion. I'm so sorry to have upset you.' He put his arm around me, pulling me close. 'We have told you too much, too fast. Shall we adjourn for the night and return to our story when you've had some rest?'

'I don't ever want to return to it,' I said.

'Oh,' said Sergei. 'But you must.'

It was at that moment that the key turned in the lock.


## Delphine

My mother had been gone so long I'd stopped even expecting her. What was it now? Three weeks? Four? She was in tears again. Loud and large enough for a concert hall. Only after pulling off her heels and tossing her coat and to one side did she notice she had walked into some sort of wake.

'What's all this?' she asked.

Hümeyra scampered across the room to embrace her. Then she removed one arm from my mother's back to wave frantically at Sergei, who just as frantically pulled away the shawls and cushions I had gathered around me to bury himself beneath them.

'Come sit down!' said the grandmother who had two names and perhaps as many murder raps. 'How wonderful to see you! Such a lovely surprise! We were not expecting you until next week, *ma chère*. What made you leave Athens so soon?'

'A man, of course!' my mother cried. 'What else would it be, but a man!'

As more tears arrived, she fled to the bathroom, eyes covered, and therefore not seeing me. Hümeyra followed, leaving me in charge of the pillows and the shawls. Now Vartuhi was summoned. Now she was rushing back and forth with tea for my mother, and tissues. Now she was running a bath, and when my mother returned to the great room in a robe and slippers, she at last caught sight of me, there on the chaise longue.

'Dora!' she cried. 'What are you doing here?'

'Waiting for you to come home, obviously.'

'Well that makes sense at least,' she said. 'But Melih. What's with *you*?'

He stood up, hands clasped. 'Ah,' he said. 'Ah.'

'Ah. Well, that's great. One day, I hope, you'll have more than that to say for yourself.' Turning back to look at the lump of shawls and cushions next to me, she added, 'Why is this place such a wreck?'

She did not wait long for the answer I was not going to give her. For by now she'd spotted Baby at the baby grand. He'd taken the black hood that usually sat on a bust of Beethoven and pulled it down over his head.

'Baby,' she snapped. 'Explain.'

'We're playing a game,' he replied.

'What kind of name?'

'It's sort of like statues,' he said. 'But not.'

'Does this game have a name?'

'Dora in the Dark.'

'Ha, ha, ha,' my mother said. 'Very funny.' She padded

off into the bathroom. The moment she was out of sight, Baby raised his arms in a silent cheer. But suddenly my mother was back again, pointing at Baby's raised arms.

'You moved.'

He gave no indication of having heard her.

'Oh, well, then,' my mother said finally, in a little voice. 'I give up,' she said, a little louder, as if to pretend she was in on the joke. 'So anyway. I'm getting into the bath. But I'll have you know I'm keeping the door open! I'll catch you yet!'

And that was when I boiled over. With what, I do not know. Fury, perhaps. Exasperation. Despair. Whatever it was, it caused me to use a word I had never before uttered in my mother's presence, or even in the silence of my own thoughts.

'What kind of spook are you anyway, if you can be fooled by your own family?'

I'd like to say I felt some compassion for my mother as she stood there swollen-eyed in her damp bathrobe, glancing wildly this way and that, as if the walls might tell her how exactly she'd been fooled. But no. I was twelve and I'd just been told about the disgusting liaison that had made me. I wanted to know how my mother had been so careless – how she had *stooped so low,* never stopping to consider what the shame of my repugnant origins might do to me.

'That's enough from you, missy.'

'You have that wrong,' I yelled. 'That's enough from *you*!'

I would like to say that I cooled off once I'd retreated to our apartment, that I felt a little sorrow, a little pity, as I stood at the side window watching the scene I'd left behind: my mother yelling, my grandmother weeping, Sergei pacing back and forth like Hamlet, Baby spreadeagled over the baby grand, Melih perched on the bench beside him, staring gloomily at his hands. I wish I'd understood how much they all loved me. How much they wanted to bring me happiness, even though they had no idea how. How this was what life looked like, if you were forced, through circumstance, to build it on ruins. But there was no room for understanding in my head that night. All I could see in my mind's eye were trigamists and ugly aunts and mad boys who thought they were horses. All I wanted was to bat them away.

## School

'Would that I could jump out of my skin.'

I found these words in an otherwise empty notebook I must have intended as a journal. The date on the front is September 1961. That was the month I started at Robert College Community School. And that was certainly how I felt that first morning, when I travelled out to the Bosphorus on the number 40 bus, among whose passengers lurked the same number of gropers, if not more.

When I got off in front of the Robert College gate, three of them tried to follow me. The gatekeeper chased them off, but one of them found another way in, and halfway up the steep and winding road to the campus, he caught up with me. A group of students came to my rescue, escorting me the rest of the way up. But they had never heard of Robert College Community School, and neither had the next eight people I asked. When I finally located it, halfway into the village of Rumeli Hisar, half the morning was gone.

And there, inside, I found America again.

The principal, with her clipped New England vowels.

The bulletin board displays, on space exploration, Columbus Day, and the evolution of our flag's stars and stripes.

The boys, with their sneakers and their crewcuts, and their fixation on Alfred E Neuman. What – me worry?

The girls, with their braces and their carefully guarded hoop skirts: Don't look now, but it's snowing down south.

The banter:

Make me.

I'd like to, but you're such a mess.

I'd been out of school for half a year, educating myself after a fashion, but I was all out of sync – way ahead in French and English, way behind in Math. Utterly nowhere in Latin, and utterly perplexed to be studying Thomas Paine and Patrick Henry again, here in this classroom half a world away from the battlefields of the American Revolution. I was in the top grade, and a head taller than the tallest boy, and no one talked to me at recess.

There were more gropers lying in wait on the bus home. So I jumped out at Dolmabahçe Palace and walked up the hill, pursued yet again by men who'd jumped off the bus with me. When I tried to fend them off by swinging my book bag at them, one of them grabbed it, and so, to save myself, I let go of it and ran. I said nothing about that to my mother when I got home. I went straight into my room and slammed the door, and every time she came to my door to ask how the school day had gone, her knock was softer, more considered.

The next morning, she was awake before I was and – for the first time in living memory – making me lunch. 'Where's your book bag?' she asked.

I told her I'd lost it.

'How exactly?'

'On the bus.'

'They weren't being fresh with you, were they?'

Something about her wide-eyed concern made me flip.

'What do you think?' I yelled. 'That I found the only bus in the city that's not crawling with perverts?'

She stepped back, in a way I had never seen her step back. As if to appraise me. As if to acknowledge that I'd grown while she wasn't looking.

'So,' she said, in a calm, cool voice, 'It's like that, is it?'

'Yes,' I said. 'It's like that. Even the principal was shocked, you know. She said she had assumed I'd have a driver. Like everyone else has, unless they happen to live around the corner.'

'Huh,' she said. 'So that's how it is, is it? Okay then. Let's go.'

Once outside, she led me to the nearest taxi stand. When I asked, 'Are you sure we can afford this?' she said:

'You can be sure of that. You just wait.'

That afternoon, I came out of school to find her waiting for me in a sleek black chauffeur-driven car. 'This,' she told me, 'is Hasan. From here on in, he'll be picking you up every morning and dropping you off home every afternoon.'

'Whose car is it?'

'Don't ask.'

'I am asking.'

'It's the least he could do.'

'Who? My father?'

'No comment.'

'If it's my father, I'm jumping out of the car right now.'

'Be my guest.'

As we bumped our way down the steep cobblestone lane

to the shore, she kept her back very straight, and her eyes on the windscreen.

When we passed our first number 40 bus, she gestured in its direction. 'Here's your chance!'

'I just can't understand why you can go crawling back to a man like that, after all he did to you. To *us*'.

'Look,' she said. 'I know I've made mistakes. I should have trusted you more. I should have explained why we had to take it slow. Sergei, for example. I should have let you in on that. Explained what an old friend he was. But I had to make sure I could still trust him. Well, I know that now. And so do you.'

'I wasn't asking you about Sergei.'

'Hold your horses. I'm getting there. So now. Your father. My mistake again was wanting us to take our time. Break it to you gently. This, I now realise, was a terrible miscalculation.'

'So was I!'

'Be that as it may,' she continued. 'I would like you to know this about your father. He has been as honourable as a man can be in his position. It was never serious, you know. We had a fling. It was fun while it lasted. By the time I knew you were on the way, it was over. And anyway, he was married. He had a wife – Elektra by name and Elektra by nature – and two grown daughters.

'But he never abandoned us. He helped your grandmother keep us hidden from my ugly aunts, who wanted to lock me up in some nunnery, and from Elektra, who on more than one occasion turned up brandishing a knife. Our big mistake was to bring Melih's sister-in-law into the secret. Mrs Doctor Semih. She was the one who delivered you. And then she tried to steal you. Remove you from the den of sin.

Place you with some deserving hardworking family. Ha ha. And you know why she failed? Because this father you hate so much caught her in the act. Pulled you away. Gave you back to me. And guess what he did next? He kicked her down the stairs! She's had a limp ever since. Ha ha.'

'But it turned into a scandal, of course. This is when his wife came into her own. Your father was a diplomat, you see. But so was Elektra's father. He pulled all the strings he had to pull. Melih got you and me out of the country before they could do *us* any damage, but they ended his career. Is that enough for now? Can you stop acting like a prig?'

'I still don't understand why we have to let him into our life.'

'Well, how's this for an answer? He already *is* in our life. Who do you think I'm working for? Who do you think *he's* working for, now his diplomacy days are over?'

"I'd rather not know,' I said airily.

'Then good. Sit back and count your blessings while your father and I get back what's ours.'

## Spooks

'And another thing,' my mother said later, back at the house. 'Don't let me ever, ever hear you say that word again. Do you hear? I am not a spook.'

'What are you then?'

'An avenger. As you well know.'

As I did, in my fashion. As for the story she'd just told me – it fell gently onto my twelve-year-old ears. To think that only days earlier I'd been thinking myself the product of incest. Not at all! I was a love child. They might not have expected me, these wayward parents of mine, but once I was in the picture they'd risked everything to save me.

All I needed to know now was what exactly my mother was out to avenge, and where this quest was taking her.

I had no idea where to begin, but as it happened, I didn't need to. Because it turned out that the car my father had made available to me did not belong to him. To whom it did belong was not made clear, but most days on our way back from school, Hasan the chauffeur would pull off the Aşiyan Road halfway down the hill to the Bosphorus and ascend a narrow lane to stop in front of a wrought iron gate beyond which sat a lovely old Ottoman villa surrounded by palms and persimmon trees. We'd wait there until someone peeked out at us from one of the little latticed balconies. A few minutes later a man would come out the door. Sometimes two men. Some were American. Some Turkish. They would greet me with gruff courtesy and then immediately look away. Never any small talk as we headed back into the city. Until one afternoon it was none other than William Wakefield, our man for all seasons. Just passing through, he told me. Glad to see me. Hoping I liked my new school. Offering no explanation for his presence. Promising, as the car pulled up in front of the US consulate, to be back in touch soon.

'Are you ever going to tell me what's going on?' I asked.

That elicited a chuckle.

'We shall see.'

How very condescending, I thought. You could brush off a child like that, but I was twelve now. I needed a proper explanation. What exactly was going on in that villa? Why all this coming and going? There came a day when I saw a way of finding out. Hasan the chauffeur had been idling outside the gate for twenty minutes without anyone coming out onto the balcony. I decided to chance it.

Ascending the steps to the front door, I looked up to see my father on the landing. As surprised as he was to see me, he was also – I could see this – tremendously pleased. I had, after all, been refusing to meet with him. But now I wanted to know about this house we were in, and he very much wanted to tell me about it.

In happier days, he told me, it had belonged to his mother, the renowned poetess.

'You know about her, of course.'

'I'm afraid I don't.'

'Ah. Then let us do something about this lamentable lacuna. You have, after all, come to the right place.'

The small library to which he led me had a window seat that followed the curve of its bay windows. For an hour we sat there, drinking the sherbets that the maid brought up for us, while my father reminisced, rising every now and then to bring me proof of yet another long-lost grandmother's beauty, art and erudition. Now it was a volume of her own verse. Now it was her translation into Ottoman of her idol, Emily Dickinson. Now it was a portrait of a dark-eyed beauty dressed head to toe in white. She had died, he told me, in the midst of the Great War. This house was all my father had left of her.

'Who lives here now?' I asked.

'Ah,' he said. 'Ah.'

I did not press him. After all, I wanted to come back. Not to see him, necessarily. But to sit here, on this window seat, watching the blue of the Bosphorus piercing here and there through the leaves of the palm trees. Drinking sherbets that the maid brought up for me. Leafing through my other newfound grandmother's books, and the cache of letters I found hidden behind them. Some were in Ottoman and therefore beyond me. Others were in French, and always asking the same sad question: *When will this war ever end?* Here, too, was a story I could embrace. A great poetess, lost to the Great War. So much easier to mourn her untimely passing than to make sense of my other grandmother, whom I loved, yes of course I did, but whose openly confessed crimes scared me.

This was the routine, then, for a few blissful weeks. Hasan would stop the car, and my father would come out to greet me. Once inside, he would make sure I was settled. Then he would climb the narrow stairs to the top floor, saying duty called. Sometimes that duty was silent. Other times there were hushed conversations. Footsteps, banging telex machines and typewriters. Ringing phones. Occasionally – when a passing ship made the whole house tremble – there was a rush to the balcony.

Once, when my father did not come out to greet me, and I went into the house, to find no one there either, I went upstairs to see my father's office for myself. There I found, in addition to the expected phones and machines, a row of binoculars hanging on hooks, and a telescope.

From this I deduced that I was observing an observation post. From the upper balcony there was a good view of any Soviet ship passing by, but the overgrown garden would give anyone watching them ample cover.

From that I deduced that my father was working for NATO or some such, reporting, perhaps, to our old friend William Wakefield. But perhaps, not reporting everything.

Pretending, perhaps, that his interest lay only in Soviet warships.

When his real interest – perhaps – was in smaller vessels carrying a more alluring sort of contraband.

That, I reflected, might explain why my mother had welcomed him back into our lives.

## My new family tree

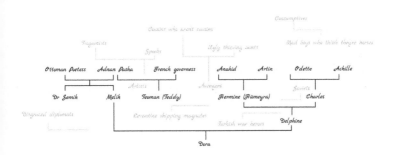

# Elektra

On my last ever visit to the Ottoman villa, I stepped into the little library to be met by a gaunt, bug-eyed woman with stiffly coiffed white hair and more wrinkles than I had ever seen on a human face. She was perched on my window seat, cradling a glass of tea.

Setting it down on the copper tray between us, she held out a jewelled hand.

'Allow me to introduce myself,' she said. 'My name is Elektra. You have probably never heard of me. But you may kiss my hand.'

She let it linger in the air for a few moments, before she withdrew it, unkissed. 'I am so very sorry,' she said. 'I had forgotten that you were raised in America, with no knowledge of our rituals of respect.'

'I don't kiss hands,' I said.

'But you have a name.'

I made to speak, but with a wave of the arm she interrupted me. 'I know who you are. What I wish to know is why you are here.'

'I'm just waiting for...'

'Waiting! Yes, I know this. But here is my question. You are waiting for what?'

I looked up to see my father in the doorway.

In silence he crossed the room. In silence he glowered down at Elektra.

'The question you have just asked my daughter...'

'Your bastard!'

He swallowed hard, as his neck bulged. When he spoke again, it was in Turkish.

'Are you asking me to kick you down the stairs?'

Elektra threw her head back in laughter. 'Is that all you're good for? Empty threats?'

'My threats are not empty.'

'Nor are mine.'

'You are currently an uninvited and unwelcome guest in my house...'

'It is my house too!'

'What? Have you lost your mind? Or is it my mind that is lost? Perhaps I remarried you in my sleep.'

'Enough with your disrespect! If you knew what I know, you would be more careful.'

'You know nothing,' growled my father. He dug his hands

deep into his pockets. He kept them there, as the woman I now knew to be my father's first wife set out to prove him wrong.

She knew what he was up to, and in this very house. Did he really think she had no way of procuring her own informers, or of planting them at his side? She also knew what he was up to with that whore of his. Why he'd welcomed her *and her daughter* back to this city with open arms...

'If you know everything,' said my father in a low and menacing voice, 'then you'll know that my brilliant daughter – my favourite daughter! – has in a matter of mere months mastered Turkish and can therefore understand your every word.'

'Let her understand!' Elektra cried. 'Let her understand what her whore mother has conspired! Let her know that you two are up to. Let us know that you will not simply fail. Unless you agree right now to share the spoils with me, you shall both end up behind bars!'

'If that is what you think, you have chosen your informers unwisely. They have been feeding you foolish falsehoods. I hope, at least, that you have not overpaid them.'

'I have paid them nothing at all. They are patriots, like me. And unless you agree to share the spoils with them as well as me, you can expect to open the papers tomorrow and find your heinous plot exposed.'

At that, my father wheeled around and bellowed, 'Ramazan! Come up at once!'

A few moments later, the janitor appeared. Together he and my father lifted Elektra and carted her outside. From the window I watched them carry her down the path and pack her into the car. It must have been an hour after Hasan reversed down the lane that he returned with my mother and Sergei.

They ran down the path as if pursued.

No sooner were they inside than Elektra came walking back down the path to plant herself between the two palm trees on the far side of the pond.

She was screaming now in a language I could not yet identify. Greek, as it turned out.

'Someone should give this women Elektra Shock Treatment,' my mother said. She came to sit beside me on the window seat. Gently she placed her hands on my ears. Gently she kissed my forehead. 'Don't worry,' she said. 'We'll be getting you someone, to keep you safe.'

That someone was İsmet.

# THE THIRD NOTEBOOK

# İsmet

In the beginning, my new minder was deferential and reserved. Uncertain, even, about his place. If, for example, I got Hasan, the driver, to stop off in Bebek on our way home after school, İsmet would escort me into the pudding shop but decline my invitation to join me at the table. Instead he'd find himself another table nearby, or linger near the door.

It was difficult to draw him into conversation. All I found out about him that first autumn was that he was originally from Adana, and spoke English like someone who had lived all his life in Kansas because he'd spent a year there as an AFS student when he was seventeen.

He'd liked it there. He'd gone back to visit, on his return visit to the US just last year.

'What for?' I asked.

'For training.'

And that was it. End of story. Two or three words, and his attention would return to the street. He was always getting Hasan to change our route. I had no idea why, or what exactly he was protecting me from. I had no idea about anything.

I longed to for my mother to give me a hint or two – who could be trusted. Who could be believed. But I had only to ask the most general question – was it true that Hümeyra had been born Hermine? Had she actually shot her husband with a Derringer once owned by none other than the Pasha? I had only to ask such a question and my mother would yelp and clamp her hand on my mouth and ask in a fierce whisper: 'What do I have to do to make you understand?

If you go around asking questions like this, you'll land me in prison. And keep me from accomplishing what I – what we – came here to do.'

'You're acting like I'm the one telling all these stories,' I complained. 'I'm not. It's everyone else. Couldn't you just tell me how much of it I can believe?'

'None of it.'

'None of it?'

'Well, okay, some of it. The broad brush stuff. So yes, your grandmother was called Hermine once upon a time. And yes, your grandfather – my father – was called Charles. He got what was coming to him, that's all I have to say. And yes, my aunts made away with me, when I was hardly one day old, and then made up wicked stories about your grandmother, to make sure they could keep me. And yes, this is a city where people will believe anything about a mother who doesn't have a husband to stand up for her. Which is why I keep telling you: people here are very good at telling tales. What they don't know they invent. What they don't like they destroy with ugly rumours. So please, Dora. Start using your brain. Stop believing everything you hear. Stop expecting stories to have more than a grain of truth in them. Instead, ask yourself this – why is this person asking me to look in the rear view mirror, when I need to keep my eyes on the road ahead?'

İsmet, I noticed, could keep his eyes on the rear view mirror and road ahead simultaneously. At Hümeyra's soirees, though, there was no point from which he could see everything without drawing undue attention to himself. He couldn't sit or stand next to the door, for instance. Even in civilian clothes, he looked like he was in uniform. He couldn't linger around the punch bowl either – that would certainly have made him an immediate object of suspicion, because in those days he didn't drink. So in the end he posted himself in the alcove I called the morning room, from which he could watch the goings on in the great front room without putting himself into the thick of things. Or had he chosen that perch because his first job was to protect me above all others? Sometimes, I would see a very sheepish-looking Vartuhi bring him in a plate of böreks. Sometimes, it was Hümeyra, or Melih, or Sergei. Each one more fawning than the last. Each taking care not to glance across to greet me.

Every hour or so, my mother would check in on him, to give him the thumbs up, or point at her watch.

Or a very bored Sinan would saunter in to join him on the sofa.

Sometimes – if Sinan was so immersed in his book as not to notice – İsmet would look across at me in my usual perch at the side window, and smile, knowingly.

He had a thin, taut face and dark, luminous eyes. His black hair was cropped so close and so precisely that I sometimes wondered if he went to the barber everyday. His head had a classical shape to it. In profile his nose was long and straight. I thought him handsome. Which shocked me: it was the first time I'd thought that, about anyone.

## A strange new friendship

One afternoon in early spring, I was sitting in the back seat of the sleek black car, lost in contemplation of the back of İsmet's head, when I noticed that we were not driving towards the city, but away from it.

I asked what was going on.

'We've been summoned.'

That was all he would say.

Just past the great castle, we pulled off the road to park in front of an old gate that led us into a maze of bushes, weeds, and flowering trees. We picked our way through it, İsmet and I, until we reached a paved walkway that ran alongside the Bosphorus. And there, to our right, was an enormous yalı that seemed to be more glass than wood.

This part of it, at least. Was it a conservatory? I wondered.

In the window closest to the water I saw the man I still struggled to think of as my father. In the window furthest away from the water, I saw his brother – my uncle – Dr Semih. Waiting for us at the open door, sporting his signature baby blue, was my other uncle, my Swiss uncle – Teddy. Or should I now be calling him my half-uncle? I wasn't sure if such a thing existed.

Air kisses from Teddy, a stern nod from Semih, and from my father a sigh and an embrace. 'Let me take you in,' he said. When İsmet made to follow, my father took umbrage. 'She is safe with me, at least,' he said. Waving him off in the direction of the kitchen, Melih led me across creaking wooden floorboards and through one palatial room after another, until we reached a second conservatory at the far end of the house. There I found an old man draped in blankets, his wheelchair positioned so that he could watch the ships rounding the point. His mottled skin was stretched so tight across his face that I could almost see his skull. His eyes, behind thick-framed glasses, were bloodshot and watery and so large as to look almost unmoored. But at the same time they were appraising, animated, alert.

Melih bent over to kiss his hand.

The old man waved him away. 'So,' he asked. 'This is Dora?'

'Yes, it is,' I said. 'And incidentally, I can speak for myself.'

The old man threw back his head in laughter. Turning to my father, he said, 'Bravo, my son. After a lifetime of disappointing me, you have at last produced a miracle. A new Hermine!' He reached for my hand, to enclose it in his. 'Do you know who I am, dear girl?'

'No, I don't,' I said. 'But I can guess. You must be my grandfather, the infamous Adnan Pasha.'

More laughter. Gales of it. Interspersed with a bit of coughing. A helping hand offered by Melih, which again the old man waved off. 'You can leave now,' he said. 'But first bring a chair for the girl.'

Defeated and deflated, Melih did as he was told.

When he had left, the old man turned to me and said, 'Is it not disgraceful, how these sons of mine are circling? Still seeking the advantage, even after all these years? They cannot bear to let me die in peace.'

'Is that what you've come back for?'

More laughter. And then, a long and disconcerting silence. 'No – but also yes,' he finally said. 'At my age, a single draught could take me. But I have not come back from Switzerland to die, my dear girl. I have come here to live, and to laugh. To drink in the beauties of the Bosphorus, while my little miracle, my Hermine reborn, keeps me entertained.'

It went on until for the better part of a year, this strange friendship of ours. Though that may not be the right word. Can you make friends with your own grandfather?

Twice a week, they'd take me there and wait – İsmet in the kitchen, and Hasan in the car – while I sat in the far conservatory with Adnan Pasha, drinking tea, and listening, taking notes in French that I wrote out in English the moment I got home. He had charged me with writing his memoir – his official memoir, as he called it. 'Let the others twist and turn the story to their own ends, while I trust you and only you with the true version.'

I'd made index cards for my questions, which covered all the chapters of his life, as I called them. Each time I visited, I would hand him the clunky red Rolodex in which I had arranged my cards, in chronological order. He'd flip through them and pick out the question he wished to answer next.

Sometimes I asked follow-up questions. Sometimes, if they occurred to me after I got home, I wrote them out on new index cards and added them to the Rolodex. Which meant that the number of index cards kept growing, no matter how many questions he answered.

This pleased him no end. 'It seems I shall need to stay alive forever,' he would laugh, 'if ever we are to take this task to its completion!'

I still have that Rolodex. I still have those notes. And despite all I know now, I still can still remember and even half believe the story they conjured up for me. So splendid and so terrifying. So strange and so full of holes.

Question 1: **Where were you born?**
Ah! That is a good one. I was born in Jaffa. But when I was one, we moved to Tripoli, and from there to the Arabian Gulf. This, I fear, is the life to which military men must resign themselves. But that last move was difficult for my mother. She was Georgian, after all, and accustomed to a certain degree of freedom.

Follow-up to Question 1: **Why was she Georgian?**

Why should she not be? After all, Georgians were the most prized of wives. It was commonplace for us Ottomans to look far and wide for the best and the most beautiful, to the edges of our empire and beyond. My own father, for example. Until the age of five, he was a simple Albanian farm boy. Then, his mother died, and his father gave him up. He was brought to this city to be educated. Thanks to his talents, he rose to the highest ranks.

Follow-up to follow-up to follow-up: **In other words, you are half Georgian and half Albanian. How, then, can you call yourself Ottoman?**

Because Ottomans can be almost anything, so long as they have entered the ruling class. My first wife, for example. Your other grandmother, the poetess. Her mother was Persian. Her father, Hungarian.

Follow-up to follow-up to follow-up to final follow-up before I throw up my hands and give up: **So what you're telling me is that my father is a quarter Georgian, a quarter Albanian, a quarter Persian, and a quarter Hungarian?**

Yes, that is correct. But also, one hundred percent Ottoman. At least, until the dawn of the Republic.

**Shall we choose that as our next card?**

Because we jumped back and forth between chapters, I took to constructing annotated timelines. These, too, still sit in my old bedroom, in their old box, in their original, never-disturbed, order:

1. Which parts of the great empire had split off when.
2. Which Muslim minorities had been driven from the Balkans and the Caucasus and by whom, and in league with which foe.
3. Which non-Muslim minorities had, after centuries of peaceful co-existence in Ottoman lands, turned against the Sultan, to sue for independence.
4. The order in which the catastrophic defeats of the First World War had occurred, together turning the empire to dust.
5. The order in which the Allied Forces had seized and parcelled out its last remaining heartlands in that war's aftermath.
6. The hard-won battles through which the patriots, among whom Adnan Pasha numbered, had won it back, beating back yet more enemies – the ones lurking within.
7. The order in which the patriots, led by their great leader, Mustafa Kemal Atatürk, had forged a republic that had gone on to become a hope for all mankind, and a beacon for the world.
8. The ugly lies, in chronological order, with which the enemies of this republic had sought to discredit it, from its dawn to the present day.

I would draw up these timelines and take them along with me, for comment and correction.

'Such an industrious girl!' he would say. 'You put your father and his brothers to shame!'

Most of the time, though, it was the old man himself who did the shaming. First he'd call one of them in. Whichever son happened to be hovering that afternoon. Then, he'd pull out one of my timelines and ask that son for the date and precise location of a particular defeat or triumph. Then, after that son had failed the test, he would ask me to supply the correct answer. But I would refuse.

'I'm not playing along with this,' I'd say. 'It's just not nice.'

This would only serve to earn me more affection, and more praise.

Question: **Why are you so mean to your sons?**
Ah. But I am nothing of not generous to these boys. Without me, they would have nothing. As they should know.

Follow-up: **Then why don't they?**
That, my dear girl, is a question you must take to them.

Follow-up to follow-up: **Why can't you just tell me instead?**
Because, it would not be fitting. The affairs of a war can be understood only by its warriors.
**But how am I going to compose your memoir unless you give me a sense of the hell that you endured?**
I have described to you this hell.

**Yes, but I still can't imagine myself into it.**
Fine, then. Fine. I bow to my queen, who shows no mercy. What can I tell you, so that you can imagine, to your heart's content?

**Tell me about the regrets that still haunt you. Speak to me of the deeds that weigh heavy on your soul.**
Ah. Such deep questions. To find the correct answers, I shall certainly need to think.

But first, we were to drink more tea, and enjoy more

kurabiyes, and I was to pretend to the others that I had eaten all of them, while also insisting that he, obeying doctor's orders, had not touched a single one. First, I had to find the dusty, clouded glass he kept hidden in one cabinet, and the Russian vodka he kept hidden in another. First I had to keep his glass full, while amusing him with tales of Hermine, and of all the characters sweeping in and out of her wild soirees. First I was to tell him of my discreet investigations into Communism and the Soviet soul, Radio Moscow and the mysteries of the Russian language, because this, more than anything, lifted his spirits. And never more than the afternoon when a Soviet tanker rounding the point failed to right itself, and seemed for a moment, to be heading straight for us, its red flag fluttering first its hammer and then its sickle.

'Why did that make you laugh so much?' I asked him, once disaster had been averted.

'Ah, but you don't understand. How many ships I have counted on these waters. How many of these ships were carrying the flags of the enemy, or even worse, the occupier. But then, what do we see? They move on! Who knows why? Perhaps we have frightened them. At least, today, you and I have succeeded in doing this. Meanwhile, behind us, the weak cower.'

'You can't keep blaming everything on your sons, you know. You really should stop doing that, while you still have time!'

This would set him off into more gales of mysterious laughter.

Question: **Are you ready?**
Yes, I'm ready.

**We can do this on another day, you know.**
Now is better. After all, I have been thinking. Additionally, I am in the mood.

**Okay then, let's go.**
I have made a list.

**Of the things that haunt you?**
Yes. It is not, however, exhaustive.

**Don't worry. I'm keeping notes. We can always return to them later, if we wish.**
Excellent.
We begin, then, with the war.

**The Great War?**
As you can imagine, I have never thought of that war as great.

**Fair enough. Can we call it the First World War instead?**
Yes, I prefer this.
Though in my mind, it remains the last war.
The war in which we lost everything. Even our pride.
It is therefore at the top of my list.
It is that long and never great war that haunts me, from its first day to the last.
**Can I ask you to be more specific?**
Certainly. If you can pour me another glass?
Thank you.
And so we begin:
A river running red.
A town in ashes, left to its dogs and its beggars.

A roadside, strewn with the remains of women, children and old men. While above, vultures circle.

A cart, laden with plunder. But it cannot move. For the horse to which it is attached is lying on its side, panting while its master curses, and cracks his whip.

Another glass. Please.

And now, the snow melts, revealing a vast field of corpses. Our soldiers. Our finest men.

There they lie, until the mist sweeps down from the mountains. Another drink.

A toast.

To friends lost.

But also:

Friends revealed as enemies. Turncoats. Traitors, lost to the Dashnaks.

The day of the Armistice.

I was in Adana. The occupiers were on their way, and so I left.

Aboard a mail boat named History.

To sail for days along the shores of our beloved heartland.

The mountains of Anatolia, magnificent, even in defeat.

The disgraceful jubilation of Christians in the towns and villages receiving the news of our defeat.

The Dardanelles, the Sea of Marmara, and the Bosphorus.

All thick with enemy ships.

Except that they are no longer our enemies.

They are now our occupiers.

No room for us to dock.

We must call for a fishing boat to carry us to shore.

We must seek in vain for porters.

Without their help we must make the steep climb, through the back streets of Pera, which are thick with jubilant Christians.

To a man, and to a woman, they are drunk.

Onwards, upwards, to the Grande Rue de Pera.

It is lined with yet more jubilant Christians, cheering, waving flags.

In the distance, a fanfare.

The British are coming!

Near the door of the apartment, a drunken Christian grabs my fez.

Meeting my harsh gaze, he crumples. Hands it back.

While the drunken Christian next to him spits.

My resolve. My resolve!

At the door, it deserts me. It returns, as I ascend the stairs.

From this moment. We shall refuse. We shall resist!

But with that resolve, the question:

In these ravaged lands of ours, is that a single Christian we can trust?


Is there?

Yes. Even on that first day of greatest bitterness, there is one.

Later, when there are again rich pickings, others come creeping back.

By then, we can welcome them with dignity and pride.

For we have their awe to savour.

We are heroes!

We have stood as one and won back our heartlands!

We can turn with pride towards the West that had betrayed us.

**Germany didn't betray you.**
Ah, but Germany lost.

**Is that enough for today?**
Perhaps.

**Maybe next time we can talk about something happier.**
Yes, that would be good.

**Shall we make a list?**
There's no need. It is all in my head.

**Shall we put them down on index cards anyway?**
Certainly. You can file them under the chapter we have named
as The First Years of the Republic:

1. The day our great leader led us to victory.
2. The day he abolished the caliphate.
3. The day he shut down each and every dervish tekke,
   thereby freeing us forever from the stranglehold of
   Islam.
4. The day he sent the last sultan and his family into
   eternal exile.
5. The day our great leader banned the fez.
6. The day he announced that in just three months'
   time, we would be abandoning the Arabic script for
   the Latin.
7. The day he announced we must all have surnames.

**That's seven. Enough to keep us busy for a very long time.**
I know! But I have more.

**I've run out of index cards, though.**
You have a notebook. So you can write this down:

These were heady, joyous years for us.
Even here.
In this city that was no longer to be our capital. It was once again ours!
In our joy, we had renamed it!
While Europe, in retreat, bowed its head.
In awe. At our magnificent achievement.
Peace at home! Peace in the world!
How happy is he who calls himself a Turk!
All this is true. All this we must discuss.
And you, record.
Nevertheless.
You had asked me what weighs most heavily on my soul.
It is the world we knew before that terrible and not great war. The world we lost, on account of our innocence, and misplaced trust.
The streets in which a dozen languages wove their way through the air with such grace and high spirits.
The schools, where the city's Christians, Jews and Muslims learned side by side. To become not just friends but allies. And sometimes, even, saviours.
The Alephs. Ah, the Alephs! Always watching over each other, always finding joy.

**Who were the Alephs?**
Who can know? Who can now say? I am talking instead of the days when we thought we knew. When from the depths of our hearts we believed that we could depend on each other through thick and thin. It is the happy memories that

haunt me, Dora.

Our picnics.

Our boar hunts.

Our afternoons at the Bourse.

Those long nights at the Cercle d'Orient.

Our escapades.

The game of the shirt.

**The game of the shirt?**
Yes, the game of the shirt.
Such laughs!
But then, it all ended.

**Why?**
There was a traitor.

**Do you want to tell me about the traitor, or should we call it a day?**
I do not wish to talk of the traitor.

**Shall we call it a day, then?**
Don't be so cruel, dear Dora. Don't leave me to languish in bitter thoughts. For once, you can ask me a question that makes me laugh, the way Hermine did, when she was small.

**All right then. Let's talk about that. Why do I remind you of Hermine, when I'm so different?**
You are taller, of course. And darker. And sometimes, too solemn.
But how am I like her?
You can make fire.
Just by rubbing together two fingers.

Like this.

Ha ha!

Your mother, she cannot do that. She can only make trouble.

**Why do you say that?**

Your mother – she comes to a wall, and she gets angry.

Not like Hermine.

My Hermine sees a wall, and she rolls right through it.

On that tricycle of hers! Ha ha!

While you, Dora.

You – you don't even see the wall.

You don't even know it's there!

**What exactly do you mean by that?**

For example, you are supposed to respect me.

**I do respect you.**

Yes, but not from fear.

**Why should I fear you?**

Raaaaaaaaaaaaaaaaaah! Raaaaaaaaaaah!

**Should we call it a day now? Or are you going to behave?**

I shall behave, of course. On two conditions.

The first:

You will accept my apology, for my silly little joke.

**Okay. Fine. I accept your apology.**

You are very kind, dear Dora. And very generous. I hope you don't mind if I now ask for your assistance. For alas, we have run dry.

This would have been in May or June – the glorious culmination of my second spring in Istanbul. As I walked through the palatial rooms of the yalı that had, as I now knew, been the childhood home of my poetess grandmother, I could almost convince myself that the Bosphorus and the Asian shores were moving in the opposite direction. The hills were pink and purple with the blossoms of their Judas trees. On the Bosphorus, a caique was fighting against the current.

In the kitchen, I found İsmet, sitting alone.

'I don't know why you stay in here,' I said. 'It's such a beautiful day!'

He gave me a studied look, as if I had said something very deep.

'Anyway,' I said, 'I've been sent by our Pasha.'

'Of course,' he said. But he did not move.

'He said you would understand. But do you?'

'I understand, of course.'

'So are you coming?'

Looking startled now, he asked, 'Of course. But where will you wait?'

'I'm coming with you, naturally.'

This perplexed him. 'Are you certain of this?'

'Yes, of course I am. We're not done yet.'

'Okay. If you say so.'

But when we reached the door of the far conservatory, he told me to stop there.

'I need to make sure,' he said.

In he went with his heavy briefcase, shutting the door behind him.

Greetings. Murmurs. Laughter, gales of it.

'Dora!' cried my grandfather. 'Come in! Come in!'

And that was how I discovered that my minder had become the old man's conduit for Russian vodka. Purloined from the Soviet Consulate by Sergei, no doubt. Passed on to my grandfather's cook, on whose discretion he could count, to be secreted to the backs of cabinets when no one else was looking.

But the cook was visiting an ailing relative that afternoon. And my grandfather now trusted me enough to bring me in on the deception.

As we sat there, İsmet and I, watching the old man knock back another vodka, and then another, and another, he told me how this minder of mine had come into our lives, and why we could trust him absolutely.

'It is a useful story for me to tell you, on this day of all days. For there is more to war than the hell and the betrayals. There are also the discoveries.'

And of all those discoveries, none had proved more heartening than İsmet's patron, Soran Bey.

'I would go so far as to say that, almost singlehandedly, this one-time factotum was able to help me understand what a great future could await the Anatolian heartlands, if its fortunes were placed in the right hands.'

**So tell me about Soran**
Soran was just fourteen when he entered my service.

**Where was he before that?**
Harput. Do you know it? Aha! I have caught you out! You shall look on the map when you get home, Dora. You shall find it on the eastern edges of our glorious Anatolia.

**How you find him there too?**

Ah. Good question. No. He was already in Istanbul, in domestic service.

**Where?**

Various places. Mostly Christians, it seems. Though perhaps there was also a Jewish family in the beginning. He had used his time in these families well, our Soran. Borrowing the schoolbooks of his masters' children at night. Listening in on their lessons. Learning their languages. And he was so good with the children. The children loved him. Celeste, my late lamented wife, came to depend on him to keep the peace. But I came to depend on him more.

**How?**

Wherever my duties sent me, Soran was at my side, keeping watch. Understanding the dangers. Guarding us from the traitors and the thieves. Thanks to Soran, all our journeys yielded satisfactory results.

**Where did you go?**

Sometimes, to Berlin. But mostly, to the East.

**Where in the East?**

Every city, every town, every desert and mountain that this Not-Great War had ravaged.

**Why?**

To bring order. And justice. To discipline the greedy! Stop the plunder! Oh Dora. If only I had the heart to tell you how many of our trusted officials had secretly enriched themselves. It was perhaps due to their treachery, not to mention the greed of the Europeans, that our Treasury was so quickly depleted. But we did our best, Soran and I. Of course, Soran spoke all the tribal languages. And a few of the Christian languages, too.

But oh! Such sights we saw! Schools and customs offices, piled high with fine carpets and furniture. Abandoned villages, destroyed factories. Empty bazaars, and herds of shepherd-less sheep. Over and over I would ask myself: where from here? Who could we trust to become the new shepherds of these ravaged lands?

The answer should have been clear to me. But I was, I fear, held back by my old attitudes. For too long, I persisted in seeing our Soran as a servant pure and simple. But then, I saw. And just in the nick of time! It was the spring of 1918. Soran and I were on our way to Adana. The fields in its environs were pockmarked with abandoned cotton mills. Later, in the city, our hosts were wringing their hands. Who could we trust? Who had the necessary education, brains, and moral character? At that moment I knew.

So I took them to one side and said, 'I have a good man for you.

Now find him a good house.'

Of course, this did not happen overnight.


**Why not?**
The Armistice of Mudros, of course! Our defeat, and the crushing, after five hundred years, of the House of Osman! The years of the occupiers! But then, in 1922, our patriots overcame them. The work of reconstruction could at last begin. By the dawn of our great republic, Soran had become Soran Bey, proud master of a thousand fields. With judicious assistance, he was able to continue growing. By the time we

joined his son in marriage with my granddaughter, he had become a figure of national consequence. Soran the Cotton King! That's what they called him in the newspapers, and even inside the family.

**But not you.**

You are correct. Not me. He and I were simply two old men who enjoyed the fruits of our labours from afar. We had joined our fortunes. Equipped his industrious son with my granddaughter and her excellent connections. We knew they would go far, these two, and we were right.

But still one question vexed us.

What of Anatolia? Where from here? It takes more than a single generation to raise a nation from its ashes. But all around him, my old friend Soran saw rapacious landowners and corrupt officials who could see no further than their own enrichment. A second regeneration was needed. Who could they count on, to be the shepherds of the new dawn?

İsmet, my throat is dry, and so is my glass. Perhaps, while you serve me, you can take up the story.

Thank you, my boy.

Are you sure?

Can this be true?

How can it be, that an event so significant cannot have lodged itself in your memory?

Ah. I didn't know this.

Certainly. It would be rare for a child to keep a memory from such a tender age.

And so. Let me continue.

Let me tell you the story as my dear friend Soran has told it.

**So. Are you ready now, to tell me this story as your old friend Soran told it?**

Yes, indeed. I am.

It was again in Adana, only a few days later. By this I mean, a few days after the conversation during which we two old men had been fretting about the future of Anatolia was still at the forefront of Soran Bey's mind. He was visiting the cotton fields of a concern that had recently been bankrupted. It was very hot, and so he paused to take shade under a tree. Here he found a small boy.

He could not have been more than five, this boy, and perhaps you are right, İsmet. You could have been as young as three or four.

When Soran Bey told the youngster that he was thinking of buying those fields, and many others besides, the boy nodded. You are the sahip, he said. Yes, Soran said. Not today. But one day soon.

The boy was not cowed by this news. Instead he pointed out his mother in the field and said, 'If you are the sahip, can you let us go home early?'

'Why?' asked Soran Bey.

The boy said, 'Because I am bored. And hungry.'

And Soran Bey laughed. 'You are a boy after my own heart,' he said. 'You know what you want, and you are prepared to pursue it fearlessly. You will go far, I'm sure of it!'

In short, Soran Bey had seen something of himself in this boy.

After he bought the fields in question, he kept a discreet but watchful eye on him.

When the time arrived, he made sure the boy went to school and stayed there.

Of course, he also provided all the books and shoes and clothes he needed. He never did let his mother leave those cotton fields early, ha ha! But when it was time for İsmet to attend a good lycee in the city, Soran Bey arranged for him and his mother to move into an apartment building he owned, not far from the school.

On weekends, and during the summer, the boy would go to work with Soran Bey in his beloved garden. Such a beautiful garden, Dora! I hope that one day you can see it. Perhaps one day, İsmet Bey will take you there, to meet his illustrious patron, and share in his rich Anatolian wisdom.

But for now, let us leave it there, dear Dora. You know now why this fine man has come to live under our wing. And now you will see. With just a little help from you and me, and perhaps a few others, our İsmet will become that shepherd, leading us to our new dawn.

Really? I remember thinking. Because instead of smiling, instead of thanking the Pasha for his lavish praise, İsmet had kept his back bent, his gaze downwards, his hands tightly joined.

It was not until he looked up at long last, first to give his belated thanks, and then to express the hope that one day he might prove himself worthy of the Pasha's trust, that I saw something else in his eyes.

It flashed, and then it was gone.

# New schemes and plans

Not long after that – this would have been in May. It was the weekend, and I'd been inside our stuffy apartment all day. So my mother suggested supper at the Park Hotel. İsmet was at his desk in the foyer, as per usual. But for once he did not make to leave with us. When I asked my mother why, she said, 'I've given him the night off.'

All the way down the avenue, we held hands, swinging our arms to the beat of her favourite marching song:

*I left my wife with forty-nine kids, and nothing but gingerbread left, left...*

In the Park Hotel bar, we were greeted with effusion, and led out to the terrace, to the table with the best view of the Bosphorus, and a welcome breeze. 'You'd never know,' she said. 'Would you? That I used to be persona non grata in this place.'

She looked so very happy when I asked why.

'I was beginning to wonder if you'd ever ask!' She went on to explain that, on account of it being practically next door to the German consulate, the Park Hotel had been a hotbed of Nazi spies, collaborators and informers, from the start of World War Two until its finish. 'While I, as you recall, was working for the Americans.' Lighting up a cigarette, gazing at the ships passing below, she asked, 'Do you miss it, ever?'

'Miss what?'

'America. New York. What we had there.'

'What was that?'

'Ha ha! As sharp a tongue as ever. Well, don't let me stand in your way. It's a good thing for a gal to have. As for what we had, when it was just you and me against the world, be it on the Upper East Side, or the Lower and Lower... Well, we had our freedom. We could go wherever we wanted, without pretty much anyone knowing. Not like here, where you can't go anywhere without everything you ever do or say becoming everyone's business. Everything you ever did or said, too. Even if it was a million years ago, it's still breaking news.'

'What are you asking me, exactly?'

'If you'd like to go back. Once I wrap up what I have to do here, that is.'

'But...'

'Come on, Dora. What do we have to lose?'

'Our family?'

'Oh, but we could take that with us. Start a new one, even, while we're at it. If things go my way, and they are going my way, finally, we could even afford a house on the Hudson. What would you say to that?'

What I wish I'd asked her:

Why she was suddenly so light-hearted.

Why her stream of gentleman callers had just as suddenly dried up.

Why things were going her way at long last.

Why she had taken to spending so many nights across the landing.

Why, when she swept back in, for an early or late morning coffee, she was always humming to herself.

Why my grandmother took to giving me tragic embraces, calling me her poor, dear child.

Why, when my mother was nowhere to be found, and I

asked my grandmother if she had any idea where she'd gone, she would raise her arms in helpless, hopeless puzzlement, but avoid looking me in the eye.

Why Sergei, in answer to the same question, would gaze at me soulfully while making as if to zip his lips.


Officially, if anyone asked, my mother was a freelance journalist. During that last spring in Istanbul, she was away on assignment more than she was at home.

It was during one of these absences that Melih arranged for the rest of us a visit to the Swedish Consulate. The consul general's wife having expressed an interest in Hümeyra's paintings. We'd picked up İsmet at his desk in the foyer downstairs, as per usual. Arriving at the consulate, he'd first stationed himself in the courtyard, but our hosts had insisted that he accompany us inside.

And there he sat, at one end of a reception room the size of a ballroom, while at the other end the rest of us sat sipping tea. Melih in his cream-coloured suit did all the talking, extemporising on art, culture, and history's great treasures, while Hümeyra sat leaning forward, balancing her portfolio on her feet.

Then suddenly the portfolio fell forward, spilling its contents, whereupon the consul general's wife clapped her hands and said: 'Such perfect timing! How we are longing to see your great works!'

Impatient as a child, my grandmother scrambled to her feet, almost falling over herself as she set her wares up against the wall.

These were all collages, in the manner for which she was best known. These having elicited polite admiration, but nothing more, Melih asked our hostess if she would like to be the first to see Hümeyra's most recent paintings, through which she was forging a daring new path.

But of course! said our hostess.

Gathering up the collages, Melih replaced them with a series so new that even I had not yet seen them. They were, he said, a return to an old preoccupation, but with a twist. Group portraits of figures arranged either around the baby grand or the chaise longue, with the human form bent and twisted in the time-honoured way. Except that now – thanks to our friend the Society Photographer, who had been taking such exquisite pictures of our soirees – Hümeyra had given them all real faces.

In each group there lurked the angel of death. Hiding under the chaise longue in one, sitting on the baby grand in another. In others, it was hovering in the window, brandishing a coarsely drawn pitchfork. Elsewhere it was pinned to the wall like a painting in its own right, or slithering across the floor.

In the last it was curled up like a fetus in the stomach of the writhing and emaciated figure that carried the likeness of none other than the Swedish consul general's wife.

Ever the gentleman, Melih took my distraught grandmother in his arms the moment we had cleared the consular gates. It was not her fault. How could she have known that the consul general's wife had only recently suffered a stillbirth? He suggested a restorative drink at the Pera Palas, but we had no sooner seated ourselves in its bar than we were asked to leave. There was an unpaid tab, it seemed. So we decamped to the shabby grandeur of the Büyük Londra, where İsmet sat quietly next to the parrots, while my grandmother wept noisily, and Melih did his best to comfort her, though I could tell, from the way he kept dabbing his forehead, that he too was agitated. Reading between the lines, I understood that my grandmother had been trying, in my mother's absence, to raise a bit of money for him.

'But how dismally I have failed!'

Later, back in the apartment, when my grandmother was playing with my hair – brushing it up into buns and plaits of all descriptions, or just spreading it out on the back of the chaise longue, to give a hundred strokes to each tress in succession – she told me why it was that Melih was a broken man.

It was because of the scandal following my birth, she explained. That episode with his brother's wife – not quite kicking her down the stairs, but almost. And oh, those infernal curses! Inevitably, brother Semih had taken umbrage. Inevitably, the story had got out, eventually reaching the ears of Melih's wife. 'Who is half Greek, as you know,' Hümeyra said. As if that alone explained her wrath, and her thirst for revenge. For this wife had gone straight to her father, himself a distinguished Turkish diplomat, despite his love for Greek sonnets, to forever blacken her husband's good name.

'What falsehoods she invented, we can never know. But since that moment, our poor Melih has never worked. Because his own father has also refused him assistance, it is I who must seek to supplement his paltry income, as best I can. But please, Dora, please! You are never to tell your mother! She would instantly put an end to this! She would never understand!'

I remember looking up at the moment and catching a glimpse of myself in the mirror near the hallway, just above the chair where İsmet was sitting. My grandmother had fashioned a ponytail at the top of my head, and now she was twisting it into a lopsided bun that made me look utterly, utterly ridiculous.

And for the first time ever, I caught İsmet smiling.

Not just smiling, I decided afterwards.

Exuding radiance.

But only for a moment.

When our eyes met, his went blank.


What must he think of us, I wondered? It was not a thought I'd ever entertained, about anyone. I'd been too much inside my mother's world to wonder about such a thing, or too much outside everyone else's to care. But from this moment on, there was always part of me standing outside myself, wondering what he might think of me, or see in me, or find lacking.

Beyond refusing or deriding whatever my mother laid out for me, I'd never given much thought to what I wore. Comfort and common sense – that was all I'd cared about. Now, though, I came into daily conversation with my mirror – trying on clothes and discarding them, fretting about shoes with heels that might seem too high, wondering if this necklace with that twinset would seem too showy.

I never asked İsmet for his thoughts. And neither did he offer them. He just carried on doing what he had been hired to do. Guarding me from dangers never described. Escorting me on outings. Ferrying me to and from my grandfather's yalı, and my more occasional overnight stays with that younger disciple I mentioned earlier who had remained my only friend at school. He never sat next to me. He always took the front seat, next to Hasan the driver, while I stared, in silence, at his beautiful neck.

I am no longer sure how much I put myself forward. I

can recall an awkward supper, sometime during that last summer, somewhere along the Bosphorus. This was one of those occasions when our man for all seasons used a flying visit to bring together our family's warring parties, and to somehow knock some sense into us. So on his right-hand side on this particular evening, there was a taciturn, leg-swinging Sinan. While on his left-hand side, was Sibel, Sinan's wayward mother, who had been away for many months, following a string of scandals. These two didn't wish to talk, but William Wakefield was determined to make them.

He had also insisted – just this once – that İsmet join us at the table. But then, when he saw me pulling on İsmet's arm, trying to talk him into a bit of arm wrestling, William Wakefield wagged a finger at me and said, 'Dora! Lay off.'

My mother was not with us that evening, either. It was William who joined me in the back seat of the sleek black car taking me home, quizzing me on the French lycee to which I would be moving in September, and acting as if İsmet was not even there.

But when we stopped in front of my apartment, William ordered him to follow us upstairs. 'There's something I want you to see.'

That something turned out to be a procession of Soviet passenger ships, sliding through the dusk towards the Sea of Marmara.

'Do you see how low in the water they are?' William murmured.

İsmet nodded, as he moving from window to window until he had reached the one with the best view of the Soviet Consulate. Its every window was lit up.

'Are you thinking what I'm thinking?' William asked.

'Perhaps,' said İsmet.

'And so,' said William, 'the plot thickens.'

Questions that kept me up that night:

What that plot was
Who was in on it
Where the danger was
What might become of us
Where my mother was
Whether or not things were still going her way
Why it was that this family of mine could never find peace
And lurched instead, from war to war
Rent asunder by its losses and betrayals
Generation after haunted generation

Questions that somehow eluded me, perhaps because I was too young:

Why İsmet, who had never, to my knowledge, been inside our apartment, knew his way around it
Why he even had a key
Why he knew exactly where to find our binoculars, and my mother's current notebook, which he used to record William Wakefield's curt remarks: the name of each ship, its location in the convoy, the exact time it appeared in our window, the number of men on deck.

It was not until October that the story broke, exposing what they had recorded on that night and quite a few subsequent nights, and I had seen with my own eyes. The Soviets had been smuggling missiles and troops through the Bosphorus all summer, many or most of them in just this sort of convoy. And William had known, and İsmet, and Sergei, and my mother, too. But when President Kennedy went on air to tell us that these troops and missiles were now assembled in Cuba, only ninety miles from the continental United States, thereby putting the world on standby for a nuclear world war, he made as if he'd had no advance warning. As if none of Istanbul's spying eyes had passed on a thing.

It unnerved me, the thought that our president might be lying. What unnerved me most, though, was my mother's matter-of-fact calm: 'So anyway,' she said. 'For the next few days – or even, weeks, if we last that long – I'm going to be pretty busy, there in the back channels, helping the crazy guys over here who are trying to get these crazy guys over there to climb down before they blow us to smithereens. So wish me luck! But don't expect me home for supper. And make sure you have as much fun as you can, while you can!'

'What do you mean by that, for God's sake?'

'I'm sorry. I didn't mean to scare you. But you never know. So think of it as insurance. Live life to the full, just in case!'

I imagine that people all over the world were doing crazy things, just in case, when the countdown to the threatened World War III began, on the night of 22nd October 1962.

My crazy thing was to adorn my mother's bedroom with candles, ribbons and flowers, and then, when my grandmother's famous End of the World Party was in full swing, to entice İsmet across the landing under false pretences. Something strange was happening, I told him, in the courtyard of the Soviet consulate, into which, as he knew, our apartment had the best view

We opened its door to the smell of burning. We traced it

to a ribbon I had placed too close to a candle in my mother's bedroom.

He knew immediately what to do. Where to find the fire extinguisher, even. I remember being impressed. It was after he had put out the fire, while he was checking the rest of the room, fire extinguisher at the ready, that he noticed all the other ribbons and candles.

'What is this?' he asked. He looked so startled at that moment. So almost scared.

Overcome by what felt like pity, I bounded across the room and threw my arms around him. Knocking over the fire extinguisher. Attempting a kiss. But not succeeding. After all, I didn't know how.

Pulling back, he stared at me. 'Why are you doing this?' he asked.

'I want to know love,' I said. 'And this may be our last ever chance.'

He stared at me, as he wiped his lips clean.

'What's wrong?' I asked.

He wouldn't say.


So in the weeks that followed – weeks we spent together in the usual way, except that he wouldn't, not even once, look me in the eye – I went over every detail I could remember, over and over, from my offer of boundless love, to his cold, cruel, heartless rejection. What had I done to deserve his contempt? Why did he think me unworthy of his love? Who did he think he was? Who did he think I was?

That November, a few days before my birthday, I wrote him a letter. I tossed it onto the front seat of Hasan's car while İsmet was standing some distance away, smoking. I had thought this would be fine, on account of Hasan speaking no English, which will give you a sense of how naïve I was.

It had been a long time since we'd last stopped at the pudding shop in Bebek on our way back from my grandfather's, but on that afternoon, it was İsmet who suggested it. He ordered us for us both. For once, we were sharing a table.

Once the waiter was gone, and for the first time in all those weeks, he looked straight at me.

'Dora,' he said. 'You must stop this.'

And I said, 'Why?'

'Because it is wrong. You are young. And I am here only to guard you.'

'Are you honestly saying you have no feelings for me?'

'Dora. This is unsuitable talk.'

'I'm just asking you for the truth!'

'The truth,' said İsmet, 'is that I have a duty to protect you. No less, and no more. So please, respect my wishes. If not – if you refuse – '

'I refuse!'

A great sigh, the likes of which I had never seen from my beloved. Burying his face in his hands, he said, 'Dora. I beg you. Please. Before it destroys us both, stop this madness.'

Which was, or ought to have been, clear enough. There was something, though, about the way he said it. Or at least, the way I heard it. As I lay in bed that night, too distracted for Radio Moscow, I went over our short exchange at the pudding shop, over and over, searching some sign of his true feelings, until suddenly, I thought I knew.

It was duty holding him back. Duty and duty alone.

I still had a chance.

The next trap I laid for him was only marginally subtler than the first. It was another Friday, another soiree. But there were no ribbons, no candles or enticements. All I did was stand in my usual window – which I'd been avoiding, ever since the End of the World Party. I stood there, thinking that the world had ended that day for me that night, if not for anyone else. I kept my eyes fixed on İsmet in the alcove opposite, in his usual chair, intent on his newspaper. I stood there for ten minutes exactly, and then I pressed my hands and face against the window, and open-mouthed, let myself sink very slowly to the floor, as if I'd fainted.

A few minutes later, I heard him letting himself in.

I kept up the act. And he knew what to do. Within moments, I was tucked into my mother's bed, with a glass of water beside me. He was sitting at my side, and when I asked if he might like to lie down beside me, for just a while, he took my hand – my hand! – and said, 'Dora. If this continues, I shall have to ask for a transfer.'

'Why don't you love me?' I asked.

And he said, 'Because you are a child.'

'I am not a child anymore! I'm fourteen years old!'

'You are still a child.'

'My own grandmother was married at my age!'

'Yes, and that was wrong.'

'It wasn't at the time!'

'Dora! I have asked you! Many times! You must stop!'

'I'm never going to stop,' I said.

'Then our friendship is over.'

'It was never even that,' I said.

He gazed up at the ceiling, as it to ask God to grant him patience.

Then he left.

Returned to the party and his chair in the alcove.

Did not glance once in my direction, while I downed the beer I'd found in the refrigerator.

I was fourteen after all.

Let him stop me, if he thought that was too young to have a drink.

I took some time getting ready. It would have been close to midnight when I joined the party across the landing, ambling across the room in a pink dress I hoped the cold-hearted cur I now hated more than anyone in the world would find unsuitable.

Unsuitable. What a word.

I poured myself a giant glass of my grandmother's infamous punch, the one with pure alcohol, boiled in not enough water, and a few fruits of the season and not much else.

I cast my defiance across the room, but – as per usual – the only one who noticed me was Sinan. He was perched on the ancient chaise longue, his face half hidden by a book. He gave me a good long stare, before returning to his reading.

In the corner, I saw Sibel, Sinan's mother, bent over the gramophone. A few loud scratches, and it was Secaattin Tanyeri, singing a Turkish tango. Plunging into the crowd, Sibel emerged with Uncle Teddy, dressed in baby blue as always, but this evening, stripped down to the waist. Having left her draped over the piano, he reached across to Baby Mallinson, perched expectantly on the piano stool. Soon he, too, was draped over the piano, as Uncle Teddy found his next partner, and his next, until he had danced with all of the most beautiful women in the room, and more than a few of the men.

I remained by the bowl, continuing to help myself. While İsmet ignored me, and I followed his every move.

Why was he refusing me?

It was when he went to perch himself on the baby grand – when Baby Mallinson looked up from the keys to blink at him flirtatiously – that I divined an answer.

He loved men.

I waited until Baby began to play again, and İsmet had moved to the window. I sidled up next to him. I took his hand. He pulled it away.

'You're drunk,' he said.

'Of course I am. Shall I tell you why?'

'You're making a disgrace of yourself. You should go back to your room.'

'Oh, I shall, I shall. I'm heading there right now. But first I want you to know that I have figured out what your problem is. And İsmet, I'm so disappointed in you! Why didn't you trust me? I would have understood!'

'You are making no sense,' he said.

'Oh, I am. You're just not listening. But listen to me now. You've broken my heart!'

And perhaps the punch was doing its work by then. Perhaps I was shouting. Or perhaps it was the way İsmet seized my arm that attracted Sergei's attention. For now Sergei bounded across the room, bringing with him the ambassador from somewhere. I reminded Sergei that he and I were not to be seen together. I set about explaining the reasons why, for the benefit the ambassador from somewhere. When Sergei tried to interrupt me, I waved away his gentle words.

'I still don't know who you work for,' I said. 'Any of you! And do you have any idea how that makes me feel?'

'Dora. Darling.'

'But I do know one thing, Sergei. All this spying is a front. What you're really after – and I mean all of you – is that gold!'

'What gold, dear girl?'

'The Armenian gold, of course! In the Kremlin! But who knows where it is by now. I'll tell you what I think.' I paused, to let the room stop swirling. And then I ventured a preposterous thought that had never once occurred to me, not until this very moment: 'About those ships that went through here last summer. You know. Carrying all those missiles to Cuba. I think there was something else keeping them so low in the water I think someone made room for Armenian gold. Six million dollars' worth. If not more!'

The room had not stopped swirling. But Sergei was laughing, throatily. 'Such a beautiful idea!' he said. 'A perfect solution for us all! Tell me more, dear girl. Tell me more!'

Nothing I could say to this man upset him. Ever.

But İsmet had me by the shoulder. 'Enough,' he said. 'I am taking you to bed.'

'To bed? Oh please. Not to bed, İsmet. Anywhere but there. Sergei, please save me! Save me from İsmet's clutches!'

'What has he done to you, dear Dora?'

'What has he not done?'

I fell into Sergei's arms. As he cried, 'Dora! Darling! Has this man interfered with you?'

'Hardly!' I cried. 'He loves men, but is too cowardly to admit it! Even to himself!'

'You are lying!' İsmet yelled. 'You are a disgrace! And you are as drunk as a skunk!'

By now the music had stopped, and so too had the dancers, the better to watch the show.

Turning now to his sudden audience, İsmet declared himself to have been defamed. For he was a real man, a true man. Unlike so many here assembled.

Drunk as I was, I could see this was not going down very well.

Especially not with Teddy. Who raised himself from the piano over which he had draped himself, to creep up behind İsmet and goose him.

Taken by surprise, İsmet let out a mousy little squeak, which was met by uproarious laughter.

Until Delphine, pushing through the crowd, came to his rescue, and mine.

'You ungrateful girl,' she said – not just to me, but for the benefit of all assembled. 'After all this man has done for you. You are going to apologise, this very moment. And then I am taking you to bed.'

I did not apologise. But she did take me to bed.

Across the landing, this suddenly officious mother of mine stopped my in my tracks to say, 'When you have well and truly sobered up, Miss Priss, you and I are going to have to have a serious talk.'

Back inside the apartment, back at my old window, I watched Uncle Teddy and two friends of his pin İsmet to the wall. The window was half open, so I could hear what Teddy said to him, as he cupped his hands around his face: How long, and how hopelessly he had desired İsmet – this Apollo he had at long last snared. All these months and months, while seeing him with 'that woman'. But hoping, dreaming, lusting, that this dear little secret policeman, who liked nothing more than to jail pederasts, might one day look his way!

Good, I thought drunkenly. And left them to it.

It was in my bed, and already half asleep, when I heard a key turn in the lock. I paid it no attention, assuming that it must be my mother, back for a cigarette, or a tissue, or a bottle.

Then my bedroom door creaked open. İsmet was standing over me, undoing his zipper.

'Is this what you wanted?' he asked, in a strangled whisper. 'Is it? Is it?'

Although he did succeed in pinning me down – first on the bed, and then, after I had kicked him off the bed, the floor, and later, more than once, against the wall – I turned out to be stronger than he expected. How I knew to knee him in the balls I cannot say. But seeing it work so well on the first occasion, I did it again, and then again. Somewhere in the middle of all this, I found the bat my mother had placed by my door, presumably for just this sort of occasion. I used it to back him into the corridor, and then, when he opened the front door to turn from a shadow into a silhouette, I cracked it against his departing back, screaming every epithet I knew in the loudest voice I could muster, but such was the noise coming from the party next door that there was no danger of anyone hearing me. So I chased him in. Screamed as loud as I could, over the music and the dancing. Only the three men near the door paid me any heed. I ran into their arms, almost. 'This man tried to rape me!'

Upon which İsmet lunged at me. Two of the three men restrained him. The other urged me gently backwards. 'Go,' he said. 'Go!'

So I did as he had asked. Once safe inside our apartment, I locked the door behind me and then I bolted it. For a few minutes, I stood there listening to the ruckus next door. The tango still full blast, syncopated now by kicks and shouts and then a struggle in the stairwell. Then a door closing, muffling the tango. Then downstairs, the door into the street creaking open, slamming closed. After that I went off to take a very long shower.

I could still hear noise next door when I finally got out. But mostly it was people leaving, and heading into the stairwell. I was still drunk, of course, and that may be why I fell asleep so fast.

It must have been four in the morning when I went into my mother's room to borrow a bathrobe. Looking across into Hümeyra's apartment, I saw that it, too, was empty, and deathly still.

Where had they all gone? And where, more to the point, was my mother? I must have still been drunk, because it wasn't until morning that I remembered the door I had yet to unbolt. On previous occasions, when I had left the door bolted, my mother had stayed across the landing. So I let myself in to my grandmother's apartment, and it was like Pompei. A night interrupted in mid-flow, now absent of life.

At noon I walked down to Kulis, to check with the bartender. The anger with which this gentle soul told me he knew nothing, told me everything. I took the fastest way to the US Consulate, even though that meant passing several side streets of ill repute. It was early, though. Their denizens were mostly still asleep, and because it was Saturday, the consulate was closed.

The marines outside gave me the name and number of the duty officer.

I made the call as soon as I got home. It was not a man who answered, but a boy.

'Dora,' he said. 'It's you isn't it. Dora from the wedding?'

'Which wedding?' I asked. I'd been to so many.

Then he told me his name, which I remembered, perhaps because I'd never met anyone else named Tallis.

'You're Sinan's friend,' I said.

'That's right.'

'Why are you back?'

'I'm doing an exchange year,' he said. 'At Robert. It's nice to hear from you! I was starting to give up hope.'

'Why are you answering this number?' I asked.

'Oh. It's because it's where I'm staying. Friends of my dad's. Did you call because you wanted to talk to them?'

'I'm looking for the duty officer,' I said.

'Are you ok?'

I paused, uncertain as to what to say.

'I'll be right over,' he said.

Tallis, who was a head taller, I thought, but otherwise exactly as I remembered him, reached the building just as I was leaving it.

'I need some air,' I said.

And he said, 'I'm coming with you.'

'I'm fine by myself.'

'No you're not. You look terrible.'

'I don't want to talk about it,' I said, as I veered left, down a steep and narrow alleyway.

'We don't have to talk. Let's go for a walk instead.'

But we were getting too much attention: catcalls, insults, remonstrations, swerving cars. So we ended up on a ferry, which we took as far as Kanlıca. In the café next to the landing stage, I ordered a yoghurt. It arrived with a mountain of powdered sugar on top. In silence, he watched me eat it. Then he ordered us tea.

It was at this point that I told him everything. Everything

142

except anything that might cast me in a bad light. I remember how much lighter I felt, with every fact imparted, and every insult named. And even all these years later, I can close my eyes and recall what I saw in his. Now confusion. Now disbelief. Now anger on my behalf. Now awe.

'You kicked him in the balls?'

When we got back to the apartment, late afternoon, there was still no sign of my mother, and no sign either of Hümeyra next door. Tallis put in a call to his host, the duty officer, who gave him some sort of talking to. 'Yes, sir. I see, sir. I understand, sir. I'll be right back.' Putting down the receiver, and hanging his head, he said, 'It's not right. You shouldn't have to be here alone all night. Should I ask my hosts if I can bring you back with me?'

'What did he tell you?'

'Your mother is being held by the police.'

He made me promise to call him. 'Any time you need me. Listen, there's a sofa right next to their phone. I'll sleep there, just in case.'

I did the same, making a bed for myself on the sofa next to our phone. He had promised to call me if he had any news. When I woke the next morning to a knock on the door, my first thought was that it must be Tallis, but in his place was our man for all seasons. Standing next to him was a woman who greeted me like we'd known each other forever, though I had no idea who she was.

Seeing my confusion, she explained that her name was Ruth.

'Dr Ruth?' I asked.

She laughed. 'Are people still calling me that?' She was retired now, she informed me, but was still, and always would be, Tallis' great aunt. She had known me well when

I was just a tiny thing, but it had ended there, which is why I didn't recognise her.

Our man for all seasons then explained that she had kindly offered to accompany me back to New York.

'New York?' I asked. 'Who said I was going to New York?'

'Listen, Dora,' said our man for all seasons. 'I'm very sorry about this. But we need to get you out of the country, lickety split. And now, if I can leave you two to make your own way, I'll see if I can get your mother out to the airport in time to say goodbye.'

When I asked him where she was, a thin smile was all I got by way of reply. But once it was just the two of us in a car, Dr Ruth was more forthcoming. 'It seems that a friend of yours – he's something in the police – got a bee in his bonnet last night for some reason. We're not quite sure why,' she added, with the sort of smile that told me she did indeed know why, but was too nice to say it. 'The long and the short of it is that he ordered a police raid. On an infamous spy's nest, as the papers have decided to describe your grandmother's lovely apartment. He acted way above his rank, of course.'

I had noticed by now that we were going in the wrong direction for the airport, but when I pointed this out, Dr Ruth raised a gentle, warning hand. 'There's something I need to pick up at Robert College.' As we drove along the Bosphorus shore, she explained that her father had taught there all his working life. 'We might almost say that he built its engineering school with his own hands!' Though she had moved back to the US for her education, she had come back to Turkey for a spell to work as a doctor. 'First in the field, and then here, in our hospital.'

'Which hospital?'

Your Uncle Semih's hospital. I helped him set it up. Surely they've told you?'

We were skirting the walls of the great castle by now. As we climbed the cobblestone lane just beyond the entrance to my old school, she pointed out the house where she was born. Here she hopped out, returning minutes later with an embroidered portmanteau.

'That's it, then,' she said lightly. 'Ready for take-off!'

My mother was waiting for us at the restaurant on the upper floor of the tiny airport. The moment she saw me, she strode across the room to strike me hard across the face.

'You little slut!' she said. 'How dare you? You should be ashamed of yourself,' she went on. 'Sneaking around with that sneak boyfriend of yours. Turning us all in. How dare you? So tell me. Are you happy now? Your dear friend Sergei's getting deported, I'll have you know. Unless they decide to lock him up for life instead. Thanks to you, he's headed for the gulag. And your poor grandmother, having to spend the night in jail – if she dies of a heart attack, it will be on your conscience!'

All across the skies of Europe, Dr Ruth did her best to comfort me, patting my shoulder, squeezing my arm, assuring me that, in spite of all she'd said, my mother loved me dearly.

'Now I do understand how angry you must be with her at this precise moment…'

'I'm not angry!' I cried. 'I'm burning with rage! I'm disgusted! And ravaged! Ripped in two! She should have stood up for me! She threw me away instead!'

'Dora, my dear girl. That she did not do.'

'Oh really? Then why did she call me a slut?'

'Now, now. She was just upset.'

'Well, that's too bad. I never want to see her again. Ever!'

'Well, we'll see about that,' said Dr Ruth. 'Let's give all this some time. The important thing is that your mother and your grandmother are safely back at home now, and you and I are heading for New York. We can see to the details later.'

With my permission, she would, in due course, set my mother straight on what this policeman person had attempted, 'as she might have been told an entirely different and utterly false story.' In the meantime, I had my cousin Sinan to thank for noticing that İsmet had had in mind to molest me. 'This was very helpful, for without his statement, we'd have had a much harder time getting people out.'

'But İsmet didn't molest me,' I said. 'I fought him off.'

'Well that explains something.'

What? I wanted to know.

'Why this İsmet was so very, very angry. He still is, in fact. Which is why we had to get you out of the country.'

'I'm not afraid of him.'

Smiling placidly, she said, 'Oh, but you should be.'

# THE FOURTH NOTEBOOK

# To Pomfret

From the airport (which was still Idlewild in those days, not yet JFK) we drove straight up to the house in Pomfret where Dr Ruth lived with her sister Mrs Mary – Tallis' grandmother – and where, it now emerged, I had spent the first two years of my life.

'Surely your mother told you? She didn't? How very strange.'

How very strange indeed, I thought. Another chapter of my life, erased. 'Well,' said Mrs Mary. 'There was that little awkwardness at the end there.'

'What was that?' I asked.

'A little misunderstanding, that's all,' said Ruth. 'When your mother got that job at the UN, we thought it might be better to leave you up here. But, bless her, she begged to differ.'

'Don't judge her too harshly,' said Mrs Mary, 'She loved you much too much to give you up.'

'And now, here you are again,' said Dr Ruth. 'With plenty of time to catch up.'

Every evening, at supper, they told me little stories about myself. They showed me pictures. The highchair I had sat in. The room where I had taken my first steps.

I struggled to believe them. I knew they must be telling the truth, but to take what they said on faith felt like learning to walk in a room that might not have a floor. It was easier, over the next few days, to think about what they called next steps. Together my two guardians had mapped out a catalogue of futures for me to choose from. Over breakfast we discussed schools. Over supper we discussed careers, or in their parlance, callings. Whenever I confessed to an interest, their faces lit up. But never as much as I saw them light up towards the end of my first week, when I went downstairs late at night for a glass of water.

They were sitting together in the middle of the sitting room. Between them sat the embroidered portmanteau that Dr Ruth had picked up on our way to the airport. Next to it was a pile of gold and glittering pile of jewellery. So enraptured were they that they did not see me. 'And look at this one,' Mrs Mary was saying. Delving into the portmanteau, she lifted up a jewel-studded crown of sorts, and placed it on her head. 'And this, from our favourite little princess,' she added. Crown still in place, she fished out the large and bulky green velvet pouch that you will hear much more about, later in my story.

'What's all this about?'

I was startled by my own voice. I was still on the stairs. I hadn't intended to speak.

And at first, they looked up at me with something akin to horror. But in moments they had composed themselves.

'Do come down and join us,' Mrs Mary said.

They observed my descent in smiling silence.

'I imagine you recognise the portmanteau?' said Dr Ruth.

'Yes,' I said. 'It's the one we brought back with us.'

'And aren't these treasures magnificent?' said Mrs Mary.

I asked whose they were.

'Ah,' said Dr Ruth. 'That would be telling. I can say one thing, though. Our Mary here has always had an eye for the jewels!'

'Only to feast my eyes on them, for just a few moments. I'd never wish to claim such heirlooms! Let alone wear them!'

'What's going on then?' I asked. 'Are you some kind of fence?'

That sent them into peals of laughter.

'Oh, I'm afraid not,' said Mrs Mary. 'We could never hope to be that exciting. It's just that so much got left behind, all those years ago.'

'People had to leave so fast,' said Dr Ruth. 'They couldn't possibly take everything with them.'

'During the Great War, you mean?' I asked.

'That's right,' said Mrs Mary. 'When so many of innocents were driven from their homes, all those many years ago. And let me tell you, it didn't end overnight!'

'Though I have to add,' said Dr Ruth, 'that most of the stories you hear about buried treasure are entirely false! The only thing we can say for sure is that there is not a square inch of Anatolia where they don't tell these stories about Armenian gold.'

'Nevertheless,' said Mrs Mary, 'What you see here is Assyrian.'

'Or so we've been told,' added Dr Ruth.

'What makes something Assyrian?' I asked.

'Oh, I'm sorry. I should have explained. The Assyrians were another Christian people. You found them in southeast Anatolia, but also sometimes on the Black Sea coast. Not any more, alas.'

'Why not?'

'Ah. Well, that's a long story. And not a tale for the middle of the night. So for now, let's just say this. Someone cruel might like to call us fences...'

Another peal of gentle laughter.

'While we prefer,' said Dr Ruth, 'to see ourselves as conduits.'

'It's something we like to do,' said Mrs Mary. 'When the occasion arises.'

'Yes,' said Dr Ruth. 'But only for dear friends.'

In no time at all, the sisters had found me a place at Miss Porter's, just an hour away from Pomfret. I was, in the meantime, to consider their home to be my home, and them to be acting in loco parentis. 'Though we must advise you that we shall insist, in due course, on your making peace with dear Delphine. In fact, we consider it to be our moral duty.'

When I asked, just this once, who was paying for all this, Mrs Mary said, 'Never you mind. You just concentrate on your studies.'

'In any event,' said Dr Ruth, 'we shall be welcoming you back for vacations and as many weekends as your school permits, at least until the dust settles.'

The dust did not settle. Instead, I brushed it away. I did not open any of the letters my mother sent me. I did my best not to think of her. Or İsmet. Or my father, or my grandfather, or even Sergei and my beloved grandmother. Instead I threw myself into my schoolwork. This being my fourth school in two years, I again had catching up to do. Along the way I discovered tennis, and track, and hiking, and swimming, and soccer – no half measures for me. Together these pastimes helped to clear my mind.

I even made a few friends. And there were moments – when we were hiking around a lake that first spring, or swimming across it when summer at last arrived, or huddled together in one of the secret nooks we used for midnight feasts – when I thought, maybe I should just talk to them, tell them about what was going on in my life, before I landed here. These girls talked openly about their own lives, after all. And the others are so generous in their sympathy and advice. Why not test the waters, at the very least?

I'd think that, and then I'd try to imagine what I could say. That my mother was a spy, and my father the son of a Pasha? That my grandmother, a brilliant but scandal-prone artist, had only learned to love her husband after shooting him in the neck?

That I was half Levantine, and half Armenian on one side, and a quarter each Persian, Hungarian, Albanian, and Georgian on the other?

How was I to explain that tangled roots like these had not been unusual in the ruling classes of this vanished empire that my lovely new friends had probably never heard of?

Or that I had nevertheless felt disappointment on discovering these roots, because it meant that my father could not therefore be a Soviet spy of whom I was so very fond?

How could I convey how jarring it had been, after discovering my father's true identity, to realise that my cousin Sinan was in actual fact my nephew?

Or that – if the paperwork was to be believed – I was born in New York City, and also in Istanbul, on exactly the same day?

Or that I had seen, from my own window, the ships that had secretly ferried to Cuba the missiles that had almost started the Third World War just a few months back?

Or that in the run-up to that crisis I had been given a minder, on account of being a kidnap risk, and fallen in love with him, or at least become besotted, and grown so very upset by his rejection of me that I had taunted him in public, calling him a homosexual, which was no big deal by the way in our circles, but a big deal to this minder, who came from a simple rural background, and who, in retaliation, had tried to rape me, and who – after I'd fought him off – had, again in retaliation, arrested every last person at the party next door, my mother and grandmother included, and charged them all with being spies, even though that was only true for a handful of them – a dozen at most?

How could I explain that one of them – the Soviet spy of whom I was so fond – may have been deported as a result, or worse? That if he was now wasting away in the bowels of the Lubyanka, or even worse, in a Siberian gulag, his fate would be on my conscience for all time?

Would my new friends even believe me when I told them that I had been rushed out of the country after this terrible scandal I had caused, for my own safety, on the very next plane?

And what would they think when I told them that my mother had come to the airport, not to say goodbye, but to call me a slut?

But why had she called me a slut? How could a mother use such an ugly word against her own daughter?

What exactly had my mother been up to? What had been the true purpose of all those trips to Athens and Rumania and who knew where else?

How could any of this have happened?

Snug and safe in my beautiful boarding school, where bells measured out the day and rules made sense, even I had to struggle sometimes, to believe that any of it had happened. As the view in the rear view mirror grew steadily more implausible, I fixed my eyes on the road ahead.

But it kept leading me back, this road.
Always when I least expected it.

## The first time

Strictly speaking, there was no first time, because the house in Pomfret was fully furnished with reminders. No floor without a Turkish carpet or kilim. No trivet that was not an Iznik tile. No sofa without a shining copper tray standing before it. No mantelpiece without a copper bowl or urn. No wall without an antique map or a nineteenth century engraving of a Bosphorus view, or a photograph of my guardians' worthy parents, who now lay buried side by side half a world away, in a city they had never thought or wished to claim as theirs.

What had compelled them to leave this house, this very house, to travel so far afield? Why had they stayed on through all those wars and famines, first to serve an empire that was of two minds about such assistance, and then to serve a republic that wasn't so sure either? Why had they chosen to stay on after retirement? Why, on returning to Istanbul for their father's funeral, had Dr Ruth and Mrs Mary found themselves unable to say goodbye to all these tiles and urns and carpets, choosing instead to ship them back to Pomfret, at considerable expense?

They led a good and gracious life, my guardians. Both were in their seventies by the time I joined their household but they had remained studiously active. Dr Ruth took care of the vegetable garden and cooked our evening meals. Mrs Mary did the baking and the jam making. Both gave time to the Congregational church down the road. As if that weren't enough, Mrs Mary volunteered at the local historical society on Mondays and Wednesdays. On Tuesdays and Thursdays, Dr Ruth drove a bookmobile, which was always breaking down. It was old, that she knew, but whenever she needed help, she found it to be close at hand, and how interesting they were, these people who came to her assistance, and even if they lived with mangy dogs in trailer parks and dressed like bikers and had never read a book and never wanted to, they were also (she'd say pointedly, looking us each in the eye) so very, very kind.

'You bring out the best in them, I'm sure,' Mrs Mary would say. 'And that, my dear sister, is not their doing but yours. You are the kind one. In fact, you are the very soul of kindness. And sometimes, just sometimes, these mangy friends of yours take advantage. Do they not?'

'Oh, do stop playing the diplomat's wife! It hardly becomes you.'

'Need I remind you, dear sister, that I ceased to be a diplomat's wife some fifty years ago?'

'You are right, little Mary. Of course you are. That said, you have continued to lead a cloistered life.'

'In your eyes, at least! Few in this world can claim to have been as intrepid as you, dear Ruth.'

These gentle sparring sessions would take place before supper, during the ritual they called sherry hour, which took place around the fire during winter, and during summer in the gathering dusk of the conservatory. It was the only time we conversed at any length. Beginning with the here and now, and looping back to the war they had once vainly hoped might end all wars.

Mrs Mary's husband had been working at the US Embassy at 1915, she told me.

'When he wasn't gambling,' added Dr Ruth.

'Goodness!' cried Mrs Mary. 'What a thing to say!'

'Well, it's true, is it not?' Dr Ruth replied.

'It was part of his work!'

'Part of his work to go to the Cercle d'Orient every night until the early hours?'

'It was, in fact. It was there that business was done. Where he made his connections.' Turning to me, she added, 'Aubrey was an Aleph, you see. And it was at the Cercle d'Orient that he made the acquaintance of the others.'

'Be that as it may,' said Dr Ruth.

Be that as it may, Mrs Mary continued, her husband had, through his work at the Embassy, been amongst the first to hear of the Armenian slaughter. His Ambassador had almost singlehandedly taken the news to the rest of the world.

Returning to New York after the US joined the war, that same Ambassador had almost singlehandedly launched Near East Relief, the biggest humanitarian drive our country had ever seen.

Dr Ruth had been one of a thousand American doctors and nurses that had set sail for Constantinople on decommissioned warships in 1919, just months after the Ottoman capitulation.

Their hope had been to heal and nourish the many hundreds of thousands of homeless and destitute Christians still lost in the wilds of Anatolia, Central Asia and the Middle East.

This they had done to the best of their ability. A task somewhat complicated by the war that had broken out not long after their arrival, between the occupying forces and the Turkish patriots who eventually drove them out.

Dr Ruth told me a great deal about those years during

our sherry hours. And I how I wish I'd had the foresight to take notes.

She began her every story with the same question: 'I haven't told you this before, have I?'

'Of course you have, my dear sister,' Mrs Mary would reply. 'But do continue. It bears repeating.'

'You are very kind. Now where were we? Oh, yes, we were in X. Running that hospital. The first of many! We woke up in the night to cannons rumbling and the sky alight. The city was almost entirely under siege! Leaving us with just one way out. We had no choice but to evacuate at once. And that, may I say, was no easy feat. We were just on our way, stretchers and all, when I remembered the costumes from the Christmas pageant. The mind is a strange thing, is it not? Most especially, when danger looms. But I didn't think twice. I ran back inside, under sniper fire, no less, to retrieve our costumes. All three bags of them. Oh, how my fellow doctors berated me! How could I think of amateur theatricals on such a day, and amid that wall of snipers? Of course, they changed their tune later, when the snow began to fall. We were three days walking through that blizzard. Some of us went warmly dressed as shepherds, wise men, and Puss in Boots, and survived.'

Some of those survivors came to visit from time to time. Doctors and nurses who'd worked alongside Dr Ruth, first in Anatolia and later in Armenia and Greece. Age was catching up with them: they rolled up in wheelchairs or leaning on canes. I'd help with the serving, grateful to be coming and going as they conversed with leaden earnestness, cleaning their thick glasses, exchanging condolences and comforting each other with phrases from the Bible at each mention of yet another of their number who had 'gone to their maker'.

A moment would arrive when they couldn't seem to bear it. But then one of their number would say, 'Do you remember the day the Soviets marched into Alexandropol?' And another would say, 'Dear Lord, how could I ever forget?' And then, how they'd laugh then about the quandaries they'd faced together – forty thousand orphans to feed, and no wheat! Operating on their patients in the dark, while outside bullets flew! Wending their way through Anatolia on the Baghdad railway, only to be stopped by bandits who turned out to be soldiers, who took them to their leader, who was deathly ill, and who, once restored to health, sent them off on horseback and under escort back to their still marooned train while he marched off to torch a dozen or so Greek villages – but this was when the laughter would cease abruptly, to plunge the company into an uneasy silence, which would end only when Ruth patted the sad storyteller on the back and said, 'You must remember that we were there to heal.'

The orphans were easier. These were the Greeks and Armenians for whom Ruth had arranged safe passage to America after the troubles. They seemed always to come to us around Easter time. They brought us red eggs. They were anxiously polite, these visitors. Eyes bright, voices halting, palm pressing against palm, as if in preparation for a prayer. They wanted Ruth to know that their children and grandchildren, who sent their very best wishes, were thriving, that if Dr Ruth or Mrs Mary or indeed her grandchildren ever needed help with their taxes or their insurance or their investments or even, God forbid, a legal matter, they should get in touch at once, because there would be someone in the family who would be most honoured to help them.

They did not like to talk about the old days, these orphans.

If the old days came up at all, it was to recall how Dr Ruth had helped them escape. In all these stories, officials loomed large. Be they Turkish, American, Armenian or Greek, you could never tell in advance which ones would be kind or cruel or obstructive. But in each and every case, Dr Ruth had won the trust of the officials by demonstrating, quietly and patiently, her absolute dedication to the living, wherever and whoever they might be:

'I cannot serve humanity unless I first refuse to take sides.'

I imagine you girls will recognise those words. Your father used them all the time, but ironically. He loved his grandmother and his great aunt very dearly. Worshipped them, even. But he saw no reason to hide his exasperation for their missionary mantras.

In fact, he never tried to hide anything from anyone. That was why I came to trust him so, and then to love him. Though sometimes – yes – it drove me to distraction, having to listen to what I didn't want to hear.

The first time, then. This would have been in June 1963. I was just back from Miss Porter's. Tallis, who was just back from his exchange year in Istanbul, had come up to visit his grandmother. And me.

There were things he needed to tell me. But also, there were things he had assumed someone else would already have told me.

And perhaps they had tried. Perhaps, in one of those letters my mother had written to me and I had thrown away, she had told me about the aftermath of the scandal I'd kick-started.

She might also have told me that my Pasha grandfather had died, of a stroke, while that scandal was still raging.

159

She might have tried to comfort me – assure me that this was absolutely not my fault.

She might also have told me about her own trials and tribulations, not just with İsmet, but also with our man for all seasons.

She might even have sent me an invitation to her wedding.

Later, she would insist that she had done all these things, but it was your father who made sure I knew where she was getting married, and when.

It was all too much, I told myself. I'd been gone only six months, but already, nothing in Istanbul was the same. This, too, became a constant. As my life in America continued in its orderly fashion – as I progressed, calmly and confidently, from boarding school to college, and from college to graduate school, and from there into marriage and motherhood without ever giving up, or ever once being asked to give up, the career I loved – there was always this other world in Istanbul, this other mad and tumultuous drama, daring me to look.

'I'm sorry about your grandfather.' That was the first thing Tallis said, the first moment Mrs Mary and Dr Ruth left us alone. And on that first day, we went no further. I was too upset, about losing this man, about never having said goodbye.

I kept imagining myself back there with him, in the yalı conservatory. Listening to his stories. Asking him questions. Taking notes. Watching that Soviet ship race towards us. Hearing his mad laughter, when at the very last possible moment, it righted its course. And then, righting my own course. Imagining the letter I could have written, to explain my abrupt departure. Imagining myself back there, apologising for never having said goodbye. Imagining the conversations that we might have had, if I hadn't had to leave. The questions I might have asked. Why did that Soviet ship make you laugh? Why do you feel most alive, at the moment you have cheated death? Why do you regret the happy days before the war, more even than you regret the war and its ravages? Who was the traitor? Why wouldn't you say?

I would imagine myself asking those questions, and then I would hear him chuckling, and saying: If you asked me the right question, I would tell you, of course! To which I would say: What question would that be, then? And he would say: The question that indicated the correct degree of maturity and understanding. In my wishful imagination, he would say this in a teasing voice. But then I would see his bony hands trembling. Clutching the armrests of his wheelchair so tightly I could see all his blue veins. I would stop with the questions. We would sit there in silence, watching the light play on the fast moving currents. Until I said, You should never have trusted İsmet, you know. You should never have invited him in. And then, behind me, I would feel İsmet's shadow.

This, too, would remain a constant.


On the second day of his visit, the sisters gave Tallis the keys to their car, and we drove up to Walden Pond. We walked the periphery, stopping here and there, sometimes to take a swim, and sometimes just to sit by the water trying to make some sense of this story he was telling me.

He began with the days following on from my enforced escape from Istanbul the previous autumn. My mother had been the first to be released – this with the intervention of

161

William Wakefield who would go on to arrange the release of all others accused of belonging to my grandmother's alleged 'nest of spies'. By Monday, all forty-three of her unfortunate guests were safe at home again. It was on that same day that every newspaper in the nation carried the shocking story of their arrests.

Except that it was a different story from the one they knew.

No mention of spies. Or nests. No mention of a secret policeman attempting rape.

Instead it named Teddy, 'the illustrious Adnan Pasha's half-French son', who lived openly as a homosexual in Lugano, but who came to Istanbul frequently to be entertained by the seven underage boys he kept in his own private brothel. According to the papers, he'd had the temerity to bring three of them to a soirée hosted by the undisputed queen of Pera, the celebrated artist Hümeyra, whose works adorned the walls of embassies the world over. Had it not been for the alarm raised by an innocent girl who was herself a relation of said artist, the good people of Istanbul might never have been the wiser. The situation had been rectified by the subsequent actions of an outraged citizen, who also happened to be a high-ranking police officer, and who had chosen to remain nameless.

'How bizarre!' That was all I could think to say. We were sitting on a tiny pebble beach by now, watching a breeze rustle across the surface of the water. Across the lake, a bank of sheltering trees exuded the peace and quiet that could be mine forever, if I turned my back on all this madness, and just stayed here.

Still. I couldn't stop myself. I turned to Tallis. 'Who do you think cooked up all this nonsense?'

'According to Sinan, it was your mother's boss. Your man for all seasons. Mr Wakefield. He cooked it up personally and then fed it to a gossip columnist. This columnist was someone who'd been at the party earlier, before leaving with someone else's houseboy. So he had things of his own to hide. And according to Sinan, Mr Wakefield made the most of that. In other words, this guy was going to spread whatever story Mr Wakefield wanted him to spread, to keep his own story private.'

'Yes, but why this story?' I asked. 'It makes no sense.'

'I agree. It's, as you said, bizarre. To me, at least. But according to Sinan – '

'Is Sinan your only source here?'

'I was there for your granddad's funeral, so when we get to that part I'll be telling you what I saw with my own eyes. But this part I'm telling you now – it's not just Sinan guessing. Something he is very fond of doing, I'll give you that. No. This is something he overheard, when Mr Wakefield paid his poor mother a visit, the day after the party that turned into that raid. He did the rounds, you know. The same day you left. Paid visits to all the major players, giving them the official song sheet, which they were to memorise, or else.

'First he took your mother home from the airport after seeing you off. Then he made sure she told your grandmother what was what. No more soirees, until further notice. Then he went to see İsmet. To berate him for having turned himself into a laughing stock. For having acted above his station. For being a fool. And then he had told İsmet that he was going to have to leave town for a while. But not in the nicest way. What he said was that İsmet had to put his tail between his legs and head back home to Adana. And this made İsmet very angry.'

William Wakefield's next stop had been Tarabya, where he'd found Teddy recovering from a bath. Together they had fabricated what would become known as the Teddy Affair, which had cheered Teddy up no end. Because of course, the investigators would never find this private brothel, seeing as it did not exist. They might, however, need to visit Teddy here at home, and some of them might be cute.

Our man for all season's last visit, Tallis told me, had been to Sibel. 'Sinan's mother, in other words.' He found her sobbing on her bed, lying under about a thousand fur coats, and he actually went right in there to lecture her. 'Sinan kept watch, of course. If you ask me, he does far too much of that. But in any event, he was there, watching through a crack in the door, while Mr Wakefield lorded over his mother. Bragging about his masterminding. Telling her everything he'd done to save the day.'

And then, while she shivered under her fur coats, he'd gone on to berate her like a wayward child, telling her she'd been hard work lately. Accusing her of being a one-woman scandal factory. Commanding her to get back on the straight and narrow, at least until the story he'd concocted had done its magic.

'And the worst thing about all this is that it worked,' Tallis told me. 'According to Sinan – '

'He's still our only witness, I take it.'

'Yes, but as you know, he sees and hears a lot more than you'd think while he's sitting there, hiding behind a book. So yes, he was there, behind his book, night after night, while your Uncle Teddy dined out on his story.'

The story he'd dined out on was not the story in the papers, but the story about the subsequent police raid, complete with all the voices. A dozen police officers! Half of them with clear proclivities! The other half with a poorly disguised taste for playing the man! All searching breathlessly under each and every divan and chair for the underage boys they all secretly longed to caress.

'Needless to say, you can take Teddy's account with your pinch of salt. I never know when to believe things in that city. The thing you need to know, though, is that Mr Wakefield was right. The story worked. Your father loved it! Your uncle, too! So did everyone else! The only one who was upset at all was your granddad, but nothing about Teddy was going to shock him. It just confirmed what he already thought. As for İsmet, he was back in town by April. Just in time to attend your granddad's funeral.'

'I still don't understand why no one told me,' I said.

'You can't be sure your mother didn't. Can you? In any event, funerals happen very fast out there. This one was actually the very next day. You could never have made it in time. And when I've told you everything I have to tell you, you'll have to agree. No way you should be going back to Turkey. Not for a very long time.'

'So tell me about it,' I said. 'Tell me what happened at the funeral.'

'Okay, then,' Tallis said. 'But first I have to tell you about Sinan's mother.'

'What Sinan told you about her, in other words.'

'Exactly. And I'll try to be accurate. Which means, of course, that I may not sound like me.'

All winter, Tallis said, Sibel had been on what Sinan viewed as house arrest. To that cesspool called Society, it was a long overdue return to married life. In their eyes, it was only right that Feridun Bey keep this errant wife of his on the tightest leash, having disgraced herself many times over with her affairs and outlandish accusations, her refusal to follow her husband from posting to posting, and most of all, that strange and unspeakable interlude only last summer at the Kilyos Hotel where night after night she had stunned respectable guests by crooning like the ghost of Piaf in that little dress, on that little stage, with those mafia goons on drums, sax, and the piano. What did it matter that she had a lovely voice? She was the wife of a diplomat. Protocol demanded silence. Protocol demanded that her husband should be called back from Cairo to fish her out of jail. Never mind that the Teddy Affair had by now been reduced to an after-dinner anecdote. Enough was enough.

On this at least, Sinan agreed. Enough was enough: with his father back at home, there was no air left to breathe. At fifteen, he felt he had earned the right to some say over his destiny, but since none of the adults in his life were of this view, he had been grateful to William Wakefield, his family's eternal and infernal fixer, for arranging a reprieve. On weeknights, he now stayed with his cousin Haluk, at his grandparents' villa on the Bosphorus, in Bebek, within walking distance of their school. It was, like so many of his fixer's fixes, killing two birds with one stone. Not only did it reduce Sinan's daily travel, it offered solace to poor Haluk, who so missed his elder brother, dead for a year now, following a boating accident.

And then, one stormy day in April, death had come to claim their great-grandfather the Pasha. The crowds filing along the Bosphorus shore and up to Aşıyan Cemetery were, Sinan supposed, a testament to his importance. But he'd hardly known this man, and neither had Sinan ever wished to know him, on account of this man's coldness towards his mother. He had heard, of course, of the Pasha's return to these shores, following the death of his French wife, but neither he nor his mother had been to visit, nor had they been invited.

It was in the yalı once owned by the father of Nuran the Poetess and later appropriated by my Pasha grandfather that the ghastly crew calling itself the immediate family gathered, after he had been laid to rest. With significant omissions: when Sinan and Haluk arrived at the yalı (with Tallis in tow, after a detour to a pudding shop lasting long enough for them to miss the Mevlut) their Uncle Teddy was nowhere to be seen. There were only the pasha's two older sons, Melih and Semih. They were standing together, but Sinan could see that they have already begun to argue. Despite the fact that Turkish law would require the estate to be divided equally among the Pasha's children.

In retrospect, Sinan would decide that they must have been discussing the other shocking development. 'About which more later.'

The three boys – Sinan, Haluk, and Tallis – had left these ageing brothers to their misery, drifting from room to drafty room and losing each other somewhere along the way. Fatigued by the unwelcome conversations and introductions into which aunts and uncles kept pulling him, Haluk had wandered out into the rainy garden, and Tallis had eventually found him there. Here they had witnessed a number of altercations, the oddest being a shouting match between Delphine and İsmet. Odd because this was the first time anyone had seen İsmet since the so-called Teddy Affair.

Sinan, after catching sight through a window of the same hostile interchange, had retreated to an almost solitary corner, next to Ekrem, another of his great grandfathers, who was bent over in his chair and snoring beside his wife, the mute Alethia. But soon they were joined by their daughter Elektra – Sinan's maternal grandmother – who spoke far too much. Until Sinan asked after his mother. Then Elektra fell silent as her face went dark.

She nodded in the direction of the window. Outside, in the overgrown garden, Sinan could see Sibel, his mother, pacing back and forth at the water's edge in her white fur coat. She stopped to take a long drag of her cigarette before tossing it into the sea.

She was wearing dark glasses. Behind her the clouds were billowing, sailing in from the Black Sea, but still she was wearing those glasses. Without pausing to button up his coat, Sinan pushed open the door and strode outside. Grabbed those glasses, and yes. It was as he feared. Yet again, his brute of a father had left his mother with a bruised and black eye.

'Where is he?' Sinan asked.

He could tell, by the way her eyes darted about, that she was lying when she claimed ignorance.

'I'm going to find him,' Sinan said.

'You can't!' cried his mother. 'Please! Sinan! For the love of God, don't make things even worse! You're coming inside with me, he said. We'll find him together.'

He could tell from the way his mother now relaxed her facial muscles that she was not worried about going inside. This must mean his father had already left. Taking his mother by the arm, he led her towards the door.

'Give me back my glasses,' she cried.

And he said, 'I will, when you need them.'

And so the show began. Seeing Sibel's bruises and black eye, Alethia gasped, bringing her hand to her mouth, springing to her feet, wrapping her arms around her daughter, while old Ekrem and mute Alethia watched through watery eyes saying nothing.

Elektra turned to Sinan. 'You're taking her home.' It was not a question. 'Where are her glasses?'

'I have them,' said Sinan, patting his pocket. But as he led his mother into the next room, that was where they stayed. Now they stopped to greet his grandfather. Melih was deep in conversation with Soran Bey the cotton king. There had been tension between these men since the Teddy Affair, but for today, if only for a day, it had all been smoothed away. As each in turn embraced Sibel warmly, Sinan did not see so much as a glint of concern in their expressions.

It was not pretence or embarrassment that kept them from asking Sibel what had happened to her eye. They refused even to see it.

As Sinan yanked his mother by the arm to march her towards the door, there were others who did see, but one by one, after staring for a moment too long, they turned away.

Outside, they found Tallis with Sinan's cousin Haluk, who was sharing a cigarette with their other cousin, the wild-haired Suna. Who gasped when she saw the state of Sinan's mother, but she, at least, did not turn away.

'You stay right there, while I get my father.'

It was while they were waiting outside that Sinan had glanced through the foliage, to see İsmet standing in the courtyard, smoking a cigarette, his back to the sea.

He did not raise a hand in greeting, and neither did Sinan. Instead, they exchanged the stares that both could read. Then events took over, once again. Their cousin Suna's father, being the good Dr Semih's son, and if anything, a better doctor, bundled them all into his car and drove them back to the city, to his office in the hospital. Dropping Tallis off along the way, and returning his story to hearsay.

Once arriving at the hospital, the good doctor examined Sinan's mother thoroughly, discerning far greater problems than her black eye. He would not be drawn on the specifics, however. There were other contusions. That was all he would say.

'Come back tomorrow,' he told Sinan. To Suna and Haluk, he said, 'Try and take the boy's mind off things.'

From the way they pursed their lips, it was clear to Sinan that they knew this to be a lost cause. But this would never stop them from trying. For they were more than his cousins. They were the only people in the world he could trust.

'Let's go to the Club 33,' they said. That being where just about every sixteen-year-old they knew would be at five on a Saturday afternoon. But Sinan had no desire to go to the Club 33. All he wanted to do was find his father and kill him.

He did not say this. He did not need to. And that was why Suna and Haluk had known better than to go on ahead to the Club 33. They went home with him, waiting in the dining room while he searched the house for some clue as to father's whereabouts. When they left the building, and Sinan said he needed to go back up to the apartment to look up the definition of contusion, they went back up with him. When they at last headed down the metallic staircase at the Club 33, there to join all the other sixteen-year-olds around its metal postage stamp of a dance floor, Sinan turned back, saying that he needed another breath of air. And they decided, without discussion, to share that breath with him.

You don't have to guard me, said Sinan as they returned to the club.

'We don't,' agreed Suna. 'But we will.'

For the next two hours, Sinan sat with his arms crossed near the far corner of the 33, watching Haluk dance with Suna, while one girl after another tried to push past her, only for Suna to reassert her claim. In the past year, Haluk had grown handsome. Every girl in the city seemed to be in love with him. Suna included. From time to time this spectacle became amusing enough for Sinan to stop wondering about the definition of contusion, which he had still not found.

At seven, they fought their way through the throngs on the metal stairs to visit, one by one, his father's favourite bars. First, the Divan, where Avni the bartender invited them to sit down, assuring them that Feridun Bey would be arriving soon. Did he guess Sinan's intentions? Did he find a way to warn his father off? When the cousins reached the Park Hotel, to be told that Feridun Bey had just left, that was what Sinan concluded. So they pushed through the crowds of Taksim and Iskiklal. Arriving at Kulis, Sinan pulled open the velvet curtains, so forcefully, they almost ripped. And there he was. The wife beater.

Sinan later claimed to have no memory of what happened next. Only that he had managed, at some point, to hold his father by his tie and spit at him. Whereupon others had pulled him off, and away, and perhaps someone also had pushed him onto the floor. Or perhaps he had fallen backwards, hitting the edge of a table. That would explain the gash in the back of his head. When Sinan came to, he was no longer at Kulis. He was lying on the ancient chaise longue at Hümeyra's. Delphine was sitting next to him, holding his hand.

She told him that the cousins had gone to get Suna's doctor father.

She told him that he could stay with her for as long as he liked.

His mother, too.

'But you hate each other,' Sinan found the strength to whisper.

'Sure we do,' said Delphine. 'But so what?'

And perhaps it surprised him, the generosity of her offhand invitation. That and the clear fact that she meant it. Or perhaps it was the next thing she said: 'I hope you don't mind my saying this. But I've always thought your father was a bastard.'

No one had ever said such a thing to him. Later he decided it must have been the sheer relief at hearing that truth spoken that caused him, for the first time since childhood, to let a tear roll down his cheek.

Did she see it? Perhaps. Or perhaps not. Filling both their glasses, she merely said, Now drink up. It's not everyday that a bartender sends me home with a bottle of Johnny Walker Black. And here. Use this napkin if you need it.

When he thanked her again for offering refuge, she waved his words away. 'It was nothing,' she said. 'It's just lucky I was there. Between you and me, though, we should have taken you straight to the hospital.'

'Why didn't you?' Sinan asked.

'Bad company,' she said, staring up at the cloud of smoke above her head. Her baleful look told him the rest of the story. So his father had also been injured. He would have had to travel to the hospital with his father. So, yes, it was better to wait for Suna to arrange this home visit.

'Sad to say,' Delphine sighed. 'But it is what it is. He beats

172

your mother to a pulp, and then he gets away with it. It's a miracle she's still standing.'

'She should stand up to him,' said Sinan. 'Make him stop.'

'And how, exactly, do you propose she does that?' Delphine asked. 'She'd be all alone, penniless and cast out. Not even her father would lift a finger. Least of all him! He's the one who married her off to that brute in the first place. She was all of seventeen! She was getting a little wild, you see. A tad free wheeling. Well, he wasn't having that! So he did what fathers have done from time immemorial. He handed her over to another man, to knock her into shape. Can't have the family name dragged in dirt, can we? Especially not our family, seeing as that is exactly where it belongs.'

For a few minutes after that, Delphine said nothing. She just puffed out great clouds of smoke and stared at them, until she turning to Sinan to ask, How much do you want to know?

Everything.

And so she told him.

'And what exactly did she tell him?' I asked Tallis.

'Everything,' he said.

We had walked the full perimeter of Walden Pond by now. We were sitting on a boulder, close to the water's edge.

'My mother never tells anyone everything,' I informed him. 'Especially when she says she is.'

'You may be right,' Tallis replied. 'And we can be pretty sure that Sinan would not have told me everything he heard. But he did tell me what your mother told him about those men who've been running her life. Mr Wakefield most of all. She never wanted to be a Mata Hari, you know! He forced her into it. And that's immoral. Thank God she can put all that behind her now.'

'What – has she come into an inheritance?'

'Not exactly. At least, not yet. But your grandmother has. It turns out that when the *Pasha* changed her name from Hermine to Hümeyra, he did actually officially adopt her. It was that French wife who suppressed that information all along. But now the wicked wife is dead. And your mother has the papers. So your grandmother will get her share of the *Pasha's* estate. The part they know about, at least. I mean, whatever's left in Turkey.'

'Well, that's good news, at least.'

'Your grandmother doesn't want to leave Istanbul, though.'

'I'm not surprised!' I said. 'She hates leaving her neighbourhood, even.'

'So I hear. But it should be okay. They've worked it out so that your mother will spend at least six months of every year with her in Istanbul. And your grandmother will be spending her summers with the happy couple, in Lugano.'

'Lugano? Why Lugano?'

'Don't tell me no-one told you!'

That was how I found out that my mother was marrying Uncle Teddy. Which didn't make sense to me, not at all. Until Tallis explained why it had turned out to be the perfect solution for them both. In Uncle Teddy's case, it protected him and his Swiss inheritance from a slew of lawsuits launched by some other relatives of ours – Tallis couldn't recall the details, which were murky and had not, in his view, added up. All he knew was that these lawsuits had originated in Paris. And were doomed to fail, again on account of Delphine having the papers. Though what papers these were, exactly, no one could say.

'As for your mother,' Tallis continued. 'Well, this marriage sets her free. She won't have to work for Mr Wakefield anymore. Or resort to desperate measures like marrying İsmet.'

That was how I found out that my mother and İsmet had been an item, a secret item, since the day he'd entered our lives. That she'd never known – never even dreamed – what Sinan could have told her, about my own secret crush. That all hell had broken loose after the scandal I'd kick-started. That my mother still must have been in shock when she called me a slut, out there at the airport. That she deeply regretted her words. And missed me terribly. And thanked me, too, for – however accidentally – exposing İsmet for the shit he was.

But now, she had a new life to look forward to. All the cousins were coming to the wedding which was to take place on the last week of August in a little church high in the hills above the villa in Lugano. And nothing would make her happier than to have her one and only daughter give her away.

'That's a lot to take in,' Tallis conceded. 'And I know what you're like. It's fine if we don't talk at all on the way back. I'll understand. But before we get into the car, let me just say that I could go out there with you, if you wanted me to. I'd pay my own my way, of course. I'd never let your mother buy my ticket, to be sure. But if you need a friend at your side, I can be there for you. Take your time, though. Think it over.'

But I couldn't think at all.

I just felt stupid.

# The wedding

In the end I decided it would be cowardly to miss the wedding. Or the *mariage blanc*, as the embossed invitation described it. At the church it was just family, but when we got back to the lakeside villa that my theatrically jubilant mother insisted was now my home, too, Teddy's friends were there to greet us. They were, if anything, wilder than he was. And they had gone to great lengths to procure the props of a Hümeyra soiree. It was vodka in the punch, though, instead of grain alcohol with not enough water. The urn with the peacock feathers was clear of cigarette ends and the dregs of drinks. The chaise longue was not ancient but brand new. The tricycle had no dents in it. But it was the thought that counted. My grandmother feigned delight when they wheeled it out, and she was happy for them to photograph her riding it across the terrace, but that was the only time I saw her use it.

Sinan, Suna, and Haluk were all secret smokers by now, and Sinan had been bold or foolish enough to bring with him a great lump of hash. So we young ones spent most of the wedding afternoon and much of the rest of our stay down on the dock, sharing spliffs and conspiratorial gossip. My mother knew but didn't care, I thought. Though the cousins insisted that she did care. She just didn't mind, because she understood. This became yet another constant during the summer weeks that your father and I would share with the cousins in the years to come. I would say something snide about my mother – complain about her ostentatious wardrobe or the wildly expensive dress in a loathsome style that she had bought for me without my knowledge or consent

– and the cousins would berate me. Even Tallis (who generally took my side in cousinly disputes, come what may) would urge me to reconsider. Together they would tell me that she alone of her generation genuinely wished them well. Shared their dreams of freedom. Understood.

And even I could see that they were right. Every time my mother tiptoed down to the dock with a fresh bottle of champagne, laughing and tut-tutting if they made to hide their spliffs – every time I ventured onto the terrace to find her conversing with Sinan or Suna or Haluk in a softly reassuring voice I had never before heard her use – I could see that understanding. In my absence, she had taken the cousins under her wing. And they were genuinely grateful. For she had genuinely come to their rescue, and not just after my grandfather's funeral. In return, they were kinder to her than I had ever known how to be.

She'd opened up her home to them, welcoming not just the cousins but also their friends. Doting on them all, including Tallis. Who had been changed by his year in Istanbul. Who was closer to the cousins now than I was. Who was, with their help, beginning to shed his illusions about the country of his birth, and instead using words like hegemony and imperialism. That was another thing even I could see – the political understanding between him and the cousins that would grow and grow in years to come. Sometimes including me, but oftentimes not.

That is my abiding memory of the wedding summer: being part of things, even in the centre of things, only to have a passing remark or an exchange of knowing looks remind that this strange assemblage I called my family had moved on without me. Only to remember that even when I'd been there, in their midst, in Istanbul, I'd understood next to nothing. Failed to read even the more glaring signs.

How could I have missed them? According to Tallis (who had it from Sinan) our very own secret policeman had been in and out of our apartment from the day he'd entered our lives. At first, for no other reason than to track the ships on the Bosphorus. But before very long, İsmet and my mother had been taking full advantage of my time away at school. Everyone had known about it. Everyone except me. Even though there must have been clues everywhere – rumpled bed sheets, men's shoes poking out from beneath the sofa, a surfeit of cigarette smoke, two coffee cups in the sink.

As if that weren't enough – once their secret became serious, my mother had tried to tell me. That night on the terrace of the Park Hotel, she had come this close. It wasn't her fault – this I knew. But still I couldn't look her in the eye.

Instead, I pretended, let her embrace and spoil and flatter me, hoping that my mask would one day become my face. The hardest thing was when she put her hands on my shoulders, and fixed me with a glassy grin, and without mentioning İsmet by name, said, 'We're not going to let some two-timing bastard come between us, are we?'

If it hadn't been for Hümeyra, I don't think I could have managed it. She alone understood. Every evening, she would find me. Wave to me from the terrace or her bedroom window. Beckon for me to come at once. And then, when I'd done so, she'd her put arm in mine, to lead me across the great lawn and into the woods that ran alongside the lake.

There, on a bench overlooking the water, she would ask me about my life. Did I like my school? Had the Blind Sisters been kind to me? Truly, deeply kind? If I asked why she called my kindly guardians the Blind Sisters, she would shrug her shoulders and say, 'Because this is how they were, when I knew them.'

But she had been happy to hear that they had at last regained their sight, and found me a good school, and how very sorry she was to have to decline my kind invitation to visit us in Pomfret so that she could see for herself that they could see as well as she could. With regret, my grandmother explained that it would be impossible for her to acquire a visa, as she had recently made herself a persona non grata at the US Consulate by setting fire to the towels in the guest bathroom during her last visit to the consul's Residence.

'Deliberately?' I asked.

'*Mais bien sûr*, she replied. 'I could not restrain myself. I shall never know how to belong.'

'Would you want to?' I asked.

'Of course not,' she replied.

'Me neither.'

'That is good.'

Our every exchange on that bench overlooking the water ended on this note, or a note much like it. Having renewed our secret vows – never to belong, never to surrender fully to those around us, no matter how kind they were, or how blind – we would retrace our steps to the great lawn and the coach house, where the man who had played the bad fairy at the wedding would be waiting for us at the card table that he'd placed on its little terrace. A plate of white cheese, and next to it, a plate of sliced melon. A bucket of ice, three glasses, a bottle of water, a bottle of rakı, and an Orangina for me.

He would greet us in silence, this father of mine, and see us to our chairs. There we would sit, the three of us, and watch the clouds over the mountains and the lake turn pink. If the spirit took him, he would recite poetry for us. When he was feeling sad, we would do no more than to listen to the soft laughter float up from the dock, to be drowned out by the party on the terrace.

From time to time, Teddy would bound into view, to chase a naked or almost naked friend with his little water pistol. Sometimes my mother would chase after him, to douse his signature baby blue short shorts with champagne. It was not that I disapproved of all this. A *mariage blanc* it might be, but even I could see that it was working. My mother and Teddy had genuine affection for each other, and whatever the details of those inscrutable property disputes that underpinned their union, it was clear that they were protecting each other, facing the world together.

And he was generous, this Teddy. He had happily agreed to give over the coach house to my father for the entire summer, even though Melih hated him, and continued to refuse to speak to him.

I didn't think that was right of my father, or worthy of him, either, and I told him so. Though I did agree that there was something shallow – even ersatz – about these incessant festivities.

In my father's view, my mother and my Swiss uncle had turned their backs on their nation and its proud past. 'I hope,' he said, 'that you will grow up to correct this imbalance. You,' he said, lifting his hands like a prophet, 'shall be our historian. Bringing together all our broken pieces into one proud and glorious entity. So tell me,' he continued. 'How much have you engraved?'

"Engraved?

'In your memory, of course.'

I told my father what I remembered of our family's sometimes proud but more often tragic history from my conversations with my Pasha grandfather, and my father told me it was an insult to a history as glorious as ours to know only its final chapter. 'I, for one, shall begin with the founding of the House of Osman.'

For the rest of that evening, and for many evenings thereafter, he took me through the history of the Ottoman Empire, century by century, sultan by sultan, slowing down for the reign of Suleyman the Magnificent, who had opened his arms to the Jews of Spain, he informed me, thereby saving them from the wicked Inquisition. Here he made what he called a detour in time, to speak at length about the great European mercantile families like the one from which I should be proud to be descended on my mother's side.

From the outset, my father told me, the sultans had cherished their Christian and Jewish subjects, entrusting them with the commerce of the empire. Allowing them to practice their religions and regulate their own community affairs. Permitting them to accumulate great wealth, and excluding them only from the military and the civil service – though in these realms, too, they could rise to the highest office, so long as they converted to Islam. 'And of course, we had no qualms whatsoever about marrying their women!' No empire on earth had achieved the same degree of religious tolerance, he assured me, while my grandmother listened in silence, her eyes sad and luminous.

On my last afternoon in Lugano, while the others were out buying fish for our final supper, my grandmother found me on the dock and led me back up to the coach house, where Melih stood waiting in a striped jacket and a straw hat. He had a camera strung across his chest.

'Let's go,' Hümeyra said.

Melih proceeded to lead us through the bushes, furtively dangling keys. Jumping behind the wheel of the oldest car in the garage, he waved us into the back seat, and soon we were bucking our way down the drive, and up a winding lane into the mountains.

Arriving at a village that was small enough to be a hamlet, we parked in front of its church. My grandmother fumbled inside her handbag, retrieving a rumpled envelope on which someone had sketched out a rough map. She led us across the churchyard, pausing here and there to consult her envelope, until she found it: her mother's grave.

Anahid. That was all it said. No surname. No dates. My grandmother knelt down to caress each letter, and then she lay down beside the stone, on her back, staring at the sky, her arms straight, and her cupped hands turned upwards.

'I'm ready,' she told Melih.

Melih sighed, as he lifted his camera. Adjusted the aperture. Adjusted it again. Changed his position. Examined the lens. Changed sides. Moved closer, and then further away. Until, with a final sigh, he began to snap.

# THE FIFTH NOTEBOOK

# A weekend in Paris

It was just three of the cousins during those first summers.

Anais wasn't yet part of our tribe. She joined us in the summer of 1976, or rather, we joined her. As did the saga that we thought we'd put behind us.

This all happened in Paris.

It was our first reunion in four years.

The cousins had spent most of the interim in an Istanbul prison, having been unjustly implicated in a political murder that was possibly not even a murder, as no body had ever been found, or even named.

Even after their release, they'd continued to live under a shadow and (in the case of Haluk and Suna) without passports.

You girls know that your father was a draft resister. But I'm not sure if he's ever told you the how and the why.

He'd been halfway through architecture school when his diplomat father opened the Washington Post one morning to find a picture of him burning his draft card at some anti war demonstration. I forget which one.

The man's first act had been to report his son to the authorities. His second had been to call Tallis, to inform him that he would no longer be paying his tuition. When Tallis had protested, asking his father if he really wanted him to be sent to die in Vietnam, his father had said yes. And that was, to my best knowledge, the last time Tallis and his father ever spoke.

He'd gone first to Canada, moving on to England and Holland, where, like most American draft resisters, he'd got by working odd jobs, off the books.

His luck had changed that past winter, after Sinan smuggled Haluk and Suna out of Turkey, and through all the other border points between Alexandroupolis and Paris, in the boot of his car. Leaving them to recover the use of their limbs in his mother's Neuilly apartment, Sinan had driven straight on to Amsterdam, to liberate Tallis from the offices of the Magic Bus and whisk him back to Paris.

And now I was flying in to join them.

Tallis and I had been serious for some time by then, so I'd grown accustomed to flying here, there and everywhere for a week or two together. But it wasn't just me accommodating Tallis. There were constraints on my side, too. For I too had left my studies – in Ottoman history – midway, in my case to look after my guardians after their health began to fail. Grateful as they might have been at the outset to remain at home in my care, they'd grown increasingly restive. It wasn't fair, they kept saying. It wasn't right. They couldn't condone my taking responsibility for everyone in the whole wide world.

It had been at their suggestion that we'd brought in another live-in carer, so that I could fly out and have my reunion with Tallis and the cousins. For a few days. After my return, they said, we would need to discuss the future. If not a care home, then at least bringing in this new carer on a more permanent basis so that I could return to Paris not just for a weekend but an entire summer, or even a whole year, and use that time to think my way back into a doctorate that was worthy of my gifts.

A lovely, lofty thought – but what did it mean? I had never lost interest in Ottoman history. There in Pomfret, I'd never stopped reading. But in my isolation, I'd lost my thread.

The smart move, I knew, would be to pick up where I'd

left off – but for reasons I could not quite fathom, I no longer believed myself to have anything new to say about the Levantines in the time of Suleyman the Magnificent.

However. Tallis had, since arriving in Paris, tracked down one of my Levantine uncles. Or great uncles. Whoever he was, this man lived in Paris, not far from Sinan's mother's apartment in Neuilly. So Tallis had arranged for me to see this man. I appreciated the gesture, even if I did not expect to glean more from this new relation than I had from any of the others I'd previously tracked down. Nevertheless, I wanted to turn up for that appointment with a few good questions.

So that was the task I had set myself for my overnight flight from JFK to Paris on that June evening in 1976. I would skim the three most recent books of consequence that touched on my area, before returning to my own unfinished and long-abandoned draft, in the hope that by the time we landed, some new lightbulb would have gone off, indicating some new way in.

According to the tannoy, our flight was full, and so I considered myself doubly lucky – first to have been bumped up without explanation to a window seat in first class, and second, to have the seat next to me still empty when the pilot called for the crosscheck. But then there was a small commotion up ahead. The door opened for a final passenger, who slipped down the aisle, fast and dark as a shadow, to take the seat next to mine.

It was İsmet.

Thirteen years since I'd seen him. His face was fuller, his complexion less olive than I remembered, but otherwise he looked much the same.

Except for his suit, which no ordinary secret policeman could ever have afforded. And his eyes, which were enjoying a joke he had no intention of sharing. He was as comfortable in his skin now as I, at that moment, was not.

Not that I let him see it.

It wasn't even that much of an effort to play along. A great calm comes over me, whenever I feel myself in danger. I might fall apart afterwards, but while the game is on, I feel relaxed, ready for whatever my opponent will throw at me next. Even, on occasion, looking forward to it.

I was the first to speak. It is always best, in such circumstances, to be the one to set the tone.

'So I imagine I should be thanking you,' I said.

'For the upgrade? Yes, of course.'

'And to what do I owe this pleasure?'

'That is self-evident, is it not?'

'Let me guess. You wish to speak to me.'

'And why would I not? Forgive me if I have taken you by surprise, dear Dora. I hope at least that once we have reached those other shores, you will agree it's for the best. Where else would we find the opportunity to converse without interference or interruption? Here at least, we are in safety but at the same time, without the distraction of an exit.'

'No expense spared, in other words! I suppose I should be flattered, that you – or whoever sent you – felt you had to go to all this effort.'

'Well,' he said. 'It's not as if you ever come to Istanbul.'

'If I'm not mistaken,' I said. 'It's because of you that I don't.'

'Oh dear,' he said, 'is that what they've been telling you, these incorrigible cousins of yours? Excuse me. I meant, of course, your nieces and nephews. In actual fact, it's the other way round. Your mother and I have been keeping you out of Turkey, to keep you from sharing a prison cell with these spoiled ingrates who refuse to learn from their mistakes, no matter how we reason with them. A favour we were never able to do for poor Sergei! I hope you remember to count him as one of your victims.'

'What exactly are you trying to say to me here?'

'I am saying that we have spent a great deal of time, picking up the pieces left by these so-called cousins, and also by your own foolish choices and misdemeanors. By which I mean to say, your mother and I have continued to work together, to the best of our abilities. Would you like to know how badly you failed with poor Sergei, thanks in no small measure to all those notes you left lying around everywhere, about Radio Moscow?'

'No, I do not,' I said. 'You'd just tell me more lies.'

'Not about your mother, surely?

To which I said nothing. I knew my mother would have been keeping İsmet warm, so as to continue having influence over him, most especially when the cousins needed to be sprung from their latest prison cell, so I did not protest or make to contradict him. I did not repeat what I had heard from Tallis – that it was İsmet who had put the cousins behind bars. İsmet who had continued to hound them, after their release.

Instead, I sat back and let the plane take off. I opened my book and read, until the seatbelt light went off and the flight attendant arrived with our champagne.

'And so,' I said, after we had clinked glasses, 'I imagine you have arranged all this because you have finally decided to apologise.'

'You will never have an apology from me,' he said.

'Oh really?' I said. 'Why not?'

'Because in my view, we are even.'

'I'm sorry to hear that. Though of course – knowing you as I do, I am not at all surprised.'

'In any event, those events are in the past. Today, we have something more important to discuss.'

He was acting, he said, on my mother's behalf. I didn't believe that for a second. At least – I didn't believe for a second that this was all there was to the story. But I didn't challenge him.

Instead I gave him my full attention.

He began by telling me where I was headed: a nest of insurgents.

'Not another one,' I said.

'No,' he said smoothly. 'In actual fact, it is the same one, though it now finds itself in a different city, with a younger cast.'

This ploy of Sinan's – to smuggle his cousins out of the country in the boot of his car – it had, he informed me – not gone unnoticed. 'But we did not see the point of lessening their discomfort. It was important for these ingrates to think that they were successfully evading us. For then they would lead us directly to our prey.'

The prey, in this instance, was ASALA.

In case you girls don't recall this acronym – it stands for the Armenian Secret Army for the Liberation of Armenia. Its aim was to force Turkey not just to acknowledge the 1915 genocide but also to pay reparations and cede to the Armenian Soviet Socialist Republic a large chunk of Anatolia. It was new to the scene in 1976. Over the next five years or so, its attacks on Turkish diplomats worldwide would result in almost fifty deaths and six times as many casualties.

The previous October, a bomb for which it took responsibility had killed the Turkish ambassador to France and his chauffeur.

All this I knew. It was big news at the time. Most especially in American universities with Near East Studies programmes, where Turkish and Armenian scholars often found themselves working side by side while refusing to converse except to exchange accusations and insults. This had been my world from the day I walked into my first Ottoman history class, and I knew from my peers that it had grown all the sharper since the arrival of ASALA.

But now, according to İsmet, something new was happening. A new generation of Turkish scholars was changing sides. Having answered to the siren call of Communism as students, they had first tried to destroy the Turkish republic from within. Thanks to patriots like İsmet, who had worked tirelessly to quell and incarcerate them, they had failed. But now they were quitting their native land to infiltrate the murky underbellies of the West where American draft dodgers joined arms with Communist agitators from across the third world, not to mention the second and the first. 'Including, dare I say it, your old friend Sergei.' It was in the unholy melange that ASALA now operated, preying upon the disaffected – by which İsmet meant the spoiled children of the bourgeoisie who had expected the riches bestowed on them to be enhanced by freedoms they'd done nothing to earn. Who slept all day and spent their nights in bars and drug dens, setting traps for the honest and hardworking. Looking for new ways to undermine the motherland. 'And now their enemy's enemy has become their friend.'

'I am speaking, alas, of your nieces and nephews.'

'Oh for God's sake,' I said. 'You cannot be serious.'

'Alas, what I say to you is true. But only up to a point. It would be more correct to say that their enemy's enemy has sunk its claws into them, without their even knowing. I am speaking now of young Anais.'

'Anais?'

It pleased him that I had to ask. It pleased him that he had to explain to me that Anais was yet another cousin, if we were to stretch that term to its limits. 'If I'm not mistaken – and I hope you will excuse me if I am – with incestuous families like the ones from which you descend, it is so very easy to lose one's way. But I do believe you and this Anais are related to each other in three different ways. Though at this moment, there are only two connections that should concern us. The first, of course, is her connection to the ingrate cousins. She is in and out of this Neuilly apartment that Sinan's poor mother should never have opened to her son. Cooking for them, caring for them, even, on occasion, cleaning for them. The poor girl has a good heart! So of course she wishes the best for them all. She has her doctor father – who is himself none other than the son of your uncle, Dr Semih, seeing to their so-called wounds. Her mother, who is just an architect, but well-endowed with powerful connections, is busy pulling other strings so that they can work. In the meantime, our little Anais has persuaded this mother to offer your Tallis an internship at her firm. Where she herself is currently interning! She is so very kind, this Anais, that she picks him up every morning, to drive him over! Our Anais is also very beautiful. I'm surprised Tallis hasn't mentioned her. On the other hand, I'm not surprised. Not in the least. Why would the boy wish to raise the hackles of his loyal fiancée?'

'We're not engaged,' I said.

'Aha. Well that makes matters more straightforward. If you and your Tallis are enjoying an open relationship – '

'I said no such thing.'

'You seem concerned, however.'

'As you know to your cost, I am never what I seem.'

'Nor am I, dear Dora. Nor am I. Shall we move on? It is, after all, your second line of connection to this Anais that most concerns me: her great grandmother. Madame Karine. The sister of your own great grandmother, the unfortunate Anahid. Now I don't need to tell you, Dora. I know you know this. But Madame Karine, who so famously married into oil, remains amongst the most monied Armenians of the great diaspora. So perhaps it will not surprise you to hear that ASALA can work with impunity throughout the world because it has her backing.'

'That's nonsense,' I said. 'I don't believe you.'

'I don't care what you believe. You can dismiss what I say, or you can listen. But for your own good, there are things you should know before you venture into Madame Karine's lair tomorrow.'

'How would you know what I am doing tomorrow?'

'Your Tallis. He's set up an interview with one of your Levantines, has he not? For your research. Am I right?'

I said nothing.

İsmet took that as affirmation. 'So, yes, this Levantine you're meeting. He's your mother's uncle on her father's side, if I have that correct. He is going to help you with your Levantine

192

family trees, so that you can return with honour to that dissertation you abandoned, too many years ago. And that would be so kind of him, so generous, even, something for us all to admire, that he should open his doors to you. But Dora, you must beware. For in addition to being your great uncle on your mother's side, he also happens to be Anaïs' grandfather, and the son-in-law of the dangerous and nefarious Madame Karine, who laughs every time a Turkish diplomat is slaughtered. Who hates all Turks apart from those whose minds she succeeds in poisoning, But of all the Turks she hates, the ones she hates the most are the descendants of your esteemed grandfather, Adnan Pasha. Do you wish to know why?'

'No, I do not wish to know why,' I said. 'In fact I've heard all the nonsense I can bear.' Our food having just arrived, I asked him to leave me to eat and read in peace. But even this didn't faze him.

'I share your ambition,' he said.

'For what, exactly?'

'For the chance to slumber safely and in peace.'

'You're after something,' I said.

'Of course I am,' he replied.

'It would make things a lot easier if you could dispense with all the slander and insinuation and just come out with it.'

'Fine. Understood. Perhaps I could put it like this. In one way or another, this woman, this Madame Karine. She will try to use you.'

'I have no plans to meet with Madame Karine.'

'Oh, but she has plans to meet with you.'

'So what if she does? What is it to you?'

'It would grieve me greatly,' İsmet now said, 'if any more harm came to your father.'

193

'Who said anything about my father?'

'Ah. So they didn't even tell you that.'

I ate my supper with my head turned. I returned to my books. He was baiting me, and the only way to beat him at this game was to refuse to play. In time he turned off his reading light, and I turned off mine. But every time I felt myself drifting off, the same question would swing in to wrench me back.

Sergei. My dear lost friend Sergei. Could he truly be involved in such a thing as ASALA, I asked myself, even as I reminded myself that the whole story must be a confabulation?

At the curb side the next morning, when a black limousine pulled up to the kerb, and İsmet offered me a lift, there was a moment of temptation. Along the way, I could ask him about Sergei. But what was the point of that? He was never going to tell me the truth. So I said, 'Thanks, but no thanks. I can make my own way. You've made it very clear to me that you know exactly where I'm going, but strangely, so do I.'

'That's good to know,' he said. 'But let us see, when the worst happens, if you can find your way back to me with the same ease.'

Arriving some hours later at Sinan's mother's apartment in Neuilly, I was greeted by Tallis draped in a sheet. When he reached out to embrace me, it nearly fell off. He grabbed it just in time, before leading me into a once grand parlour that was now a wasteland of beer cans and dirty socks. The figure sprawled across the sofa, half obscured by a quilt, I took to be Sinan.

I did not recognise the bright-eyed, honey-haired girl who came out of the kitchen to greet me, but she insisted that I would have had to be clairvoyant to do so. I'd met her only the once, after all, at that long-ago wedding, when I was newly arrived in Istanbul, and she was 'a mere girl of seven'.

She introduced herself again.

So this was Anais, I thought. 'I remember now,' I said. Though it would take me longer to connect the adult Anais with the child I'd met some fifteen years earlier.

Drawing again on what İsmet had told me, I said, 'If I'm not mistaken, we have a great great grandfather in common.'

'That's right,' Anais said. 'Monsieur Tigran. And in fact, I am named after your unfortunate great grandmother, who died too young.'

'But that can't be true,' I said. 'Her name was Anahid.'

'That is the name on my birth certificate. I am Anais to my friends and my family because my mother preferred this variation. In fact, the only one to call me by my official name is my great grandmother, the sister of the first Anahid.

'Madame Karine?' I asked.

She nodded. 'You have an impressive recollection of names.'

'I met her once. And only once, in New York, but she made something of an impression.'

'This is her usual custom, I agree! If what she tells me is true, this encounter happened in New York.'

'Yes,' I said. 'When I was a mere girl of eleven or twelve.'

'She, too, remembers the occasion well,' said Anais. 'And now she is, I fear, very eager to meet with you again.'

How, I asked myself, had İsmet known this?

To hide my confusion, I glanced at the disarray around us, and said, 'Not here, I hope!'

'Great Gods,' said Anais. 'No. Not here. In the 16th. And not right now either. I am very glad to inform you that she is presently out of town. We misinformed her about your dates, you see. With any luck, you can glean what you need to know about your Levantines before her return. Though I must warn you, time is of the essence. It would have been good, I think, if you had been able to commence your researches at this very moment. But Tallis insists that you must rest first from your sleepless flight, and I am sure he is right. So. Would three hours be enough for you to refresh your senses? It must be you to decide. I shall be here waiting. And as soon as you are ready I shall take you over.'

'Over where?'

'To the 16th, of course. Your Great Uncle Remy awaits.'

I explained to her that this was the first I'd heard of a Great Uncle Remy.

'Oh, yes. Tallis has explained. Your mother tells you nothing. You must learn everything from others. And perhaps, this is a story for another day. Suffice it to say for now that your Great Uncle Remy is my grandfather on my mother's side.'

'But how could that be?' I asked.

'It is a story, I think, that you will enjoy. But for later, yes?'

Because first there were other matters to settle. She sent Tallis back to bed, promising not to keep me away for too long. In the café on the corner, she ordered me a tisane.

'I hope you don't find me selfish for having delayed your reunion with your beloved,' she then said. 'But we all thought I might do a better job of explaining the quandary in which we find ourselves. And that you, with your superior mind, and your added advantage of detachment, might be in a position to offer us a certain number of helpful suggestions.'

The quandary, she went on to say, was İsmet. For it had not been enough for Sinan to flee his country, leaving behind him all he held dear, except for the two cousins he had smuggled out with him, in the boot of his car. İsmet was continuing to stalk him.

Hearing his name, my first thought was to tell my newfound niece – or was she a grandniece? – that this man had been stalking me as well. But then, once again, I felt the sting of the tentacles İsmet had somehow left beneath my skin. I had no reason to trust her. Best, for the time being, to hold back what I knew.

So I sat there, sipping my tisane, while she launched into the story I'd thought I already knew: five leftist students, Sinan, Suna and Haluk amongst them. Detained in 1972 for the murder of a sixth, whose body had yet to be found. Immortalised in the scandal sheets as the Trunk Murder, even though the trunk was nowhere to be found, either.

Possibly at the behest of Sinan's brute of a father, or possibly at the behest of someone else, İsmet had taken personal responsibility for the interrogation of the cousins.

This much was familiar to me. But not what came next: in the course of his interrogations, İsmet had raped all three.

'I am saying this just to you,' said Anais, 'because Tallis has instructed me to trust you absolutely. He thought you should know. Additionally, he knew you would believe it. Bearing in mind what you yourself had endured at this man's hands.'

'He didn't rape me, though.'

'I know,' said Anais. 'But didn't he try?'

'That he did,' I said. And Anais reached out for my hand. 'We are all so proud of you. For fighting back. Of course, this wasn't a possibility for the cousins.'

'In a police station? I imagine not.'

'Suna, at least, managed to jump out of a window.'

'Yes, I'd heard.'

'Of course you have. It was in all the papers. But not what I have just told you. Can I trust you never ever to breathe a word of it?'

'How did you hear of it?'

'From my father. He is a doctor, did you know that? He runs a centre, for victims of torture. He has been helping our cousins, as best he can.'

'So I've heard,' I said. Though in fact, I had not. I had just had my suspicions pointed in that direction the night before, by İsmet.

Anais returned to the story I already knew: the cousins had all been released on the same day, following a general amnesty. But despite all their family's connections (and perhaps because of them, for their fathers, despising their politics, could have been pulling in the opposite direction) neither Haluk nor Suna had been able to secure passports. So Sinan had come up with his plan, to smuggle them out of the country in the boot of a car.

Except, it now emerged, it had not been his car, but my mother's car. It had been to pick up that car that Sinan had flown out to Lugano alone, on his US passport. 'You are aware, of course, that he had this second citizenship on account of coming into this world while his father was working at the Turkish Embassy in Washington.'

I had forgotten, but I nodded, so as to keep that lapse of memory to myself. Instead, I said, 'So anyway. When did Sinan fetch up in Lugano?'

'Did your mother tell you this, at least?' '

'I'm afraid not.'

'Oh, dear. She truly must try to keep you better informed. It is not right! Let's discuss this further, when we have the chance. For now, let's keep to the bones of the story, so that I can take you back to your beloved. It was early this past spring. And Sinan had not been at the house for more than three or four days when early one morning, there was a knock on the door. Sinan was still asleep, thank God. It was your mother who opened that door. And there, in the flesh – in Lugano! – was İsmet.

'Of course he had not been invited!' Anais assured me. 'Nor was he welcome! But your mother knew that if she was to keep our poor cousin safe from his clutches, she had no choice but to play along.'

İsmet had stayed for three days, which Sinan had spent hidden in a locked room, watching the comings and goings through a crack in the shutters.

'Every night, after the others had gone to bed, Sinan would hear İsmet roaming the house, knocking against the walls. And outside, walking through the garden, tapping the earth with a rod we think to have been a Geiger counter. Such strange behaviour, don't you think? We can only be glad that our Uncle Teddy had the foresight and generosity to buy Sinan a Super 8. Because now we have such scenes on film. We have proof, and a grain of hope for our poor Sinan.'

'Of course,' she added, with a strange note of pride. 'Our Sinan kept his courage. Only the next day, he was driving your mother's car back into Turkey. Thanks to his American passport, he could enter the country quietly and quickly cross back over with our dear cousins in the boot. But did he stop when he'd brought them safely to Paris? Not at all! He was at once behind the wheel again. This time to drive to Amsterdam to rescue Tallis from the office of the Magic

Bus. Where he found the energy I cannot say. But you know how it is, dear Dora. We can find the adrenaline for a necessary act of courage, but afterwards, we pay the price.'

'Since reuniting his tribe,' she continued, 'Sinan has unfortunately been suffering a crisis of nerves. Never leaving his mother's apartment, never washing. Always trembling. And then, last night, they had found a razor blade beneath his pillow. Tallis and myself – we are now on suicide watch. We take turns staying up with him. My father helps too, when he can.'

'And what can I do?' I asked. 'How can I help?'

'You can help us keep watch, of course. But also, you can help us with the others. Exile has not been kind to them, I fear. As my father puts it, they may have lost their way.'

Again, İsmet's insinuations came back to me. How exactly had the cousins lost their way? I had been asking myself, but to my shock, I heard myself saying it out loud.

Anaïs, who was just as sweet and good as İsmet had said, somehow guessed what was troubling me.

'I think,' she said, 'that we have spoken enough for now. We have plenty of time later. For now, I had just wished you to tell you in confidence – from my mouth to yours – that the cousins, despite their bravado, are in a most fragile and perilous state. But they are not always easy. That is why I wished you to know of these other matters. So that you could understand. If need be, make allowances. Help us imagine a new way forward. That is your forte, according to your Tallis. But Dora, please. Never let them know that you know what İsmet did to them. If you can manage it, I would, in addition, beg you never to utter his name.'

I promised, grateful that she was making my decision for me.

'And now for my grandfather. Your Uncle Remy. He is quite a character, you know. So first you must rest!'

'All set?' asked Tallis in the back bedroom, as he unfurled himself from his sheet. He shook it out, and as we lay there side by side, watching it float down to cover us both.

'Absolutely. All set,' I said.

Uncle Remy, I thought, as I drifted off to sleep. The name was familiar. He'd featured in some of the stories I'd heard while in Istanbul. But where, and when, and how?

As Anais drove me over to the 16th that afternoon, taking a considerable detour so that I could have a glimpse of her mother's architectural firm, where (as İsmet had already informed me) she too was currently, alongside Tallis, doing what she called a *stage*, I continued to sift through my Istanbul memories. Until it came to me. Yes, of course. Remy was the eldest son of Achille the shipping magnate. The brother of Charles, my unfortunate Levantine grandfather. Remy had been the one to arrive on Büyükada under cover of darkness after the unfortunate accident in which both Charles and his mother Odette had died. He had then whisked the deceased off to parts unknown, along with Hermine, already pregnant with my mother.

The Levantine sisters who would go on to raise my mother were Remy's sisters, too. Though my mother had never tired of complaining about this pair, she'd never once mentioned an Uncle Remy. And this was the first mystery that my newly discovered great uncle sought to clear up for me after he had led me through a house that had the dimensions of a palace, the hush of an examination hall, and the chill of a museum.

'I must say,' he said, as he seated me at a table in an

alcove at the far end of vast and sparsely furnished parlour, 'it is such a pleasure to meet you at long last. I wish it had been much earlier. I wish, just as much, that I had had a chance to meet your dear mother soon enough to avoid all these lawsuits she has so needlessly launched against us!'

It was the first I was hearing of these lawsuits, but I nodded, as if I was fully up to date.

'We could have been friends,' Uncle Remy continued, 'had our association not begun with these misfortunes. For we share a certain fate.'

'What would that be?' I asked.

'Aha,' he said. 'Now that is a story.'

He pursed his lips and gazed up at the marble statue looming over us. Poseidon, I guessed. Poseidon in a foul mood. 'So now, dear Dora. What your mother and I have in common is that our family has repudiated us. You know your mother's story. Mine begins much earlier. Would it surprise you to hear, after what you know of our family, that after I married Rosa – Madame Karine's daughter – who is also, as you may have gathered, the grandmother of little Anais – my father commanded that my name should never again be mentioned in his presence?'

'Why though?' I asked. 'Why would they object to your marrying into money?'

Whereupon my newfound great uncle graced me with a gentle, luxuriant smile that took me straight back to Istanbul, because it withheld as much as it suggested, feared as much as it promised. Certain things I could read right away. From the dashing cut of his suit and the daring pattern of his tie, from the sheen of his bald head and his manicured nails, and most of all from his piercing, searching eyes, with the slightest hint of kohl at their edges, it was clear to me that he had left Istanbul not just to marry Rosa, but to escape his father's grip.

'Can it really be true,' Remy asked, 'what Anais has said – that you have heard nothing of me?'

'That could be fortunate,' he continued after a pause. 'Because at least, you have not been poisoned with the usual lies.

He rang for the maid. And then, as we sipped our coffee and looked out over the Bois de Boulogne, he sought to deny the most pernicious lie, just in case I heard it further down the line. 'I was not stolen. My mother-in-law – Karine the Great, as we sometimes call her – would never dream of stooping to such a mad and malicious device. Though of course it is true that she had anger for all the Alephs.'

'The Alephs?' I asked.

'Has no one told you of the Alephs?'

'They've mentioned them in passing, certainly. But that's pretty much all.'

'Aha. That explains something. We can perhaps take that up, but not yet. I was wishing to explain to you the lies they tell of my mother-in-law, the great Karine, who is also, as we both know, your great aunt.'

'My great great aunt, I think you mean.'

Yes, of course. But we meander. What I had wished to say was that Achille – my father – your great grandfather – was one of those Alephs. And Madame Karine felt great anger towards him. With good reason. But she has also had a healthy sense of humour. It is this more than anything that has helped her to prevail against the odds. *En tout cas*, there was a joke she used to share. If only, to make her foes nervous. With her every return to Istanbul, and she would return quite often, because her husband was in oil – you know this, at least. Her every return would inevitably involve social occasions with my father, our Monsieur Achille, but also, of course with your grandfather on your father's side. The Pasha. Seeing that they were all in business together, these reunions were of course both necessary and inevitable. You know what they say, don't you? Commerce, being the lifeblood of the world, can extract from war the best that peace can offer. But these were difficult occasions for our great and great-hearted Karine, whose grievances were forever being brushed aside. Even by her own husband, who should perhaps have shown more consideration. So inevitably. She would on these occasions occasionally lose her, how does one say it, her sang-froid. She would point at my father, Achille. Or the Pasha. Or on some occasions, she would point at them both. And then she would cry: "I shall make you pay for your crimes! I have already the plan! You wait and see! I shall rob you of your first-born!"'

'And did she?' I asked.

'No, of course not,' said Remy. 'She may, however, have given me an idea. After all, I did not wish to spend my life marooned inside a family shipping company, in a city that had once been the heart of an empire but was no longer. The oil world promised so much more. *En tous cas.* It was I who approached Karine the Great with my proposal. It was oil with its rich promises and daunting challenges that lit my way. It was only after my departure, and after I had been working for some time with Karine the Great's illustrious husband, that I met my dear Rosa, and fell in love. It was the same with the other first-born, you know. All those years later. That, too, was a love match.'

'Which love match was that?'

'My goodness, it is true. You do know very little. But time

204

being of the essence, we should perhaps return now to the matter at hand. How can I help you with your researches?'

'A family tree, for a start?'

'Hmmm. For that we must decamp to the library.'

On our way we passed through a small room on whose walls I found displayed several paintings from Hümeyra's DEATHBED series, alongside several others from a series that featured the building where she and my mother still lived. In this series, the image of our building was studded with fragments of coloured glass, beneath a roof that was on fire. 'You seem surprised,' said my newfound great uncle. 'Had you not known that Karine the Great is amongst your grandmother's most fervent and loyal collectors?'

'No I haven't,' I said. 'And I hope you don't mind my asking,' I added, as I followed him down a long and polished corridor. 'Does my grandmother even know how many of her paintings are now the property of Karine? Because I'm not sure she'd be so happy about it. She has nothing kind to say about her, after all.'

'But how could that be?' asked Remy as he led me into the library.

'My dear Remy,' said a voice coming from the armchair next to the furthermost window. 'The answer could not be more evident. For more than half a century, our Hermine has been fed on lies.'

There followed a tapping and flashing of silver canes, as Karine the Great rose from her armchair and crossed the room to greet me.

She looked to be dressed for a circa 1890 outing in the countryside, in many layers of linen, and just a few strings of pearls. Her white hair was pulled back into a harsh and gleaming bun.

'What are you doing here?' I blurted.

'Why am I doing here?' she exclaimed. 'You come to my house and the first thing you ask is this?'

'They told me you were out of town.'

'Who exactly told you this?'

'Anais.'

'Ah, Anais,' said the grande dame. 'She is very sweet, is she not? Wanting only the best, for us all.' Turning to Uncle Remy, she nodded and smiled. Then she turned stern again. 'I find this room too dark,' she said. 'Remy, my boy, would you be so kind as to call for the car.'

And so it was that I came to hear Karine the Great's version of our family history while driving around the Bois de Boulogne very slowly in a Bentley.

We did not get off to a good start. I think now that she must have been nervous. Or at least, trying too hard to inspire fear in me. She refused Remy's helping hand as she struggled across the library and down one over-polished corridor after another with only her two silver canes to support her. Arriving at the marble staircase that led to the front door, she fairly collapsed into an ornate armchair too narrow for her bulk. Here she heaved a heavy, panting sigh, and dropped off to sleep. As she slept, Remy rushed outside, returning with the chauffeur. Together they carried her down the stairs and into the back of the Bentley.

And off we went, Karine and the chauffeur and I, as slowly as a car could go.

We had been inching our way through the park for twenty minutes or so when Karine the Great opened her eyes again. She blinked a few times as she took in her new surroundings, but she gave no other indication that the change of scene surprised her.

'And so,' she said. 'Let us make good use of our time.' She began by quizzing me on what she had been told was my proposed course of study: why had I chosen to research the thieving Levantines, forever in collaboration with the wicked Ottomans? What had stopped me from investigating my Armenian family, and avenging the crimes committed against them?

I countered by telling her it was not all black and white. Not during a war, I said. Never during a war. This she was more than willing to concede. 'We need think no further than the dastardly Artin, my dear sister Anahid's husband. Shall we begin there, perhaps? Would you like to hear what I have to say about him?'

But I was not yet interested in this man. Instead, I wanted to know why she had been content to collect Hümeyra's paintings.

'Hermine. I refuse that other name of hers.'

'Fine,' I said. 'Hermine. 'That doesn't stop me wanting to know why you bought so many of her painting after letting her down so badly.'

'I did not let her down.'

'Oh yes, you did. You promised to rescue her, and take her to Switzerland, to be with her mother. But you never did.'

'Oh, but I tried,' said Karine the Great.

'Oh, no you didn't,' I countered.

'Is that what these liars have told you?'

'It's what Hümeyra –'

'Hermine.'

'Hermine, Hümeyra,' I said. 'What does it matter? Could

you please stop interrupting me and listen? No one lied to me. I am simply repeating to you what my grandmother told me herself.'

'My point exactly. She believes I let her down because of the lies they told her.'

'Who are *they*?'

Here Karine the Great heaved a great sigh of exasperation. 'I fear I must ask you now for a modicum of politesse. I am 90 years old, I'll have you know. And I have been kind enough to forgo my afternoon nap to take you on this drive, to exhaust myself by offering to you your own sad history. So. I shall now ask you to remain tranquil. And listen.'

I apologised. Promised to stay quiet and listen. But then Karine the Great dropped off to sleep again. When the Bentley rounded a corner just a little faster than a snail, she fell into me. For what must have been no longer than ten minutes but felt like hours, she slumbered, mouth open, on my lap. Until finally, the chauffeur stopped the car and came around to help me prop her up again.

We were just back on the road when Karine the Great opened her eyes and resumed the story she must have been telling me in her dreams.

'And so, as I was saying. We could not remain forever in the bliss that was Madame Roussana's small school...'

Madame Roussana? Who was she? And who were *we*?

Too late to ask. She had already moved on.

'...nor could we two share the even greater bliss of Constantinople College, there across the Bosphorus in Üsküdar. Oh, how happy we were in that beautiful school! But then, one day on the ferry landing, poor Nuran was sighted by your grandfather, that pasha you love so much.

And before we knew it, she'd been whisked out of school and married off. The poor girl was only fourteen!'

'Wait a moment,' I said.

'Why should I? You promised to be tranquil, and just listen.'

'Yes,' I said, 'but you've skipped ahead. And now I'm lost. Is this Nuran you mention my grandmother Nuran the poetess?'

'It is. I already told you this. How could you have forgotten so soon?'

'I had no idea you even knew each other.'

'And whose fault might that be, dare I ask? And now, let me dare to answer. It was the fault of that cretin, Adnan Pasha. The husband who never knew her worth. The father who crushed his own sons. While blinding first our poor Hermine to the truth, and then you. Of all people. I hope you are ashamed of yourself. If only it makes you listen. For I – I always knew. Always. From our earliest days together, at our schools. And I was there by her side. Without me, my dear Nuran would never have been furnished with the books that nurtured her gift. Never savoured the glories of a salon. In spite of everything, your beautiful Ottoman grandmother would go on to grow and grow as a paragon, but only because she had me, her best friend, at her side. But oh, how she suffered at this Pasha's hands! Twice she divorced the man. Did you know that? Twice he so weakened her that she had to take him back. Oh! Such horrors I could tell you of your Pasha grandfather! But today is for the crimes of the Alephs.'

'Before you tell me about the crimes,' I said, 'I need you to tell me who the Alephs were.'

'This I fear I cannot tell you. Who were these men, behind

their masks? What impelled them? We shall never know. So for now, suffice it to say that this heartless scoundrel grandfather of yours – this loathsome Adnan Pasha – was the first of our Alephs. The second was Achille, your Levantine grandfather. The third was Artin, my wastrel brother-in- law. The so-called banker. The Dashnak who was the ruin of everyone in my family, except for me.'

'What makes you think your brother-in-law was a Dashnak?'

'I do not think. I know. Others may believe that he was only in the midst of these reckless revolutionaries who brought disaster on our head, simply to inform the cretin pasha. But I, who move in high circles, all across the globe, have no need of groundless speculation. I have my sources.'

As İsmet mentioned, I almost said.

'But let us leave that to one side for now. I was speaking of the Alephs. Of the reckless, feckless Artin, and the thieving Achille, and your cretinous pasha grandfather. These three had been friends since school. It was the fourth, who was somewhat younger, and naïve in a way only Americans can be, who gave them their silly name. The Alephs. I am speaking now of Aubrey, your friend Tallis' grandfather. The husband of Mrs Mary. The brother-in-law of Dr Ruth. I have things to say about these two women later on. For now, let me tell you that I call them the Blind Sisters, and with good reason.'

'Hümeyra calls them the same thing, strangely.'

'Please. I am warning you. In my presence you are to call my niece Hermine. And as I said, I do not wish to speak of them just yet. I wish instead to speak about the gamblers.'

'The gamblers?'

'The Alephs. They met at the tables. At least, that was where they gathered, at the Cercle d'Orient. If not to play

210

cards, then to scheme. If not to scheme, to help each other out of scrapes. But my wastrel Dashnak banker of a brother-in-law, he was in the hot water a great deal more than the others. And my sweet sister Anahid – well, she was an artist, with an artist's soul. At first, she did not notice that this scoundrel husband of hers had taken away so many of her jewels, and the lout had perhaps even found his way into our father's vaults. By the time she began to notice, she'd been struck down by consumption. She was too weak to act. And I – by then I too had married. Did I mention that my husband was in oil? We were almost always travelling in those days. Each time we returned to our city, it was to a new disaster. And the architects of each new disaster were always the Alephs.'

But before she could describe these disasters, Karine the Great fell asleep again. When she awoke some twenty minutes later, she was in a panic. Leaning forward, first to tap the glass barrier, and then to thump it, she cried, 'Take me home! Take me home at once!'

Uncle Remy was not there to help us. The wheelchair that the maid carried down to us would have to do. Together we transferred Karine the Great's suspiciously moist bulk, while she ranted and railed. 'It's too late. Already! Altogether! It is a scandal! An absolute disgrace!'

Together we carried her up the stairs. As the maid was wheeling her off, Karine the Great called after me. 'These fools have forgotten my canes! Go back to the car to fetch them, Dora. Then you will please wait where you are told. Do not dare leave!'

Returned to the alcove with the disapproving Poseidon, I too had to struggle to stay awake. My two-hour nap had not been enough to rid me of that sense of time and space

211

bending. The three coffees they brought to me only served to sharpen my anxieties. Why was I here? Why was Karine the Great here, and not away, as Anais promised? Had my Great Uncle Remy lied to her, deliberately entrapping me? Where was he now, and why had I agreed to stay?

Karine the Great had been restored to her old chair in the library, by the time I was ushered back in. Dressed this time in many layers of satin, her white hair arranged now in a softer sort of bun.

She pointed me to the chair across from hers. Insisted, against my protestations, that the maid should bring me yet another coffee. Waving at the shelves stacked ceiling to floor with leather-bound volumes, she said, 'All these books will prove useful to you, should you pursue the righteous path in your researches.' Waving towards the heavy, varnished cabinets behind the desk, she added, 'And there you will find all these letters. And deeds. And documents. And photographs. And all the facts and family trees that I have gathered and sometimes stolen. All are yours, and do you know why, Dora? Not because I trust you, because how can I? We have only just met. But here is the sad fact. I have tried all the others, and I have failed.

'And so here we now are. At the precarious age of 90, I find myself obliged to take my risks with the daughter of the incorrigible Delphine. Who has still not let up. Can you believe me when I tell you that this mother of yours has again launched against me an array of lawsuits? They are fishing expeditions, as we call them. As if I, of all people, could direct anyone to those legendary caves piled high with Armenian gold.'

'She's not honestly hunting for that gold again, is she?'

'Not overtly,' Karine said. 'But this is the quest I can sense between the lines.'

'That's crazy. Especially now. She has enough now, doesn't she?'

'I would say so. Yes, I would.'

'Let me talk to her, then.'

'That would be very helpful. I would prefer not to spend my last days in a courtroom. In the meantime, I am heartened to hear that you and your mother don't always agree. That is a healthy reaction. She is a loose cannon, after all.'

'Don't expect me to be your go-between,' I said. Grateful to İsmet, for just one moment, for putting me on my guard.

'I wouldn't dream of it,' she said. And then, her head dropped forward, as she went back to sleep.

The chauffeur drove me back to Neuilly. Stiff-necked, straight-backed. In his uniform, complete with cap. There in the back seat, it was all I could do to stay upright, while everything I'd been told over the previous twelve hours did battle inside my head.

When Tallis opened the door to find me shivering in the warm summer sunshine, the first thing he said was, 'Oh no. Not again.' He put his arm around my shoulders, guided me gently into the kitchen, where Anais was at the counter, pushing down a plunger into a cafetiere.

With a gasp, she let go, raised her hands to her face. 'Can it be true?' she asked. 'Did they trick us once again? Was Karine the Great in situ? Awake and not asleep? Oh dear. Oh dear. *Quel catastrophe.*'

Now she, too, threw her arms around me. And there I stood, time and mind and body bending, locked inside this double embrace. Until together they led me to the table. Sat me down. Poured me a coffee, my fifth of the day, and certainly the last thing I needed.

Until Anais, seeing my hands shake, thought better of it, and pushed the coffee away. 'No. Not this. What she needs is a shower.'

Tallis stood up to help. But Anais waved him away. 'This is women's business,' she said. 'Leave it to me.'

She knew her way around the linen closet, and the bathroom. 'Leave the door unlocked,' she said. 'Just in case. I shall wait for you.'

And when I padded back into the bedroom, refreshed but still unsteady, Anais was indeed waiting for me, there on Tallis' bed.

She had unpacked my bag, laid out what she hoped might be the right dress to wear for the supper we would be eating at her family home.

'My father is here already. In the study, with Sinan. After they have completed their consultation, he will drive us all over.'

Anais' family home was just a few streets away. Her wiry, wide-eyed mother, who met us at the door, was effusive in her greetings, but the smile was tense, and she moved like a wind-up doll. 'You are coming with me,' she said. 'To let the others speak.' Once in the kitchen, she relaxed somewhat. 'Such terrible times!' she sighed. 'Let us hope we can get through them.'

Through the sliding glass door that separated us from the sitting room, I could see Haluk and Suna rising from their sofa to greet the new arrivals. Both looked gaunt and haunted, as if they had been to the underworld and back. An older man came in. Anais' father, I thought. He had the manner of a doctor, and he needed only to raise one hand for Haluk and Suna to settle back into their sofa, as Tallis and Anais settled into theirs.

Why, I wondered, were these two sitting so close together? I was still entertaining that thought when my hostess put a Bellini in front of me. 'I thought you might need some cheering,' she said, 'I hear you have been the victim of a surprise attack.'

'Well, perhaps not a victim,' I murmured.

But before I could continue, she squeezed my arm. 'We all adore the Great Karine, but we cannot condone her. At least, not tonight. It was unconscionable, what she did to your father on Monday.'

'My father?'

'Oh, dear. Did they not tell you? Never mind. They must not have wanted you to worry.'

'About what?'

'It was just a false alarm, in any event. A seizure, to be sure, but by the time we reached the hospital it was over. He is back in our care now.'

'Here? In Paris?"

'More than that. He is our guest. We have a flat below ground, you see. It's where Haluk and Suna have been staying. We've put Melih in the spare room.'

'That is certainly very kind of you.'

'What else could we do?' said Anais' mother. 'The fact is, our Karine almost killed him.'

'She did?'

'Metaphorically, at least. With her accusations. And harsh words. It was a mistake for us to bring them together. It was Karine's own idea, needless to say. She did not share with us her plans. Once again, we were fooled. Your French is very good, by the way.'

'French was my first language.'

'Yes, of course it was. How could I forget. And I've also

forgotten to introduce myself. What a silly woman I am! In addition to being the mother of Anais, I have a name. I am Solange. In addition, I am Karine's long-suffering granddaughter. But anyway. Where were we? Yes, Karine, and her little ambush. You see, she had heard through some grapevine of hers that we were planning this surprise reunion for you and your father. And meanwhile, through some other grapevine, she'd either learned or imagined that your poor father was launching a string of lawsuits against her – in the name of others, mind you – to place his hands on some unknown caves in some faraway land, that some fool has claimed to be piled high with gold. Such nonsense! All this she said to him, without warning or preamble. Over supper! Not a one of us touched a thing! As if that was not enough, she was also screaming, at the top of her lungs, about the groundless rumours she believed your father to be circulating against her in the name of these unnamed others. Stamping on the floor with those silver canes of hers. Threatening to countersue poor Melih, for implicating her in the ASALA bombings. When she had never, ever, supported revolutionaries, whatever their stripes! Not the Dashaks, not the Bolsheviks, and not ASALA! Over and over, she said this to your poor father, even when he began to clutch his heart.'

'I had no idea he was even in Paris,' I said.

'Oh yes. Oh dear. I remember now. It was meant to be a surprise. I'm sorry. It's been such a week. When he joins us later, can you pretend you are surprised?'

Before I could answer, we were interrupted by the sound of a chair crashing against a wall in the sitting room next door. Because the sliding doors were closed we couldn't quite make out what people were saying, but we could see that it was Haluk who had taken offence at something. And

216

Suna, who was pleading with him to sit down again, and listen, and be calm.

'Oh dear, ' said Solange. 'The poor boy is still upset.'

'About what?'

'About the altercation. The one on Monday. He was its witness, you understand. We were all witnesses.'

She poured me a second Bellini. Patted me on the arm.

'My husband knows how to deal with this. He went through his own sufferings, in his time. I know you will want to catch up with your cousins. It must be strange, watching them through the glass, after all these years apart! But we have the whole evening ahead of us. Let's wait in here, while they settle this.'

The cousins had all fallen silent now. The father was speaking. Or rather, lecturing. Gently, but in a voice that carried. He was speaking in Turkish, I now realised.

I asked my hostess how this could be.

'But you know this. You must. No matter. It has been a long and upsetting day. So let me remind you. Kemal – my husband – is a Turk. But not just any Turk. As it happens, you share a grandfather. Our fabled Adnan Pasha.'

Struggling once again to mask my confusion, I asked how she and her husband had met.

'You will have heard of this, too, I fear. But it is not as you have been told. At least, what you may have heard is true only to a point. We met, for the first time, at a vernissage. I was a student. And so was Kemal. Here in Paris. True, this vernissage of which we speak was curated or at least generously supported by my grandmother. But until that evening, she and my Kemal had never met. Had she invited him? It's possible. Perhaps. However, that was all. She could never have predicted how things would develop. Kemal's father,' she continued. 'Your Uncle Semih. He was fit to be tied. With our own Karine the Great – it was quite the opposite. After we declared ourselves, she was infinitely gracious.'

And I thought. So that's it then. The other first-born Karine the Great had stolen. Or rather the other love match.

'I would go so far,' Solange added, 'as to say our Karine adores my husband more than she does me.'

The voices in the other room were growing louder again. Haluk was leaning forward, hands clenched, red-faced and furious. Suna was chopping the air with her right hand, as she pirouetted through one of her endless sentences.

'Oh, how my heart aches for them,' said my hostess. 'Such reactions, and they have not yet heard of the great crime!'

'What crime?'

She waved a dismissive hand. 'This is for later. And not for me to tell. Because you see, these things need to be told by the right person, in the right voice, with the right intervals, in the right order. And even if all these measures can be taken, there is still so much pain. They will have to tear apart every story they've been told, our poor dears, and start all over. It was the same all those years ago, with my Kemal.'

She poured me a third Bellini, and then a glass of water. 'You should drink the water first,' she said. 'Now where was I? Oh yes. I was going to mention Sinan. Yes. We have been surprised to learn that none of it was a surprise for him. We are not sure who told him – was it your mother, perhaps? They are close, I understand. In any event, that's how this second argument started. This was, let me see. Yes, it was yesterday, while you were flying across to us, above the Atlantic. Sinan said he knew all about the genocide, and not just the magnitude of the crimes, but the story inside our own family, and when he had uttered these words, the other two – your Suna and Haluk – they wanted to know how he could say such a thing. But this thing was not the story in our family. It was his mention of the genocide itself! They wanted him to prove it. Exactly then and there. Which was impossible. Had I been present, this is what I would have said. Alas, last night, on the occasion of this second altercation, I was not in their company. I was still at work.'

Here my hostess reached across the table, took my hand. 'Let us hope my Kemal is able to mend the rift between them. And my dear, can I ask you to be gentle? This Suna. She is, as you know, my Kemal's niece. And they have trust between them. We are hoping this will help. Above all, she needs, like the others, to concentrate on her own health. Though I must warn you, and this is why you must be especially gentle with her. If Haluk is correct – and even if he is, I regret his decision during that argument to air this fact to all the others – our poor Suna was while in police custody not simply raped, but raped with a truncheon. She may never recover. She may never know the joy of a child.'

Time and mind and body were bending fast and furious by now. When the door to the sitting room opened, the roar of angry voices hit me like a gust of wind. Then it closed again. I closed my eyes, to cherish the silence. I opened them again and there they were, standing before me. Tallis and Anais, wide-eyed with concern.

Speaking almost with one voice, they asked, 'Are you all right Dora?'

Whereupon the question no person with any dignity should ever ask slipped out of me: 'Do you two have some kind of thing going?'

She was horrified. He was mortified. She burst into tears,

and Tallis took me outside, to walk around the block, while the trees around me swayed, and the pavement beneath my feet. Had he not had his arm around my shoulders, I am sure I would have fallen. Over and over he asked me. How could I even think of such a thing? What had happened to me, and the trust between us? How could I not know that I was the one, the only one, and always would be?

What could he do to convince me? What could we do together, to make up for these doubts and fears that must certainly have come from being apart far too long? Would I consider taking another year off my study, if the carers back in Pomfret could agree to step up for me? Wouldn't it be good, to spend next year together, here in Paris, instead of me there and him here, and both of us so lonely?

In the meantime, though. How was Tallis going to face Anais and her family? They had been so kind to him. So very, very kind. To all of them. All of us. But now, with this... I saw then, that I had made a mistake.

I should have told him the whole story, the moment I got off the plane.

And now, as I made up for lost time, I felt İsmet's tentacles loosening, and falling away.

Anais and her mother were waiting at the doorstep. When Tallis told them the misunderstanding was all cleared up, they burst into happy laughter. 'Come back in!' cried the mother. 'You must be famished! Can it be true, Anais, that you forgotten to give our Dora the tiniest morsel, all day long?' She pulled open the sliding doors. 'Assez!' she cried,' À Table!'

But Tallis raised his hand. 'Before we eat, there's something we need to tell people.' He led me into the sitting room, first to introduce me to the doctor father, and to give Suna and Haluk the opportunity to offer me some semblance of a welcome. Then he asked Anais if she'd mind switching sofas, so that he and I could sit together.

'Okay now,' he said, once we were settled. 'You are all going to fasten your seat belts. Dora needs to tell you what happened to her yesterday, on the plane.'

Over supper, for which my pale and limping father joined us – we pieced some things together. Not all of it, by any means. But by the time we retired to the sitting room with our coffees and our tisanes, Anais' father was ready to propose a larger picture.

İsmet had spirited me into first class, and himself into the seat next to mine, so as to undermine my trust in all my loved ones. But not just to get back at me. Not just to bring me misery. He also will have wished to use me as an unwitting pawn in his latest ruse, which was to use our tangled family tree against us – twist the facts in such a way as to make it look as if we were in league with ASALA. And in that way, to continue to pursue and prosecute us, and shame us to his heart's content in whatever scandal sheet would have him.

My story had so shocked the cousins that they'd almost lost the will to argue. But when Anais' doctor father put forward his hypothesis, Haluk protested. 'What have we done to deserve this?'

This earned him a wise but mournful look from Kemal the doctor. In later years, I would remember it often: Haluk never did quite see the point of the trouble his cousins had dragged him into. He'd only come along for the ride. He'd only stayed to help his cousins up again. To protect them, and keep them going.

He, more than anyone, longed to go back to the way life had been, before politics intruded. This saddened his cousins, who chose, for the most part, to meet his outbursts with compassionate silence. But on this particular evening, it was my father who answered Haluk's question.

'You ask what we have done to deserve this,' Melih said. 'The answer is plain and simple. We have done nothing. From the moment my father brought this man into our midst, it was clear, to me at least, that İsmet wished us ill. But not just because he comes from a humble background, while we do not. There is something more behind his envy and contempt. Even before the infamous Teddy Affair, and before…before…before the rest of it. Yes, even then, we could see its first signs. We could perhaps trace it back to his birthplace. But that would be an arduous journey. Additionally, I have never much liked Adana. It is enough, I think, to ask what lies at the heart of this new ruse of his. Of course, it is money. Of course, it is gold. The idiotic man still believes those silly stories. At the end of the day, the devil is hopelessly naïve!'

'That may be so,' said Kemal the doctor. 'But so long as this İsmet possesses facts about our family that we ourselves dare not admit, he will have the upper hand. Dear Melih,' he said, reverting now to Turkish. 'I do not wish you to suffer another seizure, or God forbid, a further spike in blood pressure. I only wish to inoculate you against the words of your enemies, so that you can better withstand them. Would you permit me to relate to you a story, bearing all that in mind? I shall do so as gently as I am able, and in the spirit of remorseful love. If ever you feel distress or pain, my dear Melih, you have only to raise your right hand.'

It was a cosy room, made more so by the plane tree brushing its leaves gently back and forth against its large window, obscuring the darkening sky. The sofas were deep and soft. We settled into them, as our hostess dimmed the lights, and her husband began to speak.

'My dearest Dora. You must be asking yourself how I, a proud and patriotic Turk, came to live in Paris, in happy matrimony with an Armenian whose family views all Turks as devils. There are so many answers I could offer. I could speak of love. Of politics. Of dreams dashed and betrayed. These are all stories you deserve to know. And know them you shall. But today I am tasked with taking you back to the story from which all these other stories flow. I am going to speak to you of a terrible crime. It is, sad to say, a crime of which most of us know something, even if we dare not say it. Even if, at the slightest mention, we begin to shout. So let me begin by saying that I, too, have wished to shout. But once I had heard the worst, I felt peace in my heart. For at last, I understood what I had spent my life watching: this beautiful motherland of ours, held hostage by liars, building their fortunes on stolen wealth, while the rest of us languished.'

My father lifted his arm, only to let it drop again.

'Melih? Kemal asked, in the gentlest of voices. 'Should we perhaps –'

'No,' said my father. 'I am ready now. Please continue.'

'With your blessing, dear Uncle,' said Kemal. 'And my thanks. So now, with no further ado. Let us pack our bags and travel back to the 18th of January 1916. The fateful day. If you will please imagine yourselves, dear friends, on a freighter that is furiously bobbing in a winter sea. The little mountain you see before you, rising out of the Sea of

Marmara is the first of the Princes' Islands. The freighter from which you are now alighting is under the direction of my wife's esteemed ancestor, Monsieur Achille. And the man in the rowboat that is slowly making its way from this ship to the calmer waters of the harbour? It is our very own Adnan Pasha.

'He sits up straight, our Pasha. Impervious to the occasional crashing waves. Only when he reaches the calmer waters does he raise his arm in greeting. For there, on the pier, is his lifelong friend Artin, the Amenian Aleph. Pale and thin he might be, but also, he is elated, impatient. Bursting with resolve. And happy, so happy, to see his old friend. Nine months have passed since they last saw each other. Those same months have seen their empire through slaughter and ignominy, humiliation and defeat. But on this, the afternoon of the 18th of January, 1916, the sun has poked its way through the frozen clouds to offer our humble waterfront the semblance of the old days and the old ways, or at least, a reminder.

'The two men embrace, before taking their places at the only table outside the only establishment that has opened its doors on this cold and windy and only intermittently sunny winter afternoon. A waiter comes hurrying out, with rakı and its usual accoutrements. For a precious half hour, the two friends speak in hushed, short sentences, the sort to suggest a plan already agreed, and now to be executed.

'The sun goes behind the clouds. The Pasha rises. Before doing the same, Artin leans down to pick up the suitcase at his feet. Handing it over to his friend the Pasha, he says, "They're all in here. The keys to the vaults and directions." The Pasha nods. They embrace, for longer than is usual. This is the point of no return. This they both know.

224

'Off Artin goes to the man who is waiting on the pier. As he boards the rowboat that will take him to the freighter that he still believes will take him to freedom, he turns around, for one last wave of farewell. The Pasha, after returning that courtesy, watches in silence as the rowboat cuts across the turbulent waters. In sadness, he notices how his old friend Artin seems almost not to notice the waves crashing over his head. He watches the fool climb up onto the freighter, to greet the captain who will now take him across the Sea of Marmara, but not through the Dardanelles, nor into the inky waters of the Aegean. By nightfall he will have performed with a kitchen knife the deed for which he has already been paid in gold.

Here Kemal paused, to look at us each in turn.

'That,' he informed us, 'is the sin from which we all were born. That is the crime.'

Again my father lifted his arm, only to lower it.

'Do not be shy, Uncle Melih. If you have a question, you must ask it.'

'You say this,' my father said, his voice hoarse with shame. 'But do you have proof?'

'Unfortunately, yes.'

'What sort of proof?'

Achille's son Remy – Dora, I believe you have met him, only today. He was present when Achille and our Pasha agreed their plan.'

'But that is only hearsay.'

'Uncle Melih. It is regret that I must inform you that we also have the waybill, signed and sealed.'

'But why would these two men commit such an atrocity?'

'To know this,' sighed Kemal, 'we would ourselves need to have suffered the slings and arrows of the Great War. We would need to have seen our own fortunes reduced to rubble. Our prospects, and therefore our families, in dire straits. And furthermore. It is highly likely that Achille and our Pasha had come to think of their old friend as a traitor.'

'A Dashnak!' cried my father, somewhat cheered.

'So it has been said,' Kemal agreed. 'Though perhaps our Artin was never a true Dashnak. He had been attending their meetings for some time before that dread April day that is now marked worldwide as that start of the Armenian Genocide. But his true purpose had always been to serve as our Pasha's eyes and ears.'

'So you say,' my father said. 'But do you...'

'Yes, we do,' said Kemal.

'What sort of proof?'

'Some hundred reports,' said Kemal said sadly. 'The last of these sent from the wilds of Anatolia, keeping our Pasha informed not just on his fellow detainees, but also on the guards who were accepting bribes from them.'

My father clapped his hands on his head as he let out a torrent of guttural curses.

'Be that as it may,' Kemal continued. 'We can still entertain the idea that Artin might by now have been playing a double game. Might, while buffeted by the wild winds of Anatolia, have genuinely converted to the Dashnak cause. He would, by now, have every reason to do so. It is possible, if not probable, that Achille and our Pasha saw themselves as ridding the world of a traitor. We can entertain such possibilities, though we cannot know. What we do know is that, after rewarding his friend Achille handsomely, but not too handsomely, for his freighter, his captain and his silence, our Pasha proceeded to keep the lion's share of those riches for himself.'

More muttering of curses from my father. Kemal waited patiently until silence had been restored.

'Uncle Melih, you were still with your poor ailing mother in Shishli at this juncture. As was your brother. So you will perhaps not know that Artin's corpse had yet to float to the surface the Sea of Marmara when your father took up residence in Artin's apartment on the third floor of the house of Tigran. And before you ask – yes, we have proof of this too. Proof, also, that within weeks, your father was travelling to Berlin with a large consignment of Ottoman gold.'

'So it begins!' Melih moaned. 'The great and infamous heist!'

'Of this we cannot be certain,' Kemal caution. We have no waybill in this instance. How much of this gold was truly Ottoman gold, liberated openly or in secret from the Ottoman Bank and bound for some secret vault of legend, we cannot know. Neither can we know how much of that official consignment was, in actual fact, Armenian gold. We can only guess how much consisted of treasures that rightfully belonged to Artin, or rather, the family of his wife. What we do know is that the Pasha set forth for Berlin with two companions. The first was young Hermine's governess, Mademoiselle Celeste, soon to be Madame Celeste, his second wife. She would be the one to make the infamous Swiss side trip.'

'That viper!' cried Melih. 'So she was in on it from the start!'

'In this you are correct,' Kenan agreed. 'According to the evidence we have been able to compile, she went first to visit Hermine's mother, the unfortunate Anahid, in her sanatorium. Having established that our Anahid was not long for this world, she had settled her bills, bought the plot that would become Anahid's final resting place, and made all the necessary attendant arrangements. Finally, she had taken our Anahid out for the day, to visit the banks and the lawyers. Once she had established herself as Anahid's cosignatory or executor, she had taken her to the famous lakeside property, so that the poor ailing creature could hand over the keys. On her last day in Switzerland, Celeste had returned to this villa, to find new hiding places for the gold she'd brought with her.'

'So we were right!' Melih cried. 'This we always expected!'

'And you are right. But Uncle, I fear you have, in your all-consuming hatred for your stepmother, failed to pay due attention to our Pasha's second companion. This, I regret to say, was the servant boy Soran. There is little we can know for sure about his early years. However, we do know that his first employer was not the Pasha, but Tigran, the father of Anahid, Artin's wife. These first masters of Soran's had valued him greatly. From a young age, he had been the confidante that each and every member of this warring tribe trusted most. But it seems this boy had no trouble switching sides when the time came.'

Here my father let out a gruesome laugh.

'Uncle Melih, perhaps I can leave you to take up the story from here.'

My father did not answer. He was rocking back and forth in his chair, humming.

'I can only imagine how it pains you, Uncle, to hear these truths openly uttered. But what's done is done. We are who we are. So let me relate this last revelation to our young ones and leave it there. This boy, Soran...'

'This parvenu!' growled my father,

'This boy,' said Kemal once more. After serving our Pasha

with exceptional loyalty from the start of the War of Independence to it finish, he would ultimately find himself rewarded in the city of Adana. For it was in this city that our Pasha arranged for him to take over the abandoned Armenian enterprise from which he built a fortune large enough to become Soran the Cotton King. Dora, you may not know this, but your father and Soran later joined their families in marriage. This was not a love match, to be sure. But it suited both parties. The fortune that Soran's son brought into his marriage with Gül – your half-sister and your father's middle daughter – is the foundation of their great wealth. Its humble beginnings are rarely discussed. But the fact of the matter is that the boy Soran, formerly the loyal servant of the House of Tigran, later to become the loyal servant of Pasha, and finally to be known as Soran the Cotton King, is our young Haluk's grandfather.

'This much we know. The rest – we can only guess. We can see, though, how the money has flowed – through subterfuge and betrayal, confabulations and acts of revenge, from generation to generation, to make us who we are.'

And then a great silence fell over the room, to submerge and subsume us. My eyes stung, my chest ached. I held in my breath, as if I were swimming underwater.

'Enough for tonight,' said Kemal the doctor. He checked his watch. 'I fear I must absent myself now. I have a patient. He is waiting to speak. You will all have questions, I'm sure. May I ask you to sleep with them? We can meet again tomorrow.'

He rose. He left. No one else moved. No one else spoke. Perhaps it was because we were all doing the same thing: thinking in slow motion, not about the crime but about all the other mysteries it might explain. Or at the very least, illuminate. I would like to say that it tore me up inside, to hear that two of my forebears had conspired to murder a third, but in fact, it was the opposite. As the doctor had predicted, the ugly tale had brought me peace.

I let my head fall back onto Tallis' shoulder. Closed my eyes and let my thoughts whirl, as Anais and her mother gathered up the teapots and the coffee cups, while making it clear – though none of us had offered – that they needed no help.

They closed the sliding doors behind them. I opened my eyes to watch them dance around the sink, the dishwasher, and each other. I imagine that you girls might find this puzzling, after what we had all just heard, but I found it reassuring, to see them so secure in their intimacy, and so light-hearted.

With a great and heaving sigh, my father rose from his recliner. Rubbing his sore hip, he limped and groaned his way across the room. Standing above me, he placed his hand on my head.

'Daughter,' he said. 'There is something I must tell you.'
I looked up. He looked down.

'It is about my father, the great Pasha,' he continued. 'I have always hated him. And now, dear daughter, we both can know why.'

Turning to face the window, as if the tree branches beyond it were the stalls of a theatre, he began to declaim:

'I should never have let you meet him!'

'Once again, I have failed!'

'But never fear. We can still expose him!'

'Revenge will be ours, dear daughter. Revenge will be ours!'

With that, he made his limping, groaning exit.

He was only just out of earshot when the giggling began. First Haluk, then Suna. Then Sinan. Then Tallis. Then me.

Haluk stood up to stretch. Suna jumped up, to massage his shoulders, but he brushed her hands away.

In a huff, she went over to join Sinan, who was lying on his back now, legs churning in the air.

'Why are you doing this, you silly boy?' she asked.

'I'm in training.'

'For what? The Tour de France?'

'Let our enemies assume this. While we hatch our dastardly plots.'

'Oh, yes,' she said. 'For ASALA.' With a great peal of laughter, she added, 'How could I forget!'

Haluk bounded across the room to grab Sinan by the legs. 'Stop, assassin! Before I take you by the balls!'

Now I laughed, too. But Tallis was still frowning, and bent over in thought. 'There's more to this story,' he said. 'And my question is this. Where was my grandfather when all this was going on? Old Aubrey was in deep with all three of them. Achille, Artin, and Adnan Pasha, too. He played cards with them every night. He was an Aleph, for God's sake! Where was he, while all this was going on?'

'Aha,' said Sinan. 'Oho. The Case of the Missing Aleph.'

'No, no,' said Suna. 'The Case of the American Friend.'

It went on like this. As if we were reminiscing about films. Which might seem strange. But for us, at the time, it felt like coming back to life again. Little by little, we were thawing.

Which may explain why I go back to that night and that room so often in my thoughts and daydreams. To the dimmed lights, and the deep sofas, and the leaves of the tree outside brushing against the window and the night.

It would be not until the next day that Kemal the doctor offered us the lofty words that would guide us, for better and for worse, through the decades to come – that there was honour in acknowledging the crimes of the past – that the truth would release us from the paralysing, terrorising conspiracy of silence that had crippled and stunted us for too long – that a better world was possible, once the liars and the thieves had been held to account. Fine thoughts, but I didn't need them. I was already a believer. I'd become a believer the night before, in that cosy, dimly lit sitting room, as we helped each other thaw.

So there you have it. This is where it all began: the dream. The dangerous illusion. My blue peninsula, if you will.

From that moment on – and no matter where I was, or what I thought I was doing – it was always there, before me. Shimmering with promises. Pulling me forward, even as it slipped beyond my reach.

## Risk

I did manage to make the necessary arrangements to return to Paris later that summer. And I stayed for the better part of a year, reading my way through Karine the Great's archives, and by way of thanks, giving them some order.

Then, on the day of his inauguration, President Carter issued his amnesty, thus allowing Tallis to return to the US to complete his studies. I went back with him, but because my guardians were heading into a steeper decline by then, I did not return to my own studies for another two years. And it wasn't until 1986 that I got to the end of them. I was lucky, though. My thesis on the Levantines in the age of Suleyman the Magnificent was picked up by a good publisher.

I doubt that would ever have happened, had Suna and I not kept up our lively back and forth over the intervening decade. She was a proper sociologist by now, and the questions she left in the margins of the drafts I sent her had been merciless. But they'd kept me awake, and forced me to better articulate the question at the heart of the enterprise: how had these ancestors of mine maintained their allegiance to France, their mother country, while serving the commercial interests of a foreign empire?

I was working on the proofs, that summer before you two were born. We were in Lugano, as usual, but the weather had been tricky, and that afternoon we had retreated to the sitting room that – though spacious – seemed cramped and stuffy after the terrace.

I was at one end of the long table, with my proofs. Tallis and Sinan were at the other end, engrossed in a game of Risk that was into its third day. My grandmother was next to me with her sketchpad, and it was not clear to me if she was attempting an abstract expression of her mood, or if she was using the clouds looming over the lake as her subject – if the inky whirlpool beneath those possible clouds could be my Uncle Teddy, taking his speedboat in ever tighter circles, and if the black log on the bottom right of each image might be William Wakefield, who had been standing at the edge of the terrace, watching and smoking, smoking and watching, since lunchtime.

My mother wafted through the room in a silken robe. She had her hair pinned up, presumably to save it from her lime-green face mask. 'Where is that boy?' she said. I pointed out to the lake.

'Honestly!' she said, as if she were truly exasperated. And I wondered if anyone else ever caught it, that undercoating of delight. I'd never known anyone so grateful to be married into money. I wondered if she pinched herself, every time she woke up.

She bounded prettily across the terrace to wave at her husband-in-name-only, as she liked to call him. 'Teddy! Teddy! The masseuse is here, and she can't wait forever!'

Teddy did his usual, accelerating towards the shore as if intending to crash into it. One day he would. But on this particular afternoon, he executed his party trick with finesse.

William Wakefield followed the couple-in-name-only inside. Chuckling, he watched them prance up the stairs. He ambled over to the buffet, poured himself a bourbon. 'It's almost that time, guys. Anyone else up for an early start?'

'No thanks,' said Tallis. He didn't like our man for all seasons more than the rest of us, but he couldn't shake off his manners.

'Hümeyra?'

My grandmother looked at him blankly, as if trying to read his lips.

'She really is stone deaf now, isn't she?'

She wasn't. She was just pretending, while the rest of us played along.

As our man for all seasons made himself comfortable in his favourite armchair, he studied her with a blank and amused sort of interest, as if to let her know that he wasn't fooled or even offended – that if this was the game she wanted to play, then he was happy to play it, too.

I returned to my proofs.

'I hope you don't mind,' he said. 'But I took a look at those last night, after you went up to bed. And Dora, I'm impressed. Truly and deeply, as my dear old dad used to say. You're the real thing.'

'Glad to hear it,' I said.

'You sound annoyed.'

'Well, it would have been nice if you'd asked for my permission first.'

'Fair enough,' he said. 'Now let's see if I can make it up to you.'

'By saying sorry?'

'I can do better than that.'

He took out a cigarette, fumbled in his pocket for his lighter.

'I'm pregnant, by the way.' I said. 'Would you mind taking that outside?'

'I'd rather forgo the pleasure entirely,' he said. He put the unlit cigarette away.

'So anyway. I wanted to reassure you on a few points, while no one can hear us. First but not least – our dear Delphine.'

'You can't hire my mother back, if that's what you were going to ask.'

'God no. Those days are over. But I do still have her back, you know. We're still friends. She confides in me. And when I can, I clear things up for her. So for instance. She's been worried about you. She thinks there's a danger you might give it all up – your career, I mean – to bury yourself in motherhood.'

Through the corner of my eye, I could see Tallis rolling his eyes. 'As if,' he mumbled.

'I heard you,' said William.

'Good, so you heard me,' said Tallis.

'So we're even,' said William. 'Now back to your game.'

'And you to yours,' said Tallis.

I could tell, from William's grin, that he was enjoying this.

'So, as I was saying. And to get to the crux of the matter. Your mother's worried what kind of Ottomanist you can hope to be, if you're barred from the archives. The ones in Turkey, I mean.'

'Am I barred from them? Am I?'

'Well, not in any official capacity,' said William. 'As far as I know.'

'False modesty doesn't become you,' I said.

'And neither does it become *you*.'

Taking out another cigarette, he lifted it, unlit, to his lips. 'In answer to your question. We've kept you out of Turkey, your mother and I, for some time now. And with good reason. But we think now that the statute of limitations has been reached.'

'By which you mean?'

'İsmet has other fish to fry these days. He's gone over to the private sector, did you know that?'

'I did not.'

'He's come into some money.'

'Oh really? And how did that happen?'

'Don't ask.'

'I wouldn't dream of it.'

'Good to hear,' said William. 'So now, back to the archives. When you're ready – not right away, of course. The babes must come first. But when you decide what you're going to do next – professionally, that is – do bear in mind that you can pretty much have carte blanche in terms of those archives.'

'You can pull some strings for me, in other words, and get me in faster.'

'Well, I don't have to tell you, do I? You'll know from the grapevine. It's not always easy to get into those Ottoman archives. Especially if, you know...' He glanced over in my grandmother's direction.

'What, I'd be a liability? On account of my grandmother being Armenian?'

'Well, not a liability. But Dora. I don't need to tell you. There's a sensitivity. Not that you would want to rock the boat...'

I angled my pen at him. 'What makes you so sure of that?'

'Let's put it like this. You do have this lovely villa here. And every summer for some years now, your mother has been able to bring you all together. But one of these years, it won't be quite so easy. Your grandmother's in her eighties now. You say she's stone deaf, but the way she's been acting, there may be some dementia at play as well. As you cannot have failed to notice, she seems to have lost the power of speech. And just look at what she's been doing in the sketchbook. I know that one man's scribble is another man's work of art. But honestly, just look.'

I bent down over my proofs, so as not to oblige him.

'Fair enough,' he said. 'Loyalty is loyalty. But when you next go into the kitchen, take a look at that gift-wrapped monstrosity she's left on the sideboard. A three-year old could have done a better job of it. But she was at it all morning.'

'What's it to you, how my grandmother chooses to spend her time?'

'All I'm trying to say is that you can't count on these Lugano summers continuing. According to your mother, your grandmother's been falling a lot lately. And struggling with the stairs. If your mother had her way, she'd move her out here to live all year round. But your grandmother, as you know – she's an obstinate woman. She doesn't like to be out of that neighbourhood of hers. Not for more than a few weeks, at most. And so we are one bad fall away from it being too late. When that moment arrives, Dora, you'll want to be sure you can go in and out of Turkey without impediment.'

'So let me get this clear,' I said. 'You're telling me that I'm fine to go in and out of Turkey, and in and out of the archives, so long as I never write about the Armenians.'

'That's about it,' said William.

'Well, that's wonderful to hear,' I said. 'You must say that to all the scholars, I imagine.'

'Strange as it may seem,' he said. 'I don't have to.'

'Why not?'

'They know where the red lines are. They know that if they cross them, they'll never get a grant, let alone a chair.'

'Why – because all the grants and chairs for Ottoman studies in the English-speaking world are funded by the Turkish government?'

'Yes, and why wouldn't they be? Turkey has its international reputation to consider. Why would it want to fund projects that might undermine its official history?'

'So then tell me,' I said. 'Tell me it never happened.'

'What – the genocide? Of course it happened.'

'So why are you so fine about letting our Turkish friends deny it?'

'Because they're our friends,' he said. 'And friends need to look after friends. Especially now, with trouble brewing in the region. We're in for one hell of a scramble, Dora, you mark my words. We can't afford to let Turkey go over to the other side, just because you and a handful of other scholars with agendas want to talk about something that was over seventy-five years ago.'

'I can't believe I'm hearing this,' I said.

And he said, 'I can't believe I have to spell it out.'

It went on. He had other warnings to issue on my mother's behalf. She wanted me to know she knew I'd been visiting Karine the Great in Paris, that she had given me full access to her papers. He would, of course, be happy to confirm to anyone expressing a doubt on the matter that in my work so far, I'd not so much as mentioned the old empire's Armenians.

'But the fact remains that the great lady mentioned you in her will.'

'By which you mean to say?'

'That no money comes without strings attached. She's an unreliable witness, Dora.'

'I hope you don't mind my saying,' I said, 'that you didn't need to tell me that.'

He did not seem to know that Karine the Great had left me just one small gift, with instructions to pass it back to its true owner. But I was not about to tell him now.

At last, he went outside for his cigarette. The moment he was out of view, my grandmother rose from the table, so abruptly that the chair fell back onto the floor. Sinan jumped up, to guide her into the kitchen, and I followed.

Tallis went bolting outside, as if on cue. From the kitchen door I watched him bound across the terrace, to join our man for all seasons, and shepherd him away.

'All done,' said Sinan, bolting the door. 'It may rain, of course. He may decide to come in early. But Tallis is going to try and keep him outside for at least twenty minutes.

239

Sit down, Dora. We have something to show you.'

He went over to the kitchen sideboard, to retrieve the gaily wrapped package that was as high and layered as a wedding cake.

'It's for you. From your grandmother,' Sinan said. 'Think of it as a very late birthday present.'

I went over to thank and embrace her, but my grandmother waved me away, before burying her head in her arms.

'Just open it,' said Sinan. 'We don't have much time.'

I unwrapped the first layer, and then second. Opened a box, to find another inside it, and another. At long last I was left with a deep and narrow box the length my hand. Inside it was Karine's small gift, which I had passed on to my grandmother, as instructed. It had now been fashioned into the strangest necklace I shall ever see. Though it was not, strictly speaking, a necklace, because it had no clasp. Some of the gems were precious, some were not. Some were cut and some were rough. Some had had holes drilled through them. Others were set in gold, or silver or brass.

'You recognise them?' asked Sinan.

'Of course!' I said. 'It's just...'

Lost for words, I held it up to the light, the better to see each gem. When I draped it around my neck, my grandmother came to life again, to help me try various solutions. First tying it like a scarf around my neck, then tying it around my head like a bandana. Draping it over my shoulder. Wrapping it around one arm, and then the other, and then both. The more she tried to find the perfect solution, the more her eyes watered.

'She's not just pretending, you know,' Sinan said. 'She really, really cannot speak right now. She's gone back in time, you see. Back to then.'

'It happens a lot these days,' Sinan continued. 'So she wanted me to be the one to tell you.'

My grandmother leaned across the table to take my hands in hers. She looked at me beseechingly.

'She can hear perfectly, of course. You can be sure, for example, that she heard every word William Wakefield just said.'

'But we were speaking in English,' I said.

'Just because you speak to your grandmother in French, doesn't mean she ever forgot her English!'

My grandmother squeezed my hands. Then she looked up at Sinan and nodded.

'Are you sure?' he said. 'You could try your voice and see.' She gave him a helpless shrug.

'Okay then,' said Sinan. 'So this is what your grandmother wants you to know. You should use your voice, she says. You should go out there and make as much trouble as you can. Don't listen to that spook out there, and don't listen to your mother either. You should try to understand her fear, of course. But you shouldn't let it stop you. Just tell the truth, Dora. The truth as you see it. If you promise to do that, your grandmother can die in peace.'

# THE SIXTH NOTEBOOK

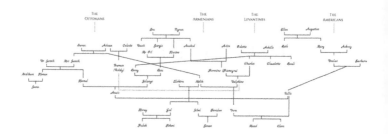

The truth as I saw it, once I had visited my antecedents' easels, desks, and windowsills, and pored over their every letter and document, imagining myself into their thoughts

## 1

It begins as it will end, with an impossible promise:

**I, Aubrey Hayes, dedicated patron of the Cercle d'Orient, shall remain forever in service to the Alephs and their great cause.**

'May I ask a few questions?' asks Aubrey after he has signed it.

'On one condition.' says the Pasha.

He winks at Achille, who with grave demeanor clears his throat. 'You must prove to us your loyalty.'

'Didn't I already do that?'

'I fear not,' says Artin. 'There is more, dear boy. Much more.'

Aubrey glances nervously around him. For a hush has descended over the entire club. Behind every palm and wreath of smoke he imagines a gentleman smirking, a waiter straining to hear.

'Our poor friend is trembling,' says the Pasha. 'We are perhaps being too harsh.' He beckons for the waiter, who needs no further instruction to come forth with the champagne.

'It being your first day in our service,' says the Pasha as he lifts his glass, 'we can afford to be lenient. You may proceed with your questions.'

'Gee,' says Aubrey. 'Thanks. So really...when it comes down to it...it all boils down to two things.'

'Things?' asks Adnan Pasha, in an ominously enquiring whisper.

'Things?' asks Achille, in a whisper laced with outrage.

'Things!' cries Artin with some petulance. 'Again, he speaks of things.'

'I'm sorry. So sorry!' cries Aubrey. 'What I meant was I had two main questions. The first one, the really big one, is about your cause.'

'*Our* cause,' growls Achille.

'Have you forgotten already,' cries Artin, 'that you are now one of us?'

'So what is it, then? Our cause.'

The three older men exchange solemn glances.

'Our cause,' says the Pasha, 'is our mutual preservation.'

'One for all,' says Achille, 'and all for one.'

'When one of us falls,' adds Artin, 'we others jump to the rescue.'

A noise from the foyer wipes the smile from his face.

He falls back into his chair as Achille and the Pasha jump from theirs.

A crash. A scuffle, followed by a furious female cry. 'How dare you stand in my way? Do you not know who I am?'

On hearing the voice, Artin slides from his chair to take refuge behind a nearby palm.

Aubrey turns around to see two waiters struggling to restrain a finely dressed lady. She bats them away with her parasol. But now the maitre d' is scurrying towards her, full of apologies. It is with immense regret that he must inform her that the smoking room is for gentlemen only.

But still this lady stays, casting her gaze across the room, over which a hush has now well and truly fallen.

'Hah!' she cries when she catches sight of the Pasha. 'So I've come to the right place!'

"Madame,' says the maitre d'. 'I beg of you...'

Madame ignores him. Waving her parasol at the Pasha, she cries, 'Where is he?'

The Pasha does not respond. It is as if he has not even heard her.

The lady turns to Achille. 'And you!' she cries. 'The great magnate. Have you no shame?'

Achille responds with a bow. 'Madame,' he says. 'How may I be of assistance?'

'Assistance,' she says, with a bark of a laugh. 'Yes, you certainly may. You may tell my worthless brother-in-law that I know exactly – but *exactly* – what he has done and is further conspiring. What's more,' she cries, pulling from her portmanteau a bundle of documents, 'I have the proof!'

With that, she turns on her heels and departs.

When Artin has returned to his chair and the Pasha has restored order with another bottle of champagne, Aubrey looks at each of his new gambling friends in turn and says, 'That was a show for my benefit, I'm guessing.'

And oh, the laughter! Oh, such pinching of cheeks and patting of backs! Such a sweet boy! they murmur. So trusting. So naïve.

'Oh, how lucky we are,' cries the Pasha, 'to have our own American Aleph.'

'That's my other question,' says Aubrey. 'Why are we called Alephs?'

'That, my dear boy, is a puzzle for you to solve.'

'A clue would be good,' he says, somewhat churlishly.

'You might perhaps begin,' says Adnan Pasha, 'by considering our names.'

## 2

The lady, meanwhile, steps out onto the street, using her parasol to clear a way for herself through the cabs, the horses, the trolleys, the crowds. This Eastern commotion is always such a shock, Karine thinks, after Lisbon and Paris. Lugano and Rome. Were she a dove or even a swan, she could reach her destination within minutes. Instead she is faced with this endless cascade of disrespect, which chimes only too well with the fury in her heart.

Until at last she steps inside the marble foyer that is still, in 1910, of an elegance that no other building on the Grand Rue de Pera can, in her opinion, ever hope to match.

## 3

In the family they call it the house that Tigran built. Though it is hardly a house. It is, in Karine's view, better described as an edifice. And neither did her father build it. He had a famous Italian architect build it *for* him in the first year of the new century amid the quarter's finest churches and embassies, to mark his ascent from Anatolian silversmith to fabled purveyor of jewels to the finest families of Constantinople, and in so doing, to launch his children into their moneyed world.

By 1910 they are well on their way. His eldest, a pharmacist, occupies the shop to the left of the edifice's ornate entrance. His second son, a photographer, occupies the shop to its right. On the mezzanine are the private viewing rooms for Tigran's most valued customers – those for whom a visit across the Golden Horn to his shop in the Bedesten would be inconvenient, dangerous or indiscreet. A small apartment on the same level is all that he needs now that his wife has died. Its windows are high on the wall and narrow, by design: as a survivor of not one but two massacres, he sleeps best in the penumbra. But the four floors above him are palaces of light.

He has given the lower floors to his sons. The penthouse he has assigned to Karine, his elder daughter, who, having married into oil, requires only a suitable base from which to entertain and impress whenever she and her husband pass through the city on important business.

Such a view it commands! But Anahid, his youngest, has a view almost as fine, with almost twice the space. On one side of the third- floor landing is the apartment she will share with the up-and-coming banker Tigran has chosen as her husband. On the other side, the studio where she will erase from her mind all worldly concerns, to commune with the beauties only she can see.

That, at least, was the plan. But as is the way of all things in this city of upheaval and intrigue, it has by September 1910 been rent asunder.

There is Tigran's health failing, his memory departing.

And only last month, while his mind was elsewhere – lost to his aches, and so not paying the necessary people at the necessary time – there was another eruption of Muslim fury and antipathy, resulting in the smashing of both his sons' fine storefronts.

And now, as he casts his weary eyes over the documents that Karine has so rudely brought to his attention, there is the shattering disappointment of Artin, the no longer up-and-coming banker that he must certainly now regret having chosen for his Anahid.

If this cretin still has a desk at the Ottoman Bank, Karine informs him, it is thanks only to the powerful friends he has made for himself while gambling, by day at the Bourse and by night at the Cercle d'Orient. If he still has a shirt on his back, it is thanks to the gems that he has purloined from his own wife to pay off his debts.

How could Anahid have allowed such a thing?

Tigran wants to know.

But he doesn't want to hear what his only worldly child has to say to this.

'Father,' she says. Do you see your favourite daughter when you look at her? Or do you see only your fondest dream? Did you never notice how her health has never rallied – not since the birth of little Hermine? Have you not seen how each time when she coughs, she leaves on her handkerchief a blooming rose of blood?'

'It cannot be,' says Tigran.

'It is,' Karine replies.

'Her husband would notice this at least,' Tigran counters.

'Her husband most certainly has,' says Karine in her steeliest voice. 'He has, since my last visit, moved her over to the studio. He has hired a governess. He has banned poor Anahid from seeing her own daughter.'

'Why am I only hearing of this now?' Tigran asks.

'You are not only hearing of this now,' Karine replies.

She raises her arm. 'Soran! Come here!'

The long-lashed Kurdish boy who serves as Tigran's ears and eyes now steps forward.

'So Soran,' says Karine. 'I trust you have been listening.'

Carefully, Soran indicates the affirmative.

'You have always done your duty day and night,' Karine continues. 'And I have always rewarded you handsomely, have I not?'

'Yes you have, Madame Karine. '

'So tell me. Have you hidden from your master the truth about his favourite daughter?'

'No, Madame Karine, I have not.'

'So I have always thought and assumed,' Karine continues. 'But what can we do. A father's fond heart cannot bear to harbour certain truths. Though there is, perhaps, another truth that he will most certainly wish to hear. Tell him,' she says.

So Soran tells him: since moving his wife across the landing to her studio, Artin has taken to consorting nightly with the Dashnaks.

'He'll be the death of us all,' Karine says. 'He must go.'

But first her sister and her little niece must be delivered to health and safety.

This part of the plan she decides not to share with her father. Which turns out to be unwise. Because young Soran is not just Tigran's eyes and ears and Karine's eyes and ears. He is willing to serve as many gods as will pay him.

So on the night when Karine leads Hermine down the

unlit stairs in stockinged feet, having already settled Anahid and her luggage on the ship that is to take them all to freedom, she finds Artin waiting for her.

Artin, alas, is not alone. With him are the three fine friends he calls the Alephs. That cur of a Pasha. That turncoat of a shipping magnate. That American fool. Behind them, another friend from the tables who is claiming to be high up in the police.

Together they restore Hermine to her rightful owner.

Together they release Karine to her only rightful duty, which is to deliver her sister to a sanatorium she has already arranged for her, not far from the house on the shores of Lugano to which she will no longer be taking her young niece.

Of course, Karine doesn't give up that easily. The penthouse remains hers, after all. The ship has yet to leave port. Twice she returns by stealth, only to be caught both times in the stairwell. The third and last time she arrives openly, securing permission to say her farewells, and in the few minutes she gleans, again by stealth, to speak to Hermine far from other eyes and ears, she passes the girl a large and laden green velvet pouch, and this note in Anahid's hand:

**The seas are wide, and the days are long, but I shall be back, my love, as soon as the mountain air cures me. If you can remember what I have taught you, then you can rest assured: you can always find your way to me, and I to you, no matter what lies between us.**

So there Hermine sits, craning her neck to watch one dark ship after another round Palace Point to vanish into the Sea of Marmara. Never knowing which ship holds her mother. Never giving up. Thinking back instead to those rare fine days when her mother had her nurse wheel her out into this same room, to sit before the easel that Tigran had had made for her specially, so that she could paint sitting down.

Never would this beautiful mother of hers paint what she saw before her. Oblivious to the sunlight pouring in, she would conjure up a view obscured by snow or night, or leaden with rain. Sometimes she would pick up her brush and pass it across her cheek, painting nothing whatsoever as the frigates and the sailboats plied the waters below, hour after hour, until the light had failed and the mosques and palaces on the other side of the Golden Horn faded into a haze of ashen blue.

Sometimes she'd take a few gemstones from her pocket. Some precious. Some not. Some rough. Some sparkling, all angles. Pink and green and yellow, blue or black or all the colours in the rainbow, all at once. She'd line them up along the base of the easel and test Hermine's knowledge.

Which gems calmed nerves and fevers, which ones protected from harm or brought its wearer good luck. Which ones could bring back the spirit of a loved one, no matter how far she wandered.

Which ones, Hermine asks herself, as she rummages ever more frantically through the large and laden green velvet pouch. Which ones?

She has a fine memory, but she has only just turned six.

4

Travelling down the Bosphorus now, to join Mary in her childhood home at Robert College some months later, in

June 1911, as she wanders from room to room, and desk to desk, wondering why her father had never seen fit build her a desk she could call her own.

She can only guess. But that is mainly and primarily because she will never ask. She's grown used to it, anyway. A desk nomad's life has its perks. She can sit in her father's study and bask in the importance that his chair endows on all who dare to occupy it. She can perch at her mother's little secretary desk in the darkest corner of the sitting room and still her thoughts, quell her intemperate desires, and for at least a few moments find genuine satisfaction in writing a thank you note in which all the Is are dotted and the Ts crossed, but not a true word said.

This afternoon, she has chosen her sister Ruth's old desk, though her legs can barely fit beneath it. The view from this window is the best in the house. It looks out over the treetops, and down the hill, to the Bosphorus and its parade of ships that do not know her, and do not judge. She is very much hoping that her sister will not judge her either.

Dearest Ruth,

I have a confession to make. I have stolen one of your shirts. Never fear! I shall replace it. Madame Aliki down the lane has your measurements. Sister, I swear to you. Next time you open up your chest of drawers – though who knows when that might be? – you shall find everything as you think you left it.

Why, you might ask, would I want one of your shirts? I shall tell you, but first let me tell you how dearly you are missed. Oh, how I wish your clinic were here and not in Maine! I have no call to complain. You are doing valuable work. We are all very proud of you, while we do our bit here. Mater and Pater make for fine company, of course they do. As do my fellow teachers at Constantinople College. Nevertheless. I miss Mt Holyoke. I long for the company of my classmates. Dear sister, I hope you won't dismiss me as too terribly frivolous for saying so, but I miss *having fun.*

And now, for my confession's preamble. This morning I went out for a walk. I had a book to return to the library, and Mater, who was off to check on one of her invalids, had asked if I could stop off at Pater's office along the way, to take him his lunch. Yes, that is the tenor of my life these days. Now that the school year has run its course, I am back to being our mother's second pair of hands.

Having performed my good deeds, I was making my way home, when there on a bench at the edge of the college terrace, I spied the College Scoundrel.

Hah! Never fear. No one calls him that except me. And this only to add the tiniest of frissons to my life. His name is Aubrey, and he graduated from Amherst on the same day, practically, as I graduated from my place down the road. His father's on the Robert College board, and that is how he got himself hired here. But the poor boy simply hasn't managed to settle in.

He's made friends downtown, you see. The embassy crowd, and so on. You will remember the Cercle d'Orient, I imagine. Well, according to the stories that Pater brings home, that den of well-heeled gamblers has become our young scoundrel's second home. He's been caught more than once trying to sneak back into the dormitory in the early hours of the morning via the fire escape. And I've lost count of the number of times he's been hauled up in front of the college president, for missing chapel, or being late for class nine times out of ten, or – dear Lord! – taking our Lord's name in vain.

So naturally – good Gibson girl that I am – I was giving him a wide berth. Until this morning when I could not fail to see the silly boy hunched over himself on that bench at the edge of the terrace, wrapped inside a woollen greatcoat.

This I found most odd! We are in the month of June, after all. The sun was shining. The heat sweltering. In spite of myself, I stopped and asked him what on earth he thought he was doing.

'You know who I am, I take it.' Those were his first words.

'How could I not?' I said. 'Your reputation precedes you!'

'Oh dear. I'm sorry to hear that. But it's my own damn fault, of course.'

(I hope you don't mind, dear Ruth, if I quote him exactly.)

He went on to explain that he'd been at the tables again. 'Until only a few minutes ago, in fact.'

'Are you telling me that it what they say is true?' I asked. 'Does this den of iniquity detain its gamblers until dawn?'

'There are always other places to go, if not,' he said. 'Though on mornings like this, I find it most regrettable. I recall being way ahead when we left for that final den. And there, I fear, I lost my shirt.'

He opened his greatcoat, just slightly, so that I could see for myself that he was not speaking metaphorically. He really was missing a shirt.

It had started as a misunderstanding, he told me. Some months earlier, at the end of a monumental losing streak, he'd used the expression, which none of his companions had heard before. They'd found it hysterically funny, these friends of his, and from then on, they'd been stripping him of his shirt whenever he lost everything at the tables, which was much too often, because his fellow Alephs (that was what he called them) were all natives of this city and therefore counted cards.

The shirt he'd just lost was the last in his possession. But now, because he'd come back so late, he was being hauled up before the college president again, and his heavy woollen greatcoat was all he had to wear.

I couldn't let *that* happen, now could I? So I took him with me back to the house. The first shirt I tried was one of Pater's. It may not surprise you to hear that it didn't fit! 'All you need now is a cap to match,' I said. 'Then you'll be ready for a long winter's nap!'

He tried to laugh at my little joke, but the gravity of the situation quelled him. He was standing half dressed in the laundry room of the Dean of Engineering, after all. 'I think,' he said, 'that I had better cut my losses and get going.'

That was when I remembered your shirts.

The one I pulled out for fit him perfectly.

That surprised him, if only momentarily.

'Are you sure your sister isn't a man?' he asked.

That, I am happy to report, earned him a little slap across the face.

'She's better than a man,' I said. 'Far, far better.'

'That wouldn't take much,' he replied. 'But I'm glad to hear it.'

He had another half hour to wait, before the hauling-in happened. So I walked him back up to the terrace, and along the way I told him all about you.

He was very impressed! His exact words being, 'We need more doctors in this world like your sister.'

And then I gave him a little lecture. About counting his blessings, returning to the straight and narrow. He agreed with everything I said. He promised to try, but with such a hangdog look that I had to laugh, and say: 'I should probably be giving myself the same lecture!'

This time he did laugh. Then off he went 'to take whatever I have coming.'

I shall keep you posted!

Your incorrigible sister,

Mary

## 5

By November 1914, in her new marital home in Pera, Mary does have a desk. She insisted on it, but she's no longer sure why. Because it really is the tiniest of tiny apartments. It is conveniently located – at least it is for Aubrey, who has, with a little help of his string-pulling father, left his desk at Robert College for another at the US Embassy.

Turn left at the entrance to their building, and Aubrey can be sitting at that desk in five minutes flat. Turn right, and in five minutes he can be at the Cercle d'Orient. Truth be told, Mary is not so very happy about that part of the bargain. But when she settles down this morning at her monstrous desk, which makes the rest of her sitting room look like a dollhouse, it is not to tell her sister the truth about married life. It is to spin a story good enough to keep her from seeing it.

At the same time, she dare not make it sound as if she is having fun! She made that mistake last time. She is still smarting from her sister's stern words. So she skips lightly over her adventures on the embassy circuit – the whirl of dinners and receptions that have seen them through the two Balkan Wars, and now into this terrible new conflagration that threatens to swallow up the entire world. Instead she talks about all the hard work Aubrey is doing. How there is more of it now than ever, now that the French and British Embassies have closed their doors. The onus is on the Americans to look out for their stranded nationals, not to mention their churches and schools. At the same time, Mary writes, they must take care not to let the mask slip: 'So long as America remains neutral, our doors must remain open to the Germans. Not to mention the Ottomans. Who are, after all, our hosts.'

'You ask me about the Alephs,' she writes. 'I was surprised to read that I'd not mentioned them all year!'

In fact, she'd not mentioned them all year on purpose. Knowing what Ruth thought of gambling, and wanting her to see the good in Aubrey, and not only the bad, she'd edited the Alephs out of her accounts. But now, at last, she has something worthy to report. For Aubrey's Alephs have shown themselves to be very useful of late. Very useful, indeed.

In times of war, it can be helpful, after all, to know one man in shipping, another in banking, and a third in the War Office. As for Aubrey, well, what can I say? As the spokesman for a civilised and humane neutral power, he has much to offer his friends in return. This thanks in no small measure to the Cercle d'Orient.

Now I know your views on this establishment – so let me say that our new Ambassador is himself a habitué. And I dare say Aubrey has come to know him rather well, thanks to this connection! He has called upon Aubrey many times now, having seen how far his connections in this city reach these days, thanks to his Alephs.

In a manner of speaking, they are now my Alephs, too.

No, I have not taken up gambling! But it is thanks to the Alephs that I now spend my every afternoon in a soup kitchen.

And now, at last, Mary can herself go. Does it matter if she exaggerates here and there? They are not all starving, these poor souls who line up in their dozens, not thousands, outside their little storefront every afternoon, and she does a mere three days a week in the place, and not seven. But it is a good thing she's doing in this soup kitchen, and it was, in fact, an Aleph who made it possible: Madame Odette, the proprietress of said soup kitchen, being none other than the wife of the fabled shipping Aleph, Monsieur Achille. And it does not end there. For it is thanks to the generosity of the banking Aleph, Monsieur Artin, that his daughter's governess Celeste can also lend a helping hand at said soup kitchen on Monday afternoons.

For that is the day when we switch roles, as it were.
Which brings me to my second line of work. For on Monday afternoons I present myself at Monsieur Artin's door, to become his daughter's English tutor! She is a sweet little thing, our Hermine. A naughty little thing, too! Though that may explain why we get along so well. I see myself in her. She is making good progress, thanks in no little measure to the games I invent for us. We are writing an adventure together. We imagine it *a deux*, and I write it out when I get home, while she does the illustrations.

And that is not all. I've been such a success with this child that my fame has travelled, and now I am *also* playing English tutor to the Aleph Pasha's sons.

You'll never guess who their mother is. Well, I'm sure you never met her, but you'll remember her house. Her summer villa, I mean. It's that dear little place below the Robert College terrace – white, with a turret, inside a formal garden.

She's promised to invite me there, come summer. But for

now, we are meeting in her dusty, draughty mansion on the edge of Schischli.

And not only for English lessons! Here I shall ask you to imagine a drum roll. For your frivolous sister has now added yet another string to her bow. She is no longer just the angel of a soup kitchen. No longer just the queen of the blackboard. For there is more to life than feeding the needy and correcting grammar. I am now the translator of a poet!

The poet in question is the Aleph Pasha's wife. His estranged wife. Now you'll recall that I never was much good at reading Ottoman, but I can understand her poems when she reads them to me, and they are very lovely indeed. If also desperately sad: they are all about the cruelties visited upon her by her husband. And the loves that will forever be beyond her reach.

You may remember her from Constantinople College. Her name is Nuran, and she was in your class, but not for very long, because she when she was only fourteen her father married her off to the Aleph Pasha.

She was already writing at that early date, and she never stopped! I would so like to translate her into English. But do I dare, dear sister? Could I ever be worthy of this task? In the meantime, I shall confine myself to a lesser, but surely more important, role: for my poet has undertaken to translate Emily Dickinson into Ottoman, and I am helping her, explaining, as best I can, the words and phrases she finds puzzling. Though more often than not, these words and phrases puzzle me even more.

Slowly but surely, we are finding our way. And last Thursday, I am proud to say, we presented our first efforts at her *salon*. It was quite an occasion! Most of the poets in attendance were elderly gentlemen or officers passing through the city, so we made something of a splash, Nuran and I.

There was only one other woman in attendance, and you'll never guess who she was. Do you remember that terrifying creature named Karine? She, too, was in your class, I recall. I'm not sure what you called her there, but we younger girls called her the Tornado. Only behind her back, of course!

And isn't it always the way? She had no memory of the little pipsqueak I was in those days. She remembered you, though. Would you like to know why? You scared her. Ha ha ho ho. Oh yes, you did.

So of course, I bragged about you. I even brought along pictures of your clinic when she and I met at the Pera Palace a few days later. Why, you may well ask, did the Tornado seek me out? Well, you'd never guess. It wasn't to discuss soup kitchens, or grammar, and it certainly wasn't Emily Dickinson! No, she wished to talk to me about my three lovely pupils. She and my poetess have been friends since childhood, you see. She fears for Nuran's two sons and wishes to help them. By which she means – save them from their father.

As for little Hermine – well, it turns out Karine is her aunt!

She's worried about her, too.

Because, you see, little Hermine's poor mother is ailing and failing, and so far away, in her sanatorium in Switzerland. And this has left the little girl at the mercy of her father, the Aleph banker, whom the Tornado does not trust, and a French governess who remains an open question.

Best to stop there, Mary thinks. No need to spell out the promise Karine has extracted from her. Time, she decides, for some evasive action. So she does what she does at the end of every letter:

Have you given any thought, by the way, to the whereabouts of that church? I've mentioned it before and perhaps you did give it some thought, before duty called, or perhaps nothing ever came to mind. So let me summarise: it was the church you and I visited with our mother, the Armenian church where all those people were hiding from the mobs.

This must have been 1895. That was the summer of the massacres, was it not? The streets were empty by the time we got there. But covered with shattered glass. I was only five years old then, so that is all I can recall, except that there was a boy who led us off the street, and into a dark hallway, and then suddenly we were in a courtyard, and then inside a church which was full of people crying. And you and our mother got straight to work, tending to the wounded. While I just sat there, sucking my thumb. Looking around me.

There was so much gold! That's all I remember. I was wondering if you might remember more? It would be typical of you, and of our mother, if you have no recollection whatsoever of this act of mercy, because you've both done so much! But I thought I'd ask, because as far as I can figure out, I must be living around the corner from that church now. I would be so curious to see it again, if only I knew its name.

6

It was fun in the beginning, but by February 1915, it's become tiring. The life of an informer is not all it's cracked up to be! Mary ought to have foreseen this, but Karine is the worst sort of taskmaster. She might be flitting across the seven seas with that oilman of hers – a new port every day, but wherever she alights, she expects results. Mary is to tell Karine everything, everything, no matter how trifling, in the letters she is to send to intriguing addresses the length and breadth of Europe and the Middle East, courtesy of the diplomatic pouch. It is never enough. 'Send me more!' Karine keeps writing. 'It is no longer soup that you fine ladies are serving! Tell me what jewels your friends prefer, what pretensions they favour. Where they go with their husbands, and without them. Remember that this work you do for me is not for our benefit, but for the children.'

And the insults – or does she intend them as gentle jests? 'Oh, how the pure are blind!' she writes. And: 'What kind of water did you drink as a child up at Robert College, to be so naïve? Ah, I have the answer. It was American water.'

Today, though, as Mary sits herself down at her giant desk, she is comforted by the thought that she has two highly dramatic pieces of news to impart to Karine the Terrible:

Our friend Nuran has lost her cook, I fear. And perhaps her housekeeper, too, though she will not say. There are times, dear Karine, when I arrive at the poetess' draughty mansion to see the dust one inch think, and I wonder when the last time might have been when it held the scent of supper cooking. Those boys of hers are getting very thin. But they are too proud to ask for help. The same goes for their mother. I do not know the last time our Nuran saw a doctor, despite this cough of hers, which worsens daily. I am not a bad nurse, I'm proud to say! But I do sometimes wonder if the only nourishment these three see sits in the picnic basket I bring with me.

As for the House of Artin. Karine, I have grave concerns

here as well. When I arrived last Monday at the usual hour, I was confronted with a sea of swarthy men. They were gathered around the table, wreathed in heavy smoke, all talking over each other. Artin seemed startled to see me. And his hurried excuses failed to impress. His guests, he told me, were from the Patriarchate. But these were no churchmen. That much was clear.

We retired to the second apartment for our lesson, but even from here, we could hear their voices. And of course, we could see them, through that window at the side.

I do fear leaving little Hermine at their mercy. She is seeing too much! I have new concerns, too, about the governess. It is not only that Hermine hates her – this we have known for some time. She now claims that Celeste has been spiriting away Hermine's mother's jewellery, piece by piece.

She has therefore entrusted me with the green velvet pouch that was her mother's present to her, before leaving for her sanatorium. Some of the jewels contained therein look precious; most do not. But of course they are all precious to little Hermine. I shall hold them for her, until you find a way to release her from this terrible pair.

To think that I once thought Celeste a friend! And Artin a man we could trust! As for the Pasha! I am simply beyond words that he could have left his two sons and estranged wife to starve. I am grateful to you, dear Karine, for opening my eyes. But now, what to do? What to do?

I await your answer in hope and trepidation.

X

## 7

There is a moment halfway through that dark night in the third week of April 1915 when Artin wonders if he should tell his in-laws the truth. Not the whole truth. That would be his death knell. But he could, very safely, prove to them that Karine is mistaken in her suspicions. Well, in some of them, at least.

If only they would let him speak.

If only his father-in-law and the two bears he calls his sons would stop hovering over him. How do they expect him to pen the confession they require of him, if they insist on blocking the light?

My dearest Anahid,

It is my fondest hope that this missive will find you well.

I further hope that the words that follow will not cause you undue sorrow.

Alas, I have fallen prey to the demon drink, and his cousin, baccarat.

I regret to inform you that I have, to pay my debts, fallen so low as to rob your father's coffers.

*Not so!* Artin mutters to himself. *It was to save our skins that I contrived, with the help of my fellow Alephs, to remove from this perilous city as much of the family wealth as I could safely transfer. I was fully intending to give it all back on the other side! Well, at least most of it. If my plan was foiled, we can blame the British Navy for blocking the Dardanelles, leaving our ship marooned in the Marmara with its bed of jewels, until bereft of food and fuel, it sank. If indeed it did sink. If the captain and his crew did not dock in secret and make away with their booty. We may never know. Our troops have amassed at Gallipoli. Yet again, the war is on our doorstep.*

I cannot begin to imagine, dear Anahid, how my words must grieve you.

Alas, I have more to confess. I regret to inform you that

I have further endangered the family by welcoming revolutionaries to our home.

*But only to spy on these Dashnaks for my dear Pasha! Oh, if only there were a way to reassure you, dear Anahid, without putting myself in further peril!*

In summary, I am writing to you today at the insistence of your father and brothers to confirm that I shall be removing my good self forthwith from the house of Tigran to seek my fortune elsewhere. I am further granting permission to Karine, your blessed sister, to restore our dear daughter Hermine to your side as soon as the winds of war clear a passage. Until that moment, I remain...

A knock on the door.

Who can it be?

The chief of police, as it turns out. A friend from the tables. At last, Artin thinks. It seems his Pasha has kept his word. Though of course, he cannot look to be seeking special favours. It is with some relief that Artin hears his friend from the tables declaring that all the men of the family must now return with him to the station. But he packs a lighter bag than the others. After all, he could be back in the morning. When he finds himself dispatched with his in-laws

266

and upwards of two hundred others to the wilds of Anatolia, he is at first confounded. But then, when he catches the first whiff of revolutionary talk in the rough camp where they have been left to starve: he thinks, of course. My Pasha still needs me. I am, as always, his eyes and ears.

## 8

In April 1916, it is Aubrey's turn to sit at Mary's monstrous desk. In the room behind him the dollhouse furniture is piled high with boxes. For America has entered the war now, and its nationals must leave this city forthwith. The room smells of dust, for it has been five months now, since a woman's hand last touched it.

Your Excellency

It grieves me greatly to be penning what will be my last report. It has been an honour, to work alongside you these past two years. I know I have not always been a credit to our embassy, and I am thankful for the understanding you have shown me, and I am no less grateful for your wise guidance and discretion with regard to the unfortunate events of last winter.

So let me take this opportunity to reiterate: at no point did my wife share with me her childish scheme. How she came to the view that my dear friend Artin was a Dashnak, I cannot say. It could have been a figment of her own overwrought imagination, or it could have been the invention of her partner-in-crime. For my understanding is that there has never been much love lost between Madame Karine and Artin, who is, as you know to your cost, her brother-in-law.

Whatever the truth of the matter, my wife and Madame Karine seemed to have goaded each other on. We cannot know for certain how much Adnan Pasha's good wife was involved in their plans, but we can assume that she too played a role: as you know, Nuran Hanoum and Madame Karine have been friends since early childhood.

How these two (or three) thought they could get away with this mad plot they hatched, I cannot say.

I am only glad that the harbourmaster was able to intervene in time, and in advance of their machinations, to ensure that Hermine and Adnan Pasha's two sons were spared the distress of being removed their homes.

At which point, I must thank you for asking after Mary. I am happy to say that she is safe and sound in Pomfret. Though still grieving, I fear, for the child she lost during the passage home.

Before I go any further, I would like to apologise, again on behalf of my wife, if not also the grand dame herself, for the letters they have been sending you.

They are entirely without justification. No one has done more than Your Excellency to raise the alarm. If the world knows of the plight of the Ottoman Armenians, it is thanks in no small part to Your Excellency's tireless efforts.

As for my own efforts: we shall never know, I fear, if the rumours spread by Madame Karine, and further disseminated by my unsuspecting wife, played a part in turning my dear, lost friend Artin into an object of suspicion.

What I do know, if only from chance remarks, and the snatches of light banter I can recall with any certainty from our evenings together at the tables: Artin did indeed consort with the Dashnaks, but only to serve as our Pasha's eyes and ears.

Was Madame Karine the very person to introduce doubts into the Pasha's mind? It could well have been another. Our

Pasha was never one to confine himself to a single informer. Always best, he said, to have several, so that they could inform on each other.

Hard to believe that a year has passed since the killings began. And still we don't know the fate of the two hundred or more friends and neighbours who were removed from their homes during the swoop that began it all. But not for lack of trying. I have, on many occasions, and perhaps too many occasions, begged our Pasha to seek some news of Artin Bey. I am sure that you are justified in thinking that I could have pressed harder or found a subtler way of gleaning a few more facts, but I regret to say that I have tried my best, only to be met on every occasion with a wall.

You are right to have your suspicions about the Pasha's true motives in all this. Did he spirit Artin Bey away, with all the men in his wife's family, because of what he hoped to gain by removing them from the scene?

It would be easy to assume the worst, seeing as the Pasha has now taken up residence in Artin Bey's apartment, and also bearing in mind that his wife the poetess had been dead for less than a week when he took the governess as his wife.

It was with those fears in mind that I paid him a visit yesterday evening. I was expected, of course. We have been friends for six years now, and I could hardly have left this city without bidding him farewell. And as you may have noticed, he is rarely, if ever, to be found at the Cercle d'Orient these days. This new wife of his has her rules!

I was afforded a warm welcome. And on this occasion, at least, I had no need to press him for answers. Though silent as usual on the subject of our mutual friend, he went out of his way to clear my mind on all my other areas of concern.

First he thanked me for helping to place his sons at Robert College. They have been boarders since September, as you probably know. What you may not know is that my wife is paying their fees from her own funds.

The next thing that he was very keen for me to know was that he had not contrived for his first wife, the poetess, to starve to death in her sons' absence. Though in fact starvation does seem to have been the cause of her death.

He insisted, at length, that he had sent over servants with large quantities of food almost daily. His new wife Celeste confirmed his words.

Finally, he assured me that Artin Bey's daughter, little Hermine, was thriving. That he loved her, as his own daughter. That his plan was to adopt her. This, too, Celeste was at pains to welcome, and confirm.

They brought her in to meet me. I can confirm therefore, that she is in excellent health. Though her relations with her former governess look to be cool, this may well be because the Pasha dotes on the child.

All in all, it was a jolly evening – a welcome respite from the war that has now claimed us, too.

We were joined by another of our old friends, the venerable Ekrem Bey – he of the Greek sonnets. He sends you his warm regards, expressing the wish that all others in attendance repeated – that once this wicked war is over, we can work together to build a world of peace.

You will never guess what they chose as my goodbye present!

9

Meanwhile, just streets away, from her perch on the windowsill in her mother's old bedroom, Hermine watches the empty apartment next door, replaying for her amusement the scenes of the previous evening. She is getting better at this: filling her life's empty spaces with remembered images, which she can alter and enhance at will: The raised glasses, the peals of laughter and the thrown-back heads. The strange man who keeps taking off one shirt to don another. That other strange man who keeps jumping to his feet to recite things. Celeste, whom her fury cannot budge. The Pasha, whom Hermine cannot anger, even when she kicks him in the shins.

She likes it that he likes that. She likes it that he calls her his little monster. But most of all, Hermine likes it that the Pasha has seen off those Dashnaks. No mention of them these days. No mention either, of her father. Where is he? Where is Aunt Karine? Where is Mrs Mary? When will she come back, to take her off to Switzerland? And her mother? Where is she, how is she? How much longer will Hermine have to wait before Aunt Karine and Mrs Mary can return her to her mother's side?

Hermine lowers her head, to stare at her slippers, silently reminding herself of Mrs Mary's promise – I shall be back, as soon as I am able – and Karine's instructions – you must never seem impatient, and yet you must also be prepared to leave in the space of a mere moment.

She shuffles over to the four-poster-bed and pulls out her little suitcase. She snaps it open to inspect the contents: her paints and pencils. A drawing pad, half full. The bracelet with her mother's name on it. Her locket, with her mother's picture. A dozen splendid postcards. A cardigan and a nightgown. An extra pair of shoes that Celeste thinks she lost, and just enough room to fit in the slippers she is wearing, when the mere moment arrives.

271

Content with her inventory, she closes her little suitcase. After returning it to its hiding place, she climbs up onto the fourposter-bed, settles herself amongst the pillows, folds her arms, and waits.

And waits.

While the war rages on, always out of sight but never absent. The Ottomans are vanquished. The Allied forces march in, while far away, the patriots meet in secret to launch the new struggle. Until one day, the Allied soldiers march out of the city again. The patriots march back in, while yet again Hermine sits on her balcony, sketching.

She has given up on waiting. Now that dear, mad Charles has been exiled to the island, she has even, almost, given up on mischief. Under Maître Refique's guidance at the School of Fine Art, she has learned to disengage, step back, and stand very still, giving her full attention to what the eye can see.

### 10

In June 1925, Hermine completes her first year of study. When she leaves the apartment of her birth to join Charles and his mother on their island of exile, she packs just one change of clothing, and enough art supplies for a lifetime.

As she steps off the ferry at Büyükada on that June day in 1925, her first thought, on seeing Charles rear up like a horse, is how to capture that pose on paper. Her tutor, Maître Refique, who has contrived to travel out to the island on the same ferry, is able to drop Hermine's bags and pull her to one side, thus saving her from Charles' forward charge. But he fears the worst. And as the summer progresses, the worst comes to pass.

Whereupon Maître Refique leaves the cool breezes of the island to return to the city, in search of a relation who might help him rescue Hermine from peril.

Only to find that Hermine has no relatives. At least, no relatives who will claim her. As for the Pasha. He has departed yet again for the wilds of Anatolia, to see to his patriotic duty. The French wife he's left behind seems almost pleased to have to inform Maître Refique that while the Pasha did take the trouble to furnish Hermine with a Turkish name, he never formally adopted her. As for letting the little wretch back into her home, the answer is an emphatic no. For she, Celeste, has enough on her plate, now that she is expecting, now that she is forced to fend for herself while her esteemed husband goes from one unsuitable Anatolian posting to the next.

She directs Maître Refique to a Monsieur Achille. Having set out his concerns to him and his son, Maître Refique is stonily informed that there is nothing they can do. 'It is Hermine herself who has engineered her downfall, and with it, our own.'

He calls upon an Armenian colleague, a normally rambunctious fellow who on this occasion meets his enquiries with a studied silence. Only when pressed does he suggest that Maître Refique ask around the churches. 'Generally, they know where to find the families.' But if they do, they are not about to share their thoughts with a Turk, not even a Turk like him, who was born to a Maltese mother and spent the war in with her family in the Maltese capital of Valletta, serving first as a hospital orderly at a British hospital, and later, after the British brought its Ottoman war criminals to trial in that city, as a courtroom artist and interpreter. He, of all men, has no illusions about the evils visited on the empire's

Armenians. But still, in the eyes of these churchmen, he remains a Turk, to whom nothing must be said.

He does not give up.

It is while taking coffee at the Pera Palace on the eve of his return to the island that a friend tells him of a friend having mentioned in passing that Hermine has an aunt who, having married into oil, is now living in Alexandria, or Monaco, or was it Paris.

Within the hour, he has an address. Returning to the Pera Palace, and availing himself of its stationery, he sits down at a desk to pens his letter to Madame Karine.

He begins by describing Hermine the student. When they first met, he writes, she was a primitive, heavy with her lines, and not so much ignorant of perspective as refusing it. But when, 'after no little persuasion', she applied herself to the study of technique, she came to approach this task with a most astonishing devotion. It was, Maître Refique said, as if no world existed for her beyond the easel. At the same time, it was a world hemmed in by horrors. 'Each tree, each rock, each wave and figure she attempted bore an element of the grotesque.' But then there was the sky, and the way she arranged the other elements of her drawings danced against and around it, so that the overall effect of each completed composition was one of 'redemptive, if also rebellious, joy.'

Having met with her current custodians, if that is what we are to call them, I can only surmise that she has, in the past, had a similarly taming and inspiring influence on all whom she chooses to take under her wing. Endowed as she is of a generous and all-accepting spirit, she has sought out the mocked and the wounded, the ostracised and the dispossessed, to create for them a world in which, if only for a time, all are loved, and all are welcomed. It may not please you, Madame Karine, to hear what I am about to say, but I beg you to suspend judgement, if only for a moment: during my recent wanderings through the backstreets of Pera, I have not encountered a single beggar, tavern owner, or lady of the night who does not love her dearly.

They also had kind words to say about the idiot child who was her companion on these nocturnal wanderings. To a man, and to a woman, they described this Charles as her utterly devoted, and besotted, protector. However, I regret to say that this is no longer the case.

Maître Refique goes on to describe the current situation. Sparing no detail. Taking care to give each fear its proper name.

The crux of the matter is that Hermine has no family to protect her. I am sure you do not need me to explain to you, a daughter of our city, what happens here to those who are left, for whatever reason, without a family. This Pasha who took her in, and who arranged for her a birth certificate bearing a Turkish name that she has never, to my knowledge, used – it seems that this Pasha never formally adopted her. He dotes on her – everyone I've met insists on this – and in my humble estimation, he has treated her well enough. He did, after all, encourage her in her studies. But he has also, with the not entirely innocent collusion of his French wife, allowed her to cavort around the least salubrious streets of Pera at all hours of the day and night, like an urchin. This is not what any man of his distinction and reputation would permit of a child he loved as a daughter.

Even so, his presence in the shadows of her life would once have offered her some protection. But now, with the Pasha far away, in whatever corner of Anatolia his duties have assigned him, and with his wife refusing the role of stepmother, Hermine has been left at the mercy of a boy who was born without a brain and a mother who has lost whatever brain she formerly possessed. Though who are we to judge? The war has ravaged us all, each in a different way. In a city such as ours, with its newly restored veneer of peace, it is easy to forget the scars that still remain. The thefts that are left unrecorded. The victims left wafting with the tides.

Our dear Hermine is penniless. Imagine that! Penniless! The granddaughter of a celebrated jeweller! The daughter of a banker! I therefore beg you, as the one member of her family who has escaped the horror and the devastation, to come and save her from perdition.

I understand from the mutual friend who has furnished me with your address that you are currently, in your capacity as a departed Ottoman Armenian, barred by Turkish law from returning to our city. That said, I understand from the same source that your husband, being in oil, may have a way to effect a change of heart in the relevant bureaucracies. In the meantime, I shall do my utmost to watch over your esteemed niece, who is, in spite of all her sufferings, a free and independent-minded spirit, having forged a hard-won unity in her life through the genius of her art.

Having offered his most distinguished salutations, the so-called Maître signs the letter with his full official title, reaching the post office just minutes before it closes.

## 11

On that same afternoon, over on the next hill, Dr Ruth is sitting in an office that is bare except for a battered desk and a chair that won't sit level, and a clock that moves too fast, and far too noisily.

Spread out before her is a letter from her sister in Pomfret.

It does not contain much news, and how could it have done. Nothing ever happens in Pomfret. Ruth would go so far as to say that is the point of Pomfret.

How very far away it seems to her. For in August 1925 Ruth is just back from five years with Near East Relief, a tour of duty that has taken her from Marash to Sivas, Aleppo to Alexandropol, and Smyrna to Lesbos, Chios, and Macronissi, through sieges, blizzards, epidemics, pitched battles and midnight evacuations. And no time in between to rest. After each miraculous escape, she has had to grapple with new versions of the impossible: vast orphanages full of starving and diseased children; packed, wrecked hospitals lacking even the most basic supplies; blazing cities, and hill after hill of refugees with not a tent in sight.

And now she is back in the city she still thinks of as home: the city of her birth, the Constantinople of her childhood. No rest for her here, either. No time, even, for a single day of peace with her parents on the campus of Robert College. For six months now, she has been on perpetual call, working, or rather, struggling, to save a hospital that was, during the occupation years, an entirely Christian establishment. Serving not just as its director, but all too often, as on this very morning, seeing to the emergencies that come through the door at times when she is the only doctor in the building with a free pair of hands.

Most of the other doctors left with the Allied forces, taking with them most of the nurses. It has been a struggle to replace them. Despite the need, the urgent need. The scourges felling all that cross their path, regardless of their nationality or religion.

Near East Relief can no longer help her. Its money now flows directly from the pockets of good Americans to the centres of greater Christian need. This despite the fact that the weak and infirm in this still mostly Christian city have needs just as great.

And now –

As she passes her eyes once again over her sister's letter, she reminds herself. Mary could not have anticipated, could not have known. But still, it irks her. To be urged, yet again, to find news of Hermine. Why such urgency? Why the barely concealed impatience?

I hate to be banging yet again on the same drum [Mary writes.] But I made this girl a sacred promise, and she is not answering my letters. I need you to track her down for me. Could you do your little sister this one tiny favour? Never mind about that church you still haven't found for me. That can wait. But Hermine – she was nine when I last saw her. She must almost be a grown woman by now! If you could ask your colleagues at least, I'd be so very grateful. Eternally grateful! I promise.

A better person would have overridden her petty irritation, long enough at least to impart to her sister a gentle and dignified account of their mother's passing.

But it is not to be. The clock is still ticking, and it is time to go and see her brother-in-law, who is back in town for some sort of business. She will be taking along her begging bowl to the meeting. As Ruth prepares to leave her airless office on that hot August afternoon, she rehearses her lines. As she walks down the corridor – which is clean – which is, in actual fact, immaculate – she gathers up more details. The cracks in the ceiling, and the walls, the floor. Her good colleagues, gaunt and rushed. The supply room, almost bare. The patients, four to the room. Only inches between the beds.

But her father, in the room next to the nurse's station, seems happy to have company. Two of his three roommates are former students. The other is not himself a graduate of the Robert College School of Engineering, but he is the son of one. When Ruth walks in, the four are discussing bridges. Or rather, her father is holding forth while the younger men raptly listen. Which warms Ruth's heart as, once again, it breaks. For here father does not yet know that the fever from which he has now recovered has claimed his wife.

She will tell him when he is stronger. When she is sure enough of her voice to keep it from breaking. When they can walk together to the cemetery just down the road, to visit her grave.

Which is next to the graves of their firstborn, Barnaby, who never saw his first birthday, and their youngest, Sarah, who never saw her second. When the time comes, Ruth will not have to explain to Augustus why they could not wait for his recovery before burying his wife. He knows the customs here. He understands why they can't embalm.

All that is for another day. Today, she sits down on her father's bed, takes his hand in hers, and lies. Her mother is still feverish, she says, and still in isolation. But rallying. Definitely rallying. In the meantime, Augustus must concentrate on building up his strength.

With that, she sets off for her appointment on foot. Practicing her smile along the way. The problem Ruth has with Aubrey at this precise moment is not so much the man himself as the company he keeps. To be precise, the US High Commissioner. Admiral Bristol, who after shafting the old empire's Armenians, has gone on to shaft its Greeks. But no one can say a word, for the dead are dead. The departed are departed. All that matters to the Admiral is the new Turkish Republic. And the interests of their own Republic. In deference to which, they all must collude in the Admiral's lies and obfuscations.

She pushes through the crowds as indignantly as if they are treading on her memories. Which, in fact, and whether they realise it or not, they are. Where have they all come from, these fez-less, Homburg hat-wearing men? These veil-less women in their fine spring coats? Where are they now, the desolate rows of homeless waifs? She cannot stop herself from glancing through the windows of what was once their Relief Store. She cannot quite accept that it is now a shoe shop. The Greek milliners across the avenue are still there, still in business, but when she peeks in to wave at the man behind the counter, his smile is tinged with alarm. He doesn't recognise her. He must be a nephew, or a new husband.

Never mind, she tells herself. Never fear. As she passes what was once the Russian and is now the Soviet Embassy, and what is still the church of St Antoine – though for how much longer? – she keeps her eyes on the cobblestones ahead.

It is typical of Aubrey to have chosen to stay at the gaudy Pera Palace. The silly man cannot bear not to be seen. But when he catches sight of her, he seems to lose all sense of himself. He rushes over, knocking into tables in his haste. He throws his arms around her. Steps back to take her hand in his. 'I'm so sorry,' he says. 'So very sorry. Dear Ruth. Dear, dear Ruth. Oh, your poor mother! Such a loss? How is your father holding up? And you?'

For a moment, she longs to unburden herself. But just in time, she pulls herself back. 'How kind of you to ask, Aubrey. But you are not to worry. And neither should my dear sister. She has been such a treasure. Of course she still is. You must tell Mary that Pater is rallying and we at the hospital are fine. Doing our duty, in sorrow and in unison. Needs must.'

'As always,' he says, 'I stand in awe.' Taking her by the arm, he guides her to his table. Here she is greeted by a second gentleman. It is only after he has kissed her hand that Aubrey introduces him. 'This is Melih. The son of my great friend Adnan Pasha.'

Fluttering his eyelashes just slightly as he lowers his gaze, Melih murmurs, 'Though of course, strictly speaking, he is no longer a Pasha.'

Aubrey nods, a bit too vigorously. 'He's going great guns, though. As indeed is his son.'

The waiter is called for. Ruth asks for tea. The men continue with their rakı as they discuss Melih's studies and his future plans. He is training to be a diplomat. It is his turn to serve, he says, in what only Americans would call perfect English. And now, Ruth remembers her sister telling her about this Melih, whom she'd tutored during the war. No wonder he sounds so American!

The new Republic will need strong alliances with the West, Melih is now saying. Intoning. As if he were a gentleman of the world, and not a slip of a thing in his twenties. 'And so I shall venture out into the world,' he now says. 'But meanwhile, there is also the home front. But why am I teaching you to suck eggs?' he laughs. 'You are fully aware of the challenges. Our hospitals, for example! We must not turn away the West!'

Clasping his hands, he beams as if he is about to offer her a gift. To her surprise and consternation, she hears herself phrasing that thought as a question. Whereupon Aubrey lets out a genial, almost carefree laugh. 'In actual fact, he *is* offering you a gift!'

There is a building, he explains. A fine building. Solid and new and built for purpose.

'For what purpose?' Ruth asks. Balking at the sharpness in her voice, and also the gormlessness.

'It is a hospital,' says Melih.

'Oh goodness,' Ruth says.

'A hospital for our people,' Melih goes on to say. 'A hospital we are hoping you will agree to direct.'

'But my father...' she says.

'Your father,' says Melih. 'Of course we must consider his preferences. And of course you must talk to him. When the time is right, when his health demands, you must take him home with you, to America. But for now... Well, let's see what he will say. He has done so much for our country. He may not wish to leave.'

Here Aubrey interjects to say, 'We can do this, Ruth. We've found the money.'

'You've found money? Goodness! Where?'

'My father is a generous man,' Melih says. 'And also, he is a patriot. He wishes to guide our new Republic to vigour and good health. It is thanks to him that we have sufficient backing. What we do not have, and what we most desperately need, is your wise direction. Not for long, I promise you. Only for a time, while the new generation finds its feet.'

With a slight wringing of hands, he goes on to explain

what she knows full well already. The education of so many fine young people has been sadly, badly interrupted by the war. There is at this moment a deficit of new doctors, and of established doctors under whose auspices they might learn. A deficit also of hospitals in which the latter might pass on their expert knowledge to the former. 'If, for example, I had the ambition of becoming a surgeon...' says Melih. He looks across the opulent room, his eyelashes again fluttering, as another young gentleman approaches.

This one is sad, slow. Hesitant. He does not wish to be here.

This Ruth can see.

'Allow me to introduce my brother Semih,' says Melih. 'He is not yet of your profession, but he soon shall be.'

Ruth offers bright words of interest, which Semih seems not to hear. Except – he does hear them. She can see the comprehension in his eyes. It is just, she decides, that he does not wish to speak. To converse. To be false, like the rest of them.

And so it is Melih, smooth and charming Melih, who apologises on his behalf. 'My brother is a patriot of the highest order,' he says, as he offers Semih a cigarette. When Semih declines it, the smooth Melih explains that while his brother's English is – though not perfect – certainly adequate, he prefers to converse in French. 'Though of course, he would prefer it if all citizens spoke Turkish!'

Semih winces. Melih laughs and pats his shoulder. Semih tries and fails to smile, whereupon Melih smiles for him, before explaining that it is Semih's ambition to become a surgeon.

'He could work alongside you,' Melih says lightly. 'Until the time has come for you to take your father home. By then, I am certain, Semih will be ready to stand at the helm.'

'Will you now?' says Ruth. She looks Semih in the eye. And what she finds there is the anguish she shares – the lives not just lost but forgotten, the new order not so much sweeping the old aside, but stamping on it, spitting on it, crushing it into pulp.

Never mind that he is and still might be on the wrong side. Might still hate all that she holds dear. They are both lost in this new world. In this silly and opulent room, with its puffed-up waiters and its puffed-up drunken dealmakers, they are the only two still grieving.

And that is why, when she has gathered her wits, and readied herself to accept this desperately needed gift of unknown provenance, with all its strings attached, she ignores Melih and turns instead to Semih, to thank him in Turkish.

## 12

As she sits in her old bedroom at Robert College in June 1927, hunched over the desk that was always a little small for her, even when she was a child, Ruth is seized by an old longing:

To set down her pen, fly down the stairs, push through the garden gate and race down through the village, so fast that the cobblestones barely touch her toes, and then faster still, until she can fling herself into the Bosphorus, whose blue waters she can only just see from this desk in her old bedroom, peaking through the trees.

She closes her eyes to recall the adventures she once imagined starting there, in the shadow of the great castle. Her head bobbing in the swirling currents, as they hurl her past the palaces, and the yalıs, the ferries and the mosques. Past the new city and the old city into a sea dotted with ships. Past wooded islands, and through the Dardanelles. Into the Aegean, the Mediterranean. Past the Rock of Gibraltar, and into the Atlantic.

The dream fades there, as her thoughts pull her back. Across the same seas, and through the same narrow straits. Over the past six years, she has seen their waters darkened and their shores stained red by war, but she cannot, must not, allow these memories to overtake her. Duty calls, even on this, her first mandated day of rest since coming home.

She picks up her pen.

Dearest Mary,

Though I know you to be the most understanding of sisters, I still feel I must apologise for my long silence. In the many months since my last letter, you have indulged me with almost weekly bulletins, each one bursting with energy and joy. I cannot begin to tell you how much it has cheered me, to know that little Lachlan continues to thrive. It will have taken considerable strength of character for you to decide to stay put in Pomfret, rather than follow Aubrey to Washington – though I never doubted that you would rise to the occasion. Nevertheless it is comforting to know that you have found a welcoming community through your church.

I am writing to you from what I am learning, with some difficulty, to call our father's house. For it is here, especially here, that my mind can trick me into thinking our dear mother is still with us. Every chair, every vase, is where she left it. And Pater still speaks of her as if she is in the next room.

He and I have not yet spoken of the future. But I shall be staying the weekend, and if the right moment presents itself, I shall broach the subject. If he is indeed open to the idea of joining you in Pomfret, I promise to write to you at once to let you know.

There will, I am glad to say, be other weekends, if he needs more time to settle his thoughts. Young Semih – the Pasha's son, whom I believed you once tutored – is insisting on it. And what a fine fellow he is. Though I still have much to teach him, he has shown himself to be a most diligent assistant, attentive not just to the needs of our patients but to those of the hospital itself. I am in no doubt that he will make a fine director in due course.

If our move to the new premises was largely painless, it was thanks to him. And he has already made good use of his family connections, not to mention their deep pockets, to bring in doctors – European and American as well as Turkish – of the calibre we require. We are drawing upon the same resources to lay the foundations of the nursing school that will, with a bit of luck, open its doors this fall.

All this is a far cry from the hospital as I first knew it, little more than a year ago. And here I must bare my heavy heart and come out with it: My dear sister, I have failed you. All I can say in my defence is that I did not come to understand how badly I failed you until just a few weeks back.

I'd been in the operating room that morning. It must have been eleven by the time I reached my office, there to find two rather dour looking ladies and a child I took to be ten or eleven months, a year at most. A rather lovely creature with golden curls and a laugh to match, who after scuttling across the room on her derriere, set about pulling herself up on a chair.

No apologies from the dour ladies for entering my office without invitation, or taking up my valuable time. Instead they went straight to the point: they were concerned for the health of the child. They did not ask me to examine her so much as command me to do so. When I asked, somewhat lightly, Why now? Why here? Why me? they exchanged furtive glances, before informing me that I had been the one who'd delivered the lovely little creature. By Caesarean, no less.

Had I? I was still struggling to remember when at long last they thanked me. Not for delivering the baby, but for having been good enough to 'observe discretion' in the aftermath. They went on to say that they hoped they could continue to trust me.

Still mystified, still racking my brain, I took the child into an examination room, where I quickly established that the little sprite was in the best of health. Returning her to the ladies, I ventured to ask if they had any particular causes for concern. Whereupon one of them took out an embroidered handkerchief to daub her eyes, while the other described what she termed 'the tragedy of the child's parentage.' Or rather, the tragedy of the child's father, one of life's innocents -- their brother – who, rendered half-witted by fits and fevers, had fallen into the grip of the child's mother, a moral degenerate, who had, after years of involving him in her deranged activities, propelled him to an early death.

Reassured though they were to hear that the child's unusual way of scuttling across floors on her derriere was not an early sign of moral, spiritual, or physical turpitude, they would not leave me in peace until I had promised to continue to examine the child regularly in the months and years to come.

With that agreed, I returned to the pressing matters of the day. These were so pressing that I almost forgot to mention this curious visit to young Semih. But when I did, he at once connected the dots. And I must say, he did so in a spirit of great fairness, as I understand that he and Hermine had never been particularly close.

For yes, the golden-haired creature I found to be in perfect health turns out to be none other than the daughter of Hermine, whom you tried and failed to rescue all those years ago. And now that I, too, have failed, I must do my best to make amends.

For all is not lost. With Semih's help, I have at last succeeded in tracking Hermine down. She was, I understand, living hand to mouth for some time, more on the streets than off them. But now she has been taken in by a Maître Refique, who first entered her life some years ago, as her tutor, and who has kindly undertaken to oversee her return to the School of Fine Arts. In this he hopes to have some assistance from an aunt, currently resident in Paris, with whom he has been in correspondence.

And Hermine? I was told that she had put on weight since her restoration (as Maître Refique calls it) but to me she seemed all skin and bones. Ready enough with a polite smile for the visitor, but subdued, even depleted.

She's happiest when she's sketching, Maître Refique tells me. And it is here where he is working to establish the sort of discipline that a sound mind requires of a sound body. Thereby guiding her away from the little studies with which she has been amusing herself since joining his household. She is ready to do portraits, he believes. We've agreed that I shall sit for her when I next visit.

No mention of the child. Having heard from Semih what is being said about Hermine – be these rumours true or false, or a mixture of the two – I see little likelihood of the little girl being returned to her. And forgive me if I sound callous, but after years of witnessing destitution at first hand, I do think this may well be for the best. The child will lack for nothing with these Levantines. While Hermine can offer little more than a drafty studio and the charity of friends.

It is shame, I agree, dear sister. And my own shame at having failed to recognise Hermine at the outset, on the operating table, at a time when you and I might have helped her to a different life, and a different fate – this shame knows no bounds. But the deed is done. To keep herself fed, Hermine has walked the streets. To put a roof over her head, she has sold her body. So they say, and even if what they say is untrue, or exaggerated, I cannot imagine any court giving her the benefit of the doubt.

In sadness,

Your loving sister Ruth

## 13

As the rain pelts against the windows of her host's great library in Kandili on a stormy afternoon in November 1928, Karine watches the Bosphorus wash up against his pier, and dreams of breaking something.

A tea glass, even. That would do. To see it smash against the floor, and across the floor. To watch its smithereens sparkle.

In fairness. She had agreed to come here. Before her husband would so much as raise the matter of a visa with his fine new business partners, he had made her promise. If she wished to accompany him to this city they could no longer call theirs, she would have to put the past behind her. Erase all memory of the evils that were little more than a decade old. Pretend to rejoice in the new republic. Forget that it was founded on stolen money, remembering instead that – thanks to her husband's acumen and cunning – this republic, with its thirst for oil, stood to bring them great gains.

He would be back soon. He and their host, the diplomat poet Ekrem Bey. Later on, to be joined by the other bandits – the Pasha and his sons, Monsieur Achille and his, and as if that were not enough, their American idiot, Aubrey! Oh, how her will is to be tested, not just by these pickpockets in fancy dress, but by Ekrem Bey's handmaidens: his wall-eyed wife, and his preposterously pregnant daughter, who make such a show of conversing in Greek. What exactly do they wish to say with this? That they are sorry their leaders saw fit to chase all the Greeks of Smyrna into the sea? Only to expel another million from across Asia Minor, without so much as giving them the time to gather up the bones of their ancestors? The entertainments she'd had to endure after supper last night – Ekrem Bey with his Hellenic sonnets, the wife with her tuneless lyre – it had been all Karine could do to keep from throwing herself into the Bosphorus to let its currents take her far, far away.

It had been a mistake, though, to pretend dizziness, for no sooner had she retired to this same library than she was joined by the lumbering daughter, who had put her arm around her, and pointed across the Bosphorus, first to the lights of Robert College, high on the hill, and then to the patch of night that would, with the sun, reveal the towers of Rumeli Hisar, and below them, to the Aşıyan Cemetery. 'Your dear Nuran is buried there, I understand. The poetess. Is it true what my father says – that she and you were lovers?'

The impudence of this woman. Glancing up, Karine sees that she is not yet rid of her. Here she is, hovering in the doorway and broad daylight, waiting to be invited in.

Why? Karine wonders.

Then she remembers.

The elephant wishes to avail herself of that daylight to point out where exactly in Aşiyan Cemetery her lost friend Nuran now lies.

Karine musters up a smile as she lifts up a warning finger. 'Not quite yet,' she says. 'I still have one last letter.'

My dear Mrs Mary,

You may be surprised to receive a letter from me.

No less, surprised, I imagine, to have it delivered to your hands by your husband on his return from the gates of Hell.

For yes, we are all here together. Not just the Alephs – the three surviving – but their fresh-cheeked sons. Such are the indignities that my husband is requiring me to witness with a smile I cannot feel.

All I can say, my dear Mrs Mary, is that we are living in a new age, where old enemies can put the past behind them, if ever there is a chance of a fat profit.

But that, for the moment, is neither here nor there.

There is another, urgent matter of which I wish to speak.

First let me clear the air by saying that I forgive you.

To this, I must of course add a caveat. I shall never forget how you failed me. That said, I have come to accept that you acted in good faith, and in innocence.

In addition, I know you to have an open mind.

Sadly, this is not a quality you share with your esteemed sister.

With that, let me move to the matter at hand.

You will have heard from this sister of yours, this Dr Ruth, that after losing our dear Hermine yet again to the perils of this city, we have found her, and that she now finds herself in the care of an older man who first entered her life many years ago, as her art tutor.

In your sister's estimation, this is a respectable arrangement, to be left as it is.

I beg most vociferously to differ!

The man is a philanderer of the worst order. For it is not her body that he wishes to possess, it is her mind. It is her soul.

Once in possession of these treasures, he wishes to wipe their slates clean.

Permit me to explain how I made this disturbing discovery.

I went to her. I went by myself.

I recognised the house. In fact, I knew it very well indeed in those old days that new minds must take care not to remember. But I digress. For the moment, let me just say that I found the building with ease.

And there, in a dank back room, I found my unfortunate niece.

Oh, such tears we shared! An hour must have passed, as we wept in each other's arms.

And when at last we had cried our fill, I made to her my promises.

The next day, a trusted associate would escort us to the relevant authorities, to arrange for her passport. Equipped with that passport, we would board a ship to Marseilles. Upon reaching my home in Paris, it would become her home too.

This news brought yet more tears into the eyes of Hermine.

But then, this self-styled Maître stepped in.

He did not like my plan at all.

Why not? I dared to ask.

Because, he said. Hermine had her studies to complete.

Are you telling me, I asked, that these studies could not be better pursued in Paris?

Of course, he could make no such claim. So then he began to talk about the child. Hermine was a mother. And mothers could not just up and leave, he said.

But what are you saying? I enquired. The child is lost to her!

My choice of words was perhaps unfortunate, because now poor Hermine wrapped her arms around her skeletal frame, to moan and rock.

Explain yourself, said the huffing, puffing man. Explain why you think you can come into my home and wreak havoc.

And so I did.

I began by pointing out that this home called his was not strictly speaking his, for it had, until the great heist of 1915, belonged to a close friend of my family. In short, it had been stolen from an Armenian.

The Maître looked surprised to hear such news. When I described the sad fate of this man, deported on that dark night in April, to be lost to the wilds of Anatolia, never again to be seen, he raised his hands to his chest, as if to stifle a deathly cough. He was so sorry! He'd had no idea.

He went on to tell me of the courtrooms he'd sketched in Malta, of the trials he'd witnessed, of the slaughter's architects, there before him in the docks, of the terrors he'd heard described. Of his horror when the Great Game changed, almost overnight, and all were acquitted. The Maître then reached for my hand, as if to share the sorrow. As if it could all be swept away, now that he had established himself as a good Turk. As if, now that I had seen him so saddened by our catastrophe, I would not mind him sitting in a building he had no intention of leaving, even now that he knew it had come to him through immoral channels.

Hah!

My dear Mrs Mary, knowing as I do that you have not visited these shores since those dark days of the war, I should perhaps describe the city as it is now. The city that basks in an amnesia that carries the full force of the law. No one must mention the horrors they visited on us. No one must ask for the vaults and banks they plundered, the lands and properties they seized. On pain of torture, imprisonment and death. Instead, we are to speak of these things as ashes. The ashes of the empire, from which this bright new nation has so effortlessly risen.

My dear Mrs Mary, I cannot begin to tell you. How my heart aches, to walk down our old avenues, remembering what once was, and I alone can name.

I am barred even from my own apartment!

My own sister-in-law has refused to let me in!

She does not want to upset the Pasha!

My own husband refuses to understand why I myself should be upset by this!

He points out instead that this old Pasha is our business partner now. Let us fleece him openly! he says.

I should add, perhaps, that I do not believe he means to do this.

He simply wishes me to behave.

And I shall, I shall. Even this evening, I shall.

My dear Mrs Mary, imagine the hell awaiting me this evening, when I must share a dinner table with my husband's new associates. Imagine the lengths to which I shall be obliged to go, to keep myself calm. With every false smile, I shall be imagining my revenge. Yes, this is how I shall keep myself sane and smiling: I shall be imagining their faces, some years hence, when they understand I have successfully conspired to rob them of their precious sons. I assure you, I am serious!

This at least I shall do! Mark my words. I shall make these thieves pay. A first-born from each! And do not think for a moment that I am saying this in jest. To the contrary, I shall consider it my life's work.

But in the meantime, I must sit with them all. Your husband Aubrey, who has not improved with age. Ekrem, the poet diplomat you might remember from Nuran's salons, with his ridiculous sonnets in Greek. Monsieur Achille, and his son Remy, who will be mine one day. I shall be laying my traps as I endure the entrance of Nuran's two sons, and with them the Pasha, to complete the ghastly group.

Can you imagine? My husband expects me to dine with this man, who did nothing to protect the men in my family from their deaths. This man who, after robbing Hermine of father and her fortune, went on to adopt her without really adopting her, and to care for her without caring where she spent her days, or for what, or with whom. Who has not lifted a finger for her, in her hours of need. Who retains close ties with the family that has not just stolen away her child, but spread the most vicious rumours about Hermine, if only to ensure that she is ostracised by all respectable persons in this city until the end of days.

This Maître who has set himself up as her new moral guardian: he takes, or pretends to take, another view. All will be well, he says. With a little patience, and perhaps a modest allowance from her wealthy aunt, Hermine's fortunes will change. She will complete her studies at the School of Fine Arts. She will wait for her child to come to her, busying herself in the intervening years with portraits he will commission on her behalf. Everyone wants portraits in the European style, he assures me. With the clients he brings her, he says, 'our Hermine' will not want for work. All that stands between her and this dream is a certain lack of discipline, a certain reluctance to paint in the expected way. But this will pass, he assures me. Under his direction, and in anticipation of the child who will one day come back to her, she will learn forbearance.

My dear Mrs Mary, I do not need to tell you how just the memory of these words sicken me. And with them, the memory of our Hermine, once so lively, bright and wild, clutching her skeletal frame and rocking, moaning, refusing my embrace.

I shall try again. As early as tomorrow. If I survive the ghastly dinner that is fast approaching, I shall set out again tomorrow, seeking to visit and persuade her. But because I fear the worst, I am sending your husband back to America with this missive, and this abject request: could you please write to our Hermine, to let her know that she is forever welcome, with her child or without her, at your fine home in Pomfret?

I know you will do this for me. Fearing as I do that my own efforts have again failed, I am thanking you in advance from the bottom of my heart for doing right by this poor young woman, who has been left too long at the mercy of those who have robbed her of her future.

Your despairing friend,

Karine

P.S. You will also return to me the velvet pouch of jewels that I now understand Hermine to have entrusted to you, when she was a mere and unsuspecting girl of nine.

P,P.S. They are not yours to keep!

## 14

As she sits at her secretary desk in January 1928, gazing out at the rolling hills of Pomfret, which seem so close and flat this morning with their new coat of snow, Mary imagines herself back to those other hills, where there was always more to see:

The wooded groves, concealing palaces. The cobblestone lanes, winding up and down, and back and forth, skittish and unhurried. The latticed windows, and the shadows flitting behind them. The slow and endless traffic of donkeys and horse carts, milkmen, junk men, and vegetable sellers. The dogs barking behind them. The cats, in their hundreds. The tortoises crawling into the foliage, the phosphorescent beetles scuttling out.

The man in the graveyard, praying over an emerald-studded dagger. The door floating open to reveal a girl pouring silver, or is it water, over an old woman in a tub. And there, in the gap between the houses, the Bosphorus. The ferry fighting the current, as it rounds the bend. The caique fairly flying in the opposite direction. The rowboats, tugging against their anchors. The fishermen on the shore, dropping their lines in a chorus of yells and shouts, as they pull one sailor after another to safety, as beyond them an abandoned galleon sinks, dragged down by its red sails.

Dear Hermine,

Let me begin by saying how sorry I am to be writing you this letter. How much better it would have been, to knock on your door, and visit. But I fear my horizons have narrowed considerably since we last met. I should not complain – this I know. For I have everything a women can wish for. A home to love. A nest to feather. A providing husband and a darling son.

But I envy you, I truly do.

At this moment, there is nothing I would like more than to knock on your door and suggest a walkabout. That street where my sister tells me you now live – I know it well. It is just around the corner from the little snuggery I shared with my husband in the first years of our marriage.

I can still picture the bakery that must be just a few buildings down from you. I bought our fruits and vegetable from the shop across the street. My seamstress was just next door. Those around you must never tire of telling you how unfortunate you are. But let me just say that there are riches in your surroundings that I can only just remember. And only you can see.

My dear Hermine, I am so very, very sorry to hear of the trials you have endured in recent years. The world is so very cruel to us mothers. But our children are not. I know in my heart that your daughter will find her way back to you.

In the meantime, let me do what little I can.

Hermine, it is my understanding that the gentleman who has so kindly welcomed you into his home, and who has such faith in your talent, has refused to accept on your behalf an allowance from your Aunt Karine, having somehow taken umbrage after a brief but cutting altercation with her.
I have therefore undertaken to do so in her place.


Hermine, you may know by now that my husband has paid in full your tuition at the School of Fine Arts. We shall, to the best of our ability, aim to supplement that with a monthly stipend, to be delivered to you by my sister.

You will, I trust, also know by now that the Levantines will be in regular contact with my sister Ruth, having somehow engaged her services as your daughter's personal physician.

An odd turn of events, I agree. But at least, we shall never be short of news.

It goes without saying that you are always welcome in

my home should you wish to take refuge with us. You and your daughter both.

As I write these words, I cannot but wonder why it is that I alone am appalled by the situation in which you now find yourself. How a few ugly rumours can remove a child from her mother's loving arms.

It should not be allowed. It cannot last.

But while it does, please remember that you are in my prayers, morning, noon, and night.

Do you pray, dear Hermine?

Have you lost your faith after all you have suffered, or are there times if you still wander into a church?

When I go on my imaginary walkabouts, I imagine you happily shunning the churches from which Charles' cruel relations seem to have barred you. I see you going back to that lovely Armenian church between the fish market and the flower market.

I went there once as a child, you know. With my mother, and my sister. This at the tail end of a massacre. It must, I think, have been the one following the Dashnak assault on the Ottoman Bank.

Not that I knew that at the time, of course. I was all of five years old. But I remember very clearly the shattered glass and pools of red amid the cobblestones.

We went into the city that day by ferry. A boy we knew from our village led us into the church through a secret passage. Inside was a great milling crowd, crying and praying and beseeching, all in whispers. A robed man led us to the benches on which they had laid the injured. My mother and my sister did not so much as pause to look at them before rolling up their sleeves to get to work.

While I sat and watched.

Do you know? It's the strangest thing. I spent the first two years of my marriage living almost around the corner from that church, but never once did I go inside.

Perhaps I thought I didn't need to.

Or perhaps, I was afraid to discover that it was not as I remembered it.

This is how I remember it. Still, to this day: On the ceiling, angels hovering between clouds. On the walls, saints with flowing hair and robes, straining to reach up to them. Above me, great and golden chandeliers. Before me, a great and golden altar.

I did not yet know what altars and chandeliers were, of course. So all I could see was the glitter and the gold, and the robed man I now understand to be a priest, helping my mother remove the medical supplies from the trunk we'd brought with us with yet more gold for us to take away and hide.

You grew up surrounded by precious stones, my dear Hermine. But I, the daughter of plain Protestants, had never seen the like.

It opened up a door in my imagination. And that is why I'm wondering. My dear Hermine, if you ever have occasion to wander into that church, could you let me know what you see there? Could you write back and disabuse me, if my memory has misled?

Behind her, a door slams. There follows a parking of shovels and stamping of feet, a throwing off of coats and pulling off of boots, and then Mary's little boy comes careening into the room in his stockinged feet. Lingering in the doorway, her husband tells her that the drive is clear now, and the snowman built.

A good hot coffee and he's off, Aubrey says. Parking the car in New London so she doesn't have to drive him, and then the train back to Washington. 'If you've finished that letter of yours, I can mail it for you,' he says. He holds out his hand in that sheepish, hopeful way he has, when he thinks he has just about convinced her that he will be boarding that train alone, and not with his latest conquest.

Such nonsense! Too silly even to fret about. All she wants is to see the back of him. In the meantime, let him at least send this letter. Scribbling a hasty salutation, Mary seals the envelope. But as she watches her husband's car roll down the drive, she almost calls him back. She should have chosen her words more carefully. Spoken less about herself. At the very least, she should not have ended with such an odd, abrupt request.

## 15

As she sits at her easel in the back streets of Pera, contemplating Mary's letter on the first fine day in April 1928, Hermine sees nothing odd in it at all. Instead, she jumps to her feet and grabs her coat, taking the Maître by surprise.

'Where are you going?' he asks.

'To seek an answer,' she replies.

'To what?'

'You know. You were reading over my shoulder,' Hermine says.

'But the portrait,' the Maître protests.

He reaches out for shoulder, as if to stop her. It annoys her, when he does this. She does not pause to tell him the obvious, that it can wait. Stepping aside, she buttons up her coat. Meeting his dull metallic stare with dispassion.

'It's good news, at least,' he offers.

'What is?'

'The fees. And also, the stipend this American friend will be sending.'

Hermine shrugs her shoulders.

'When will you be back?' the Maître now asks.

'When I am done.'

With that, Hermine strides out into the street, which is bright with the first scents of spring. The salt in the sea air. The implausible hint of fresh grass. The sun playing on the windows stings her eyes, just a little, just to scold her; she has been sitting in the dark far too long.

With each new step, she is greeted. The beggars. The tavern owners and their waiters. The chestnut roasters. The porters. The flower sellers and the fishmongers. They raise their arms, to ask where she's been. And she raises hers, to say she hasn't a clue.

Reaching the church, she settles herself into a bench at the back. Slowly, she looks it up and down. She must have been here before. With her mother, certainly. To be baptised.

And it is not at all – at all – the way Mrs Mary remembers it. Yes, there is gold everywhere. Enough, she sees, for three altars and seven chandeliers. But the walls of this church are white. She can see no angels fluttering above, no saints straining and failing to touch them.

She tries to imagine praying. But she's lost the words. Or perhaps, she always lacked them.

Mrs Mary's faith in her is all she has, and her power to conjure up what no one else can see.

So she sits there, head bowed, hands joined, eyes tightly shut. Until she can hear Mrs Mary padding down the aisle, returning to her the daughter whose name is now to be revealed.

## 16

Ten years pass, the most tranquil Hermine will ever know, and also the most tedious. By 1939, she has been the Maître's wife for seven years. She has given him two sons and supported the family with the portraits she has painted under her husband's strict supervision.

Until one fine summer day when Hermine opens the door to find a woman of a certain age pointing a gun at her.

A pistol, to be precise. A Derringer, the same kind the Pasha had once kept in his pocket. Perhaps that very one? Sold to a junk dealer? To pass from hand to underworld hand? Only to turn up, so many years later, at her door?

This pistol, it looks familiar. Could it be the one used to teach her how to shoot? Taking it from the woman's trembling hands, she examines its captivating lines more closely, seeking in its surface the tell-tale nicks that might prove her theory right.

Yes, Hermine says finally, more to herself than to her unexpected guest. I do think I have guessed correctly. She goes back inside, and the older woman follows.

Over coffee, the two exchange notes. Almost without effort, the pieces fall into place. For more than a decade the Maître has been a bigamist. The woman sitting opposite is the rogue's first wife. Until this year, he had, it seems, given equal time and support to each of his betrayed families. But it has been many months now since his last visit to this first wife and her son. And Hermine has hardly seen him either. Reaching into her portmanteau, the first wife pulls out a stack of unpaid bills. Venturing for the first time into the bigamist's study, Hermine discovers an even larger stack of important-looking envelopes. Together, the two wives rip them open. More bills.

Where can the man be? Asks the first wife. Hermine says, I think we both know. Together they board a ferry for the island that is now known as Büyükada, though Hermine still calls it Prinkipo. Arriving at the studio high in the hills, creeping up the last steep steps in silence, they are met with a locked door.

Hermine lifts her finger to her lips. 'Hush now! Give me the gun!' Dropping it into the pocket of her painting smock, which in her haste, she has forgotten to remove, she deftly scales the Judas tree beside the house until she is level with the great, bright studio where she, too, had once worked.

And there he is, the Maître, standing behind an easel, looking over the shoulder of a lovely young girl to examine the sketch she has made of the view from the window.

Hermine makes herself comfortable on her chosen perch, one hand on a higher branch, and the other fondling the pistol.

It is almost, she thinks, like gazing at her own past.

The window is open, and the Maître's clear, commanding voice sails through it. He is informing this poor unsuspecting girl that her sketch, though riddled with flaws, shows promise. Under his tutelage, she could go far.

Do you really believe that? asks the girl in a plaintive voice. Even now? She places her hand on the belly that Hermine can now see is swollen.

The Maître chuckles as he places his hand on hers.

And Hermine fires.

She feels lighter, so much lighter, as she slips down out of the tree. As she uses a neighbour's broom to ram open the front door, she marvels at her strength. The joy pulsing through her veins clears her mind on arriving at the scene of her crime, to find the paramour convulsing, and the Maître unconscious at her feet.

She can see, from the location of the pool of blood that she has shot the trigamist in the neck. And from this point on, she plays doctor, nurse, and angel. No one could have guessed, from the calm and compassionate way she directs the Maître's stretcher and its bearers through the jostling crowds and onto the ferry, that she was the one to pull the trigger.

Arriving in the city, she again leads the way through the hustle and the bustle with her head held high. Arriving at the hospital, she cannot bring herself to leave her victim. She sends the first wife away, to see to their children, their houses, and the Maltese mother-in-law they share. Once alone, Hermine parks herself outside the operating room while a tight-lipped American doctor removes the bullet from the Maître's shattered neck. When she does her rounds later that day, she finds Hermine is still there, at his bedside, holding the Maître's hand to her chest.

'Do correct me if I'm wrong,' says the doctor. 'My understanding, Hermine, is that you did this to the man.'

Hermine sighs. Serenely. There follows a brilliant, thoughtful smile. Yes, dear Dr Ruth. I did.

Dr Ruth frowns, before saying, 'In a fit of passion, I take it?'

'Yes,' Hermine replies. 'At least – perhaps.'

Nodding sadly, Dr Ruth says: 'And now, I take it, you are full of regret.'

Again, Hermine sighs. Lifting the Maître's hand, she kisses and caresses it, before saying: 'I regret only that I have not loved him with a full heart until this moment.'

The police arrive soon afterwards to cart Hermine off to the station. But in the end she spends only three nights behind bars, this thanks to Melih, who after arranging for all charges to be dropped, returns her to the apartments of her birth.

These have been sitting empty since 1935 – ever since the Pasha and the grasping Celeste left for Switzerland, initially for the education of their late-born son Teoman. But latterly to sit out the Second World War. Or so they said. In Melih's mind, it was a plot to deprive him and his brother, Semih, of their inheritance. All their father's money is there with them in Switzerland. Together with all the money their father stole from their mother, the great poetess. All will now go to Celeste's darling son, Teoman, or Teddy as the little brat has taken to calling himself.

All Melih and Semih can hope to inherit following the Pasha's departure are the lands and the properties that the grasping Celeste was not been able to take with her.

Which was why – to Melih, at least, if not to his kind but somewhat joyless brother – it has felt like a vindication to restore Hermine to the apartments that a creature more worldly than she would have considered to be her birthright.

There is something of his mother in this Hermine. From time to time, when Melih catches her at the window – staring into the night, seeing things only she can see – he can hear his mother whispering to her. Sharing secret poems, lighting the way.


## 17


But then, within weeks of her return to the apartment of her birth, Hermine engineers a second scandal. First, by removing the Maître from hospital before his wound has fully healed – at his request, but against all medical advice. Then, by installing him on the ageing chaise longue in her great front room, there to nurse him, until his death some months later. While some (like the Maître's Maltese mother) are outraged by the turn of events, and others (like the doomed union's two sons) are mystified and rendered mute with hurt, the gossip columnists are overjoyed. For the door is open, and not only to them. All who wish to cheer the Maître with their company are welcome. The tavern owners and the beer hall owners. The waiters and their dishwashers. The chickpea sellers and the flower sellers. The lottery sellers and the man who roasted chestnuts outside their doors most days. The journalists looking for one last drink before they stagger off to bed, the cartoonists who need a drink first thing to stop their hands shaking. Not to mention the Maître's old colleagues from the School of Fine Arts, and all the loves of Maître Refique's life, not excluding his first wife, or even his most recent paramour, who visits weekly, first with her bump, and later with their son – her first, his fourth and last.

Nourished by chestnuts, chickpeas, and great Argentines of beer, they puzzle over the future direction of art and humanity. The Maître propped up on pillows, and draped in shawls, and Hermine in the corner, sketching.

With time, even the gossip columnists have half fallen in love with these wild creatures, and their readers, too, but then comes the next scandal: Hermine's first exhibition. Because no gallery will have her, this exhibition takes place in the apartment. Because only weeks have passed since the Maître's demise, Melih has not put her name on the posters he has happily run up for her, and then arranged to have pasted on every wall in Pera. Instead, he has billed her as the Divine Hümeyra.

Hümeyra is of course the name the Pasha put on her revised birth certificate. But no one has ever used it. And now, no one is fooled. They all know Hümeyra is Hermine. And so they says: How dare this Armenian upstart appropriate one of the most beautiful names of Islam! Never mind that Turkey is a now secular nation. There are sensitivities. There is also the title she has given to her exhibition:

DEATHBED.

Never mind that she has used the English word. Whatever the language, it shows disrespect.

But great crowds turn up for the opening regardless. If only to gawp at these mad and gaudy tableaux in which the artist has arranged for the cream of society and its dregs to stand together, and laugh and drink together, artfully grouped around a skeletal man tightly wrapped in shawls and propped up on pillows reclining on a chaise longue, His face in profile. His eyes on the monstrous fish-filled waves implausibly beating against the windows.

The gawpers come and go. Only a few of them linger, but they are the right ones, and because they later exchange notes, agreeing that their last visit was the best party ever, they keep coming back. Soon the gossip columnists of Istanbul can barely remember what they did with their Fridays in the days before Hümeyra threw open her scandalous doors.

## 18

In the beginning – during the war years – Hermine-Hümeyra sets herself apart as the crowds file in, sketching whomever agrees to be sketched. Melih at her side, ever the diplomat, makes sure they understand what this artist might choose to do with their likenesses. Assuring them that when she has finished stretching and twisting their features, and cutting them into little pieces, and rearranging them into new and preposterous shapes, even they will struggle to know which nose belongs to them, and which to someone else.

But what is her purpose? they sometimes ask. What does it all mean?

That, he insists, is for them to decide.

An evasion.

Surrounded though Hermine is now by friends and admirers, it is Melih alone who fully understands her, Melih alone who sees the shards of Hermine's broken heart in her every painting and collage. He has always nurtured an excessive passion for the arts – how could he not, as the son of Nuran the Poetess? But of all the great works he has seen in the greatest museums of the world in the course of his diplomatic career, none has spoken to him as hers do.

Safe now from the authoritarian rules of portraiture, she is free to bend and twist her colours and her shapes, disassembling the masks of the quotidian to excavate the soul. Such fury she sets loose, with each slice of the scissor and each new splash of paint! Melih's kindly but officious doctor brother might not approve, but the fact is that the soiréés Melih now hosts with Hermine-Hümeyra have become madly, wildly popular, not only with the diplomats who become Hümeyra's first buyers, but also with the city's poets and the journalists, its singers, actors, and musicians. Since the beginning of the war (which, though never reaching these shores, has still plagued its nerves) these soirees offer a rare respite from worldly concerns. And that is why the city's most celebrated names and intellects flock there every Friday, to laugh and dance and down lethal homemade spirits with the inevitable travellers of unclear purpose and society's most flamboyant rebels.

For Melih they offer yet another kind of solace. For his marriage to Elektra has become a hollow shell. And to make matters even worse, he has been obliged, through a series of accidents and misfortunes, to move in with his in-laws, in their creaking, storm-blown yalı in Kandili where his morose wife and their two daughters can find no purpose in life except to gang up on him, and his mother-in law strums endlessly on her tuneless lyre, and his father-in-law walks around spouting the same Greek sonnets that made him such a laughing stock when he was a diplomat.

Despite the fug of grain alcohol in Hermine's great room, and the heavy wreaths of smoke, it has been the one place where Melih has been able to breathe with ease. He has, at the same time, profited in no small way from the alliances forged at these soirees, and the intelligence gathered. While officially resting between postings, Melih has been unofficially asked to report on the doings and dealings of the city's diplomats, along with their less salubrious hangers-on. Thanks to Hermine, now reborn as Hümeyra, he can bring them all together into one room.

In 1944, he has at last found a way to thank her.

Because he has made it his business to keep Hermine-Hümeyra informed on the welfare and whereabouts of the daughter she has never met, he is among the first to hear when the girl is expelled from her lycee-convent at age 16. And also, the first to suggest to his friends at the US consulate that, with her five or six languages, this girl might prove useful to them, if only as a secretary. Since hearing that she is delightful in every way that a nun might find hard to bear, he has been curious to meet her. But when he persuades his American colleagues to bring her along to a soiree one Friday, his first thoughts are for Hümeyra. Ever since the Maître's death, her two sons from that marriage have shunned her.

How good it will be, to reunite her with at least one child. To see her happy once again –

that is his fondest wish.

Until the lovely Delphine comes floating through the door, and everything changes.

19

Sergei is there to see it all happen, having washed up in Istanbul in 1943. A stowaway, searching for his father, a high-ranking officer who'd last been seen at this city's Soviet Consulate. Arriving at said consulate late one night, Sergei was denied entry, and it was here, at its gate. that Hümeyra had found him. Hungry, cold, and penniless, and just fifteen years old. Without so much as a moment's pause, she took Sergei home with her, and that is where he still is on that fateful evening in 1944 when Delphine sweeps in to attend her first soiree.

She is barely eighteen and new enough to adult society to be delighted by all those eyes turning towards her – for she has only just grown into her beauty, Sergei sees, and this is the first ever time she's dared to venture out in the low-cut, backless gown she acquired on the sly. It is a thrill – of course it is. At home with her aunts, at school with the nuns, and now in the secretarial pool at the US Consulate, she is met with weary sighs. This is much more fun, she thinks, as she clings, somewhat nervously, to her escort's arm.

His name is William Wakefield. He's still new to the consulate. Delphine is not yet working for him – she is still in the typing pool – but he has noticed her qualities, and also her potential. Which is why he has agreed to bring her along with him to this soiree.

The first to greet her is Melih. So entranced is he by her beauty that he has to struggle to find his breath. But he is not a diplomat for nothing. And this evening, he is a diplomat with a sacred duty. So he takes it upon himself to part the waters, leading the enchanting creature across the room to be reunited at long last with her mother.

For a moment she stands there, arrested by the shock of recognition, while around here the crowds fall silent, while Hermine wraps her shawls all the more tightly around herself – as if a great gust of wind has blown in from the north with no other purpose than to fell her.

And then, as if by magic, Delphine takes Hermine's hand, and kisses it, saying, 'Mother, I have missed you so!' All in the room gasp. Whereupon Hermine raises her arm to say, 'Sergei! My prince! We must have a toast! Would you kindly bring my daughter a drink?'

Sergei does his best to look princely as he places in Delphine's hands a goblet filled to the brim with what is – he knows to his cost, the most dangerous punch the world has ever seen – grain alcohol boiled up with not enough water, and given the illusion of substance by the fruits of the season.

From that Friday on, Delpine is a fixture at her long-lost mother's soirees. And soon, Sergei has become her most loyal and devoted confidante. This, too, is a first for the poor girl. For though Delphine has always managed to make herself the centre of attention, at home and at school, she has never before had a friend she could trust with her secret thoughts. In the beginning, she has little to disclose to her new confidante, beyond her spats with her grandparents and her misadventures in the typing pool at the US consulate, and her little stories from childhood that Hermine-Hümeyra so loved to hear. It is young and wayward Sergei who does the lion's share of confessing.

But all too soon, a great cloud comes looming: the threat of marriage. For Delphine is nineteen by now. And those Levantine aunts of hers are busy matchmaking. They need to find her a husband before she gets herself into more trouble.

For Delphine's cousins and former classmates, the wedding season is already well underway. There is hardly a weekend without its nuptials. Delphine finds them all so dreadfully dull, these would-be suitors who lead her on and off the dance floor. They see the world through their fathers' purse strings. She must struggle just to breathe. The walls are closing in! Her new confidant urges her to find a pretext. Use your languages, he says. You have so many of them, after all! And so Delphine talks herself out of the typing pool, with more than a little help from Willian Wakefield, and in no time at all, she becomes the interpreter that no one at the US Consulate can do without.

20

Her new job involves frequent trips to Ankara with her boss who, despite his many flaws, is a diligent custodian of her honour. Melih is but one of the figures of consequence she and William meet, as if by chance, on the overnight train back to Istanbul. Before retiring to separate cabins at a respectable hour, they often dine together in the club car. But on one particular occasion, in the depths of the winter of 1948, Delphine walks into the club car to find Melih waiting for her alone.

He informs her that William Wakefield has been called away on an urgent errand, with promises to return well before the time of their departure. Of course, this gives Delphine pause. For it is utterly and entirely out of character. But then Melih clicks his fingers, and the waiter steps forward with a bottle of champagne. *French* champagne.

They are onto the second bottle when the train lurches

forward, so suddenly that Delphine might have fallen from her seat had Melih not reached out to steady her.

Still no William. Glancing anxiously at the clock on the platform, Delphine wonders out loud what might be keeping him.

Taking her hand, Uncle Melih tells her not to worry. The night train to Istanbul rarely leaves on time. Their friend is sure to turn up any moment.

No sooner has he said that, than the train again lurches forward. This time, Delphine remains steady in her seat, thanks to Melih's tight grip.

And the train keeps going.

Whereupon Melih says: 'Oh dear. It seems that you and I have been left to our own devices.'

## 21

It is her busybody aunts who notice first. They corner her one Saturday at St Antoine, within hearing distance of the confessionals. So this is how she's repaid their trust? This is how she has thanked her employers, by opening her legs? Pulling her by the arm, they take her across the street to Markiz for a coffee Delphine is too ill to drink. Here they carry on hissing: they always thought it a bad idea to let Delphine work. They'd said as much to their husbands. Always too wild, this girl. Always a problem. But thanks to their sharp eyes, time is on their side. They know of a clinic whose director is discreet.

Delphine says nothing, thus feigning agreement. But that evening, she goes back for the last time to the apartment where she's lived since infancy, and gathers up her things. In their place, she leaves a note: she has arranged to go to Europe where her American bosses will help her with her problem.

Arriving at her mother's apartment only minutes later – for as strange as it might sound, their dwellings are that close – Delphine is hardly halfway through her sad confession when Hermine raises her hand, commanding silence. For there is no more to be said.

Lifting a heavy key from a hook near the front door, she leads her daughter across the landing to the apartment where she will spend the next six months in uninterrupted safety. For Hermine has taken great care with Delphine's alibi, with the expert assistance of our man for all seasons. William Wakefield, meanwhile, has managed to hoodwink even the poisonous aunts, inventing for Delphine a minor automobile accident in the Alps following her sojourn in a certain clinic, resulting in injuries that, though they would leave no lasting damage, have necessitated a long period of hospitalisation in Vienna which the US State Department will of course cover.

To Melih he's told both the truth and the cover story. The problem and the solution. The affair is well in the past by now, having lasted little more than a fortnight. But now, there is a future unfolding. In silence, the two men wait and watch.

And so the months go by. Claiming illness, Hermine calls a stop to her soirees, leaving it to William Wakefield to keep all concerned parties fully misinformed. Whenever he passes through town, he takes care to drop by on Delphine's aunts, to reassure them with false updates, and then he drops in on Hümeyra. He is one of three people whom she allows in to see Delphine during her remaining months of pregnancy. The second is Sergei, who is by now back in the good books of the Soviet Embassy which at last understands his potential as an informer. Or so they think. Most of his reports are fictions he's concocted with Delphine to make long afternoons shorter.

Sometimes for the benefit of the Soviets. Sometimes for the ears of our man for all seasons. What fun it is to see how far they can take him! Because it is never as far as they might like, they sometimes mix a few facts in with the lies. They can then have the occasional pleasure of watching their minder doubt what was true. If they never succeed quite as brilliantly as hoped, it has remained a game that gives them daily pleasure.

The third and last permitted visitor during Delphine's months of seclusion is Melih's sister-in-law, the doctor Delphine knows only as Dr Mrs Semih. She had balked on first hearing that a relation had been called in. Only to be reassured. This kindly doctor had come to the rescue of more than a few of Hümeyra's friends over the years. Though harsh on the outside, she is, Hümeyra insists, most gentle in her care. And discreet. Utterly and absolutely discreet.

## 22

The birth, in the autumn of 1949, passes without complication. A week later, Delphine is healing nicely, but still too fearful of the creature in the cot beside her to let herself sleep. How has it come to this? At what point was it decided? And by whom? But what sort of a monster is she, to question the existence of an innocent child? These are the questions she is asking herself when she hears her front door creaking on its hinges.

She calls out for Hümeyra. At this hour, who else could it be? Receiving no answer, she drifts back into a haze that is not sleep but might be mistaken for it. Or perhaps she really does doze off. For when Delphine opens her eyes once again, and reaches over to the cot, to check if the baby is still breathing, she finds only blankets.

Somehow she knows that her life and her baby's future now depend on her staying silent. Her heart might be pounding, but she makes no noise, no noise whatsoever, as she pads through the darkness, out the door, and onto the landing. There she find Dr Mrs Semih, babe in her arms.

And there, across the landing, is Hümeyra. In neutral tones, she welcomes the doctor, the baby, and the new mother with gentle words, as if it were the morning or the afternoon, and not the middle of the night. Ushering them inside, and sitting them all down, she turns to the doctor and said, 'I fear there may have been a misunderstanding. It's not like the other times. On this occasion, we have, as I have told you, no plans to give up the child.'

'But she is a bastard,' cries Mrs Dr Semih. 'A stain on the family, which we cannot permit'!

Whereupon a deep voice floats in from the corridor. 'Is that so?'

The voice walks into the room, looking most majestic in a red velvet robe with matching slippers.

Melih.

Calmly, he sits down. In smooth diplomatic tones, he asks his sister-in-law if she can explain why she has taken it upon herself to clear the family name in such an abrupt manner.

'There is the danger of attachment,' declares Mrs Dr Semih. 'We must separate the child from the mother before the bond is set'

'Aha,' said Melih. 'How very thoughtful. May I ask you to share with me your plans for this child'?

She has a childless couple waiting in a car downstairs,

she says. Like all the other couples she has lined up in the past for Hermine's various wayward friends, they are good people, honest and hardworking, who will give this baby the future it deserves.

'So now tell me if I have understood you correctly,' Melih says. 'You have stepped into the breach to save my family the agony I might have caused it.'

'But also,' says Mrs Dr Semih, 'to bring happiness to another, to be sure.'

'A family more deserving than our own, I take it,' says Melih. 'More honest and hardworking than we could ever be.'

The doctor nods. 'They have, additionally, been so kind as to overlook the risks.'

'From which I take it,' says Melih smoothly, 'that some concerns remain.'

'Well, of course', agrees the doctor.' The child's blood is far from pure.'

'From which I am to understand,' says Melih, 'it is your hope – and theirs – that a healthy, purely Turkish upbringing will wipe away the stain.'

Another nod from the doctor. Briefly she shuts her eyes before fixing them on Melih. 'I am grateful for your understanding. I had not expected it,' she says.

'Why ever not?'

She waves an uncertain hand. 'At this point, does it matter?'

'Most certainly,' says Melih. 'Most certainly, it does.'

Slowly, he coaxes it out of her. Everything she thinks about Melih's philandering. Everything her husband – Melih's brother – has said about his wandering eye, his penchant for foreign luxuries and travels, and most of all his failure to devote his life fully to the national cause. He is not alone, Dr Mrs Semih assures him. These are, after all, the flaws of decadence from which Atatürk has sought to rescue the nation,by moving the capital from Istanbul to Ankara. With each new condemnation, Melih offers his most abject apology, thereby goading the doctor on to greater frankness. Until, with a glance at her watch, she rises from her seat. 'It is later than I thought,' she says. 'I must go. I have kept my kindly couple waiting long enough'.

Briskly, she dons her coat. Briskly, she makes to divest Delphine of her little bundle. But before she can take two steps towards the ancient chaise longue, Melih's hands are on her shoulders. In vain, the doctor struggles to extract herself from this iron grasp, while briskly and brutally Melih pushes her towards the door. With one arm, he pins her to the wall, while with the other he flings the door open. Picking her up now by the waist, he carries her out onto the dark landing, and hurls her down the stairs.

Through the darkness she screams and shrieks. Through the darkness he drowns out her accusing words with his. There are curses that Delphine is hearing for the first time. He is promising to piss first in her mouth, and then in her husband's. He is threatening to lodge an umbrella in her infidel grandmother's cunt and open it. If Mrs Dr Semih so much as walks past the entrance to this building, Melih says, he is going to kill her, right in front of her dog of a husband. While her dog of a husband watches, he is going shit on her corpse. And then it will be the dog's turn to find out what his decadent brother was made of.

Only when a tenant comes up from the second floor to the doctor's rescue does Melih fall silent. No one inside the apartment or outside it says another thing until, down on the ground floor, the heavy iron door slams shut.

Smiling as calmly as if nothing untoward had happened,

Melih returns to sit beside Delphine on the chaise longue.

'Dearest,' he says, as he places a hand on her shoulder. 'Dearest, how very beautiful you look tonight.'

This takes Delphine by surprise. She isn't feeling beautiful. Not in the least!

'May I see my son?' Melih asks.

Delphine corrects him. 'Your daughter.'

'Ah. A daughter. But I am right in thinking it is mine?'

He taps the infant's nose, declaring her to be adorable. The infant wakes up. Time, he says for mother and child to retire to their own quarters. Turning to Hermine, he suggests a chat.

### 23

Not long after dawn the next morning, Hermine, Delphine, and the new-born child board a ferry for the island that is no longer known by its Greek name, Prinkipo. But, as in a previous chapter of this story, it is again out of season, leaving the fugitives safe from prying eyes while Melih and William Wakefield arrange their papers. When all is done, Delphine and her new-born board a ship bound for Marseilles.

From there to America. But they'll be back soon, Melih promises. As soon as the dust settles.

'You wait and see,' he says.

And for twelve long years, that is what she does.

# THE SEVENTH NOTEBOOK

# The question

I can't remember which one of you girls asked it. And it's quite possible that neither of you can help me here. It was, in any event, a question one of you hurled at me during a long-ago argument on an airport concourse. It's only stayed with me because it cut so deep. It only cut so deep because I couldn't give you an honest answer.

You were still so very young, that June afternoon at the airport. And angry – justifiably angry – about having to travel halfway across the world without me. But not because you didn't want to see your father in his new life. You had missed him terribly, and you were looking forward to seeing him, and your stepmother, too. No – you were angry because – even though you were thirteen or fourteen or fifteen years old by now, and therefore old enough in your view to take care of yourselves – the airline was still insisting that you wear those clunky signs around your neck, identifying you as unaccompanied minors.

I could understand how humiliating that was, but it was out of my hands. I was handing you over, and it may well be that I was more than tight-lipped about the whole thing, because – as much as I wanted your father to be an active presence in your lives – it tore me up to let you go.

And it may have seemed to you that I was hurrying you, when in fact I was just trying to get you to security without breaking down and saying something foolish.

It was there, just outside security, that one of you asked if it had ever occurred to me that it might come to this, back when I 'decided to write whatever came into my head, no matter what the consequences'.

'Oh, please.' I shouldn't have said that. So perhaps I deserved the next question that one of you hurled at me, after I'd added that I was not in fact writing whatever happened to come into my head, but doing right by my grandmother:

'Why couldn't you keep it simple then, and just write about her?'

Somewhere in the cellar back in Pomfret, in a box that I probably left unlabelled, you will find a typescript entitled *Hermine*. I began writing it in the months before you were born. I took it up again when you started nursery school, and you were in second or third grade when I finally went out in search of an agent.

And I hope you have some happy memories of those years. For me, there are none happier. My life revolved around yours, and yours around mine. I was working on Hermine, but only when it suited us.

I'd billed it as a novel, but I'd dedicated it to my grandmother, making it clear that it was her story, as I'd reimagined it, at her express invitation: the truth as I had come to see it.

Of the many objections expressed by the dozen or so agents who wouldn't take me on when I sent it out with naively high hopes, this was one I heard the most:

'If it's a true story, why not bill it as a true story?'

So in the end, I did. But which I mean I took out my Olivetti and typed up a new dedication page:

To my grandmother, for this is her story.

But that didn't work either. For the next dozen agents were in agreement that there was no market for my grandmother's story, even if I billed it as a true story, because no one would be able to place it. They themselves knew next to nothing about Turkey – they would struggle to place it on a map. For them, the word Ottoman called to mind a footstool. A few were aware of a sizeable Armenian community in a handful of American cities. One or two recalled that these communities harboured a virulent hatred of the Turks. 'But outside those little pockets,' one of these agents asked me, 'who even remembers what the Turks did to them?'

'That's what Hitler said,' I said.

Which was true, though it did not endear me. I am certain that I would find many faults in *Hermine*, if I found the courage to read it through again. I was young, and new at writing, and perhaps my telling of the story was too flat, and my portrayal of Hermine too idealised. Whatever the reason, a number of these agents failed to empathise with her or believe in her as a character. One went so far as to describe Hermine as a social deviant.

I did not endear myself to her either.

How I felt at the end of all this: deeply, deeply disappointed and almost, almost defeated. Had I not made that promise to my grandmother, I might have packed my dreams away with the typescript, in that unlabelled box.

But because I had made that promise, and because I was not just disappointed and defeated, but also furious to have had my way blocked, and determined not to let the gatekeepers of history have their way, I returned to the academy.

You would have been nine or ten when I published my next book, on the great Near East Relief campaign that had sent a thousand American doctors and nurses to the lands of the former Ottoman Empire in the four years following

World War I, only to be erased from memory soon thereafter. My target in this book was not the Turkish state but our very own American amnesia. We had, after all, been among the first to bring news of the genocide to the world, but our government's position from the 1920s on was that the genocide never happened.

There were two distinct camps among US-based scholars dealing with the last decades of the Ottoman Empire and the first decades of the Turkish Republic: there were those who either denied the genocide or arranged never to mention it, and there were those who made it their primary focus, or even their only focus. By using the word genocide in my account of Near East Relief, I'd left the first camp for the second.

But here, in this second camp, I discovered a number of Turkish scholars who had also crossed over. They had come to the US as students, never having been exposed to any thinking inconsistent with official history. But once they'd been exposed to such thinking, they'd begun the painful process of unlearning that official history and figuring out what might replace it. A few of us began to work together – you can find the books we co-published in my study in Pomfret. They are, I recall, on the top shelf of the glass cabinet, between the monographs I wrote before and after. And that is how I got around the archive problem: my co-authors were as yet unpublished and generally making several trips back to Turkey every year, and because there were not yet any black marks against their names, they had no trouble gaining access to the Ottoman archives, such as they are.

Even after our books had come out in English, my co-authors were able to travel back and forth to Turkey without impediment. Occasionally they were taken aside for questioning. But nothing came of it. The one consequence for us all was that we were barred thereafter from seeking funds from the only body with an interest in funding research in our area – for that body, though based in Washington DC, was funded by the Turkish state.

It was while we were seeking other sources of funding that Suna made us a proposal.

She had just helped to found a small publishing concern. They were planning a new series on the late Ottoman period and they wanted to translate the three collections that my co-authors and I had published on the empire's Armenians.

We said yes, of course.

But then your father received his own offer. Or rather, the Parisian architectural firm that Anais had now taken over from her mother had been awarded the contract for rebuilding and expanding the hospital that Uncle Semih had now passed on to his firstborn son, Suna's father, back in Istanbul.

How very incestuous, I remember saying when I first heard the news. Because of course there was the matter of your father's own involvement. For he was the one who had won the bid for them. If, that is, there had even been a genuine competition. After all, this was the hospital that his great aunt Ruth had helped to found, back in the 1920s. I am not saying that your father and Anais and the others did not do splendid work. But even so – this is what nepotism looks like.

I very much regret pointing this out to your father. With hindsight I can see that this did not get our negotiations off to a good start. He wanted us all to move back to Istanbul, at least until the work on the hospital was completed. He had been assured that I'd have no trouble getting myself a university affiliation, so long as I back peddled on what he later regretted calling my 'abiding obsession'. I reminded him of the three collections soon to appear in Turkish, courtesy of Suna's publisher. He suggested that perhaps we could put these on hold.

'Or maybe you can just leave your name off.'

If, having read all this, you remind me that I could still have compromised, for the sake of the family, I shall be obliged to half agree. Your father was not asking me to leave my name off any books I published in English. Just the ones published in Turkish. But it was Turkish readers we cared most about. The taboo we wished to break was rooted in Turkey.

So too was our fury.

Looking back I can see how I might have chosen my words more carefully, but at the time, I felt hurt and insulted, deeply so. Whatever the truth of the matter, it seemed to me that your father was disrespecting my career and failing to give due importance to the cause to which I had dedicated myself.

If you wished to point out to me that I expressed similar disrespect for his work, and his career, I would again have to agree. The fact is that we each knew where the other's vulnerabilities were, and we were both very angry. But if you ask me to mark the point of no return, it was when he dismissed what he called my 'abiding obsession'.

My mother didn't help. That next summer in Lugano, she took me out to lunch for that express purpose. 'You're going to lose him,' she predicted. And I was angry enough by then to say, with feeling, that I really didn't care.

'Fine then. So long as you understand that you're handing him over on a platter. To Anais.'

'That wouldn't be so bad, you know. And it would hardly be a surprise. It crossed my mind many years ago, that they might make a better couple.'

'I can't believe I'm hearing this. And such a fine man, too!'

'Anais is just as fine a woman, you know. If she wants him, she can have him. I have better things to do.'

'All my life,' said my mother, 'I have slaved to make you happy. And now here I am, watching you throw it all away.'

'Since when,' I asked, 'have you slaved away for anyone but yourself?'

It pains me, to relive those words. Especially as I didn't mean them. Of course I appreciated all my mother had done for me, and of course I loved your father, and of course, when I said Anais could have him, I was only defending myself against my worst fears.

And yes, I was afraid of losing your father to Anais – all the more so, after my mother had put the thought into my mind. It may well be that it was to quell this fear that I pushed your father away. I didn't hand him over on a platter, but neither did I wait to see how things might progress.

I pushed him away, only to regret it afterwards, and all I can say to you girls is that you are right to be angry at me, for leaving your father in a huff of pride, for putting myself first, and my lost cause. And despite my best efforts, for failing you as a mother, in the long run, for the same reason.

That afternoon in Lugano, though, I wasn't choosing anything. Or thinking. I was on automatic pilot, sparring with my mother in the way I always had. Hurting her as much as she hurt me. Our argument continued into the evening, though by then we had gone into silent mode.

My grandmother, understanding, sat next to me at supper, patting my arm.

Afterwards we went out to the terrace together with her bag of spectacles, to watch the sunset. You girls were with us – this I remember clearly. So I'm hoping you'll remember that patchwork bag of hers, with its twenty years' worth of spectacles.

Somewhere deep inside it would have been the only pair with lenses strong enough for her failing eyes, but she wasn't interested in finding it, not in the least. All she wanted was to watch the sunset as distorted by the lenses in all the other spectacles, and then to pass each pair on to me, and then to you, to share the delight.

She was wearing the wrong spectacles later that night when she fell down the stairs.

Was she on her way out to watch the moon, I wonder?

Or had she been sleepwalking?

We'd found her before, wondering the hallways in the middle of the night. Talking to the chairs and the walls and the ghosts only she could see. In the morning, she would claim no memory of it.

I was the first to hear her, that night of the moon and the wrong spectacles. I was with her, as she lay there dying. Or rather, she was there with me.

And you girls were with us, too, when, some days later, we buried her alongside her mother, in that little churchyard up in the hills above.

I went back up there by myself, before we packed up to

fly home. To take her some flowers, and lie down next to her, and look up at the sky as she once did, and renew my promise.

## In Absentia

There were so many times, though, when I almost caved in.

From that very first time I put you girls on a plane, I asked myself. What was stopping me from going with you? It tore me up, to hand you over. You were so little when all this started. I couldn't bear the thought of your travelling all the way to Istanbul without me. Even though I knew the attendants would take good care of you. Even though I was sending you to your father, who loved you just as much as I did, and to your stepmother, whom I trusted absolutely. Every June, as I stood there waving you off, I would tell myself that this was insane, to be handing you two over, and staying behind, simply because I had chosen to devote my life to a hopeless cause.

I would ask myself: what if I just risked it? What if I wasn't actually on some kind of list? What if no one cared what I'd written about the genocide? What if no one was keeping track? What if my mother was exaggerating the dangers? Yes, it might be against the law, to write or speak about the genocide in Turkey. It might be true, that just to use the word was to ask to be prosecuted, or worse. But if the worst did come to the worst, my mother would find some way to bail me out of jail, wouldn't she? Just like she'd done for the cousins, more times than I could count?

Every time I put you girls on a plane, every time the

cousins had a trial coming up – especially, especially when Suna was prosecuted for publishing my books – these questions plagued me. And then I'd ask myself: why am I being so precious about my safety, when the cousins go into prison and out of it and still refuse to bow their heads, even though they know full well where their refusal might lead them? Every time there was a bomb while you were there, or an earthquake – I died a little, hated myself more than just a little. Even though your father or more usually your stepmother picked up the phone then and there, to assure me you were safe and well. Even though they would offer to put you on the next plane back to me, if I thought that best. Still I would ask myself: why are they bending over backwards for me? Why, if I'm this anxious for our daughters' safety, am I not just getting myself on the very next plane to Istanbul?

In my mind, I was there already. In my mind, I had never left. From my perch of safety, I followed the news and read the books. I went to the conferences, and the workshops, and the symposia. I was there, in the thick of things (at least to the extent that an American university campus can ever be in the thick of things) when the little opening my co-authors and I had helped to create for constructive dialogue between Turkish and Armenian scholars became a bigger one.

I'm not sure if you remember this – it is one of those things that gain significance only in retrospect – but Hrant Dink even came to our house once. His name still means something here, but just in case you can't place it: Hrant was the editor of a Turkish Armenian newspaper called Agos, and the man who did more than any other to open up that space for constructive dialogue – not just in Europe and

America, but in Turkey, first and foremost. And not just for scholars and writers and journalists, but for everyone else, too. *Hepimiz*, as he liked to say. All of us.

His visit to our home would have been in 2003 or thereabouts. He was in America, going from university to university, and mine was one of them. He was there to remind us that our area of study was not just an academic matter. The slaughter of Anatolia's Armenians and the eradication of their legacy and way of life were wounds that all Turks carried. The only way forward, he said, was for all of us, all of us, to acknowledge that tragedy, and weep together, and reconcile. What a beautiful, impossible dream, I remember thinking.

But then, it happened. The fury took root and grew. The flower opened.

Suna's publishing house was ahead of the game, of course, having already brought out many of the most important books on the subject in Turkish translation. But there was also the wildly popular radio station that the cousins had founded together – it played its part, too. Hrant was in and out of their studios. Speaking openly, and forcefully, and never without wit or humour. So much so, that even from my perch of safety, streaming those programmes from half a world away, I had to gasp. At his daring. But also, at the unbounded compassion he showed to the multitudes phoning in. 'I know,' he'd say. 'They taught you differently in school.' 'I know,' he'd say, 'what a terrible thing it is, to hear from your parents or grandparents the truth of your origins, and at the same time to know that if you speak about those origins outside the house, you face persecution and prosecution, or worse.'

He's speaking to me, I remember thinking when he said that. He's speaking to me.

332

But then, I asked myself, how long are they going to let him – them – *hepimiz* – all of us – get away with this?'

They were already dragging him through the courts, for insulting Turkishness, and other thought crimes. The cousins were being prosecuted, too, along with many others in their circle. The bigger danger lay in the media hate campaigns that cast them all as traitors in league with the liars of the Armenian diaspora and invited good citizens to take the law into their own hands.

But they kept on talking, Hrant and his friends. Many others joined them. People who had spent their lives with their hands clapped over their mouths – every week, every day, more of them spoke up.

Until 18th January 2007, when I tuned in to the cousins' radio station to hear that Hrant had been assassinated, just outside his newspaper.

It was Sinan's voice I heard first, speaking from the vigil that had by now grown to many thousands. From time to time, Suna and Haluk interjected. They directed me to the live stream. And that was when I had the shock of my life: standing next to the cousins was my mother.

She was angrier than I had ever seen her.

But also, strangely regal.

Everyone was listening to her. Everyone was taking her seriously.

Everyone fell silent when she raised her fist, declaring herself ready to hunt down the assassins and drag them to justice.

She too had been friendly with Hrant, you see. So friendly that she'd called him Leapfrog, which was the pen name he used for his weekly column. She claimed now to have had fed him a number of what she called 'juicy tidbits'. It was during this same live stream that I heard for the first time that my mother had been one of the speakers at a now legendary 2006 conference at which a dozen or more Turks had spoken in Turkish, and in most cases, for the first time ever, about their Armenian roots.

Hers could not have been the saddest story, though (because no one has ever been able to tell me quite what she said) I can only guess.

But whatever her story, she told it well, and it had turned her into something of a star in those circles, sometimes for the best reasons, and sometimes – as I was later to discover – for the worst.

## Why does he hate us?

I'm not sure if you ever had a chance to see Sinan's last documentary. But if, having read these words, you decide you'd like to see it, I can find you a copy. In any event, that's its title: *Why does he hate us?*

The 'he' in that title is İsmet.

Sinan shot the film in 2008, a year after Hrant Dink was assassinated, and some months after İsmet was one of several dozen figures to be arrested in connection with the Ergenekon affair. This was allegedly a plot to overthrow the Islamist government – an unsuccessful plot, I might add, as the government in question is the same one under which we suffer today.

It was, people now say, a plot about a plot – a way of locking up the most important power brokers of the previous regime. Most had blood on their hands, to be sure. Hrant's blood included. But the Ergenekon plot turned out to be a fabrication.

In those early days, though, there was a strong desire in my circles to believe that at least some of those detained were guilty as charged.

İsmet in particular.

And now, with İsmet behind bars, Sinan must have thought the time had come to ask why this man hated us.

'Us' being an entire generation of Turkish leftists like himself.

The documentary opens as it closes, with a close-up of my mother. She is waving her usual cigarette about, and as she speaks of İsmet's early life, the camera follows the trail of her smoke to dissolve into a collage of old photographs. But we still have my mother's voice, describing the tree under which İsmet had first met Soran Bey, aka the Cotton King, who, having taken a liking to young İsmet, perhaps because he saw something of himself in him, had become his lifetime patron, sending İsmet along to Istanbul in due course, officially in the employ of the secret police, but unofficially, under the wing the same family whose patronage had proved so beneficial to Soran Bey in the years following Independence.

Alas, my mother said, the family had proved too wayward and sophisticated for the country bumpkin İsmet then was. In the aftermath of a misunderstanding, which had involved İsmet attempting the rape of an underage girl, and going on to accuse another member of her family of hosting parties for a nest of spies, while accusing yet another member of that family – Teddy – of running a secret bordello, housing seven young boys – in both cases without evidence – İsmet had been sent back to Adana in some disgrace, and it was here that we heard from a woman of about my age who had been a servant in Soran the Cotton King's Adana home at the time.

İsmet had gone to visit Soran Bey just once during his three or four months of exile, she recalled. The two men had sat together in the garden, drinking the sherbets she served them.

'I shall now tell you what I happened to overhear, while tending to the ironing, just a meter or two away,' this witness informed the camera. But first she described her master's villa.

It was a large modern villa, she said, which he had decorated in the old way. Kilims on every wall, copper trays and divans and a marble floor in evidence only here and there, between the carpets. There was no courtyard, but the garden, which was thick with fruit trees and fragrant blossoms, was enclosed by a high wall. It was here, in the lingering cool of the morning, that İsmet told his benefactor of his recent misfortunes.

He had struggled to find the right tone. This had been clear to the woman who had once been the girl ironing in the next room. And while she could say with full certainty that İsmet had listened respectfully to the wise counsel his benefactor then imparted to him, it had been difficult for him to hide his true feelings.

This was what his benefactor had told young İsmet: In this land of corrupt officials and drunken landowners, it was not an easy thing for a boy without prospects to get ahead. But it was not impossible, as Soran Bey's own case proved.

Had Soran Bey's father not won the trust of an Armenian silversmith in Harput by safeguarding their wealth during the 1995 massacre, Soran Bey would never have found himself working for that silversmith son's on the finest avenue of Istanbul at the age of six.

Had he not had the foresight to shift his allegiance from his first master to the illustrious Adnan Pasha at the apposite moment, he would never have been placed in charge of the small cotton concern that he and his sons had now grown into a financial empire, with its main office in Istanbul, just a few hundred yards away from the building where he'd worked as a child. Nor would the Cotton King's son have had the good fortune to marry Adnan Pasha's granddaughter.

But every rise to greatness had its pitfalls. The greatest mistake was to overestimate one's position. This, the wise Soran Bey said, was what İsmet had just done. The most prudent course would be to stay in Adana with a bowed head until the scandal sheets had moved on to their next outrage.

I cannot bear their mockery, İsmet had then said.

To which Soran Bey had replied, Do they really mock you? Are you certain they even pause to think about you? Be strong, my boy. Be sure to profit from their inattention. As you will discover, unless you have already done so, privilege has a way of making people blind. And where there is blindness, there is opportunity.

He had leaned forward, to tap the ground between them with his cane.

I did not send you to Kansas for nothing, Soran Bey then said. Alluding now to the expensive education he had provided for this man, expecting nothing in return. As in due course to could do for this woman who had once been the girl ironing in the next room. Though not quite as expensively.

This is the American century, Soran Bey had told İsmet.

It will not last beyond that, I assure you. But in the meantime, there is money to be made. It cannot be hard for a bright boy like you to find new ways of making himself indispensable. In the meantime, there is no dishonour in bowing to those who hold the power. In fact, it is the only way to get ahead.

İsmet had then bowed his own hand, according to our witness, for he wished to accord his benefactor with all the respect he deserved. But in silence, the witness said, İsmet refused his benefactor's words.

The next part of the documentary gave a swift but damning overview of İsmet's long career as the crusher of idealistic youth. There was a clip of Suna, offering the view that it had been the shame of his origins that had fuelled this career in general, and though the scandal known as the Teddy Affair had perhaps sharpened his animosity towards the family that had, while acting as his patrons, contrived to humiliate them, she could still not understand why he had felt compelled to single out the children of this family for special punishment.

It was left to my mother to offer an explanation.

There she sat on the terrace in Lugano, in her sleek white suit, and her bright pink scarf, and matching shoes, gazing pensively at the emerald on her finger and the smoke rising from her Soberanie.

'It was money, of course! Isn't it always? He wanted what we had. How else to explain his obsession for buried treasure? Even here, in Lugano!' She then told the story of İsmet's long-ago visit, when he had prowled the property after everyone else had gone to bed. 'With a Geiger counter.'

'So how knows?' she added with a light and lilting laugh.

338

'Perhaps somewhere along the way, he did actually find something.'


## The first attack

It was Anais who alerted me. It was, she said, a unilateral decision. The others having decided to respect my mother's wishes. 'Of course, she never wishes to worry you,' Anais explained. 'But it was a very bad attack.'

Some vagrants had managed to get inside my mother's building. They might have been glue sniffers. Or boys from the outskirts, on their way to find transvestites to rape and knife. Whoever they were, the consensus was that they'd been sent. 'If that is the case, then it could be anyone behind this attack,' Anais said. With that new platform of theirs, the cousins had been making everybody angry.

What new platform was that?

'Oh dear, haven't they told you? It was Suna's idea, of course. But they're all involved. It's an oral history project. Linked with the radio station. In the same building, at any rate. On the floor just below. It's doing excellent, valuable work. But my worry is that they have been encouraging your mother too much. It has been her contributions most of all that have made people angry.

'Now we all know your mother would never, ever wish to put you at risk on account of her actions. But my dear Dora, the fact is that your mother has been somewhat reckless – I think the fame has gone to her head – and now, alas, she has sustained serious head injuries. In addition to being kicked and punched, she was hurled down all those stairs. And it may have been some time before she was discovered in her stairwell. By the time the ambulance arrived, she was already very cold...'

They had taken her first to a municipal hospital. The tardy transfer to Anais's care had perhaps complicated her condition. But she was now in the hospital that Ruth had started all those years ago with my Uncle Semih, and that Anais now directed. Here my mother was receiving the best of care, Anais assured me. They had induced a coma, to allow her brain to heal as best it could. The chances of a partial, if not a full, recovery, were good, if not in any way guaranteed. 'But how much better it would be if on the day of her awakening she could open her eyes, and see her daughter beside her.'

And so, at Anais's urging, I flew back. By a circuitous route – it was August, and the direct flights were fully booked, so I ended up flying via Orlando, Madrid and Zagreb, landing in Istanbul some 45 hours later, after an absence of as many years.

I had travelled enough in other parts of the developing world to be familiar with the jagged, cobbled skylines of cities that had been allowed to grow too fast, with too little regulation, but they did not prepare me for new suburbs stretching deep into Europe as well as Asia as my plane made its final descent into Istanbul three mornings after the attack on my mother. In my time, this had been a city of a million. Now the metropolis that had long ago spilled over its limits was thirty million, if not more.

The airport of my childhood had been a two-storey stucco building with a single tower. Occupying half its upper floor had been the restaurant where my mother had slapped me back in 1963 and accused me of being a slut. Two customs officials had stood guard at the door on the ground floor that led on to six gates. Porters had carried bags to and from planes on their backs. The new airport was a sprawling global hub that emptied onto a smoggy network of two, three and four lane highways on which the traffic could do little more than crawl.

On clear roads, it would have been a half hour's drive to the hospital. That morning, it took us two hours through unmitigated concrete to reach the neighbourhood and another hour to negotiate its side streets.

The hospital was new, occupying the same space as the hospital of the same name where I'd had my appendix taken out at the age of twelve. In my mind's eye I could still see its speckled tile floors, its off-white walls and metal bedsteads. I could still remember walking down the corridors that were no longer, to be greeted by other patients' relatives, as they pulled me into their sickrooms to pour cologne over my hands.

Now I walked in to find acres of polished marble, hanging glass sculptures, and orchids in slender glass silos flanking the glass lifts.

Upstairs, outside my mother's room, I was stopped by a security guard. He couldn't seem to find my name on his list, so I went downstairs to the reception, to ask for Anais.

The receptionists told me that Anais was in conference. They would relay my message as soon as she was free. They directed me to the very grand cafeteria – more marble, more glass, like nothing I had ever seen in this city, though the food in the trays was just as I remembered it, and the aromatic steam that met me at the door.

It was lunchtime, and the place was packed. I sat down

at the only free table with my cup of tea – in a glass, they still served tea in glasses! – and took out my laptop. The wifi was slow. But while I was waiting for something – anything – to configure on my screen, I kept noticing gestures. A man in a doctor's coat, closing his eyes, as he lifted his chin to say no. A father reprimanding his child, by slicing the air with his hand. A matron twisting her open hand in one direction, and her head in the other, as her eyes asked for news. They took me back to the city I'd so decisively left behind. They made me feel fourteen.

So did the words jumping out at me, fully formed and wholly intelligible, from random conversations. Someone somewhere turned up the music, and a male singer who had formerly sounded no more than faintly annoyed now ejected such a cry of anguished ecstasy that I could only marvel at the way it seemed to go unheeded.

The song ended. I closed my eyes. When I opened them again, I found Anais standing over me.

I had not seen her in twelve years, but she had the same kind smile, and the same open face.

'My dear,' she said. 'At last.'

Together we went back upstairs, where the old security guard had been replaced by a new one who sprang to his feet at the sight of Anais and did not ask to see my ID. And there, beyond the door, lay my mother. Or rather, a blank replica of her. Head bandaged, eyes closed. Surrounded by bleeping machines and draped with tubes.

'Try as best you can to make yourself comfortable,' Anais said. 'If you wish, you can hold her hand. In fact, it would be so very excellent if you could do this!'

She had the nurse move my chair to one side of the bed, and then, immediately to the other, to put me next to the right hand, which was free of tubes. And then Anais just stood there, smiling but also waiting, until I did what felt so very unnatural, and took my mother's bony, leathery hand in mine.

'Yes! Excellent!' Anais whispered, her eyes lighting up. She turned away to offer a few instructions to the duty nurse. As I watched through waves of jet lag, I wondered idly why it was she wore a white coat. She might be the director of this hospital, but she was not a doctor.

It was your father who came for me, I don't know how many hours later. I was dozing, bent over awkwardly and still holding my mother's hand. I awoke to the sound of clinking keys. And there was Tallis, standing at the foot of the bed.

It had not, of course, been that long since I'd seen him, but he looked happier, more alive, than I could ever remember.

'You didn't have to come,' he said, once we were settled in a taxi. 'She's in good hands here, as you can see.'

'I can indeed see,' I said. 'But the fact remains that I'm her daughter.'

He cocked his head to one side, as if what I'd said demanded some reflection. 'Okay, then, fair enough,' he said finally. 'But don't take offence if when she wakes up, she isn't so happy to see you. She made us promise, you know. Things here are really heating up, and she didn't want you coming to any harm.'

'I hear İsmet's in prison,' I said.

'Yes, well, that's one good thing, at least. We're into the tenth big Ergenekon swoop by now, but it won't surprise you to hear he was one of the first to be taken in.'

I told him I'd been following all that very closely.

'Perhaps even more closely than you have,' I added.

'You may be right,' she said. There followed a long pause, ending with a sigh. 'There's something else I need to tell you,' he said finally. Hands clasped, eyes on the blocked road ahead, he announced in a grave voice that he and Anais were no longer together.

'Why not?' I asked.

'What do you think? I messed up.'

'Don't tell me you left her for a younger woman?'

He shrugged his shoulders. 'Strictly speaking, I didn't leave her. She kicked me out.'

'Because you were, let me guess, cavorting with a younger woman.'

'I'm afraid so. Yes.'

'Tallis!' I said. 'Really!'

He hung his head, muttering, 'I know, I know. I'm an asshole.'

'You certainly are.'

'It didn't work out, you'll be glad to hear. But Anais isn't taking me back.'

'Nor should she,' I said.

He agreed, with a hangdog nod. 'So anyway. I'm living around the corner from your mother these days, in my very own bachelor pad. Not what I wanted, but there you go. It's all very amicable, I assure you. I'm in and out of the hospital all the time. Anais still counts on me to advise her. We even eat together at least twice a week. Perhaps it's easier, if you were friends to start with.'

'Like you and me,' I said.

'Exactly,' he said, with a rueful smile. And then, with a sigh, he said, 'I wonder what that says about me.'

'That you're a typical man?'

'I should have seen that coming,' he said, 'but I walked straight into it.'

And then, without missing a beat, he began to tell me about the new project he and Anais had dreamt up, only a few days earlier – a chain of women's refuges, to be built by Tallis and integrated into a specially designated centre in the hospital.

'It's a great idea, and we have the money to do it,' he said.

As I nodded in agreement, I heard the echo of what his grandfather and my father had once said to Dr Ruth, all those years ago, when they made their deal for the hospital, at the Pera Palace.

Our first stop was the radio station, which was hard for me to understand on that first day, because its headquarters on Sıraselviler had been altered very little with the shift from residential to commercial use. The old wrought iron doors were still in place. Inside, across the marble entryway, was a matching cage lift. On either side of it was an old wooden desk. The receptionist sat at one of them. At the other sat a guard. Behind the receptionist was a banner carrying the radio logo. Behind the guard was a second banner, carrying the logo of the platform that according to Anais was making everyone angry.

Hepimiz. That was what they'd called their digital history platform. All of us.

Suna was the first to come downstairs. 'Auntie!' she cried. 'You have come!' Her embrace was genuine, if also smothering. By the time I pulled away, the lift had gone up and down again, bringing Sinan and Haluk.

These two were markedly less friendly. But there was no

time to find out why. Off we went down the hill – Tallis with my suitcase, flanked on either side by Suna and Sinan, who were talking over each other, and remonstrating, but not once losing their footing, even though the pavement narrowed almost into nothingness at some points, widening elsewhere only to catch the unwary with potholes, protruding iron rods, and ill-marked steps.

Haluk was kind enough to stay at my side, alerting me to upcoming obstructions. But he said nothing until we had left the main road for the also crowded backstreets. 'You must forgive them,' he said then, nodding in the direction of the trio ahead. Who were no longer talking, but shouting and waving their arms. Especially Suna, who stopped short now and again to stamp her feet and raise her eyes, as if to beseech the heavens.

'They are tense, of course,' Haluk went on to explain. 'At the platform, and also at the radio station, we have had an eventful day. But this evening, we shall relax.'

On we walked, up one cobblestone alley and down another. Past bakeries and hardware stores, coffeehouses, kebab restaurants and furniture depots. Wending our way past cars parked illegally and cars reversing at full speed, boys playing ball, men selling lottery tickets, girls and women hanging over railings and windowsills, nudging and giggling, or raptly silent, and as I write these words, I am back on those cobblestones, subsumed again with the giddiness of inhabiting a space through which time flows like the sea, answerable only to the tides and the currents.

The meyhane to which we decamped was on a side street that had, in my time, belonged to the red light district. Now it was it was full of students and weekend bohemians. But I could not contemplate these carefree crowds without also seeing the hawkish pimps who had once patrolled these streets. What would they have made of our scant clothing, loud laughter, and open displays of affection?

The arguments that had begun on the way over did not end when we sat down, though the cousins would interrupt them now and again, reverting to English for my benefit, for my Turkish had grown rusty. 'What has become of us?' Suna would say. 'We must remember our honoured guest! But before we close the subject, I have just one more thing to say.' And then she'd be off again, leaving me with plenty of time to savour the food, which had not changed, and the gestures people made while talking or walking, which hadn't either, and the buildings looming over us on this side street, still standing and still dark. I remembered how it had felt, just to flit past them as a girl of twelve or thirteen, muffled by a heavy coat. I had learned, without motherly instruction, never to rest my eyes on a single point for long. The memories now returning unbidden were imbued with that same anxious haste. The beer halls where no respectable woman set foot. The neon lit foyers of hotels that were really brothels. The dark doorways announced by cracked plastic signs depicting popping champagne bottles, or cartoon sophisticates sipping cartoon cocktails. The billboards of nearly naked women with nipples that sparkled like stars. The shop windows in which dismembered mannequins flaunted leather gloves, conical bras, and stockings that somehow managed to stay up without suspenders. The traffic that never flowed, the vendors perched on the edge of the narrow pavements, the better to look up your skirt, the gentleman strollers who stopped short, apparently to study an advertisement outside a cinema, or a haberdasher, or a buffet, or a lottery shop, but really to plunge their hands between your legs.

Looming over these malingerers had been the blackened, crumbling remains of imperial Constantinople. The no longer grand hotels where Graham Greene and Agatha Christie had once mingled with murderers and spies. The tearooms whose heavy drapes protected art nouveau nymphs from public view. The restaurants whose upper galleries had once boasted entire orchestras and were now repositories for broken chairs.

When, after our stormy supper, my receiving committee took it upon itself to guide me up and down the avenue before returning me to my mother's apartment, they pointed out the establishments that had been rescued and restored: the consulates still nestling behind their old imperial gates, the churches – Greek and Armenian, Catholic and Orthodox – that had somehow survived. We jumped over the tramlines that had been restored to İstiklâl after it was pedestrianised. We noted the new cafes and boutiques and bookstores and galleries. We peeked in on the fish market, which hadn't changed at all, and the Passage of Flowers, whose beer halls now looked too clean and neat. But as we pushed through the crowds, past the tumble of neon signs, and the dull roar of a thousand voices mingling with the music flowing out of every entrance, what surprised me most were the buildings themselves, for the facades of İstiklâl had been cleaned and backlit. It was even possible, if you kept your eyes raised, to imagine how this street had looked before the First World War, when it was still the Grande Rue de Pera. Even my mother's building was golden bright.

As Tallis lugged my bags up the three flights of uneven marble stairs, Anais warned me that she could not guarantee the apartment was in a fit state. She told me that I would be more than welcome to return with her to the hospital.

There was a bed for guests in my mother's room. I shook my head, saying that I doubted my mother would want me in the same room with her.

We were resting on the second landing when I said that, and though I noted an exchange of looks, I could not read it. And this was when I felt the first pang of envy for the lives they had shared, the silences they did not need to break. I was almost grateful when Suna informed me that – 'modernity notwithstanding' – it was still the custom in Turkey for families to keep vigil over their infirm.

Brought up short by her didactic tone, I said, 'How admirable!'

Shaking her head, she said, 'Perhaps.' After a thoughtful pause, she added, 'We, too, have been known to harbour murderous thoughts.'

'And then?' I asked.

'We murder our thoughts.'

This brought forth cries of exasperation, and a cascade of chastisements, which I could not yet follow, though their voices' every rise and fall brought me closer to words I had known and lost and would soon enough regain. As they carried on up the stairs, laughing and nudging each other, and raising their arms – now this way, and now that – they almost looked as if they were dancing.

The lights went off. But Tallis was already on the third floor, and on the case. 'Do you remember these things?' he asked, when I had climbed as far. 'The minuterie, I think it's called. Giving you light, but just for one minute. 'But anyway,' he said, as he gestured towards the open door. 'Welcome home.'

It did not feel like home, nor did I feel welcome. But when I walked into the dark, dank apartment for the first time since

1963, I knew at once where to find the switch for the overhead light. As I took in the cluttered and disordered room, whose drapes and sofas looked as if they'd not been dusted since my departure, I was overtaken by a very old despair. Walking into the kitchen, and finding the sink piled high with unwashed glasses, I unthinkingly set to work on them. I returned to find the others perched on my mother's collapsing armchairs and sofas, perusing the pictures on the walls.

Some were of me, at various awkward and unsmiling ages. Two were early portraits of you girls. But most were old and un-dusted versions of my mother. Delphine in a ball gown. Delphine in a chic suit, flanked by men in fedoras. In a cocktail dress, kicking off her shoes. On the deck of a ship, waving a glove. On a stool, interviewing and outshining Her Highness the Princess Soraya of Iran. Gazing downwards, as if to smile at the overflowing ashtrays and wastepaper baskets, and the books, slips, and slippers that she had tossed onto the floor at some point during the previous half-century, and that the others seemed not to notice.

I found Tallis in my mother's bedroom, staring her fourposter bed. 'It must be strange to be back here, after all these years,' he said.

'Obviously,' I snapped.

'Listen,' he said, as he put a hand on my shoulder. 'I understand how discordant all this must be, but it will be a great deal easier, Dora, if you try and lighten up.'

'I'm sorry. You're right. I'll try.'

It was not, I think, what he'd expected me to say. As he moved to the side window, he looked almost lost. He nodded in the direction of my grandmother's old apartment across the way, he said, 'It's even more of a mess over there. But would you like to see it?'

350

'Why not?' I said. But when – again with a facility that unnerved me – I'd found the key to let us in, I had to wonder if my mother had even once ventured inside since my grandmother's death. We struggled just to find a path through the piles of musty furniture.

We returned to my mother's apartment to find the others preparing to leave. 'Are you going to be all right here, all on your own?' Suna asked. 'I'm thinking about this intruder. I'm thinking that someone unsavoury might also have the key to this place. You can come stay with me if you like.'

'I appreciate your concern,' I said. 'But please, don't worry me. I'll be fine.' It wasn't long, though, before I was very much not fine, for the sheets in my old room gave no indication of having been changed in several decades. The sheets in the cupboard seemed just as old. In desperation I dabbed a shawl with the vial of lavender oil I took with me everywhere and cradled it around my head, but it proved no match for my mildewed pillow. I was soon back on my feet.

Under the kitchen sink, I found a duster and a dusty bucket. In the bathroom, I found the washer and dryer that looked to have been my mother's only domestic purchases since 1963. Why, with all her money, had she kept this apartment like a museum piece? Next to the front door, at the back of the coat closet, I found an ancient vacuum cleaner. Behind it, beneath a pile of bags and shoes, I found a box of my mother's old notebooks, numbered, dated and cross-referenced.

Some listed names, or rather, initials, alongside cryptic observations and abbreviated questions: 'Saw CS step into P unescorted, and who did he meet but WT and QM-R?' The old bankbooks I found stacked up beneath the notebooks dated back to when it had cost millions of Turkish liras just to buy a coffee – something my mother had complained about at length – but the whole business felt shabby, spoke of a life spent trying too hard, so I put them back where I had found them and went back to my spring clean.

By dawn, I had made the place habitable, but for the row of bin bags lined up in the hallway. It was while I was making my bed with my thrice-washed sheets that my hand grazed against what turned out to be my long-forgotten Russian journal, wedged between the mattress and the springs.

I say journal, though half its pages were devoted to vocabulary lists. The rest were filled with practice sentences, with the words from the lists underlined. Taking my coffee to the little table I had placed between the French doors, I set out to test my memory: I had not read a Russian sentence since age fourteen.

A gust of wind rattled the French doors, bringing with it the roar of the city. Beyond the cascading rooftops, a ferry was making a wide arc around a tanker. Beyond Palace Point, I could see a dozen other tankers, hanging in the haze.

How rounded, how careful, my handwriting had been. How certain my ambitions. Today I am studying Russian, I'd written. Tomorrow I shall master it. Today my teacher is a man named Sergei. Tomorrow we shall work together, in English and in Russian, to foster world peace.

There is no other point to life, I'd said.

I read those words and wept.

## The apartment

Having spent so much of my adult life despairing of my mother, for all sorts of reasons but mostly for her continuing to insist on spending half of every year in a city that had no place for her, I cannot blame you girls for wishing that I, too, might agree to leave Istanbul. But I do hope that the day will come when you consent to visit me here, if only to put flowers on your father's grave, if only to see what I have done with my mother's apartment, and even more, with the one next door. I had my helpers, of course. I still do. But it was Anais who, in those first weeks, got me started.

Whenever she managed to escape from the hospital, she came right over. We would go across to the furniture depot that Hümeyra's great room had become, and make our way back to the back bedrooms, go through the old collages, and the stacks of prints that the Society Photographer had left her. The rooms were full of boxes that, when opened, revealed great treasures mixed with junk. Whenever we found something Anais thought might be interesting, she'd take it away to be valued. And some were very valuable indeed. But it was always the stories she brought back with her that I valued most.

All that took time, though. In the beginning, I also had my work. Of course I did not know then that I would never be returning to my job at the university. I wasn't teaching summer school that year, but I still had articles to write.

It was Anais who suggested I use my mother's office at the platform. It would prove impossible, she said, to concentrate on academic work in the apartment, with its memories and its dust, or the hospital, with all its comings and goings. However, she added: Should I base myself at the platform, I needed to be sure to make my way through the noise generated by the cousins, who seemed to like nothing more, she said, than to stir up ancient wasps' nests.

Instead I should devote myself the young ones, who had been working with my mother on the platform's more quiet and deserving projects. Tracing family histories, for example. Mapping them against the buildings of the city.

Historian that I then still was, I did not share Anais's illusions about this sort of work. Quiet investigations into families and their former properties did not necessarily stay that way. But her gang of volunteers – most of them students of Suna's – turned out to be as lovely as Anais had said.

Sinan was of two minds about having me in the office. Your father stood up for me, though. And so I stayed.

I stayed, but during those tumultuous months I shared at least in part with the cousins and your father – months I think back upon with such longing and regret – I never lost the feeling that I had landed without warning or preparation in the life I should have had. It was as if the archives and libraries in which I had spent my entire working life had served as hiding places from my destiny. As if all my years in Pomfret, years I'd spent quite literally tending to my own garden, had been wasted. And yet I had no idea where I stood in this new life. It was like starting to read a novel at Chapter 63. No matter how much I tried to catch up on what I'd missed, or how much those around me tried to explain, I lacked the wherewithal to exercise proper judgment. I had no idea how to filter what I heard. I was left foundering between contradictions. Moment after moment, I was knocked sideways by the little beauties I encountered everywhere, nestling between the atrocities of the modern age.

The sea especially. They couldn't ruin it. The Bosphorus, the Golden Horn, and the Marmara – I could lose myself in their currents for hours on end. But that, I think, was another kind of evasion. There are things I should have noted. Things that even then, without the benefit of retrospect, I should have recognised as odd or off-key.

I could give you a hundred examples. I might, one day, fill an entire notebook with my recollections of those three short months, if ever I find the courage to ask what I thought I was doing, plunging headlong into a family I'd never truly inhabited.

But for now, let me just tell you about the island.

## The island

We had reached the tail end of that summer. My mother was still in her medically induced coma, and Anais, having decided that we both needed a break, had accepted an invitation to the private island next to Büyükada, which I understand you both know well from your visits here to see your father.

Our host was a poet: it goes without saying that he, too, belonged a branch of a branch of our gnarled family tree. We had come out expecting to spend only a night but ended up spending a week.

At first it was just Anais and me. Then she left, on the ferry that brought Tallis. Then Sinan arrived, with his young son, and his American wife, who no one had thought to tell me was the daughter of our man for all seasons, not until after she was gone. She alone had been worried about imposing, worried about their young son making too much noise, and utterly undone by the bomb we'd heard explode that Tuesday evening, across a flat sea, somewhere in the vast suburbs of the Anatolian city. The next morning, she and the boy left, having decided to spend what was left of the summer on Cape Cod.

We were joined that same evening by Haluk's wife Lüset, whom I'd likewise never met or even heard about. For reasons undisclosed, she was now living in Tel Aviv. She had her own extended family to tend to on the nearby island of Burgaz. The next morning, Haluk ran her back there in his speedboat, returning in the afternoon with Suna and Anais.

Sinan arrived soon afterwards. He would be there one night, and gone the next.

This meant a lot of changing sheets for the housekeeper, though she seemed to enjoy all the coming and going, too, despite her bad back. There were cheese poğaças every morning, fresh from the oven, fresh as the tea. At midday there was cherry sherbet, made from fruit she had pitted and crushed with her own hands. For lunch there was menemen, for supper fish and beans and stewed aubergine and salad and finely diced fruit. In between there was the laundry she insisted on doing for us all. Not to mention the dishes, sheets, and floors. The only time I saw her sitting still was at five in the evening, when she took an old transistor radio out to the back terrace, to listen to Turkish choral music while sitting under the grape arbour with the newspaper that her employer, like the rest of us, denounced as the epicentre of right-wing evil. As she perused whatever pack of lies they were brandishing on the front page, she'd grimace wisely. Moving on to the crossword, she'd remove the pencil from behind her ear. Holding it in mid air, she would hum along with the chorus.

There was one night when everyone was away except for me, until Tallis turned up with one of the interns from the office. He was somewhat taken aback to find me there, but

I told him it didn't matter. She was a nice girl, I said. I knew her and liked her. Of course, she deserved better than a man approaching sixty, I said, to which Tallis readily and unabashedly agreed. 'I know,' he said. 'But Anais won't have me back. So what can I do?'

'Tell the poor girl to try dating someone her own age, perhaps?'

'She doesn't like men her age. They're too competitive and too selfish. Their egos get in the way of everything.'

'Believe that if you wish,' I said. 'I'm still going to tell her to keep looking.'

'Fair enough,' was his reply.

It was odd, I'll admit it, the evening that followed. I did like this intern, as I've already said. And it had been years since I'd felt uncomfortable about being with your father while no longer being married to him. In fact, I enjoyed being his most trusted critical friend. But there were times when (as with Anais, in earlier years) I just wished he'd not chosen such and such a moment to kiss this new friend's forehead, or put his arm around her shoulders, or yawn, and pat her on the shoulder, and say, 'What do you say, Miss Tiddlywinks. Time for bed?' I wished, at least, he could have found some other term of endearment. He'd called me Miss Tiddlywinks. Anais, too.

We were swimming when the others arrived with the morning ferry. By the time they had joined us on the jetty, two friends from next door had joined us, too. Inside, the housekeeper was busy cooking. More guests were expected on the midday ferry. By the time we sat down to eat on the veranda, there were a dozen of us or more.

It was the sort of mix you only find in societies where friends are rarely made in adulthood. Many of those present were in business; just as many others in the arts. There were as many at the table who put their faith in the army, the state and the nation's founding fathers as there were those who harboured grievances against them.

This led to the usual sparks at the dining table. That day the sparring was about our Islamist prime minister, soon to become our president, who had once again raised the taxes on alcohol, and banned smoking in public places, as well as advising the nation's women to have at least three children each. After an old-guard secularist asked Suna when she was going to stop making excuses for him, she – and the rest of us – were treated to a long lecture. For Suna never was, and never would, make excuses for a virulent opponent of women's rights, not to mention LGBT rights, or freedom of the press, to mention just a few of our Islamist president's defects. But our prime minister was right in seeking to reduce the power of the military, which had done the nation such harm.

'He's only doing this to increase his own powers!' cried the old-guard secularist. 'Watch my word, we'll end up with a dictator who forces headscarves on us all!'

There ensued a spirited discussion about headscarves that was far from resolved when I interrupted to say that I still didn't understand what all the fuss was about. Since my return I had of course noticed that the fashion amongst devout Islamist women was to use their often very expensive headscarves to cover every last strand of their hair. I had noticed, too, that this fashion was very widespread indeed. 'But it's not like Saudi,' I said. 'You can see them behind the wheel in traffic, and behind the counter in expensive stores, and sitting in mixed groups in cafes and restaurants, and on many occasions I've seen covered girls arm in arm with female friends in miniskirts! I'm wondering, therefore, if we shouldn't just let them all be.'

In the silence that followed, there were sighs, pinched smiles and exchanges of weary looks. Until the old-guard secularist glanced at her watch and cried out, 'How time flies when the conversation turns to women's dress!'

Off they went, most of them, on the five o'clock ferry. Our generous host then played his usual ruse, suggesting for the rest of us the island boat that left for the mainland at half past six, only to lure us back to the little shingle beach on the island's southern tip. Here we sat, watching the sun sink ever lower while we lost ourselves in talk.

I imagine, looking back, that there'd been an undercurrent of tension all day. But it was only at this beach that I picked up on it. First a hushed but angry-sounding exchange between Tallis and Anais while I was changing out of my wet swimsuit, just out of earshot. Then, when I joined them, an uneasy silence, which we filled by skipping stones.

No sooner had I formed this thought than Anais made to skip a stone that might better have been called a boulder. It crashed against an outcropping of rock before tumbling into the water.

'Which reminds me of the time,' said Tallis. 'We'd better get going!'

But once again, we were too late for the ferry. We would have to stay another night.

I needed to check in on my mother. Anais needed to call the hospital about other matters, too. Suna and Haluk had their own things to rearrange. Our host gave us the use of his study in the eaves, and I can still recall waiting my turn for the phone, and looking down at the terrace, where Tallis had stretched himself out on the sofa with his book.

While I watched, Sinan joined him. Stretching out on the chair with his back to the sea, he propped his feet on the edge of the sofa. Until, with a swift and sudden kick, Tallis pushed them off.

'What's this now?' Sinan said.

To which Tallis replied, 'I got here first.' '

'So what?' said Sinan.

'So go take your feet somewhere else,' said Tallis.

'Why should I?' asked Sinan.

And Tallis said, 'Because I said so.'

To which Sinan said, 'Who do you think you are, the king of the castle?'

At which point Tallis feigned a yawn. 'But I am the king of the castle!'

A split-second pause, before Sinan burst out laughing. Standing up, he leaned over, to give Tallis a light slap. Light but sharp.

'I'd watch my step if I were you,' said Tallis, in a light voice with an edge to it. 'The king does not take challenges lightly.'

Placing himself in the chair opposite, Sinan leaned forward.

'In that case, the king will have to show us what he's made of.' '

So be it,' said Tallis. He returned to his paper.

A slamming door in the apartment below told us that Anais would not be joining us that evening.

One by one, the rest of us came out to the veranda. First Suna, then Haluk, then me. When Tallis shifted to make room for his unlucky new girlfriend, Sinan said, 'Oho! The king has a fickle soul. He has found a new favourite.'

To which Tallis said, 'A king has to do what a king has to do.'

To which Suna said, 'Please! Boys! I have had enough of this nonsense.'

But the boys had not. The game went on into the night. The king was offered tea after tea, cordial after cordial. Beer after beer. He was asked if the cushion on his sofa were satisfactory. He was asked for his verdict on each and every subject the others broached, and if he said that he had no verdict, that he was, as before, just trying to read the paper, Sinan would nudge Haluk and point at Tallis and say, 'Forsooth, the king is reading.' At the end of the evening, Sinan put his hand on the poor, embarrassed girlfriend's shoulder and said, 'Treat our king well tonight. Do not betray us.'

Turning to Tallis, he bowed and said, 'Is there anything else I can do for my master, before he retires with his concubine?'

'That's not very nice,' said Tallis.

'My king,' said Sinan, as he performed a sweeping bow. 'I fear I have offended you! Oh please. Dear king! How can I ever make it up to you?'

'Don't apologise to me, you asshole. Apologise to her. You really don't know where to stop, do you? This is no longer a joke. You cut this out now, or else.'


So there you have it. That week on the island, so perfect, until it ripped. Only for the rip to disappear, long enough for me to believe that peace had been restored, until suddenly, without warning, it ripped again.

There was never any chance to ask myself why, or even to reflect on how very odd it was, to be back in the thick of things, jostled at every turning by sights I had edited out of my memories, and brought up short by new developments I could never have anticipated. An argument would erupt, and before I had the time to count the fissures, something else would happen to send me flying.

The very next day, for instance. The day we left the island.

We all left together, because that was the day would have been Hrant Dink's 55th birthday, and the foundation that his family and friends had set up in his name after his assassination was hosting a concert to celebrate his legacy. There were more than 700 people in attendance. Between the musical performances were stirring speeches, in which taboos were again broken and Hrant's dream restated.

I knew that dream by heart. For years, I'd lived and breathed it. After his death, I'd nearly lost it. In the years following, I'd kept faith in his dream, but more through obstinacy than hope. But now, after all those years when we dared not say a thing in public, and all those other years when we did, and no one outside Turkey seemed to care – now here I was, in an Istanbul concert hall with seven hundred others who cared about that dream as fervently as I did. Who had ached in silence as I had, until today, when at last we could share our grief, and perhaps, perhaps, move on. That was the first time in my life that I was able to look around and believe that change was on the way. Not just possible, but powerful. Not just beautiful, but true.

I do honestly remember entertaining this exalted thought: that by rewriting the past, we could and would redeem ourselves.

There is nothing more dangerous than the history you think you know.

Suna had not been similarly moved by our evening of fine speeches. After so many years spent in the thick of things, while I watched on from a distant screen, she had come to the view that Hrant's dream didn't go far enough. For it wasn't (as Suna put it) enough to weep and reconcile. There was also the question of consequences: the wealth that some had lost and others gained. So it was not enough to repudiate the crimes of our grandfathers and great grandfathers. To make amends, true amends, it would be necessary for the younger generations to take full responsibility.

'And that,' Suna said, 'is not a beautiful thought. Neither is it a thought that can draw a large crowd.'

'Too true,' I said. But that, I regret to say, is why we thought there might be a book in it. Or at least, a pamphlet. 'A pdf for our platform?' I said. 'Best to be modest.'

'A worthy thought,' said Suna. 'But only if you agree that this pdf pamphlet of ours should bear our platform's name.'

"Hepimiz,' I said. 'Of course. That's perfect.'

'Two versions, though. One in Turkish. And the other in English.'

'All of us,' I said. 'Let's get to work.'

It seemed so simple. Hubris always does.


## Hubris

By late September, my mother had emerged from her coma, and according to her doctors, she was making steady improvement. But whenever I visited, and I visited at least twice a day, she was sound asleep.

I wonder now why I gave so little thought to what that might mean, what that might say about us. It gave me space and air to breathe, certainly. Time to claim the city as my own, or at least, to think I was.

I was continuing to base myself at the platform. Making up for my mother's absence, and perhaps also making the most of it. I had put my university work to one side by now, to turn my attention to the projects my mother had been pretending to lead, while her lovely volunteers did all the work. Once they had my full attention, I was able to help and even guide them, and this small contribution had engendered in me a surge of false pride: I even thought I knew what 'we' were up to.

This despite the fact that the pdf/pamphlet idea had not gone down well with the boys. The boys being what Suna and I began to call Sinan, Haluk, and Tallis after they informed us that the time was not right for a widening of the struggle, that the order of the day was still to win hearts and minds.

And here began another fissure, as Suna and I shared our frustrations: it was happening again, we agreed. The boys pretended we were all equals, until we thought of something before they did, or got in their way.

Along the way, we shared our misgivings about Sinan's İsmet documentary. These misgivings found their way into new quarrels. Why, I now asked, had it never occurred to Sinan to ask my permission before referring to the attempted rape? Why had he chosen to portray me as a victim, instead of letting it be known that I had been the heroine of the piece, by kicking İsmet in the balls?

Those questions were still hanging unanswered in the air on the morning when Sinan wandered into my office to ask me to look after a few Norwegians he'd invited in. So naturally, I was surprised.

They were journalists, he said. With a couple of potential funders in tow.

I at least had the presence of mind to ask why he saw no need to entertain a group of journalists and potential funders personally.

'I would normally have asked one of the others,' he said. 'But today they, like me, are too busy.'

'Too busy to grovel for money?' I asked.

This earned me a shrug. "These Norwegians are amusing,' he said. 'At least, this is what I've been told. If nothing else, you will find them sincere. And they, of course, will find you fascinating, with all your history. It should not overtax you, in any event. No need for the usual travelogue. They have been here before, so you can relax. And then, after lunch, you can come to our board meeting, to help us solve our fundraising problems, which are in fact serious.'

'Do you mean that?' I said. This being the first time I'd been asked to attend a board.

'It was Tallis' idea, but yes, it is nevertheless a good one. You can be our new fundraising officer.'

'Just like that?'

'Yes, exactly. Just like that.'

Fool that I'd become, I took the bait.

Over lunch with our potential funders in Cihangir, I dispensed, as advised, with the travelogue, and even with the latest political developments, in which the Norwegians were already well versed. We moved straight on the larger picture. They, too, had been surprised, as well as intrigued, by the rise and rise of oral history as a form of political protest. As seasoned journalists who had covered human rights organisations worldwide, they were, perhaps, amongst its most informed witnesses. They were now in active conversation with more than two dozen groups in other countries that had, like us, set out to challenge state lies with first person testimony, acquired by diverse means, but mostly via the internet.

What an unexpected boon this had been! But also, as I now pointed out, and they agreed, it had brought with it a host of new problems. For the truthfulness of our witnesses could never be assumed. So many were, of necessity, occluding their real names. Anonymous or signed, these claims needed to be tested. And that took time. It required a cool and critical eye. It was evident, and perhaps inevitable, that some such organisations were driven more by historical grievances and present-day agendas than by any desire to establish the truth. There was also, I ventured, the question of funding. So much of what was on offer had strings attached or hidden.

But there was no denying the flood. Neglecting to mention that I myself was a very new arrival to this platform, I told the Norwegians that over the past year we (we!) had heard from witnesses in the tens of thousands. The challenge facing our little platform now was to make some sense of what they'd given us. And then, how to disseminate it. On returning to the office I had so swiftly claimed as mine, I showed the Norwegians what 'we' had done so far.

After taking them through a few of our 1980 project's interactive pages, I told them about the pages still under construction, that would (once we had worked out how to avoid instant prosecution, if not for insulting Turkishness, then for inciting racial hatred or promoting terrorism) house our work on the fate of the Kurds during the same period, and the Alevis, as well as the country's dwindling Greek, Jewish, and Armenian communities.

I even spoke to them of your father's project, as yet to find its shape, laden down as it was with hard and undigested facts about US involvement in matters Ottoman and Turkish going back a hundred years.

'So many minefields,' said one of the Norwegians. 'How will you find your way across them?

'By remaining true to our principles,' I said staunchly. 'By which I also mean our principles as scholars – as historians. We do not publish what we have not tested. We do not take the money with the strings attached. Above all, we aim to hold ourselves to the same standards we expect of others.'

More sage nods and sighs. It was, I think, to bring some lightness back into our conversation that I gestured at the back wall, and the family trees our volunteers had been helping us build.

'Here, too, there are so many evasions, half-truths, and lies,' I said. 'When I first came to Istanbul as a twelve-year-old,' I said, 'almost everyone my age I met seemed to claim me as a cousin. So imagine my surprise when I turned out to be their aunt!'

I pointed to the trees on the blackboards, there on the far wall. They changed shape almost daily, I said. Whereupon Suna walked in to prove my point. Walking over the far wall, she erased a name from one branch of the Pasha Tree, as we called it, and moved it to another branch. After which she turned to me to say: 'I paid a visit to this aunt last night. After several hours of tedium, she confessed that her father's brother was actually his cousin.'

It must have been something about her deadpan delivery that made our visitors laugh. Whereupon one of the journalists asked if we two would mind going on the record. Suna and I looked at each other. 'Why not?' we said. Whereupon the journalist set up his cameras, placed us on either side of the Pasha Tree, and got us talking. For what did not feel like a full hour but was, we entertained our captive audience, speaking over each other, finishing each other's sentences, and courting their ready laughter. But nothing brought us as large a burst of laughter as when the Norwegians touched on Sinan's latest documentary, which they had seen.

They wished to know more about these misunderstandings the film had passed over so very quickly. 'The nest of spies,' they said. 'The rape. And the Teddy Affair. What was that?'

'Aha. Oho,' I said. 'How much time do you have?'

They claimed not to be in any rush, so Suna and I again set about talking over each other, painting for the Norwegians an impossibly romantic picture of Hermine-Hümeyra's famous Friday soirees, until Suna said, 'But enough of that. Dora, tell them what you did to our İsmet, when he tried to rape you.'

'Don't you dare misrepresent me,' I said. 'İsmet never came close to raping me, because I kicked him in the balls.'

'And so here we are,' said Suna, when the uproarious laughter had subsided. 'Who could have thought we would turn a century of tragedy into a stand-up routine?'

'Don't do yourself down,' said our journalist. 'You have made us all weep with mirth.'

With the embarrassed pause that followed, there came the chance to glance at watches, phones and clocks. The Norwegians were late for their next appointment, and so, too, were we.


## The onslaught

An argument was already in full swing when Suna and I walked into the boardroom. It concerned a new cache of documents we'd just been sent, about a string of dubious expropriations of minority foundations in the years following the 1980 coup. This time the alleged culprit an industrialist to whom Haluk was related.

In Sinan's view, and Suna's, the only course of action was to treat these documents in the same way we treated all that came to us.

In Haluk's view, this would be a most dangerous move. 'If we let ourselves be led by what we are sent...especially when it has no name attached to it, then we are, without a doubt...Without a doubt, I say!' He leaned forward, eyes bulging. 'We might as well blindfold ourselves. For we are walking into a trap.'

'Whose trap?' asked Sinan. Too softly – always a bad sign.

Haluk sat back but kept his gaze steady. 'As if you had to ask.'

'From which we can only assume,' Suna now added, 'that –in addition to these larger concerns – you also fear the anger of your maligned uncle, should we disclose his dark doings.'

'Your uncle, too,' Haluk hissed.

'By marriage only,' Suna snapped. 'But please, my dearest, my one and only...'

'This is no time for jokes.'

'Then let me rephrase. You are afraid that your uncle's anger will lead to actions on his part that will draw us deeper into an intrigue, though what that intrigue might be, you wish us to use our imagination. Rather than do what we have sought to do from the outset with this platform, which is to subject all evidence we receive to the same scholarly scrutiny.'

'I am not a scholar!' Haluk growled.

'Evidently not! But my friend, my dearest friend – and I choose these words with the utmost sincerity – it is what I most cherish about you. That you act, and think, and support us, from the heart.'

Hitting the table hard, Haluk said, 'Enough of your insinuations! As if my work requires no intellect! As if you could do the first thing without my help!'

'Haluk, darling. I am insinuating nothing. I am simply trying to clarify the situation.'

'The situation is that we should not be delving into these financial stories. This was never our aim!'

'But how could this be so,' Suna cried, 'when there is money involved in every piece of dirt we touch?'

Now Haluk lunged forward. Though there was a table between them, Suna raised her arms to shield her face.

'After all that my wife has suffered!' Haluk roared.

Suna roared right back. 'How dare you claim her pain as your own! How dare you assume I myself do not share it! Don't forget that Lüset has been my closest friend and soulmate from our earliest schooldays, many long years before you deigned to welcome her to your bed.'

'And is she still your friend?' Haluk said. He had lowered his voice, but his face was flushed, and his nostrils flared.

'How dare you ply me with false questions? You know full well that Lüset and I still speak to each other morning, noon and night.'

'Then, in that case,' Haluk hissed. 'I can ask you to respect her suffering, and her family's losses during the vile and never corrected anti-Semitic persecutions of World War II!'

'The Wealth Tax was not just levelled against the Jews, my one and only. The Christians suffered just as much from these levies.'

'What if they did?' bellowed Haluk. 'The fact remains! My wife's family, along with all this city's Jews, suffered ruination from those monstrous and discriminatory taxes! And yet, they bore this injustice with such dignity. They never lost their loyalty to the republic. And for what? Look how they treated her poor grandfather, after he came back from the work camps! Look what happened to her father, in the racist riots of 1955! Look what she herself has suffered, and me with her! Do you think it is easy, to have to go all the way to Tel Aviv, just to have supper with my wife?'

'Haluk, dearest, we all know these things,' Suna said. She took his hand. When he pulled it away, she used her other hand to pin it down. 'And not only do we know these things,' she said, as she lifted that hand to place it on his shoulder. 'Also, we respect them. Is it not in this same spirit of respect that we established this platform? Has our dear Lüset not delved into her own pocket to help us?'

'Only to open us to allegations of covert Israeli funding!' Haluk cried. 'When every kuruş was from the wealth her family built up here, against all odds, to the benefit of our entire economy!

Now it was Suna's turn to lean across the table. 'But Haluk,' she said softly. 'This is not what we are here to discuss. Our problem today is not Lüset's family, but our own.'

'I cannot be held responsible for every relative under the sun,' Haluk muttered.

He fell silent. We all fell silent.

Until Tallis cleared his throat.

'I think we're all missing the point here,' he said.

He went on to explain how, and why, in a voice I now recall as being too confident, too sure it was right, firming and raising it notch by notch until Sinan, who had been playing sulkily on his phone, at last set it down, and listened.

It was inevitable, Tallis said, that a platform such as ours would become a lightning rod. All a person had to do was acquire a few incriminating documents, and press send. But we on the receiving end could choose what to examine. As more and more flowed or flooded in, we could also choose what to read. The truly urgent question was to decide how we stored the hundreds and thousands of new documents and rumours and allegations that were coming in every day now.

'I don't need to remind you that everything we store online is insecure. I don't think any of us would relish the prospect of others hacking into our archives for their own purposes.'

'In fact,' said Sinan. 'We are already being seen to have been misusing these archives ourselves.'

'How so?' asked Suna.

Tallis looked at Sinan, who was again checking his phone.

'There have been threats,' Sinan said evenly.

'What's new about that?' Suna scoffed. 'Since the day we opened our doors, there have been threats.'

In a dry, collected voice – a voice I recognised as his way of hiding panic – Tallis explained that there had been a new onslaught, with upwards of a hundred irate emails having arrived in the past hour alone.

'And thirty more,' Sinan added, 'since we last counted.'

'They are all in response to something that was posted on another site I've never heard of,' Tallis said. He named it. No one else had heard of it either. This post had referred, in Hebrew, to the same rogue uncle we had been discussing – the one who might have been enriched by the expropriation of minority foundations during the 1980 regime. The allegations detailed in this post had then been picked up by another site no one had ever heard of. In this retaliatory post, the finger had been pointed at our own platform. The allegation was that we ourselves had set up the first site, writing in Hebrew to give the impression of Israeli backing, but in fact to dishonour and expose the rogue uncle on behalf of the backers we had acquired through Haluk's "Jewish wife'.

This twisted tale was met with cries of consternation. 'Aman! Whatever next!'

'What we can expect next is, of course,' said Sinan, 'more of the same.' Here he turned to Tallis, who was already passing around a few of the newspapers we would never wish to read over our morning coffee. Ruling party rags, all of them. Some more strident than others, but all pushing the same line. Each carried a story about our platform, along with the new fictions about our backing. And other fictions, too.'

'Ha!' said Suna, in a mocking voice. 'So now the truth is out! Haluk, my dear, no wonder you are angry. It seems your wife is actually a lesbian. It seems we have recently reignited our passionate affair!'

'You'll have noticed, no doubt,' Tallis added. 'That according to this rag here, I am just back from a secret visit to my masters in Langley.'

'Again,' said Suna.

'This must be the fourth or fifth time since March.'

'Maybe even the seventh,' Suna laughed. 'Tallis, my child, how can you justify such a carbon footprint?'

'All jokes aside,' said Tallis. 'I think we can agree that it would be madness to respond to this.'

'I agree,' said Haluk. 'It *would* be madness. But there are other ways to clear our name.'

Sitting back, and tapping his pen against the table, he turned to Sinan, reverting to Turkish to ask, 'So? Are you going to ask her?'

Now they all turned to look at me. But it was Tallis who spoke.

'First, I'd like to thank you on behalf of everyone, Dora, for agreeing to step in as our new fundraising officer.'

'Who was your old one?'

'Your mother.'

'Aha.'

'And I'm afraid things may have gotten a little out of hand.'

'How so?'

With a sigh, he explained that significant funds of unknown origin had found their way into the platform's main account, most of it since the time of her attack. 'So this is yet another matter we have to clear up, and fast, before it does us real harm. We need to take out the legitimate funds and put them into a new account, and freeze the rest, until we know what to do with it. And also,' he said, 'it would be a great help if you could help us draft an ethical fundraising policy.'

'In due course,' I said.

'Absolutely. No rush. The point is not to be reactive. We need to get this right. But in the meantime, it would be really, really helpful if we could find some way to flag it.'

When we adjourned an hour later, I had agreed to draft a paragraph acknowledging, albeit somewhat vaguely, our concerns around fundraising, and our intention to formulate an ethical policy in the near future.

Tallis had undertaken to draft a parallel account of the storms we'd endured following various groundless, and therefore best left unspecified, allegations about our funding base on social media.

He would clear this text, as translated by one of the young ones, with Haluk, who along with his wife had suffered most from recent calumnies, while Suna would redraft our mission statement, so that there was absolute clarity around our never accepting funds from foreign governments or entities with links to the same.

Together we had agreed to look into better encryption. Just how we hoped to combat other, less technical forms of surveillance, we could not say. But one thing was certain: we five had agreed, almost without discussion, to carry on regardless.

We five.

I belong, I remember saying to myself. I've been admitted. To the heart of my family, and my history. And yet, I did not wish to follow the others down the stairs. Instead I waited for the lift, engrossing myself in messages of no consequence on my phone. The next time I looked up, it was to see Tallis, opening up the elevator cage for me.

'I'm sorry,' he said.

'For what?'

'For dragging you into this.'

'Stop worrying. You didn't.'

'It's a nasty business. And it's about to get nastier. If you decided to get out, now, before it's too late, I wouldn't blame you.'

'There's the little matter of my mother.'

'Yes, you're right. There's that.'

He dug his hands into his pockets. At the same moment, just half a floor from the ground, the cage lift stopped. He pressed a few buttons. No movement. He pressed the alarm, saying, 'I have no idea if this even works.' When again nothing happened, he rattled the cage door, crying, 'Is anyone there?'

There didn't seem to be. Then his phone rang.

'I'm still in the elevator,' he told it. 'We're stuck. Listen,' he said into the phone. 'Where exactly are you?'

'Then in that case,' he said. 'You might as well come in.'

The metal door in the foyer swung open. In came a young woman I had never seen before. Almond eyes. A very long face, redeemed by a small mouth and an ivory complexion. Her smooth, black hair was pulled back by a red silk scarf that she had fashioned into a sort of hairband.

After she had gone off in search of the janitor, I turned to Tallis.

'Another one? Already?'

'No, of course not. Listen, it's not what you think.'

'Oh, really? Then what is it?'

'It is Adliye. The new receptionist. And by the way. Someone left a voice message for you this morning. And Adliye wants you to hear it.'

It was strange, hearing İsmet's voice after all these years. It was as I remembered it, but huskier.

He wanted to meet, but I didn't. I told him so, perhaps more harshly and archly than I should have done. I left it at that. Or rather, I thought I did.


## The reckoning

I am at the radio station, maybe two or at the most three days after the one I've just described to you. In any event, not much time has passed between that day and this. But a lot has happened. A lot has happened because the nice Norwegian journalists must have posted our Pasha Tree performance on YouTube within minutes of leaving our platform. And now we are in every newspaper, and on every screen, ridiculed for our airs, and condemned for our hypocrisy. In the most extreme Islamist rags, there are calls for rough justice. No longer, they say, should the whores of foreign powers be allowed to parade their wares as Suna and I have done before the cameras of the world. The god-fearing public should take matters into its own hands.

We find this threat alarming.

But the boys – as Suna and I are still calling them – do not seem to care so much about our safety.

Instead, they join the accusing chorus.

We have cheapened our family, they tell us.

We have taken what Sinan, the illustrious filmmaker, had hoped one day to spin into a tapestry of gold, and defiled it with our shit.

Despite our lofty degrees, we have no idea what we are up against.

After all Sinan's efforts to leave me out of the story, for my own safety, I have put myself right back into the middle, with this story of the balls.

And to tell the story to foreigners, to make them laugh, and to laugh with them!

Such a cheap trick. But also, such bad timing.

We could not have chosen a worse moment to expose our platform to yet another hate campaign.

We should have spoken to them first, at the very least.

It is their family, too, is it not?

Which is typical, in Suna's view. Once again, the boys are to decide when the personal can or cannot be political, and how it must be fashioned, and whose imprimatur it can bear.

We have no choice, says Suna, but to defend ourselves without their help. To this end, we are taping an interview so as to explore our new gender concerns more deeply. This with the assistance of Adliye, the new receptionist, who is sitting in on the interview, having agreed to stay on after I've left for my afternoon visit to the hospital, speaking my lines in Turkish, which is still just a little too rusty for the radio, while Suna translates her own.

Suna gets us started with a summary of the story so far. Then she asks me what about this story I find most puzzling.

And I say: the hypocrisy. How can we presume to set up an oral history platform in which we aired everyone's secrets but our own?

'Of course, we cannot,' Suna replies. 'Unless we are indeed hypocrites.'

'You and I, at least, are not,' she continues. 'Our manly friends, on the other hand, prefer to hide their own cards under the table, while they mine their new database to pursue their old quarries.'

'It's always the same, isn't it?' I say. 'They're angry at me for telling that story about the balls. Why? Because they're worried for my honour?'

'It's worse than that,' says Suna. 'They're worried for their own honour. Because, as you know, what happens to me sexually and happens to you sexually reflects on them, too.'

'I've never really understood that,' I say.

'Neither have I,' says Suna. 'We can simply observe, however, that if our cousin Sinan had shown more interest in the events of that fabled and long-ago evening, he would have wished to talk about more than just balls. He would have wished to mention that İsmet had come into your room to rape you as a punishment for your branding him a homosexual in front of all those people, in that nest of spies. If you ask me, that is the crux of the matter. It was never the money that turned İsmet against our family. It was the sexual humiliation, pure and simple. This, my dear friend, is why the personal is always political. Always at the heart of every enmity. But our cousins seem unwilling to acknowledge this. Why is that, I wonder?'

To which I say, 'Because they're men?'

'We may laugh,' Suna now says, 'but the fact remains that these are dangerous times. They say they must protect us, these dear cousins and former husbands of ours. While in fact they are leaving us poor females unprotected before the Jihadist mob. But we don't need them, do we, my dear Dora? Yet again, we must protect ourselves without recourse to male assistance. So shall we proceed?' she asks.

To my shame, I agree.

Whereupon Suna issues her challenge to the Jihadists. 'You cowards,' she says. 'Hiding behind your putrid scandal sheets. And you call yourselves men. Show your faces, for once! Dare to speak to us females as equals, and let's see what you can learn!'

That is where I stop her. Even I, in my whirlwind of lost bearings, can see the danger.

She agrees, and we wipe the tape.

'It was fun, though,' she says, with a girlish giggle. 'Wasn't it?'

And that's where we leave it: in the past tense.

As I step into the hospital twenty or so minutes later, I receive the summons. I am to report to the platform as soon as humanly possible, Tallis informs me.

When I ask why, he says, 'Do you really not know? Are you joking?'

'We've been hacked,' he says. 'At least, I hope we have. I know you and Suna are angry. But not enough to put up something like this.'

I am sitting in the main concourse now, just outside the lifts.

I open my laptop and wait for our homepage to configure. I read the new paragraph, entitled Manifesto.

In circles committed to bringing forth the truth about the heinous events of 1915, resulting in the genocide of the Ottoman Empire's Armenians, there is much talk about the three Rs: Recognition, Reconciliation, Reparation.

We at this platform can boast of a few small achievements with regard to the first two of these Rs. The third appears at times to be an idle and somewhat wistful dream.

This, we have now decided, is due to the absence of another R, that in our view needs to be the third R, shunting Reparation to fourth place.

That R is Responsibility, and not just for the crimes of our forefathers. We must also take responsibility for the consequences of these crimes, amongst both the beneficiaries and the losers: the secularists and the Islamists, the Kurds and the Armenians, the Greeks and even the Turks, whoever we might come to understand we are, after we have been honest with ourselves and each other about our cryptic multicultural heritages.

We must count the cost of lying about these crimes to three successive generations. To the culture of impunity that these lies have engendered. To the curse of ultranationalism.

The curse of patriarchy, and the woman who have collaborated and colluded, opening their legs to give birth to yet another generation of liars and thieves.

I pick up my phone. But Suna is already ringing me.

She is hyperventilating.

She knows, as I do, that most of the text for this manifesto came from her first draft of our pdf/pamphlet-in-progress.

But not the part about women spreading their legs. That part has been added. So, too, had the long list of financial mis-dealings that the hacker manifesto went on to list – offered, it claimed, in a spirit of transparency. Detailing the growth and growth of the Cotton King and his descendants, among whom both Haluk and Suna number. Also including the false, malicious, and virulently anti-Semitic reports about the family of Haluk's wife and Suna's lifelong friend, Lüset.

Struggling to keep my voice level, I ask Suna if she'd been called to the same meeting as I have.

She has.

We agree to meet in an hour's time, at the café across the street from the office.

I hang up. I enter the lift, feeling giddy. I must be in shock, because all I can think is that I must find a new pair of shoes, because the ones I'm wearing are pinching my toes.

I walk into my mother's room to find her lying in bed, on her back, and staring at the ceiling.

I gasp, because her eyes are open. Turning her head sharply, she mouths a warning. A not quite whispered command:

Hush!

With a flick of the hand that is free of tubes, she beckons

me over, and in a strangled voice, she tells me to get out while the going is good. 'Leave me to deal with him. Don't worry. I'll play dead.'

'What on earth are you talking about?' I say. In a normal voice. This sends my mother into something like a seizure.

'You were never meant to be here in the first place. Now get out, while you can!'

'OK, OK, but first I'm using the bathroom.'

She throws her free hand up in despair. 'You never listen to me, do you? Do what you want. I give up.'

When I come out of the bathroom, my mother has gone back to playing dead, and İsmet is waiting for me on the sofa by the window.

He is thinner than he was when I last saw him from up close, by not by much. His eyes are still bright, but his skin is so taut that when he smiles, I half expect it to split open.

It does not.

'What are you doing here?' I ask.

'Like your mother, receiving treatment.'

'But I thought you were in jail!'

'Do you honestly think that this nation is still so backward that it denies medical treatment to the incarcerated?'

'Of course not,' I said. 'But still, that doesn't explain why this hospital and not another.'

'I see you still don't trust me,' he says.

'You're right,' I say. 'I don't.'

'But you trust those vermin and the lies they spread on that piece of filth they call a platform.'

'They're doing important work.'

'They're making enemies. Unnecessary enemies. Enemies, dare I say it, who are far more dangerous than me.'

Here he pauses, to subject me a long and searching look.

And then he sighs, while searching my face for some sign of the girl I once was, only to fail, and give up.

'What they have never understood, these cousins of yours…'

'Nieces and nephews, actually.'

'Cousins, nieces, nephews, you can call them what you want. It doesn't matter. Whatever you call them, the fact remains that they do not understand their privileges. More crucially, they do not understand that, in spite of all our differences and everything they believe, I have always protected them.'

'Oh really? I say. 'By raping them and pushing them out of windows, and locking them up for crimes they didn't commit?'

'So,' he says. 'You believe all that, too. But never mind. You were always gullible. In fact, it was what I treasured in you, when you were a girl.'

I suggest it might be best that we not go there.

He bows his head, in acquiescence.

In the smooth tones of a peace offering, he launches into a lecture, about the winds of change that are fast changing the country into one we shall not recognise. The new guard, as he calls them, who with every new day, are tightening their grip. The Islamists, who want the secular state crushed, and its supporters silenced, if not dead.

'Oh good,' I say. 'Another conspiracy theory.'

Leaning forward on his cane, he responds to my taunt in the calmest of voices. 'It is not a theory, my dear Dora. It is a fact. And do not think that – just because I am in prison, just because I additionally have cancer, just because I am only able to leave my prison cell on days like this, for treatments or medical consultations, it does not mean that

I do not still have my ear to the ground. In fact, with the recent multiplication of sources inside as well as outside, my information is better than ever. And as luck would have it, I have a message for you.' He pauses, for theatrical effect. 'Your mother used to help me at such moments,' he says finally. 'But now that she is playing dead, I have no choice on this occasion but to use you as my intermediary.'

A strangled cry behind me. My mother, begging me to get out, leave, skip the country while I still can.

Pleased to have called her bluff, İsmet relaxes into the sofa and chuckles.

'Do not worry your lovely little head, my dear Delphine. You can give me the finger, and shop me to your little platform friends, and encourage them to publish a veritable compendium of lies about me, but you shall, nevertheless, always have a special place in my heart. As will you, my lovely Dora. In spite of all our differences, we share a history. Most especially, this. Would it interest you to hear my own answer to the question our Sinan posed in his recent film? The crux of the matter, as I said, is that you and I have suffered the same injustice. Do you wish to know why? The answer is as terrible as it is simple: that cotton mill that your pasha grandfather gave to Soran Bey, this man who was soon to be known across the breadth of Turkey as the king of that fibre. Until the spring of 1915, that mill belonged to my grandfather. My Armenian grandfather. Until, like the banker Artin Bey, he was killed. In his case: decapitated.'

'I can't see how to believe that,' I said. 'Back in the day, you hated the Armenians more than anyone.'

'Ah,' he said. 'You have that wrong. I hated only certain Armenians. The Dashnaks. The revolutionaries, who went over to the Soviet side. If not for them, they would have left us in peace. My mother, like your grandmother, would have been an heiress. She would not have toiled her life away in those cotton fields. She would have owned them. But never mind. My story, like your story, is more complicated. We must take responsibility for all our forebears. And in my case, on my father's side, this includes many Kurds.'

'You hate them, too!' I said.

'No. Again you are wrong. I hate only the revolutionaries, who have again brought death and destruction on the rest of us. Though today, with my current trials and illnesses, those hatreds mean less to me. I have conserved my dwindling energies for the things that matter most. Which is why I wish now to return to the question your Sinan asked in that filmsy and absurd documentary, in which he reveals to the world his lack of professional decorum. He asks why I hate you. I wish to say to now, that I do not, in fact, hate all of you. I hate only the men. I excuse the women.'

'Because we spread our legs?'

'Please, Dora. Coarse talk does not become you. I excuse the women because I have had occasion to share the same indignities, at the hands of the same men. And it is in deference to those shared indignities that I have undertaken to come here this afternoon, firstly to delay your departure, by making the most of this encounter, for who can say if or when we shall have another chance? My guards will be turning up any minute now. My cellmates in Silivri await me with impatience.'

'So that's firstly,' I say. 'What's secondly?'

'Secondly,' he says. 'Why the rush?'

'I need to get back to the platform.'

'Oh yes, I forgot. You're the fundraising officer now, aren't you? As of Monday, I recall. And also, as of Tuesday, you have joined forces with Suna to fight her latest battle with her boys.'

'I'd have thought you'd have better ways to use your time than listen in on everything our office says or does.'

'You're right,' he says. 'I do. Which brings me to my thirdly. Your shared concerns, so eloquently voiced at your last board meeting. About the money that is suddenly pouring in from God only knows where. Strings attached, of course, but you can't see them. Not to mention the many thousands of allegations and accusations, not a single one from a trusted source. Worst of all, these allegations of financial misconduct. Crimes that would seem to dwarf any of the crimes of which your mother, and Sinan, that boy for whom she is now pimping, falsely accused me of last January in that film of his, with her ridiculous tales of Armenian gold.'

Some rustling behind me: my mother is having an increasingly hard time playing dead.

But İsmet doesn't notice this time. He is too busy telling me how little I understand the Islamists now in power, who will stop at nothing to have their way. 'While we, at least, had our limits.'

'Oh really?' I say.

'You're all still alive, aren't you? That must be proof of our mercy, if nothing else.'

'But here's another question,' I say. 'Why are you so dead against the Islamists? You used to be very religious, as I recall.'

'That was then,' he says. 'But also, when it suits me, now. It is a safe mask to wear these days, after all. Certainly, it has enhanced my list of contacts.'

Again İsmet pauses, this time to look at his Rolex watch. He checks his phone.

He reads a text or two.

He puts it back into his coat pocket, with the slip of a smile.

He lets out a sigh, and catches it halfway.

'But you are right,' he says. 'I have digressed. So. Enough beating around the bush. This is the message I wish you to take to those cousins of yours who are actually your nephews, and that man you once called your husband. The deep state they have spent all their lives hating is locked away in prison. The cretins who call themselves Islamists have been let loose, and now there is no army to stop them, no faithful servants of the state to amass the necessary intelligence. They are primitive, these monsters. They take their money from Salafis for whom an eye must be paid for with an eye, a tooth with a tooth. It was very stupid of these cousin-nephews and nieces of yours, to further offend them. Your nieces and nephews should have ignored that silly smear about the Israeli funders, instead of responding with more vitriol. And you. You of all people should have known better than to speak indiscreetly to those Norwegians. And then, on top of it all, to exchange loose words on the airwaves with that silly Suna!'

'But I didn't!' I say. 'If you do in fact know everything that happens in our offices, you must know that the interview we did this morning has been erased.'

'My dear girl. After all these years, are you still so American as to believe that words unwisely spoken can ever be retracted?' He pauses, to gaze at me sadly.

Leaning forward on his cane, he says, 'Listen to my lips for one last time, my dearest. The game has changed. The penalty for mindless dissidence is no longer simple punishment. In the reign of our new masters, it is swift and merciless death. You can go now,' he says, with a sweep of his free arm.

But I refuse to leave him alone in this room with my mother.

So in the end he stands up and says, 'I'll drop you off.'

As we head through the door my mother gives up at last on playing dead. 'Don't you dare get into his car!' she hisses.

But out in the street it is raining, and there are no taxis, and in his car, sitting behind the driver, is an armed gendarme. So I agree to be taken as far as Taksim, and then, with the umbrella they have loaned me, I head down the hill.

I can remember the rain pelting down on the pavement, and taking extra care not to slip. But I cannot remember finding Suna in the café across the street, or crossing that street, or entering the building, or how long we waited together for the cage lift. All I remember is walking with her into our little foyer, to find Adliye the new receptionist gathering up her things.

She seems surprised to see us. Flustered, even.

She is changing out of her stilettos into flat shoes. She has taken off the red silk scarf that she fashions into something akin to headband each morning, and at the end of the day, reshapes into an Islamist headscarf for her journey home. After tightening the little bun at the top of her head, she unfolds the scarf and spreads it over her head, covering all her hair.

'Do you really have to do that?' I ask, as she knots it tightly around her chin.

'If you saw my neighbourhood,' Adliye replies, 'you would not ask.'

In the hallway I hear voices.

'We had a film crew in,' Adliye tells us.

I make to go and find them, but with a forcefulness I find puzzling, Adliye bars my way.

'They are just going,' she says. With a glance over her shoulder, she barks, 'Boys! We're leaving! Now!'

Three men emerge from the narrow corridor. One is carrying a television camera. Another is holding a boom. The third, who has the look of a newscaster, has his hands behind his back.

They seem surprised to see us. But when Adliye introduces us, they smile politely, shuffling their feet, until Adliye barks, 'That's enough. Now get out.'

They do as she asks. 'What's wrong with you?' I hear her cry, as she follows them out onto the landing. 'Do you really want to get stuck between two floors in that old lift! Go down the stairs, you lazy boys!'

The door swings shut. Their voices fade. Suna's phone rings. As she goes into the corner to take the call, I continue on down the corridor.

# THE LAST NOTEBOOK WITH
# PAGES STILL TO FILL

# This afternoon

I went back to the office this afternoon, for the first time in many weeks. The first time since sitting down to write this story, in actual fact. I'd run out of notebooks, and I knew I'd find some there.

It was snowing, snowing onto hard, uneven ice, so I took my time, stopping for a coffee along the way. It was odd, if also pleasant, to be out and about again, after those days inside, chasing shadows across the page. The clatter of spoons and cups, the bursts of steam from the espresso machine, the waitress taking orders, the customers waving, to catch her eye – singly and together, they restored me to the beauty of the everyday.

I remembered, then, that Hermine had once felt just like this. Or rather, I had imagined her feeling just like this, the day she left her studio for the first time in many months, to walk along these same streets, greeted each step of the way by porters and chickpea- sellers, waiters and pimps, to slip into the church where Mrs Mary had believed there to be frescoes of angels, but where she had found only white walls.

As I sipped my coffee, I thought back on the story I've been telling you, remembering with a jolt that almost everyone in that story is dead now. In most cases, long dead. And then I posed the question you girls must have been asking all along: What good has it done me, to trace this path again, all the way to its gruesome finish?

As I nursed my second espresso (having somehow forgotten that even one espresso was more than my nerves could take) I thought about them all. The Alephs, whose game of secrets was still playing out. The women – Anahid in her sanatorium, Nuran, marooned in her untended bed, Odette, chasing after the son who would be the death of her, Karine the Great, always conspiring, rarely succeeding, Dr Ruth, making the best of things, Mrs Mary, parked in Pomfret. But then, I reminded myself. There was more to it than that. There were the poems and paintings and mad dreams that no one but me remembered. There were the children they'd cherished and protected.

There was Hermine.

As I cupped my hands around my third espresso, I wondered, as I often do, where I would be now, and who I would be – what my name would be, what I would know of my past, what beliefs I would hold to be self-evident – had Hermine not prevented Dr Mrs Semih from stealing me from my mother's arms when I was just a few days old to place me with that honest and hardworking couple she'd lined up as my adoptive parents. But I couldn't bend my mind that way. I couldn't even imagine their faces, or how my face might have been, in that other life.

My head was buzzing by now. My heart was racing, as my thoughts chose their own way. Why I thought a fourth espresso would be the solution I cannot say, but as I sat there, stirring in the sugar, the café door flew open, and I was seized with the idea that it was Hermine wafting in with that blast of cold air. I could almost see her, taking her place across from me. Smiling as she reached out for the little candle on the table between us. Rubbing the wick between her thumb and her forefinger. Lighting the fire that only I could see.

And then, very gently, admonishing me, for pulling back when she made to put it in my hands, for failing to understand the gift she was offering me: the fire that had, from the moment of my birth, been mine to claim.

I called for the waitress. Threw on my coat. Returning to the drifting snow and the hard, uneven ice beneath it, I kept my eyes on the ground, testing it with each step. But even thus preoccupied, my mind kept spinning, looping wildly back to the trick my mind had just played on me. Asking what this figment of my imagination had wished to tell me. And why that new gift, the fire that she or I had conjured up, had so unnerved me.

On my way down Sıraselviler, I kept losing my balance. And then righting myself, only to imagine the worst: what might happen to me, if I fell and banged my head, or tripped and fractured my shoulder, or slipped off this ridiculously narrow pavement and into the path of that bus I could hear careening towards me.

Reaching my building at long last and pushing open the heavy metal door, I stupidly let down my guard. Because there, inside the cage elevator, was that nice girl who'd taken such good care of me last time I was here. The one who worked for one of the dentists upstairs. She wasn't wearing a red headscarf though. This time it was green.

I couldn't remember her name but I waved and called to her to wait. Too late – she had already pressed the button.

'I'm sorry!' she cried. 'I'll come right back!'

'Never mind!' I said, 'I'll be fine!' But because I was looking at this girl ascending, and not at the marble floor with all its pools of dirty melted snow, I did what I had been so careful not to do outside. I slipped.

Luckily, I didn't hurt myself. But I felt such a fool. I was still picking myself up when the girl and the cage lift came down again, as promised. So once again she had to help me up to the office, where she was good enough to make us some tea.

Linden tea, thank God. Somehow, she could tell that I'd had enough caffeine. As we sat there together in the box-strewn anteroom, sipping tea from our little tulip glasses, she told me she'd been worried about me. First because of my ankle, and later because there'd been people here, trying to get into the office, saying that they were the new tenants, insisting that all had been paid and agreed.

Whereupon I apologised to my young friend for any trouble I might have caused. Explaining that these tenants had been in touch with me directly after the fact. That we'd sorted things. I was the owner of the building, I told her. And I'd decided to take the office off the market for the time being.

She nodded carefully, before saying, 'Yes, this is what I was told.'

'When?'

'Afterwards,' she said. She paused, before adding, 'They also told me what happened here.'

'The attack,' I said.

'Yes,' she said. 'The attack and the needless, senseless slaughter.'

She looked up at the poster still hanging behind the reception desk. Your father at one end and me at the other. And between us, the three friends I used to think were my cousins, and continued to call my cousins, even after I found out they were not. We were at a party that day, at the Museum of Modern Art. You can see the Bosphorus behind us, its breezes ruffling our hair, just days before the attack. To weather its aftermath, Suna and I had turned the image into a poster of resistance. Along the band at the bottom, it said, 'All of us forever.'

'Tallis,' said my young friend, reading out the names beneath us. 'He was your husband, wasn't he?'

'Once upon a time,' I said.

'And the ones next to him. The other martyrs. Haluk and Sinan. They were your cousins?'

'My nephews,' I said.

Seeing the confusion mixed in with the pity and the compassion, I added, 'It's a long story. But we did feel like cousins. We were pretty much the same age.'

'But Suna,' said the girl. 'She survived?'

'That's right,' I said. 'For as long as we could, we carried on our work here.'

Lost for words, my young friend gazed up at the poster.

I could guess what she was imagining – the bodies as I had found them. The heads.

Finally, she looked back at me. 'In spite of everything, you have not changed,' she said.

Pointing at my likeness, she added, 'You have not lost your courage, I can see that. You are still the same person.'

'You're right,' I said. 'I am.' Because it seemed too hard, at that moment, to explain to this nice young woman why I wasn't.


But now that I am home again, safe inside this new notebook, let me try and explain this to you, girls, as best I can: I am no longer the person in that picture. I feel as little connection to the confident and purposeful Dora depicted there as I feel to the infant Dora you can find in the pictures on the walls of my study in Pomfret. The same goes for the girl she grew into. The woman she became. She died the day the others died. If I've been able to conjure her up for you in these pages, it has been less from memory than from the clues she left behind. The diaries she kept, the letters she wrote, the books she read, the pictures she collected, the rooms she furnished and refurnished. The objects this other Dora placed around her, and the lost world to which they return me, as I struggle to imagine how she saw it. And how it felt, to be the person I once was.

Can you imagine yourselves back here, dear girls? Can you put aside your worries and misgivings for now and stand here with me, to contemplate the confluence of seas?

The sun has just set. The evening is upon us. The Asian shore is fading, fading fast, into the darkening sky. As the street lamps light up, now here and now there, the domes and minarets of the historic peninsula recede into their blue mist.

Here inside, it's again a mess of painters' ladders and tarpaulin. I'm not sure I mentioned that I have at last located the architect's original drawings from 1901. I cannot imagine which of our antecedents could have been crass enough to remove or paint over so many of the special features. But there you are. I am slowly reversing the damage. The next time you see this apartment, its restoration should be complete.

The larger project will go on and on, I fear. The other apartments will have to remain as they are until my tenants move or die. In the meantime, I have been continuing with my salvage work, in preparation. This, too, I need to explain.

You girls will remember how hard it was for me to say goodbye to you, so soon after we had laid your father to rest. On that day, at least, I had wished away all the harsh words we had thrown at each other, in the wake of the funerals. What I wanted more than anything right then was to leave with you, and leave forever. But none of us even said the words, did we? We all knew it would have been unconscionable. After all, I had my mother to care for.

I'm sure I told you this. Your grandmother Delphine is buried right next to your father, in the far corner of Feriköy Cemetery. And this is a giant break in tradition because that side of Feriköy is Protestant cemetery, and not a Catholic one. What's more, it is not a cemetery for the city's Levantines, but for the later-arriving Europeans, including more than a few of your father's Robert College antecedents.

How it happened: Some time after the funerals, when my mother was back in the apartment, and also, precariously, back on her feet, she went to her old church – St Antoine – for confession. She told the priest that she blamed herself for the deaths. And the idiot priest agreed. He told her she'd had no business messing with politics, so shame on her. Staggering out of the church in tears, she had fallen into the providential arms of her friend, the Anglican padre. He had taken her off to the Pera Palas for a fortifying drink or two. It had ended with her deciding to convert.

At the time, I thought this to be capricious, even bizarre, but now, whenever I go to visit, I thank her, for it is a very green and peaceful corner she chose for herself. And since we laid her to rest there, she's been joined by the couple who became my very close friends in the years after the funerals. I'd known them as a girl – their daughter had been that one and only friend of mine during my first spell in this city, at least to the degree that our age gap allowed. But this daughter rarely visited the graves, so in the years after the funerals I became a sort of stand-in for her.

It was thanks to that couple's encouragement that I started

up the foundation in Hümeyra's name. I hope you'll have a chance to see it with your own eyes one day. It's in her old apartment, which I've turned into a sort of gallery. The ancient chaise longue is the genuine article, reupholstered. The baby grand is a replica – the original being irreparable. But I'm ready to swear that the bust of Beethoven sitting on top is the self-same bust I knew as a girl. I found it under a thick skin of dust on the back shelf of an antiques shop, just down the road.

The room at the back that Hümeyra used as a studio is still a studio, enjoyed now by several young artists, all women, on a rota. We use the great room for our events series – talks, mostly, and the occasional bit of chamber music. The walls we use as our exhibition space, rotating what turns out to be a quite extensive collection of paintings, collages, and photographs.

People seem to like the photographs the most.

In time, I'd like to expand, either into the apartment just above us, or the one just below – whichever tenant dies or moves out first. I'll have more time to devote to this project, now that the platform has finally shut its doors.

On the subject of which. I know you both think I should have shut it down as soon as we had the funerals behind us. And I do understand how perplexing it must have been, to see me (as you put it) soldiering blindly on. That said. It was something I had to do. I couldn't leave Suna in the lurch. We've all suffered our losses, but Suna has no one left. No children. No cousins. No one to stand at her side in our fruitless search for the culprits.

We both acknowledge the part that we ourselves might have played, and the ways in which we might have played into some larger plot. We rehearse almost daily what we wished we'd done, or known, or not said. You will know, of course, that we are no closer to identifying your father's assassins than we were seven years ago. I doubt we shall ever know for sure who dispatched them. When İsmet died, just months after our funerals – in Anaïs' hospital, of natural causes – he took that secret with him.

On clear days, we see him as the man who gave the order. On other days, we see İsmet as the puppeteer, the man who had only to flick an invisible wrist to get Adliye the receptionist and unknown others to do his dirty work for him. That said, we cannot forget that we were and continue to be capable of setting any number of Islamist groups against us just by speaking our own minds.

And that is why Suna and I have, over the past decade, concentrated on projects that keep us well beneath the radar. The personal that is political without the politicians knowing it, as she likes to put it. We've had more than enough to keep us busy over the years. Particularly during and after the Gezi protests in 2013. As you may recall, though I don't think you overly approved, we opened up our offices to the protesters as a refuge. Anaïs came as often as she could to help us. I know you followed this saga to some degree, so you may have read that Anaïs opened the doors of her hospital to protesters who had been overcome by teargas or injured by water cannons, and treated them for free – always knowing that this would enflame our prime minister, soon to be our president and would-be Sultan.

I don't know how closely you stay in touch with her, but just to say, in case you don't already know that she's retired now – she had no choice. She had to sell the hospital to a holding company controlled by one of our president's sons, or else see it shut down. She's safer back in Paris. Just as

Suna, who retired just last month, is safer in her new house on the Aegean coast, near Assos.

She would have come back to help me pack up our office. But I told her, perhaps foolishly, that I'd be fine doing it on my own. Or perhaps not foolishly. If I'd not been on my own, I might never have found the will to write all this down for you. I have called it your legacy. As indeed it is. But there is, I fear, another one, and I think this must be the moment to tell you this other story, even though I still have no idea what to do about it.

## The other legacy

It must have been a year after my mother died. Two years at the most. I heard someone knocking. Feebly. Very feebly indeed. I opened the door to find a breathless Sergei, leaning against the wall.

I knew from my mother that they'd kept in touch. In the years since the Cold War, he'd made himself rather rich. Something in shipping, my mother said. He spent a lot of time on his yacht, stopping by to see her, she said, every time he passed through the Bosphorus.

As he leaned against the doorframe, catching his breath, I counted the years since I'd last seen him. Forty-seven.

I would have recognised him anywhere, though at this precise moment, he looked like a waxwork.

'I fear to say,' he said, 'that I have aged beyond these stairs.'

When I had fed and watered him, he leaned forward, as if to share a secret. 'The time has come for us to plan a cruise.'

Why not? I thought. But it would be a few more years before the time actually came.

The yacht that came to fetch me on that fine June day was a monstrosity. From a very great distance – from the town of Thira, looking six hundred meters down into the volcanic bay, from the cliffs of southern Crete, or from the walls of Valletta, it had the graceful lines of a sailing vessel from another century. The illusion faded the moment you stepped on board to find industrial scale steel, glass and radar.

But his crew were good-hearted and eccentric. Although I am pretty much a vegetarian these days, I ate what was put before me, so as not to upset the chef. Wherever we anchored, I swam. Whatever Sergei caught me sketching – the rocks of Hydra, the fishing boats of Corsica, the forts of Sicily – he would smile and say, 'I knew it was a good idea to stock up on my art supplies! You had such a good hand when you were a girl, you know. It does my heart good to see you return to it. For it is never too late!'

'And now,' he said, on our last day in Malta, 'the time has come for a little side trip.'

Early the next morning, we flew by private plane to Zurich.

Arriving in Lugano, we spent the first day airing out the old house. On the second, we chartered a sailboat. On the third day, Sergei called for a taxi to take us back into Zurich. 'The time has come,' he said, 'to honour my sacred promise to your mother.'

On the way in, he explained that she had not wanted me to know about her bank account in Zurich until I was safely out of Turkey, with all ties cut.

'But now, with me at my age, and you still clinging to your platforms and foundations, I have decided it would be foolish to wait any longer.'

On the way back, when I was still reeling at the obscene sums that my mother had bequeathed to me, he confessed, with a sad, embarrassed smile, that she had invented most of the stories about Armenian gold with which she had taunted İsmet online following his arrest for treason. She had done so, he said, to ensure that his entry into Silivri would be met with mocking laughter.

'But also,' he said, 'she did it to distract İsmet and also others from her own dealings.'

Which were? It was only that evening, on the veranda of the old villa, and only after knocking back a glass of straight vodka, that I found the courage to ask.

'Oh, well. Let's see. There was, first and foremost, her legacy from Uncle Teddy. Which was, for the most part, his legacy from his father, the great Pasha. Not to mention his grasping French wife. If it hadn't been for her, I am sure that their little or in fact not so little cache of Armenian gold would have been lost to the tables.'

'Which cache was this?'

'This, too, is obscure. Certainly some of it came from the vaults of Tigran, the old jeweller – Hümeyra's maternal grandfather. It was, as you know, your mother's lifelong mission to get that back. But a great deal of it, if not most of it, we may trace back to the gold that the great pasha siphoned off for his own use, while overseeing the transfer of a very large portion of the empire's assets to Berlin, for safekeeping. Some of this may well have come to him through the offices, witting or unwitting, of your great grandfather, the infamous Artin Bey. He was at the Ottoman Bank, after all. And didn't our celebrated Pasha step right into his shoes, no sooner than he was deported? Didn't the Pasha contrive to feed his old friend to the fishes, not long afterwards?

'Now of course, your mother regarded any monies deriving from Artin Bey as rightfully hers. And of course, I must agree. Though I fear the court case, if there ever were one, would be complex and long-lasting. Some would argue that the gold belonged to the state. Some might brand Adnan Pasha as a traitor, which could be distressing for you and your daughters, seeing as you are all descended from him.

'And then,' he said, filling my glass with more vodka. 'There is the question of what that gold was worth then, and what it is now. Inflation has ensured that it must now have multiplied in value by a factor of 43, if not 44. There are also the wise investments made over many years by that grasping but very clever French wife. Largely in mines, I understand. In South Africa, for the most part. But also, in Turkey.'

He paused to knock back what was left in his glass, before replenishing his and mine. 'There is, as a sort of postscript,' he now said, 'my own little empire. This, too, requires explanation. When the Cold War ended, your mother was kind enough to make me a substantial loan, and with this loan I was able to buy my way into the shipping business. Dora! Don't look so horrified! This loan I paid back to her many moons ago. My billions are my own!'

He reached for the folder on the side table, right next to the vodka. Inside was his will. 'This is your copy. You can keep it. I have no children. In my day, they were not for men like me. But you have always been close to my heart, and your mother closer. I therefore name you as my one and only heir.'

One final confession: he asked if he could adopt me, and I said yes. He did not live long enough to see to the formalities – not all countries take kindly to the adoption of adults –

but I think it brought him some happiness in his last years, to hear me introduce him as my father.

## In conclusion

So there you have it. I am obscenely rich, and one day, you will be too. I have been thinking and thinking about what to do with what I've been left, and how to have at least some good come of it. But every time my thoughts go back to the beginning and the story I so long to rewrite. I conjure up Adnan Pasha on the wintry island, embracing his friend Artin. I imagine him changing heart, at the very last moment, and deciding not to send him to his death. I imagine the different story that might have unfolded from the right decision, until I remember that in this brighter version, I would have no part to play. I would never have been born.

How would I have lived my life, I wonder, if I'd known my family's histories sooner?

If I had acted more wisely, if I had known the difference between embracing your history and inhabiting its every twist and turn, could I have saved your father, and Sinan, and Haluk?

Could I have been a better mother to you girls, if I hadn't got lost inside my head and my obsession?

As I sit here in the building that was built by one side of my family and stolen by another, as I watch the mist sink into a Sea of Marmara that grows greyer with every call to prayer, I grieve for the days when I could point a finger at a single man and blame him. When I could roll time back to an original sin.

Those days are over. Now I have only my ghosts. During

the weeks I've spent setting down these words, they've been keeping me company. The Alephs, at their card tables. Anahid, wasting away. Soran, serving his masters. Mary, doing what good she can. Hermine, becoming Hümeyra. My mother, finding her way back to her. But then, falling for Melih. Falling pregnant.

The cousins, who turned into nieces and nephews. Tallis, who believed that you could build your way out of any problem. The woman I was, when I believed the truth could set you free.

Here in this room, they have no idea what awaits them, and – except when I am recording their fates in these unadorned black notebooks – neither do I. Instead, I just sit here, listening to my great grandmother, Anahid, laughing in the next room – laughing between coughs – as she bends over to embrace the daughter who has crept in to see her, against all orders.

I catch sight of my great grandfather, Artin, who is holding his glass of tea, watching a ship sail into port in 1910, while he dreams of sailing in the opposite direction.

I watch my grandfather, the Pasha, as he falls back into the cushions of another day, another time, luxuriating in the view that even he must accept is not rightfully his. But enjoying it anyway, while also feasting his eyes on his lovely French wife, and their young son, Teoman, who is a little lion of a man, even at the age of three. If only he could stop the boy's mother from addressing him as Teddy!

He is, without knowing it, looking straight though Hermine, now Hümeyra, who is perched on her tricycle, leaning over its handlebars as she cuts up a magazine for her next collage. She is in her element, and so long as she can stay in it, she could not care less about this legacy that ought to have been hers. There, in the next room, is my mother, who thinks about little else. Though she has other things to see to first. How best to arm herself? Will it be the black knock-'em-dread dress, or the red? She really needs to know – a gal like her can't leave things like this to chance. Especially not on a night like this, with the stakes running so high. But who can she count on, to pick the right dress? Not myself at twelve, certainly. Not this sulking, glaring spindle of a girl propped against the door, passing judgement! Who would have thought that the devil-may-care daughter of a bohemian legend could give birth to such a killjoy?

Outside, dangers lurk. Crimes and betrayals. Secrets and lies that can kill, and will. But here, in this room, I can savour my moment, as my ghosts savour theirs, while together we watch the seas converge beneath us, turning blue and black and silver all at once, while a century of ships and ferries pass us by, through swirling currents becalmed by silken sheets. The domes and minarets of the old city turn grey and gold and white, now against a leaden sky, and now against a turquoise so bright and pure, that not a single one of us can imagine the storm that's on its way.

Until we are joined by Nuran the Poetess, dressed head to toe in white. She is wringing her hands. She turns to ask her entourage if this wretched war will ever end, but no one can hear her. Karine the Great with her jewels, Melih and Semih with their wives, Mary with her sister Ruth – they are locked inside their own moments. They can see no further. They do not even notice the trio rushing in from another time and ploughing right through them.

Sinan first. Then Haluk and your father. Oblivious to the rest of us, they hurl themselves onto the ancient chaise longue. They've brought with them a new dossier of damning facts. This must be the last straw, they promise each other. Finally, they can exonerate themselves by stringing together the crimes committed by others over an entire century. String them across the sky, in lights. They map them out, huddled now around my easel, their whispers mingling with the tango music flowing in from next door.

They cannot hear it, and neither can the fierce old man who comes striding across the room, not so much leaning on his cane as using it to claim as his own all that it touches. Behind him is a younger man, elegantly dressed and anxious. In his hands flaps a blueprint, for he is our architect, and the imperious old gentleman leading the way is my great great grandfather, the old jeweller. Tigran.

It is 1901, and the building is which we sit is at last completed. Tigran is conducting what was to have been his final inspection, but on each floor he has found a number of small defects, and here on the third floor it is an unacceptable gap between the French doors and their frame. The flustered architect sets about making the necessary measurements, so that he can rectify the matter this very afternoon. And while he dashes to and fro, Tigran closes his eyes, the better to savour the sea breeze.

When he opens his eyes once more, there is that moment of exultation, as he measures how far he has come in this life. How much he has overcome. From his father's ancestral lands in eastern Anatolia, to this grand edifice that could hold its own in Paris, Rome or Vienna, but instead stands in proud counterpoint to the imperial city.

For those who stand atop the domes and minarets of that blue peninsula to gaze across the Golden Horn, from now on it will be this very balcony, this very building that draws the eye – this, the beating heart of the Grande Rue de Pera. Which is as it should be, he tells his imaginary audience of rulers. For where would this empire be without its Christians? Scaremonger all you wish, he hears himself telling them. Send in your regiments to murder our innocents, wrench our tradesmen from their roots, disperse us to your hearts' content. But look. You have brought us even closer. We are here, and here to stay.

This edifice from which I address you, o rulers, and which I have named after my dear departed wife – it's built on bedrock. Its foundations are sound, and in them are vaults full of jewels that you could spend a lifetime seeking but never find. Do not however, think that I plan to sink my hopes in jewels. The future lies not in what is buried, but what can flow. I am not like my brothers and their ilk. I have not plundered our ancestral lands of its precious stones and minerals to flee for safer harbours. I am, and shall remain, in service to the empire that my forefathers and I have helped to make rich.

Here, in this building, we shall continue this proud tradition. Tradesmen no longer, we shall make our mark in the professions. My son – he's a pharmacist, did you know that? I am giving him the ground floor for his shop. I had him trained in Paris, I'll have you know. He has brought back with him the science that our empire so sorely needs. My younger son, he will be bringing you photography, to record our glories and yours. My elder daughter – you will wish to curry her favour too – she is marrying into oil, and you don't need me to tell you that there is no future in these lands without it. My youngest, an accomplished artist, is engaged to a banker. So there you have it. Four seeds, from which our future prosperity will grow. Hail the new century!

It belongs to me and mine. I can see them now: my grandchildren, crowding around me on this wrought iron balcony, and my great grandchildren, too.

Here they are already, reaping what I've sown. Singing my praises, rejoicing in my wealth. It can be your wealth, too, if you heed my wise words. Look on my work, ye mighty, and understand what I am offering. Affirm my worth.

# THE FAMILY TREES

## THE ALEPHS

Adnan Pasha, the Ottoman grandee
Artin Bey, the Armenian banker
Monsieur Achille, the Levantine shipping magnate
Aubrey Hayes, the American diplomat

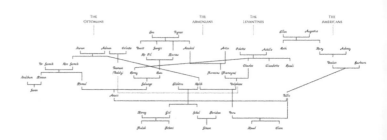

## THEIR FAMILY TREES DISENTANGLED

### THE OTTOMANS:

**Adnan Pasha**

Has two children (Melih and Semih) with his first wife, the Poetess Nuran, and one child, Teoman/Teddy, with his second wife, Celeste.

His first son, Melih, who becomes a diplomat, has two daughters (Sibel and Gül) with his wife, Elektra, and a third (Dora) out of wedlock, with the much younger Delphine.

His second son, Dr Semih, has two sons (Kenan and Kemal) with his wife, Dr Mrs Semih.

Moving on to the next generation:

Melih's daughter, the wild Sibel, has one son (Sinan) with her husband, the diplomat Feridun Bey.

His second daughter, the dutiful Gül, has two sons (Fehmi,

who dies early in a boating accident, and Haluk) with her husband Koray, Soran the Cotton King's sole heir.

Semih's elder son Kenan, who follows his father into medicine, has one daughter, Suna.

Semih's younger son Kemal, who likewise follows his father into medicine, not in Istanbul but in Paris, has one daughter, Anais, with his wife Solange.

## THE ARMENIANS
### Artin Bey
Has one daughter, Hermine, with his wife, Anahid.

Hermine has one daughter, Delphine, with Charles, the Levantine Aleph's younger son.

Delphine has one daughter, with Melih, son of Adnan Pasha.

Dora has two daughters (Maude and Clem) with her husband Tallis, grandson of the American Aleph.

## THE LEVANTINES
### Monsieur Achille
Has four children with his wife, Madame Odette.

His eldest son, Remy, leaves the family business for Paris, where he marries Rosa, the daughter of Karine, the Armenian Aleph's sister-in-law.

His younger son, Charles, has one daughter (Delphine) out of wedlock, with Hermine.

His two sisters bring up Delphine after Charles' untimely death.

## THE AMERICANS
**Aubrey Hayes**
Has one son (Declan) with his wife Mary.

Declan, a diplomat, has one son (Tallis) who after being disinherited by his father, is taken in by Mary, his grandmother, and her sister Ruth.

Tallis, an architect, has two daughters (Maude and Clem) with Dora.

AND ALSO:

## THE HOSPITAL
Was initially funded by Adnan Pasha, the Ottoman Aleph.

Dr Ruth (sister of Mary, sister-in-law of Aubrey, the American Aleph, and great aunt of Dora's husband Tallis) was its first director.
Semih, second son of Adnan Pasha, was its second.
After his retirement, it was taken over by his elder son Kemal.

On his retirement, a decision was made to replace the old hospital with a new one. Tallis was its architect, and Anais (great granddaughter of Adnan Pasha, granddaughter of Semih, daughter of Kenan, and Tallis' second wife) stepped in as its director.

## THE HOUSE OF TIGRAN
The building on the Grande Rue de Pera was commissioned and paid for by the jeweler, Monsieur Tigran, for himself and his four children.

Tigran's elder son was, until his deportation and disappearance on 24th April 1915, a pharmacist.

His younger son was, until that same date, a photographer.

His younger daughter, Anahid, had one daughter, Hermine,

before departing for a Swiss sanatorium, never to return.

Hermine had one daughter (Delphine) out of wedlock, with Charles, the Levantine Aleph's younger son.

Tigran's older daughter, Karine, married into oil and moved to Paris.

She had one daughter (Rosa) who married Remy, the elder son of the Levantine Aleph. They had one daughter (Solange).

Solange had one daughter (Anais) with Kemal, grandson of the Ottoman Aleph.

As for the building itself, it passed from Monsieur Tigran to Adnan Pasha after the First World War, and through him back to Hermine in 1963, and in 1995 to Delphine, and in 2010, to Dora.

AND FINALLY:

## THE DESCENDANTS

The cousins (Sinan, Suna, Haluk and Anais) are all descendants of the Ottoman Aleph.

Additionally, Sinan and Haluk are descendants of Nuran the Poetess, while Haluk and Anais are descendants of Soran the Cotton King.

Dora is a descendant of Monsieur Tigran, and of Nuran the Poetess, as well as the Armenian Aleph, Levantine and Ottoman Alephs.

Tallis is the descendant of the American Aleph.

Maude and Clem, Tallis and Dora's twin daughters, are descended from all of the above

This book is dedicated to them, and to all those others descended from such gloriously tangled roots, for it is their legacy.

# CAST OF CHARACTERS BY GENERATION

## The First Generation

**Achille**

The Levantine Aleph; husband of Odette; father of Charles and Remy

**Adnan Pasha**

The Ottoman Aleph; father of two sons (Melih and Semih) with his first wife, Nuran Hanim and another (Teoman) with his second wife, Celeste; adoptive father of Hermine

**Anahid**

Daughter of Tigran, wife of Artin, mother of Hermine

**Artin**

The Armenian Aleph, husband of Ahahid; father of Hermine

**Aubrey**

The American Aleph; husband of Mary; father of Lachlan; grandfather of Tallis

**Celeste**

Hermine's governess; Adnan Pasha's second wife; mother of Teoman

**Ekrem**

Ottoman poet and diplomat; husband of Alethia; father of Emel aka Elektra

**Karine**

Anahid's sister and Nuran Hanim's closest friend; wife of an Armenian oil magnate

**Mary**
Daughter of Augustus; Ruth's sister; Aubrey's wife

**Odette**
Wife of Achille; mother of Remy and Charles

**Ruth**
Mary's sister

**Soran**
Servant first to Tigran and later to Adnan Pasha, later to be known as Soran the Cotton King; his son marries Adnan Pasha's granddaughter Gül

The Second Generation
**Charles**
Son of Achille the Levantine Aleph and Odette; Hermine's childhood friend and later her rapist; Delphine's father

**Elektra**
Daughter of Ekrem and Alethia

**Hermine/Hümeyra**
Daughter of Anahid and Artin the Armenian Aleph; impregnated by Charles, the son of the Levantine ship owner; mother of Delphine

**Melih**
Diplomat; elder son of Adnan Pasha and Nuran Hanım

**Semih**
Younger son of Adnan Pasha and Nuran Hanım; husband of Mrs Dr Semih

**Maître Refique**
Hermine's art teacher and later her husband

**Remy**
Oil man; son of Odette and Achille the Levantine ship owner; marries Karine's daughter Rosa

**Teoman**
Son of Adnan Pasha and his second wife Celeste; also known as Teddy

**Vartuhi**
Maid first to Adnan Pasha and Celeste, and later to Hermine/Hümeyra

The Third Generation
**Baby Mallinson**
Blacklisted American pianist

**Declan**
American diplomat; son of Mary and Aubrey

**Delphine**
Daughter of Hermine and Charles; brought up by her paternal aunts; Dora's mother

**Gül**
Melih's daughter

**İsmet**
Intelligence officer; protégé of Soran

**Kemal**
Semih's son

**Kenan**
Semih's son

**Sergei**
Soviet man of mystery

**Sibel**
Melih's daughter

**William Wakefield**
American intelligence officer and fixer

The Fourth Generation
**Dora**
Delphine's daughter; Tallis' first wife

**Haluk**
Son of Gül, grandson of Melih; great grandson of Adnan Pasha

**Anais**
Daughter of Kemal, granddaughter of Semih, great granddaughter of Adnan Pasha; also daughter of Solange, granddaughter of Rose, and great granddaughter of Karine

**Sinan**

Son of Sibel, grandson of Melih, great grandson of Adnan Pasha

**Suna**

Daughter of Kenan, granddaughter of Semih, great granddaughter of Adnan Pasha

**Tallis**

Son of Declan; grandson of Mary and the American Aleph, Aubrey

The Fifth Generation

Maude and Clementine, Dora's and Tallis' daughters, who are descended from all four Alephs